A NAKED
BEAUTY

A NAKED BEAUTY

Book Two of the Perfectly Imperfect
Series and The Conclusion to *Fat Girl*

BY LEIGH CARRON

Published by Mountain View Press
www.leighcarron.com

ISBN: 978-1-7782806-0-3

Copyediting by KB
Proofreading by Michelle Browne
Interior design by DigiWriting
Cover design by DigiWriting

PRAISE FOR
A NAKED BEAUTY

Leigh has done it again. *A Naked Beauty* builds on the epic love story of Dee and Mick. Not only is it sexy and full of the physical love we all dream of experiencing, their story is complex and weaves in secrets from the past, the love of family and friends, and how people come together to build one another up, and support each other through the toughest of times. The story also takes the reader through Dee's journey of self-acceptance and self-love. A smart, beautiful woman who strives to love her body for all its wonder. We can all come away learning something from Dee and believing we deserve a love like Mick's.

I cannot recommend this book enough. Curl up with a mug of tea or a big glass of wine. Make sure you have time because you won't want to put it down as you get swept away by a story that contains everything you could ever want as a reader!

– CARRIE FLETCHER

Leigh Carron weaves a beautiful and sensual story of love's triumph over adversity. I felt like I was on this journey with Dee and Mick. I laughed when they soared and cried when they battled.

Dee is a reflection of my inner struggles, and she reminds me that my biggest advocate should always be me.

I'm so excited to sail off on the next adventure that Leigh Carron has on deck!

– SAMANTHA HOFFMAN

A Naked Beauty was fantastic! I loved the plot, the friend and family dynamics, and the main characters—strong female lead and devoted alpha male. It was steamy and detailed, and showed the beauty of unconditional love. I can't say enough about how much I enjoyed *A Naked Beauty*, and the way the storylines unfolded, tying it together from *Fat Girl*. I could not put it down. I'm so excited for the next book from Leigh Carron.

– ANGELA LEAFI

Leigh Carron hits it out of the park again with the conclusion to *Fat Girl*. This book is full of emotional angst and steamy love scenes. Dee and Mick are characters you fall in love with. From their shattered past in *Fat Girl* to the hope for a second chance in *A Naked Beauty*, Leigh Carron takes you on a passionate journey of healing old wounds, the heart of true love, and the power of self-acceptance. This absorbing read was well worth the wait.

– CAROLYN KNIGHT

OMG, Leigh Carron has done it AGAIN!!!! *A Naked Beauty* raises the bar above where you would ever think. Dee and Mick's reunion after fifteen years is hot and heavy, but they have issues in their way. There's Dee's body insecurities, and Mick's hot little neighbor, the persistent reporter, and dear ole dad. This book keeps you on your toes. It's a page turner that I couldn't put down, chomping at the bit to find out if Dee and Mick would get the happily ever after they deserve.

With the outstanding writing and amazing sex scenes, this author is able to bring the reader right into the room. You can picture everything that Leigh writes. It's amazing. This is the second book in the series and her best work yet. Please do yourself a favor and get a copy of *A Naked Beauty*. You won't regret it. Thank you, Leigh, for providing me an advanced copy of your book.

– DARLENE SUBER,
Mousey Books

Leigh Carron's first novel, *Fat Girl*, changed how I viewed romance novels. I confess to never having read one prior. But her book gave me a new perspective. I could not put *Fat Girl* down. I was hooked. Mick was every woman's fantasy and Dee was every woman.

A Naked Beauty is the very enticing continuation of their renewed relationship. Leigh Carron has a gift for writing vivid characters, and deftly captures that mix of love and passion. She portrays their past hurts and their battle for a second chance with compassion and understanding that bring Dee and Mick to life.

Every woman, regardless of their size, can relate in some way to Dee's body issues. Leigh Carron shows her journey in an inspiring and believable way. Every woman should read this book. And by the way, the sex scenes are really hot!

– HELEN MARTHA

This book is dedicated to my returning readers.

Thank you for sticking with me.
I'm excited to have finished *A Naked Beauty*,
and to share Dee and Mick's continued
journey with you. I hope you'll enjoy seeing
how their story unfolds as much I did.

ACKNOWLEDGMENTS

Writing a book takes a village. I have been very fortunate to have so many good and wonderful people in my camp.

First and foremost, I want to thank my husband. We tease him about being a diva princess with his pastel polos, pedicures, and enjoyment of the finer things in life. The man makes me laugh without intention. He has been one of my biggest supporters. He encourages me to follow my passion, and never complains when I'm holed up for hours in my writing chamber. A lifelong partner like that keeps my dreams and hopes alive.

Thank you to my daughter, who is kind and witty, and thinks far more deeply about the meaning of life than I do. I'm a lucky mom. She was a great sounding board when I was stuck, and bestowed on me one of the best compliments from a teenage girl when she said my writing was as a good as Colleen Hoover's. High praise, indeed. Big smile.

To the rest of my rock-solid family, thank you for always having my back. My mom is like those extra shots you can order at Booster Juice. She fuels my energy and drive with her unwavering belief in me. My dad is a source of practical wisdom and I have him to thank for my love of music. Look out for an eclectic playlist for *A Naked Beauty*. And last, but by no means least, to my brother and sister-in-law, who didn't even know how much they were contributing to the book. All those pictures and videos of my nephews—seeing their sweet faces and silly antics—were often the spark of light I needed.

To my cheerleaders, Carrie, Gilly, and Sam, whose friendship, support, humor, and virtual hugs I could not repay, even with a lifetime of heart emojis. But I will try.

To my incredible beta reading team for taking the time to review my draft manuscript, offering insightful feedback and loving my project. This book is far better thanks to you.

To those who have read an advanced copy of *A Naked Beauty* to form my street team of supporters, your awesomeness proves it takes a village.

To my editor, KB, thank you for your keen attention to detail, and aiding my development as a writer by educating me along the way. I know how understated you are but you cannot edit this out! :)

To my character, Dee, I may have created you, but you inspired me.

And finally, to all my readers, who wrote reviews, who sent me tear-jerking notes, and waited for *A Naked Beauty*, you are the caramel and almonds in my chocolate. I write because I love it, but it's your enjoyment that gives my writing purpose and validation.

"IF YOU ONLY SHINE A
LIGHT ON YOUR FLAWS, ALL
YOUR PERFECTS WILL DIM."

– Colleen Hoover

CHAPTER ONE

Dee

I DRIFT OUT OF SLEEP into heated pleasure.

The soft brush of lips along my neck and rasp of stubble teases my skin.

I might have thought I was dreaming except the feeling is far too potent.

Still, I keep my eyes closed and savor the velvety kisses that Mick scatters down my chest and across the pushed-up swells of cleavage. The hot ache of arousal billows inside me, blooming with a love and desire that had been too-long denied.

His mouth moves over my breasts, encased in the fitted cups of my nightie. He drags out my moan when the tip of his tongue plays a butterfly rhythm against my taut nipples. The gentle laps and friction of the dampened lace add another layer of exquisite sensation.

I've lost count of how many times we've made love this weekend, endless hours of exploration, relearning all the sweet spots, and discovering new and exciting delights.

He slides his hand between my legs, distilling the world into this moment. Into this space.

"Mick," I beg.

"Right here." He groans roughly, testing me with one finger, then two. His touch is intimate. Reverent. His strokes surge into my quivering sex, working me with deliberate intent while the pad of his thumb circles the nub of delicate nerve endings.

Mick's self-restraint seems absolute on the surface, his seduction singularly focused on me. And yet, his breathing is harsher than my own, his body trembles just as hard. Being aware of how much pleasuring me turns him on, of how acutely attuned he is, makes me hotter, wilder. I writhe, bucking my hips and riding his hand.

"That's it, baby," he urges, his breath a hot trail on my skin, his fingers working their blissful magic. "I can feel you. So close. So sexy."

One more stroke and rapture explodes. The release is dizzying. I open my eyes, and the only thing clear and steady is Mick. My beautiful lover. The other half of my soul, returned to me after fifteen years of heartbreaking separation.

"I can't get enough," he whispers and eases his fingers from my body to push the nightie up my torso and over my head.

Bared, I have a fleeting moment of self-consciousness, but it dissolves when his chest replaces the material, and he covers me in delicious heat. I run my nails up and down the ripples in his back, worshiping the weight of his hard body pressed against mine, the feel of muscle and hot flesh.

He lowers his head, and takes long tastes of my mouth, sliding his tongue along the open seam, nipping my bottom lip before he deepens the kiss with soft, skillful plunges. He curled my toes at eighteen. He curls my toes still.

His hands push beneath my thighs, raising my knees up and spreading them. Then in one fluid movement, he shifts his hips downward and thrusts into me, stealing my breath.

"Ah, Dee…" He slides out to the tip then slides back in. "You always feel so damn good."

Everything in my core tightens greedily. I claw at his back and wrap my legs around his waist.

The tempo he sets is slow and measured, a smooth, erotic grind. No matter the pace, Mick's brand of lovemaking is possessive in the best way possible. It's what I crave. Him loving me, reclaiming me. I didn't know how lonely I was until he bulldozed his way back into my life and filled all those empty places. Even through our anger—even after it built to an ugly boiling point and the devastating secrets and losses came spilling out—his pursuit was relentless, his love unconditional. No matter how many times I ran, afraid to risk my heart again, he caught me, held on, and proved with words and deeds that I was his and he was mine.

Now bound to his sweat-slick body, my arms and legs sealed around him, I rock into his rhythm, our rhythm—a harmony of hearts and breaths and hips. I close my eyes, listening to his rumbling groans and feel their vibration against my mouth. My hands squeeze the flexing muscles in his back, and I glory in the way we fit together, a key into a lock that opens up treasures, both the familiar and the new.

Urgency spools inside me, and my nails bite into his skin as his powerful thrusts massage me from the inside out.

"Don't stop," I plead, between our breathy kisses and throaty moans.

"Not ever," he rasps. "I was made to love you."

His impassioned words, the fervor of his movements...I climax again. The intensity of my orgasm violently shakes my body and clenches my sex. Mick shudders through the hard contractions. Then quickening his pace, he drives me into the mattress with erotic abandon, and comes, pushing so deep inside me, I feel it through to my soul.

Shuddering, he buries his face in my neck and holds me so tight I can hardly breathe. But I don't need air when I have Mick. I just need him and the way he makes me feel. Safe. Cherished. And beautiful.

When he recovers and his head lifts to stare down at me, I have to smile. He looks sexy and sated. His dark, wavy hair is all mussed. His skin is damp with sweat, and his espresso-brown eyes are at half-mast.

"Mm. I could get used to waking up like this." I touch his whiskered cheek. "You're way better than an alarm clock."

"No programming required." He grins lazily. "And I come with extra features."

"Excellent features," I say, with him still thickly nestled inside me.

I wouldn't have thought it was possible, but for once in my life, I reject the notion that my happiness is the light before the dark, the foreshadowing of the black clouds I've come to expect. Instead, I invite it in with the morning sun. A new day. A new beginning. My second chance to have everything I've ever wanted: Mick and my family.

We're all having brunch today at Maria's. I'm excited and nervous at the same time. It's been fifteen years since I've seen my foster sister. She was only eleven when I left. Now, a grown woman, a wife and mother, who owns an organic farm with her husband, James.

"Are brunches still the same?" I ask.

"What do you mean?" He rolls onto his back and brings me with him.

I snuggle into his side. "Does everyone still help with the preparations? That was the best part." Even though as a teenager I hovered along the perimeter, apprehensive about joining in, Sunday brunches were still my favorites.

. "Yeah." He smiles in a pure gesture of how much he loves them too. "Mama T wouldn't have it any other way."

"I remember you always tried to get out of doing the dishes," I tease.

"Not always. I never tried with you."

"Why was that?"

"It gave me an excuse to be with you."

I draw the sheet up to my chest and push to one elbow, searching his face. "Seriously?"

"I'd use any opportunity to be next to you. To pretend to accidentally touch hands, brush shoulders...."

"I didn't know that was on purpose." My insecurities being what they were, I had no idea that the gorgeous and popular Micah Peters had any interest in me other than as the foster sister to his best friend. "I used to get all tingly and hoped you wouldn't notice."

"I noticed." He glides his fingers down my arm causing me to shiver. "Seems I still make you tingly."

"Mick..." I draw a breath of willpower. "We should get ready."

He eyes the clock on the side table and returns with a gleaming gaze. "We have a little time."

"Not enough for that."

"I do my best work under pressure."

I push at him, laughing. "I bet you do, but I don't want to be late."

"Shower with me then." He stands and takes my palm in his.

I pull the sheet around me with my free hand and hold it to my chest as he leads me to the bathroom, the white cotton train trailing my steps.

He turns on the taps, adjusting the water to the near scalding temperature we both prefer. The tiny confinement soon billows with steam.

"Just a shower," I warn, knowing my weakness for him.

Mick's hot grin penetrates the vaporous cloud as he tugs away the sheet. "I make no promises other than to get you to brunch on time."

SHOWERS ARE EXTREMELY AWESOME WHEN they end with Mick on his knees and his mouth on me. I'm still flushed as I shimmy a pair of sheer pink panties up my legs and under my robe.

Regardless of how far I've come this weekend—showering together, skimpy lingerie, making love in the light of day—I still don't have the nerve to parade around the house naked or to even look at my body unclothed. When in the throes of passion, I let go. But I still have my insecurities.

Mick, on the other hand, immodestly naked—with good reason—has no trouble strolling across the room. I watch the play of muscles in his very firm, very fine ass. He sets his duffle bag atop the bed and rummages through it to retrieve a pair of underwear.

I've never had this before. The intimate day-to-day stuff.

"What?" He catches my stare.

"This"—I gesture around the room—"is new for me."

His thick eyebrows quirk up in question. "What is?"

"Getting dressed with someone...spending a weekend together... sharing living space. I realize that most people by the age of thirty-three have experienced that, but I haven't."

He gives me an exultant smile. "Glad to know I'm your only."

"You are. What about you?"

He drops his boxer briefs on the tousled sheets and moves toward me. My eyes roam the expanse of toasted caramel skin and the fire tattoo around his right bicep that, when in motion, resembles leaping flames. Mick is large and lean. His long, muscular body a striking work of art—broad defined shoulders, sculpted chest and abs, carved thighs, and an impressive package between them. He isn't hard, but his virility still commands attention.

"Eyes up here, Dee, or we won't be going anywhere soon." My cheeks warm and he laughs. "Embarrassment from the same woman who left scratches all over my back."

I can't help being wild with him, it's what he does to me. "Are you trying to distract me from having to answer the question?"

"No." He pulls me into his arms and cups my fleshy bottom. "But you're distracting me. I'm imagining what you look like beneath this robe, in those pink panties."

It never ceases to amaze me that Mick can be this enamored by my body, especially by my behind.

"Now getting back to your question." He gives me a playful squeeze. "It's a first for me too."

My jaw drops in surprise. "You never shacked up with any of your gorgeous supermodels? Not even for a weekend?"

He takes my chin between his thumb and forefinger and looks into my eyes, his gaze intent. "They weren't mine any more than I was theirs.

17

Comparisons between you and other women are impossible because they don't exist. I have never spent a weekend with a woman, let alone shacked up with one, as you put it. I've never wanted that...until now.

"I love sleeping with you, Dee. Feeling you curled up against me, waking up to your soft body and beautiful face...watching you slip into sexy panties, sharing a toothbrush holder with you, seeing your soap next to mine...all of it."

On a burst of joy, I wind my arms around his neck and blurt out, "So you'd be good with having a drawer?"

He answers with a lush, wet kiss. I pull back, panting, and smile up at him. "Should I take that as a yes?"

"You should take that as a *hell yes*."

I empty the third drawer, and my heart gushes as he places the items from his duffle bag inside. He meets my stare, and warmth fills his eyes.

I know one drawer doesn't equal cohabitation. That I'm even considering it this soon only proves to me how fast and hard I've fallen.

Since my teenage romance with Mick, my subsequent relationships had all been distant. It was easier to keep men at arm's length. Safer. I picked guys like me—reserved, tedious, workaholics, consumed with their careers. No one that stripped me bare, revved my dormant sex drive, fluttered my heart, or made me yearn for a future together. I slept alone with no dirty whispers among the sheets, no cuddling through the night, or spontaneous wake-up sex.

With Mick, everything is different. On that thought, I step inside the walk-in closet and feel myself frown. I'd stocked up on pretty undies to embark on my affair with Mick but my wardrobe was still sadly lacking. Aside from an assortment of dark business suits, the few casual pieces I own are loose and concealing. Except for the items I'd bought on a whim, for when...if...I ever developed the confidence to wear them.

Channeling the self-assured woman I want to be, I reach into the back of the closet where I store the maybe-one-day outfits and retrieve black jeans. I'd worn them once to the Glam Bar, the night Lexie and Jordyn forced me into the unforgiving denim and dragged me out to forget about Mick. Today, I'll don them under happier circumstances.

I tug the stretchy jeans over the thick thighs and pear-shaped hips I've always despised. It's for that reason that I have never purchased a full-length mirror. I'm not comfortable looking at myself. Now, I glance over my shoulder and wish I hadn't. The spandex that's supposed to act as a fat suction doesn't do any such thing. On the contrary, it shellacs the material to my huge bubble butt, making it even more pronounced. When that mocking inner voice starts to get loud in my head, telling me I'm not good enough, not slim enough or perfect enough, I stop, take a deep breath, and negotiate with my balking self-consciousness. Rather than ditch the jeans, I pull on a long, oversized sweater.

Still battling myself, I step back into the bedroom. Mick blows out a soft whistle. "I haven't seen you in tight jeans before."

"They're not something I wear often." Or at all.

"Let me see." He reaches for me, attempting to lift the sweater.

"Later." I laugh, batting at his hands, feeling better than I had moments ago.

"Come on. Just a sneak preview."

Since Mick likes my big butt, even if I don't, I give him a quick flash.

"Jesus, Dee." He adjusts himself. "You are seriously dangerous."

"And you're not?"

In low-slung blue jeans, aged to perfection, and an army-green Henley that hugs him just right, Mick packs a danger all his own. If we had more time, I'd strip him down—with my teeth—and lick him all over.

His lips twitch, equally aware of his effect on me. "Before I forget my promise, I'll go make us some coffee for the road."

I spritz on perfume, add moisturizing hair gel to help tame my curls, and run the mascara brush through my lashes. Satisfied, I stare at my head-to-shoulder reflection and decide to forego the blusher. It's as if the joy I'm feeling is shining out of me and making my olive skin glow.

When I join Mick in the kitchen, he pockets his cell phone and hands me a stainless-steel travel mug. "Light on the milk and three sweeteners."

I take a cautious sip of the steaming coffee through the lid opening and smile in appreciation. "Mmm. No wonder I adore you."

"I'll keep giving you reasons, beauty."

"Beauty?"

"Mm-hmm. You're my beauty. That's the way I see you. Not just because of the way you look, but because of everything you are."

Aw...how can I not love him?

He brushes his fingers over my cheek. Mick is such a physically strong and powerful man, yet he can touch me with such gentleness.

I lean into his caress, smitten with him. "We should go," I eventually say, torn between having to break the moment and excitement to see my family. "I really don't want to be late."

"I know." He kisses me—a sweet press to my lips before he pulls back and reaches for his baseball cap and dark shades on the counter.

I'd been too absorbed in him to notice them a moment ago. For the past two days, it has been just us, secluded in our safe haven, absent the threat of media attention. But now I'm reminded of how our first date at the Lemon Lounge ended. Reporters unexpectedly showed up, and Mick had Stiles—a bodyguard of sorts—drive Jordyn and me home, to protect me from his fame.

I'd blocked it from my thoughts for the weekend, wanting nothing more than to shut that part of our world out while locking ourselves in. But seeing him lower the brim and slide on the opaque shades to disguise his identity hits my happy bubble with a needle-sharp prick.

The world I wish to avoid could be waiting outside my door.

CHAPTER TWO

Micah

WHEN I FIRST MET DEE, I was a hormonal fourteen-year-old.

I thought she had sexy hair. It reminded me of those lost-on-a-desert-island movies where the girl is found in two swatches of a tiger print bikini and her hair is all wild and untamed. I wanted to reach out and touch the long sable-brown curls that curtained her face. I wanted to see if they felt as soft and springy as they looked.

Next, I wondered about the body that she hid behind baggy jeans and a sweatshirt several sizes too big. She wasn't straight or skinny, that much I could tell. When her nervous fingers tugged the bulky material at her chest, I tracked the movement to the hint of plump, round breasts. I wanted to touch those too.

Wrong, wrong, wrong, on so many levels. Papa T had already given Victor and me a stern man-to-man talk about our responsibilities as her brothers. Nothing about my reaction to Dee was screaming brotherly.

As I stood there in the living room among my surrogate family—that lives next door—welcoming the newest member, I knew I had to drag my head out of the gutter. And fast. But my brain wouldn't cooperate.

Dee tucked a cluster of curls behind her ear, giving me a glimpse of honey smooth skin and a full, pink mouth. I thought her bottom lip looked like a ripe, juicy strawberry and the upper indented like a pretty bow. I thought: *I want to kiss her badly.*

As wrong as my thoughts were, they continued on that lusty, narrow track until Mama T introduced us. Dee looked up at me with these big eyes, more golden than brown. I'd never seen eyes that rare and luminous or more beautiful. It was like being swallowed by the sun.

In an instant, everything inside me warmed. Shifted. I couldn't call the unprecedented feeling *love*. I was just a kid. But there was a quiet sadness about her that tugged on my protective strings. I understood something of her grief, having lost my mother too. And yet I sensed there was something inherently more drawing me to her. Some connection I hadn't known I was searching desperately for, that might explain why this girl had such an immediate and profound effect on me.

Later that night, I huddled inside my closet with a flashlight. I couldn't risk having my old man catch me in the forbidden act. I stayed there and wrote until the wee hours. It wouldn't be the only time that Dee would inspire my writing.

The story came alive with every word I penned on paper about a demon son born to the dark side who encounters an angel that changes his world. He knows he has no right to claim her, but unable to resist the beauty and light she possesses, he marks her heart.

In real life, our differences weren't mythical, yet no less divisive.

I couldn't betray the Torreses. Dee was off limits. She was Papa T's foster daughter, sunshine and innocence. And I was Malcolm Peters' son, dark and damaged.

I couldn't have her. I didn't deserve her. But neither stopped me from wanting her. When I started dating, all the other girls were fillers, temporary distractions. Dee was my every thought, my every breath. I invented reasons to be around her. Every day. To get my fix, to catch a whiff of vanilla and flowers, to touch her in subtle ways.

It didn't take me long to fall in love with the rare smiles that playfully tilted up one side of her mouth. Or with the single-minded determination she had to attend law school and become an advocate for foster children. Or with the way she bit her bottom lip in internal debate and chewed the end of her pen when thinking through a homework problem.

I discovered that Dee wasn't shy at all. Rather, she wore a cool reserve as a self-protective shield, but beneath it she was generous and warm.

I knew she had her secrets. I had mine too. All I wanted was to protect her, please her, impress her. I loved that she looked at me and saw past the façade of the popular jock. Loved that she believed in my talent as a writer. Loved the way I didn't feel the darkness when I was around her.

I loved her silently for four long years. And the day that I confided in her my ugly truths and she bandaged my cut and tenderly traced my bruises with her delicate, healing lips...*Christ*, I couldn't silence it anymore.

I kissed her. In the midst of one of my darkest days, one in which I thought I might die, that kiss—a simple touching of lips, of sharing breaths—was my oxygen, my salvation.

I couldn't get enough. Of her sweetness, her passion, of the way she numbed my pain and gave me hope.

I'd written about it, but hadn't allowed myself to expect that Dee could ever be mine. She'd suffered through so much neglect and rejection. Afraid to trust, she didn't form any friendships and even with her foster family she sat on the sidelines. Yet she'd let me past her guard, giving me her sweet, untouched body and her battered and scarred heart.

I promised to make her happy...to always be there for her.

But I fucked up on both counts.

The guilt from failing Dee all those years ago is still speared in my gut like a hot, damning poker. So, hearing the sudden shift in her breathing and seeing her anxious gaze as she watches me pull on my cap and shades, plunges the spear in deeper. I know what she's thinking. I can feel it resonating between us, tangible and intense—the intrusion of my fame into our perfect weekend. I hate that.

"They're just precautions, Dee." I shove away a flood of regrets. "No reporters are outside. There's nothing to worry about."

I'd made sure of that.

I'll do everything in my power to protect you from the media.

A promise I intend to keep, no matter what I have to do. I want our relationship to be a harbor of happiness and pleasure. I want her to feel safe and secure. I want to give her a life insulated from the stains of our past and the threat of my fame.

She looks up with those amber eyes. Trusting in my assurances. Trusting in me.

I press my lips to hers and feel all the tension unwind.

Dee

THE HOUR-LONG DRIVE UP north is a scenic treat. Cows graze in sprawling green meadows and dense woods are filled with autumn trees that resemble giant puffs of yellow and red cotton candy.

I watch Mick across the console. Once we hit the country roads, he'd removed his cap and shades. The breeze through the slightly ajar sunroof stirs his inky waves, and his grin crinkles the corners of his eyes as he entertains my many questions about the family and shares the funny stories he's so good at telling.

But beneath the laughter, my nerves frizzle. It's the lingering doubt that I don't deserve all this after the way I left. It's seeing Maria for the first time in fifteen years, meeting her family...little Mason. I haven't been around many babies. What if the haunting memories overwhelm me? What if I can't hold it together?

"We're here," Mick announces a short time later, giving my hand a quick squeeze before he unlinks our fingers to gear down.

I look through the windshield at the white wooden sign painted in green block letters. *Whole Fresh Organics.* I'd learned from Mama T that Maria, studying agribusiness, and James, agriculture, had met in a Harvest for the Future student group during college, and married in their final year. Maria got pregnant almost immediately, and James took an environmental job with the government. But their dream was to own an organic farm.

Mick turns onto a long, gravel driveway. His Porsche rocks over the uneven surface, kicking up dust clouds. I crane my neck to take in the rolling acres on either side, lined with a split-rail wooden fence. The property is a mix of orchards and growing fields.

My eyes widen when a large single level ranch house with a wrap-around porch comes into view. It's built on a rise and nestled among a canopy of trees. Set farther away, separate from the living space, are several outbuildings, tractors, and a barn.

"They operate all this?" I ask.

"Every acre," Mick says proudly. "Last year their sales to grocery stores and restaurants grew by 112% and their new online farm-to-table business is on an upward trajectory too. Maria is great with social media, but mostly it's word of mouth from satisfied customers. They're doing what they love."

"With help from you."

"It was no big thing," he says with a modest shrug. I know better.

"Mama T said they couldn't get the kind of loan they needed so you bought the farm for them."

"It was a good investment. Plus, I'm fortunate that it was in my power to give them a start."

When his face angles from the driveway to briefly glance over at me, I smile. "You're good to your family, Mick. They're lucky to have you."

"Not as lucky as I am to have them." He lifts my hand to his lips and kisses the back of it. "Or you."

I start to respond, to tell him how much he means to me too, to let him know how much I appreciate my second chance, but the instant he pulls up beside Victor's sedan, Justin and Danielle come barreling out from around the side of the house.

I stare out the window at the two energetic children, bouncing impatiently, and wring my hands.

"Dee?"

I hear the concern in his voice. "I'm fine."

He appears no more certain of that than I am. Nevertheless, I give him a faint smile, then on one, two, three deep breaths, open the door.

Maria's five-year-old son gazes up at me in wonder. His front tooth is missing, his chin has a dirt smear, and his jean-clad knees are covered in grass stains. He's adorable.

"I seed your picture," he says.

I blink away the swell of tears and bend down. "I've seen your pictures too. You must be Justin."

"Yup. I'm the biggest," he boasts, standing taller. "I have a baby brother. His name's Mason. He's sleeping now. This is Dani." He jerks his thumb at his sister. "She's only four."

"But Mommy says I's going on twenty," inserts the pint-size version of Maria.

I smile at the little girl dressed in a lavender princess gown that's paired with polka-dot rain boots. She's cute as a doll, round sun-rosy cheeks, dark pigtails, and wide, inquisitive eyes. "Hi, Dani."

"Hi," she says. "You're pretty."

"Thank you. I think you're pretty too."

Justin disagrees in the way of brothers by sticking out his tongue to mimic gagging. Mick swoops in with tickles that effectively distract him.

"Aunt Gabi tolded me you're Uncle Mick's girlfriend," Dani continues.

"Um...yes, I am."

She scrunches up her nose. "How come we never meeted his other girlfriends?"

Before I can think how to answer, Mick tucks the siblings under his arms like footballs. "Because your Aunt Dee is special and mine for keeps." Then winking at me, he feigns a toss, making them shriek with giggles.

I watch him with a bitter sweetness. He'd be a great father, playful enough to make it fun and loving enough to make a child feel valued. I lift my tote bag containing gifts for everyone, and with my heart rattling in my chest, follow him and his bundles to the house.

Inside is wonderfully noisy and chaotic. Shoes litter the tiled foyer. Backpacks and jackets overflow the coat rack. Off to the side is a family room where a lived-in sectional and an area rug are scattered with toys and books. A doll sits in a high chair and there's a Tonka truck on the food tray. Patterned overstuffed armchairs designed for comfort don't match the couch or each other. There is no attempt at coordination or order in this room and that makes it all the more inviting.

Along the narrow hallway hang the children's drawings, and detailed sketches that must be Dwayde's. The aroma of good home cooking wafts through the air. I can actually identify the smell of authentic ranchero sauce. Mama T's version was always the right balance of tomatoes, chili powder, and jalapeño to give it just enough heat. My stomach growls over the tremble of nerves. I feel excited, anxious, happy...*terrified*.

Mick stops when we reach the kitchen. Papa T used to call it the eye of the storm and Mama T its wind force. She issues orders in a mix of English and Spanish. "Apaga el quemador...the burner, James, turn it down...the eggs...oh ja ja! Gabi...Gabi! Dios mío. Get off the Tickie Tok and stir the sauce."

I've missed this.

It's the same in so many ways. Yet the changes are staggering. My foster sisters aren't little girls anymore. Gabi is now a senior in high school, living with Victor and Isabelle. Maria has a husband and children. Papa T is gone.

Last week, I'd been able to explain the inexcusable and apologize to everyone, except for Maria. I'd get that chance with her today. But for Cayo Torres, I was too late.

Catching whatever look I must have on my face, Mick sets down Justin and Dani to take my trembling hand in the comforting calm of his.

The kids run in, announcing our arrival. Mama T pauses mid-stream and turns toward the archway. Escaped wisps from her long, dark braid, streaked with gray, fall around her lovely face.

"Mis hijos preciosos!" She drops the dish towel on the counter and hurries over to throw her arms around us.

I hug her hard. She's cushiony soft and smells like nutmeg and sweet memories. "It's so good to see you again, Mama T. Thank you for inviting me."

"You are not a guest, mi hija. You are home." She dabs beneath her eyes with the crook of her forefingers. "Let me look at the two of you together...ah...perfecto. I wish Cayo were here to see this."

"I'll take good care of her, Mama T. Make you and Cayo proud."

"I have no doubts, mi hijo." She lifts up on tiptoe to pat Mick's cheek. "You both picked well."

My emotions are reeling when Maria comes from around the center island. We openly stare at each other. Getting height from her father, she's almost as tall as my five-feet-nine, and adulthood has rounded out her once coltish body. I can't stop the flow of tears. We both reach out and converge in a swaying embrace.

"I'm sorry." It's not the most private time to voice my apology, but the words pour out of me. "I'm sorry for leaving, for missing you growing up...for hurting you."

"Ssh..." She cries too. "All that matters is I have my big sister back."

Gabi and Mama T join, circling us in a group hug, their tears falling just as hard.

"Why's you all crying, Mommy?" Dani asks, tugging at her mother's pant leg, her tiny voice distressed.

"These aren't sad tears, honey." Maria sniffles and squats down to assure her daughter. "We're just happy to see your Aunt Dee again."

"How come you haven't seed her? Was you lost, Aunt Dee?" She looks up at me in confusion.

"Yes, Dani. I was lost for a while, but your Uncle Mick found me."

My eyes seek out his. They hold me in a deep caress as we share this special moment, the reunion that if not for his persistence, his love, may never have happened.

"Don't get lost again," Dani warns sternly, shaking her finger.

I swipe at my wet cheeks. "No. I won't. Not ever again."

"Gotta keep our girl-to-boy ratio even around here," Maria says, lightening the mood.

"Like you alone aren't army enough." Maria's husband steps forward. Clear blue eyes full of humor, ginger hair that's tied in a stubby ponytail, and a thick mustache and beard covers the lower half of his face. He's about five-ten and burly; brings to mind a mountain man. His apron reads: *In this house only 2 rules apply. #1 She's the boss. #2 See Rule #1.* "Hi Dee, I'm James. Welcome home."

"Hi, James." I go to extend my hand but he wraps me in a bear hug that squeezes the breath out of me.

My foster brother, Victor, similar to Papa T with his dark features and laid back style, strolls over for a familiar ruffle of my curls. "Hey, Brat. Is Mick taking good care of you or do I have to beat him up?"

"He's doing okay," I say with a smile.

He taps his fist to Mick's and they share a half hug. Two tall, strong, handsome men, that couldn't be more like brothers.

"What a pair they make," Isabelle says, coming up beside me.

"I was just thinking the same."

I don't know Victor's wife well yet. I've only met her twice. First, at my office with Dwayde, and then last Thursday when I showed up at her house to tell all to Victor, and he invited me to stay for dinner. True to what I've seen of her affectionate and optimistic nature, she gives me an exuberant hug.

"I'm so glad you and Mick found each other again."

"I wish it could have been under better circumstances." Not the custody case.

"I have faith. You and Mick will get your happy ending. And Victor, Dwayde, and I will get ours."

I give her another hug because more than anything I want both to be true.

Justin and Dani jump around among the excitement and Mick engages Dwayde in a tussle that has him snorting with laughter. When I approach, his laugh skids to a halt and a wary look overtakes those big Franklin eyes.

"Hi, Dwayde."

"Yeah…hey." He hunches his thin shoulders.

Although I'm his lawyer, I had hoped that my inclusion in the family might thaw him toward me. I need his trust for the case, especially since I suspect he's hiding something key. But he still remains aloof.

At twelve, I was the same, suspicious of anyone in the system, even those who claimed to be on my side.

"How are you?" I ask.

"Aw'right."

"Ready for your game this Friday?"

He lowers his head. The cornrows are gone, now replaced with buzzed sides and a curly top. "I guess."

Though he's braced against me in self-defense, I persist. "I'd like to come cheer you on."

His shoulders hitch again.

I hear Mick's sharp indrawn breath that is likely a signal for manners as Dwayde quickly adds, "Yeah. If you want."

"I do. I haven't been to a basketball game in years." Not since watching Mick play in high school from the back of the rafters.

"Then we'll have to win this for her, won't we?" Mick says, nudging Dwayde's ribs and managing to pull a dimpled grin out of him.

Maria strides up and hooks her arm through mine. "I'm stealing your girl away for a while."

"No problem. As long as I get her back." Then catching me off guard, Mick leans forward and drops a loud kiss on my stunned mouth in front of everyone.

"Eww." Justin's face turns to a grimace and Dwayde's expression shows equal complaint.

"Don't knock it until you're old enough to try it. Better than ice cream." He winks at his nephews, pleased with himself, and I feel my cheeks heat at his outrageousness.

"Okay, lover boy," Maria teases. "How about you strap it down and go set the table?"

"Strap what down?" Dani asks, as I'm beginning to see is her nature.

"I'll leave that one to you," Mick says, chuckling as he saunters over to the eating area with Dwayde.

Dani waits for her mother's explanation, her little head angled in question.

"Um...the napkins, sweetie. We need Uncle Mick to strap down the napkins with forks and knives. Now go help Aba with the tamales."

Satisfied, Dani runs off and climbs up on the footstool beside her grandmother.

"Good save," I say as Maria leads me arm-in-arm to the island.

"She's such a Curious George, I have to watch everything that comes out of my mouth. Here." Maria lays out a cutting board, knife, and strainer filled with washed apples she says are from their orchard. "Peel and chop these into cubes about this big." She shows me the size with the space between her forefinger and thumb. "You're going to make the filling while I prepare the empanada dough."

I bump her shoulder, amused. "You've gotten bossy."

"I come by it honestly," she agrees with a laugh, not the least offended.

We watch Rita Torres rule the kitchen—instructing James and Victor, and putting Justin and Dani to work fetching items from the fridge.

"James calls me a drill sergeant."

"Explains the apron."

"Mick bought that for him. Jerk." But there's only affection in her voice.

"You've done well, Maria—the success of your farm...your lovely home. James...the kids. I'm looking forward to meeting Mason," I insert with more enthusiasm than I feel.

"Thanks." She smiles in a way that tells me she's proud of her achievements and pleased with her life. "He'll be up in an hour or so. I put him down just before you got here, so you wouldn't be hit with all of us at once."

I'm grateful for her thoughtfulness. With my emotions running high, the delay is a relief. I catch up with my sister, make apple filling and immerse myself in the familiar scene of brunch preparations that could only be more complete if Papa T were here.

This is what I wished for as a child—a family to call my own. To have as mine. To last. After ten foster homes, I had been so afraid to let myself get too close...afraid that like trying to catch lightning in a bottle, the Torreses were a dream I could never hold on to.

I stayed back, protecting myself. Convinced it would be easier when they rejected me. Only they didn't. Not ever. I'd been the one to leave, to run without any explanation.

And now through a twist of fate I've been gifted with Mick and my family again, their unmitigated acceptance and forgiveness, the crowning jewel. I won't take a second of it for granted this time. I'm going to cherish it all.

CHAPTER THREE

Micah

WE MAKE ONE LIVELY, LOUD puzzle. All of us are firmly interlocked, whether by blood or not, it doesn't matter here. And Dee, no longer the observer who used to watch and want from a distance, seems to slide right in.

Good at juggling multiple conversations, over brunch she gives everyone attention. Laughs at James' dry humor and Dani's non-stop chatter. She thumb-wrestles with Justin—his new favorite thing; engages a reluctant Dwayde in questions about school and video games; talks to Victor about his work; shares a robust exchange with Maria, Mama T, and Isabelle about the political issues facing women. And just as easily switches gears to a lighter topic when Gabi asks her opinion on getting caramel highlights, which they discuss as if world peace hinges on it.

I like seeing her here. Connected and happy. But I note that she only eats a small portion of the huevos rancheros and none of the tortilla. It might have been lost on me if not for Dee's confession just days ago about her ongoing issues with food and her weight, a battle she's been fighting since childhood.

I can't profess total understanding. I know many women face similar issues with varying degrees of insecurity. I've dated models whose livelihoods were based on their looks. I've heard Isabelle and Maria talk about the latest diet or make some complaint about their so-called imperfect bodies. I've witnessed James and Victor shake their heads, perplexed by their wives' perceived flaws.

Dee is beautiful to me. I couldn't care less how much she weighs. I love her round curves. Love that she's warm and soft. Love the way she feels beneath me. I love her for so many reasons other than just her body. I watch her take a small bite of the tamale filling and talk animatedly with Dani and Justin. She's so pretty with her bright smile, and those plush rosy lips that I wanted to kiss the first time I saw her. She may not be the same girl I met almost twenty years ago, but my response to her hasn't changed. Constant, hot, and craving.

When the meal is finished, Maria sends Dee to the walk-in pantry and storage area beside the kitchen for Tupperware bowls.

"*Mick.*" She startles when I follow her inside and cage her against a wall of shelves. "What are you doing?"

"I must be losing my touch if you have to ask."

"Go, before someone sees you."

"You're cute when you're all flustered." I dip my head, tracing the curve of her neck with my nose. "Mmm. You smell good."

"Stop it." She pushes at my chest. "I have to get the bowls."

"In a minute." I slide one arm around her waist, frowning because I can't get a good feel of her. "Why did you choose this long sweater?"

"So, I wouldn't distract you," she quips, though I doubt that's the real answer.

"It didn't work. You always distract me." I close in on the fullness of her mouth. "I'm hard with wanting you."

"Ssh..." She puts her finger to my lips. "I did leave you high and dry in the shower, didn't I?"

I nip at her finger. "I'm not complaining."

"I'll take care of you later."

"I'll hold you to it. But for now, just one kiss."

She pecks my lips.

"Uh-uh. Make it count."

"Not with our family right outside."

"They won't care. All the couples fool around in here."

"You're making that up."

"It's tradition." I move back in. "Now give me a kiss, beauty. Something to tide me over."

Her eyes dart to the opening to ensure no one's there. Then she threads her fingers through my hair and—damn—there's nothing but

32

her lush mouth and the sultry sweep of her tongue. Dee's taste is a wicked sweet heat that spins my head and sends my entire system into overdrive. Her breasts crush against my chest. I slip my hands beneath her sweater and cup the round, meaty curves of her behind tucked into tight denim.

"Micah Anthony!"

We jerk apart and my eyes swerve to Mama T's grin.

"Busted." Maria laughs.

Dee's cheeks flush with embarrassment while she tugs her sweater back into place. She never experienced this as a teenager, getting caught in the act of a steamy kiss and furtive grope. Our previous relationship had been secret, and now that we're out in the open, at least with the family, I make no attempt to keep my desire for her under wraps.

"She's irresistible," I say, treating myself to one last kiss.

Dee glares at me. "I'm sorry you saw that, Mama T."

"Bah." Rita Torres cuts off her needless apology. "Passion is good for the heart, mi hija. Do you know how many times I've caught Vittorio and Isabelle in here? Or James and Maria?"

"Or," Maria interjects, "the time we caught you and Papa."

"Hush up." Mama T smiles wistfully and swats her daughter with the dish towel.

"*See?*" I mouth to Dee. When she attempts to maintain her scowl, I add, "*Your fault for being so sexy.*" That effectively coaxes her mouth into a one-sided grin.

When we return to the kitchen, the women work on storing the leftovers, and I join Victor and James at the sink.

"Dumb rookie." Victor snorts. "Getting caught your first time." He tosses the sponge to me. "You wash."

Here, no one cares about my celebrity. I'm just Mick. The way I like it.

After the kitchen is tidied, we bring the hot chocolate, Mexican coffee, and apple empanadas out to the family room where the kids are watching a Disney movie and Dwayde's playing a sword fighting game on his iPad. I settle next to Dee on the couch and put my arm around her shoulders. She leans over to watch Dwayde in action. Before long he's showing her how to capture the gems to score points.

With his guard down, I can see the tiny threads interweaving, the connection starting to form. Not between client and lawyer but between nephew and aunt. They're both laughing at her eager, yet failed attempts when the high pitch of Mason's cry crackles through the baby monitor.

Dee's smile collapses and her palm moves to her stomach. The kids are oblivious, but all adult eyes turn to us. I read their compassion.

"I thought he might sleep a bit longer," Maria says apologetically.

"It's fine." The same sturdy words Dee said to me in the car don't hold up to the tremor in her voice.

"Should we go get him?" I ask to give her the opportunity to deal with this moment privately.

She nods and tells Dwayde she'll be right back. I take her cold hand in mine. Mama T gives us an encouraging smile that's tinged with sadness. When we reach Mason's room, I stop to cradle Dee's cheeks between my palms and give in to my protective urge to whisk her away rather than have her face the reminder. "If you're not ready—"

"I'm as ready as I'll ever be. This is my family and Mason is a part of that. I have to do this."

She's right, but that doesn't make it any easier to watch the cloud of grief move across her amber eyes. With great reluctance, I release her and open the door.

Mason's wails and the smell of baby powder hit me all at once. I've smelled that scent and heard his cries a hundred times, but never before have they threatened to buckle my knees.

Dee stays rooted on the threshold taking deep, audible breaths as I manage to cross to the crib and lift the screaming five-month-old onto my shoulder, and pat his back. "It's alright, little man."

Mason chokes out a few more cries before he quiets and snuggles his chubby body into me. I think of the baby we lost. Would it have been a boy or girl? Have brown or golden eyes? Would our child have grown up to be shy or outgoing? Studious or the class clown? An athlete? A writer? A lawyer? A future president? The possibilities are endless. The guilt gripping.

I shake my head and focus my attention back to Dee, who still hasn't ventured into the room. *I have to do this*, she'd said. I clear my throat and attempt to get her inside.

"Could you pass me a jumper from the second drawer?"

She nods and enters the space-themed nursery and steps over to the white wooden dresser. Above it is a mural Dwayde painted with bright colored planets and monkeys in rocket ships. She pulls open the drawer and brushes her fingers over the tiny outfits before selecting a navy striped one-piece and walking it to the change table.

She watches me pin on a clean cloth diaper, but doesn't look directly at Mason. "You're good at that."

"I've had lots of practice with three kids. Even when I played for Miami, I got back here often."

"What were they like?" Dee asks as she's been doing all weekend, peppering me with questions to fill in the gaps of what she's missed.

"Justin was stubborn as a toddler."

"Sounds like Gabi," she replies.

"Yeah. He wanted to do everything himself. Would get mad if you tried to help. Still does. While Dani is more like Maria, a chatterbox as I'm sure you can tell. She babbled nonstop before she could even talk, and said her first word when she was less than a year old. She never stops. Mason, here, reminds me of Victor and Papa T. He has a great set of lungs when he's pissed off, but otherwise he's pretty chill."

She lets her eyes wander over him. Her expression carries a note of longing.

I finish dressing Mason and take a chance hoping it might...hell, I don't know, be cathartic. "Want to hold him?"

She gnaws her bottom lip. "He might cry with me."

"I doubt it. He likes being held."

"Okay." She rubs her palms down her sweater then stretches out her arms to receive him. Handling Mason far more carefully than I do, she lays him in the crook of her arms, supporting his head with one hand as she lowers herself onto the glider.

I watch Dee, mesmerized—so maternal, so at home with a baby. She coos to him and lifts his small palm to measure it against hers. When he wraps his fist around her forefinger, her laugh of pure delight punches straight to my gut.

She studies his toes and leans in to kiss the crown of wispy dark hair. He releases her finger and extends a bunched hand toward her face. She nibbles at it, laughing again when his mouth opens on a toothless gurgle.

Dee glances up at me through the shine of her unshed tears and I fall impossibly more in love with her.

SOMEHOW DEE KEEPS IT TOGETHER, helping Maria feed Mason homemade baby mush, assuring everyone that she's fine, discussing what she can about the custody case when Dwayde is out of earshot; gently rebuffing any false hope that the Franklins' week of silence could mean they are backing off.

She distributes the gifts she'd brought and receives hugs of thanks from everyone and a heartfelt smile from Dwayde when he unwraps his new art set. She colors with Dani and Justin and compares college options with Gabi.

Mama T and Victor comment to me on how strong and brave she is. What they don't see is how hard she's working to maintain that brave front.

After another hour, I make our excuses to leave. The drive back to Brockville is tensely silent. Dee leans against the window with her eyes closed. I doubt she's sleeping, rather lost in her thoughts and seeming to want to be alone with them.

Once we arrive at her house, she dumps her tote bag and keys on the hall table and heads straight to the bathroom. When she emerges, face scrubbed and in her robe, unable to bear the silent distance anymore, I reach for her.

Only then does she let the tears go.

We slide down to the bedroom floor and I gather Dee onto my lap, tuck her head beneath my chin, and rock her against me. Sobs hammer through her body, pounding their way up her chest and into her throat. She clutches my neck and wets the front of my shirt with heavy, mournful tears.

They rip me to shreds. No matter how much I want to fix it and protect her from the pain, I'm powerless to do either. I just hold her and wordlessly share her grief.

When she's cried herself out, she lays exhausted in my arms, her voice hoarse. "I'm sorry."

"Don't be. You needed that."

"It doesn't do any good."

"Sure it does. Better than keeping it bottled inside."

"I'm used to bottling."

"Does that help?"

"No." She laughs wetly against my neck. "Just habit."

"Maybe time for a new habit." I gently urge her up. "Come lie down with me."

"K." When Dee attempts to walk, her balance is slightly off. I catch her around the waist and lift her into my arms.

"*Mick.*"

"Just go with it." I brush my lips across hers and carry her to the bed.

36

Faded sunlight filters through the curtains, the weak remnants of an early autumn evening. I ease her onto her feet beside the mattress. She looks at me with big, tear-dampened eyes that are hauntingly beautiful.

I untie her belt and feel her nervous energy as I slide the robe off her shoulders. She dutifully shrugs out of the sleeves. Her pink panties are sheer except for the triangle, whereas the bra is translucent and does nothing to cover her magnificent breasts. My intention isn't to seduce, but I can't help but appreciate the sensual picture she makes. I drop the robe onto the bed and fold back the comforter. Dee crawls beneath it.

I quickly strip off my own clothes down to my boxer briefs and climb in, pulling her to me.

She lies across my torso, her cheek on my chest. I fold my arms around her. "Cold?"

"Uh-uh." She wedges her chilly feet between my calves to siphon off my heat. "You're nice and warm."

I kiss the top of her head. "Talk to me."

"About what?"

"About whatever you're feeling."

I hear Dee's conflicted breath. Opening herself up, letting the pain out, doesn't come easy for her.

"Have you been around babies much?" I prompt.

"Not really."

"You were a natural."

"Was I?"

"Yeah, you were." I raise Dee's hand to my mouth and kiss the pads of her fingers.

"His skin was hot."

"Babies retain more heat than we do."

"He was so soft."

"Mm-hmm." My lips move across her palm.

"While I held him, I wondered..." She pauses.

"What?"

"I wondered what our baby would have looked like."

"I wondered that too. What did you imagine?"

"Dark hair for sure."

"And brown eyes. Maybe more golden like yours."

"It was..." She pauses again for a pained swallow. "Our baby was a girl."

I screw my eyes shut. Dee hadn't told me that before.

"I carried her...talked and sang to her for nearly six months, but I never got to see her or hold her in my arms. I wish for that...if even just once. I would have told her how much I loved her. How much I wanted her. As scared as I was, I wanted my baby. I wanted to be her mother."

My chest feels like it's being sliced with razor blades.

"How can it still hurt so much?" Her fresh tears trickle onto my skin. "Many women go through miscarriages and they aren't a mess fifteen years later."

"You're not a mess. You kept it in for so long and never gave yourself a chance to fully grieve."

Her head raises and her sad gaze fuses with mine. "You're grieving too. I can see it."

Denial fails me. I work to rein in the images. But they persist across my mind like a rolling montage of my wrongdoings. Making nasty accusations about her inability to love when she told me she needed time to figure stuff out. Mistaking her fear for rejection, I stormed away, leaving her in the rain. Throwing a party, drinking to nurse my misery. Kissing another girl, letting her ride my lap. Dee seeing it. Running. Alone and pregnant. No money. No support. Stressed and scared. Then the loss. Our baby girl, gone. Scraped out, leaving scars inside Dee's body, and deep in her soul.

"It's not your fault, Mick," she says as if reading my thoughts. "You can't keep believing you're to blame."

I can't believe anything else. We were engaged. She was mine to take care of. To protect. I let her down. I let our baby down. And I can't do anything to change it. Not one fucking thing to ever make it right.

"I'm so sorry, Dee."

"Oh, Mick. You are not the one who should be sorry. I didn't tell you I was pregnant. Instead I made you think I was having second thoughts about us."

"That's no excuse. I hurt you."

"I hurt you first. We were young. We made mistakes."

"And you paid for them all."

"We both did. But no amount of self-recriminations will bring her back. We have to put the loss behind us. Not to ever forget, never that, because she mattered. But to let go of the self-blame and all the guilt."

"I don't know how to do that."

"Me either. But we'll figure it out together." She touches her mouth to mine. The kiss like gentle rain. Parted lips merely brushing. Soothing.

I'm not sure how long we stay that way, for the moment feels timeless, a fraction of eternity that belongs only to us. Nor do I know in what catalytic minute or second that our kiss turns from comforting into something wanting, needing.

"Mick…" she whispers. "Love me where it hurts."

"Where does it hurt?"

"All over."

I ease Dee onto her back and cover her tear-streaked cheeks with kisses, returning again and again to the dark honey of her mouth and delicate arch of her throat. I work the straps of her bra down her shoulders and bury my face in the fragrant fullness of her cleavage. I kiss her through the sheer cups, then flick open the front clasp. Her breasts pop free, ripe and round, topped with hard chocolate centers. She fists one hand in my hair and pulls my head down. I close my lips around her erect nipple and tug the other between my forefinger and thumb. I suck her gently until her breaths become labored and urgent.

I slide downward to paint her skin, nuzzling my mouth into the softness of her belly, my tongue tracing the white faded lines that are a sign of her strength and struggles. I slip my fingers into the waistband of her bikini panties, and Dee, moaning into my touch, raises her hips as I peel them off. I run my hands over her long, plump legs and hook them over my shoulders. Her skin feels like sun-warm satin. She arches up and the heady scent of her arousal wraps around me.

I cup the curves of her hips and taste her in slow strokes, chasing her distinct flavor from the bottom of her cleft to the top, wanting to eat her alive. To lose myself to the grinding hunger, to the delicacy of her flesh and the primal need to possess it.

I plunge my tongue inside her sweet essence and she lets out a moan that drowns out everything else. Her hips churn and her breaths quicken. I slide my fingers over her clit and her knees fall outward, opening herself up to me. Fire rages through my blood. When she's almost there, her hands grip my hair and her body coils tight. I circle my fingers faster and hasten the thrusts of my tongue.

"Mick! Oh God." She comes with hard, quaking spasms that I feel down to my bones.

Not done yet, I kiss my way back up to her breasts, her neck, her lips, before I roll us over. Dee stares down at me, her breathing rapid. I slide my hands under her ass and bring her spread legs up my chest. With her knees braced on either side of my shoulders, she's hot and silky wet against my skin. I pull her closer and flutter my tongue over her clit still pulsing from her orgasm.

"Ohh." Dee clutches the iron rungs of the headboard.

It's a thing of beauty, her flushed and naked, head thrown back, eyes closed, lips parted, breasts bouncing as she bucks into my mouth.

Boiling with lust, I could come just from watching her, but it's Dee's mindless pleasure that I'm after. I swirl my tongue, circling that little nub, and softly sucking it. She comes again, shaking and gasping, rubbing out her orgasm against me.

I hold her hips, settling her with soft kisses to her inner thighs. When she recovers her breath, Dee's dark fringe of lashes slowly lifts. The shadows of grief eclipsed by the dreamy haze of afterglow.

She slides down, aligning our bodies. Her nipples poke into my chest as her mouth ghosts over my lips to the column of my throat. I swallow hard.

"Dee…" My conscience vying for control, I pull her head up and look into her eyes.

"Let me," she whispers. "Let me make you feel as good as you made me feel. I need that."

Maybe a better man would hold out, but the fire barely banked, roars back to life. I drag her up for a long, feasting kiss. She runs her fingers across my shoulders and chest. Then her mouth follows, snaking a moist trail down my torso and over my abs. Her hands stroke my throbbing cock through the cotton, then beneath it.

I sit up as our fingers tangle in an effort to divest me of my underwear. She tosses them aside and returns to me. Kneeling on the floor between my parted legs, her curls brush my thighs and I feel her warm breaths seconds before I'm encased in wet heat.

Her going down on me is always intense. I push the hair away from her face, holding it back with my hands, and groan roughly as I watch her pink lips flow over my head and down the length of my dick.

Her muffled moans and the way her eyes close telegraph how much she enjoys pleasing me. Dee seals her soft palm around the base of my hard shaft and jacks me tight and slow. Her head bobs up and down as she takes me in deep then withdraws to the tip, licking the slit and curling her tongue around the rim before taking my length again.

"That feels…ah damn, that feels so good."

Her mouth is indescribable. A close second to being gloved inside the creamy, hot suction of her body. Flames lick under my skin and my blood scorches. I mean to pull her up, to make tender love to Dee while looking into her eyes, to kiss her as we come. But she starts squeezing and sucking faster, taking me deeper, rolling my tight sac with one hand and pumping my cock with the other. The switch tripped, a vicious tension twists up my spine and shoots through my balls, stealing any attempt at self-control.

About to go off, about to fucking explode, all I can do is tug her hair in warning. When she still doesn't move, I jerk away from her mouth and, wrapping my hand around hers, thrust brutally into our combined grip, cursing, grunting, my breath in tatters, my words incoherent as ropes of semen blast all over her chest.

And Dee, so reserved and composed on the outside, but so raw and unrestrained in here with me, leans forward and takes my cock between her plush, slippery breasts, and squeezing the sides with her hands, moves them up and down, drawing out my orgasm with a mind-blowing breast fuck.

Only after she drains me of every drop does my breathing descend out of the red zone. I look at her—hair a halo of curls, lips wet and swollen, and the mark of my desire glistening across her tits. It's fucking sexy.

I reach for her upper arms and haul her onto my lap, taking her mouth in a hard kiss that makes my blood burn all over again.

"God, Dee. I intended to be gentle, to make love to you."

A satisfied smile curves one side of her lips. "That rocked just the way it was. I like making you lose control."

"You made me lose my mind." I kiss her again, softly this time.

She closes her eyes and sighs into me.

"Tired?" I ask. She's had an emotional day.

"Not really."

"How about a bath?"

"That would be nice."

"I'll wash your back."

"Even nicer."

I stroke my fingers down her spine to the dip in her waist and over the lushness of her ass. I give her a light pat, then set her off to the side. "Wait here."

In the bathroom, I find some scented bath stuff and drop a capful of white crystals into the running water before returning to the bedroom. Dee has raised the sheet up to cover herself. She watches me with a seductive glint in her eyes. "Best view in the house."

I tug the sheet away. "Not better than mine."

"Mick!" she shrieks, trying to wrestle the sheet back as I move it out of reach.

"I love your body. Curves everywhere."

"What are you doing?"

41

"Stop squirming," I say, lifting her into my arms. "Although the boob jiggling action is working for me."

"Put me down!" She smacks my arm. "I can walk to the bathroom myself."

"Uh-uh. First off, I like sweeping you off your feet. And second, carrying you is part of the Peters' TLC Program."

"I'm heavy."

"You're perfect." I strengthen my grip under her knees to keep her from wiggling free, and deposit her into the tub.

I get in behind her and ease her against my chest. The sound of the lapping water and Dee's contented breaths are calming. I lazily glide the loofah sponge over her shoulders and down her arms.

"Something else I could get used to," she says, sighing.

"What?"

"Being pampered."

"I like taking care of you."

"I like it too." She taps her fingers in the bubbly water. "So, tell me what else you have planned as part of the Peters' TLC program."

"A massage."

"Mm."

"Then dinner on a blanket by the fireplace."

"An indoor picnic. Very romantic."

"Ladies' choice of menu."

"Something light and easy to prepare." She ponders. "What about the chilled lobster and salads you brought from Mort's?"

I freeze. I still haven't told her what happened at the deli yesterday. About Paul O'Malley, gunning for a story, confronting me with his knowledge of my "mystery woman." About the steps I've taken to keep her safe.

"Mick?"

"Yeah."

"Everything okay?" She angles her head up at me.

"Everything's good." I shift back into motion, circling the loofah across her shoulder blades, determined to have a night of peace with Dee.

A night where there is nothing and no one but us.

CHAPTER FOUR

Dee

MONDAY MORNING, I WAKE DRAPED over Mick. Our legs are intertwined and one of his arms is curled around my hip. After years of being apart it's no mystery as to why we now sleep attached to each other.

I ease up onto my elbow just for the pleasure of watching him. The blanket is bunched at his waist. Deep breaths move his chest up and down. His right arm, with the ink of flames—a tattoo he'd gotten when he joined the Miami Heat—is flung across the pillow, above his chiseled face.

He honest-to-God looks like a Calvin Klein model that has just been plucked from a magazine ad and injected with a triple dose of testosterone and sexuality. By any standard, Mick is gorgeous. But he's so much more than his looks and celebrity jock image. Beneath the packaging is a man of integrity. Of honor. Devoted to his family, to Papa's Kids. To me. Even the scar on his right cheek is a symbol of his character. He survived his father's abuse. He could have been cold and bitter. Violent and cruel. But he isn't any of those things.

He is totally red-blooded and his passion runs hot. Yet he is also kind and gentle. Protective and strong. Last night, he took care of me. Loving me through the pain of our past to pave new ground for our future.

My finger trails along his jaw. In sleep, he looks relaxed and unworried. No guilt furrows his brows. I breathe him in. His skin is warm and smells so good. I could stay like this all day. But duty calls. I place a light kiss on his breastbone and slip naked from his arms, reaching for my robe.

WHILE WAITING FOR THE coffee to brew, I power on my cell phone since turning it off Saturday afternoon. Quickly scrolling through a half-dozen texts from my friends in our group chat, the final one from Jordyn, sent ten minutes ago, has me laughing out loud.

Holy shit! doesn't the man let u up for air?

Me: *Occasionally ;)*

She responds in seconds. *I need details. Dinner 2nite?*

Lexie: *Count me in.*

Jordyn: *We'll live vicariously…I didn't get any either.*

Lexie: *Who says I didn't get any?*

Jordyn: *You're dating doctor snooze…zzz*

Lexie: *Bitch :P*

I'd missed their banter. I'd missed seeing and talking to them. I needed this time to reconnect with Mick and my family, but these women are my sisters-of-the-heart.

As part of my therapy, Dr. Roland had suggested I try something physical to help me deal with stress and anxiety; triggers to a life-long pattern of binge eating. I knew from their advertising that the Brockville Women's Fitness Center, located near me, offered an array of classes, and on the plus side, was for women only.

Still, I was apprehensive. I feared I would feel the same way I did all those times in high school when I entered gym class. As if every critical eye would be on the fat girl whose heavy thighs rubbed together. But with Dr. Roland's encouragement, I finally agreed to give Pilates a try.

That Sunday morning in June nearly two years ago, I walked into the studio, hesitantly, wearing black leggings and a men's XL T-shirt that covered my hips. Several women turned toward me. My knee-jerk reaction was to escape the sea of trim, fit bodies and stares. I might have bolted if a petite auburn-haired woman hadn't smiled up at me, probably smelling my fear.

LEIGH CARRON

"Your first time?"

"Yes." I nodded envying her tidy, athletic frame.

"It's a little awkward initially, but…" she lowered her voice conspiratorially, "like sex, the more you do it, the better you get."

"Jordyn!" chastised a tall brunette rolling out a mat beside her. She looked the way I always wished I did. Straight dark hair that doesn't require taming, and a long, svelte body with high, perky boobs, flat stomach, and slim hips—all shown to their excellent advantage in a snug peach tank top and matching yoga pants.

"I'm sorry…" Her manicured nails tucked several strands of her shiny bob behind one ear. "You'll have to excuse my friend, she doesn't have a filter."

"It's okay." I tugged at the front of my shirt. "I wasn't offended." But I was nervous. I didn't make friends easily, wary of being judged and rejected. I settled for work acquaintances, people who knew me professionally and respected my knowledge and skills.

The class began then and I couldn't leave without calling attention to myself. Being the good student I've always been, I listened attentively to the directions and watched the instructor demonstrate the moves. Despite my self-consciousness, I managed to keep up with the basics and actually enjoyed it. Stretching my body was grueling, but discovering strength in muscles I didn't realize I had felt good, empowering even.

At the end of the sixty minutes, Jordyn and the brunette, who I learned was Alexandra or Lexie for short, commented on how well I had done. It was the first time I had ever been praised for accomplishing anything physical.

The next Sunday, I returned carrying a little more confidence. I was surprised when they invited me to join them in the health club bar for smoothies. As smart, professional women, I related to them on an intellectual level. What I didn't expect was the emotional draw. While Lexie was like an elegant flute of champagne and Jordyn, a fiery shot of sambuca, there was this deep and genuine friendship between them that made me long to be a part of it.

That's why I accepted their standing invitation for Sunday after-class smoothies and why I barely hesitated when they extended the invitation beyond the health club. I think they saw the loneliness in me; a deep-seated desire to belong. Although I wasn't nearly as open or giving of myself as they were—my trust was slow in coming—they never gave up on me. And I'll forever love them for that.

45

I return to our thread of messages and send: *Dinner sounds great!*
Jordyn: *the village spoon @ 7:00?*
Lexie: *Works for me.*
Me: *Me 2. See u then. xo*

I drop my phone back into my purse and turn to see Mick enter the kitchen looking sleep-rumpled—his chest bare, the waist of his sweatpants slung below that *happy trail*, telling me he's commando beneath them.

"Morning," I say, aware of how badly I want him even as my body is still pleasantly sore from the night before. "Sleep well?"

"Mm-hmm," he murmurs, stepping closer to hug my waist and tug my earlobe between his teeth. "Why didn't you wake me?"

"Because I have an eight o'clock meeting."

"Morning quickies were invented for eight o'clock meetings." He backs me up against the counter and sneaks in a lusty, mint-flavored kiss.

"I have to go," I moan, calling upon the deity of willpower to twist away and pour him coffee. "It's strong and hot the way you like it."

"I'd rather have your hot body."

I toss him a smile over my shoulder. "You'll have to settle for a cold shower."

"Is that a challenge?" he says, full of male-determined I'll-prove-I-can-have-your-skirt-up-to-your-waist-and-you-up-on-that-counter-in-ten-seconds. And he would. Another touch here, another kiss there, and I'd be gone.

"Don't you dare." I stave him off with my outstretched hand holding a full mug. "You'll wrinkle my suit and ruin my hair. It took me forever to get it into this bun."

Amusement dances in his eyes. "Ms. Chase is nothing if not practical."

"Practicality is my only defense against you."

At my admission, he hums cheerfully, and taking the cup, backs off to the opposite side of the counter, drinking his coffee while I fill my travel mug.

"Have dinner with me tonight. There's this place I want to take you to...great food and candlelight. Private. Just you and me."

My heart thumps. "I'd love that, Mick. It sounds wonderful, but I already made dinner plans with Lexie and Jordyn."

"Can you reschedule?"

"No." I shake my head. "It would be very uncool to break the chicks before dicks code."

His mouth opens for a booming laugh. "Being the one with the dick, I'll demand equal time, but I get your point. How about tomorrow?"

"Definitely." I add milk and sweeteners to my mug then turn to face him. "Will I still see you later?" The thought of climbing into a cold, empty bed isn't a heartening one.

He sets his cup down and draws me to him. "Nothing could keep me away."

"Good." My hands snake into his messy hair. "I want you here."

"Should I take that as an open invitation?"

"You should."

"Think you can spare another drawer?"

"Maybe." I lay my lips against his.

"Some closet space too?"

"Now you're pushing it."

We share a goofy grin before he seals his mouth over mine and I sink into his soul-melting kiss.

Micah

THROUGH THE WINDOW, I WATCH the black sedan discreetly pull out behind Dee's Lexus. Adding security was a necessary precaution. Without knowing what O'Malley is up to, I'm not taking any chances.

I saw the relentlessness in him at the community center when he pushed through Dwayde and several of the boys I coach, knocking them down to get to me with questions I had no intention of ever answering. On impulse, I reacted. I come from violence. It's inside me. But most of the time, I know how to control it, channel it. Not that day. Like my old man, fists were my first response. I busted O'Malley's lip. A costly mistake.

He blogged about me for weeks. More than usual. He talked to people in my hometown, my former teammates; stirred up old shit about my drinking in college. He posted pictures of his injuries, alleging that my violent reaction only proved I had something to hide.

Then Saturday, after seeing a photo taken by the paparazzi of me coming out of the Lemon Lounge the night prior, he followed me to Mort's Deli from the community center where I'd been coaching. His so-called intention was to make a deal.

I'll forget about filing a lawsuit against you in exchange for an exclusive.

I'd laughed it off, telling him he was reaching.

Oh, come off of it, Peters. You quit the NBA at the height of your career and then invest a load of cash into building Papa's Kids in honor of Cayo Torres. Meanwhile, you rarely mention your old man and he's as tight-lipped about your lack of relationship as you are. After all your fame, you suddenly just fade into the background. And you expect me to believe there's no story here.

I struggled to keep my cool. *I don't give a fuck what you believe.*

Tough words, he'd taunted. *But everyone has a weak spot.*

And he had honed in on mine.

I checked around and guess what I found? A friend of Alexandra Townsen's. A woman you couldn't seem to keep your hands off of. My source told me about the intimate dances...the passionate kiss. And most interesting of all, she's said not to be your usual type.

It will make interesting headlines. Micah Peters, Closet Chubby Chaser.

I'd seethed, holding on to my temper by a frayed thread—my fists clenched, my knuckles white with the roaring urge to beat every breath out of him. Only bringing more trouble to my family had held me back.

I walked away and went home to Dee. I couldn't tell her. Our renewed relationship was barely twenty-four hours old. She was already wary of any publicity, and skeptical that we could make this work. I wasn't going to add to her doubts.

Restless and on edge, I get dressed and head out for a run. Brockville is a charming, middle-class neighborhood. Older style homes and bungalows bordered by large trees sit close to the lake, then give way to modern low rises and brownstones. Its appeal has attracted an influx of young professionals seeking living space outside of the city.

The waterfront is empty at this hour and I'm alone on the path that hugs the shore. I lose the cap, but keep on the shades. Near my downtown condo, I usually jog around Lincoln Park at night to avoid recognition. I've missed this, running in the morning with the sun on my face.

Ten miles—the fresh lake air fills my lungs, the pound of my shoes on the pavement blocks out my thoughts. When I return, I slip my cap back on and get out the lawn mower I find in the garage next to my car that's hidden inside from view. Another precaution I've taken.

After the lawn is mowed, I trim the hedges and repair the leaky faucet in the laundry room. Things I can do, fix, control.

After I'm out of chores, I take a shower and pull on a pair of jeans and a sweater. While downing a protein shake, I finally listen to the string of ignored calls from my agent: Beckett "Let's Make a Deal" MacAllister—a man to whom *no* is merely a challenge.

I tap the screen to call him back. After ten years, I owe him that courtesy.

"What the fuck, Mick? I've been trying to reach you all weekend. ESPN is on my ass for a meeting time."

"It's not going to happen, Mackie."

"Goddammit." He erupts in a bout of barking coughs that reverberate through the phone.

"I thought you quit."

"You'll kill me long before the cigarettes ever do."

"You're being dramatic."

"I'm serious, man." He hacks up another lung. "You gave up the NBA against my better advice. But okay, wear and tear on the body, all the travel, time for a change. Then you turned down offers to coach pro ball and to be the spokesperson for a line of men's products that would have garnered you and me a small fortune. But, hey, buh-bye to another lucrative contract. You told me you wanted to focus on this thing with homeless and abused kids, so I left you to lay low for a while…do what you needed to get over your grief.

"But it's been five months, man. This is a talk show deal with a prime network…huge coin. They want *you*. You've got that X factor. Did you see the number of tweets and retweets from a picture of you coming out of the Lemon Lounge Friday night? You're still a big draw, Mick. Great for ratings."

"I don't give a shit about ratings."

"Well, ESPN does. Your face was made for the screen. Men will watch because they want to be just like you. And women will watch to cream their panties."

"As flattering as that sounds," I say sarcastically, "I'm out. Not just with ESPN. All of it. No more deals. I'm going to put my effort into building out Papa's Kids and investing in businesses that pique my interest."

"You're just going to throw it all away to become an investor and philanthropist?" His tone is incredulous. "Everything we worked for down the drain. That's batshit crazy, Mick."

"Why? Lots of professional athletes follow that track after retirement."

"But they aren't Micah Peters. The public loves you. You look like a movie star and they eat that shit up. One call to the press and look how they come running. Like it or not, you're a superstar. You can't just walk away from that."

Through the noise of his rant, there's one thing that sticks out: *One call to the press and they come running.*

"You called the press." Hindsight is as clear as a fucking bell. I had spoken to Mackie on Friday, rushing him off the phone, telling him I had to be at the Lemon Lounge. Never did it occur to me that the bastard would stab me in the back, all in some self-serving exploit to get me back into the spotlight.

"It's how this business works, Mick," he says without apology.

"And the community center, did you call them there too?"

"What are you getting so pissed about?"

"You knew I was coaching my nephew's team and didn't want publicity."

"That's my job. I did it for you."

Anger twists in my chest. That incident with O'Malley at the community center going viral had brought the Franklins right to Dwayde and my family. The custody case is stone cold proof that my fame can hurt the people I love.

"You didn't do any of that for me." I push the bitter words through my clenched teeth. "You did it for yourself. For the money. But it's over."

"Mick...Jesus...listen to me, man—"

"Fuck you. I'm done listening."

"*Mick!*"

Fuming, I hang up and call my lawyer. Nolan Taylor confirms what I already expected, that it's going to cost me to break the contract early. "Do it," I tell him. Between an absurd former eight-digit salary, major endorsements, and smart investments, I have enough to last me several lifetimes. Enough for what matters: Papa's Kids, my family, and my future with Dee. Enough to keep Malcolm Peters away from the people I care about. That alone is worth every drop of blood and sweat I left on the courts.

Nolan goes over the terms and promises to have a draft of the letter for my review by 4:00.

I SLIDE ON MY SHADES and cap and make the short commute to Chicago. Though it's early afternoon, downtown still bustles with energy. Cars and people surge through the busy streets, while tall glass office towers loom above as if watching the activity below.

I park underground, and lowering my brim, catch the empty elevator to the twenty-third floor. The car stops several times during the ride with people getting on and off. A few furtive glances are cast in my direction. Some whispers. People are curious about celebrities. Enamored by the sheen of fame that disguises how truly human we are.

Leaning against the gold railing hand support, I keep my shaded eyes trained on the mounted TV screen that loops through the stock numbers, weather, and news until I'm alone again. It's not basketball I resent. Only the reason I'd chosen it.

I exit the car on the last stop and walk down the hall to Pivotal Consulting. The friendly receptionist shows me to the boardroom where Nadia Singh is waiting. I remove my cap and shades and set them down on the credenza.

"Hello, Mick. It's good to see you." With her professional demeanor and confident efficiency, Nadia wears her role of Project Director with ease.

"Good to see you too." We shake hands.

"Coffee?" she asks. "Just black as I recall."

"Yes. Thank you."

"No, thank you for choosing Pivotal again. Papa's Kids is a fabulous program. We're so pleased to be a part of the expansion project."

"Glad to hear it." I take the cup she offers and wait until she sits before lowering onto the chair set up next to her. "You did excellent work with the first location. This one's larger and more complex, but I'm expecting the same."

"We won't let you down," she assures and starts her PowerPoint presentation.

For the next hour, we go through the initial stages of the plan that Nadia and her project team have prepared to manage the delivery of my vision. With one hundred and nine acres of land, I want a multiple residence community that will provide transitional shelter and support services to boys and girls currently homeless or living in some other untenable situation.

After Cayo died, I quit the NBA and threw myself into creating a legacy for him. I thought if I could help even one kid rise above their dire circumstances—the way Victor and Isabelle were doing for Dwayde, and the way the Torreses had done for me—I would have accomplished something meaningful. Honorable. Something that would make me deserving of all Cayo and Rita had given to me.

"Any other questions?" Nadia asks when she gets to the end.

"No. You were very thorough," I say, appreciating her attention to detail and the commitment to meet my aggressive timelines.

"Great." She beams. "If we're going to break ground before the winter, we need a design ASAP. I can email you the profiles of several architects that we highly recommend for this assignment."

"Sure. I'll use them as a comparison, but I already have someone in mind."

"We'd be pleased to work with whomever you chose," Nadia says as she walks me to the door. "I'll send the profiles over today."

"Thanks." I slip my cap and shades back on. "Like before, my PR firm will handle any of the press on this project. If you're contacted, please direct the media to Asher Dumont."

"Will do," she agrees, aware of the drill. "I'll call you later this week."

We shake hands and I head to my condo located in Gold Coast, an affluent neighborhood just north of the downtown Loop. Since I won't be long, I leave my car with a valet at the front of the building.

"Good afternoon, Mr. Peters." The doorman tips his cap.

"Hey, George. You're on early today."

"Filling in for Juan."

"Is he alright?" I ask.

"Oh yes. He just took a long weekend with his wife for their anniversary."

"Nice." I smile, having celebrated an amazing weekend myself.

"I haven't seen you out jogging lately, sir."

"I've been away."

"Ah." He nods. "That explains why Ms. Manning has been inquiring as to your whereabouts."

Annoyed, my jaw clenches. "Has she now?"

"Every evening."

The last time I saw my neighbor, Lisa Manning, was the night of the storm when she tried to scheme her way into my condo...and my bed. Catching sight of Dee, she created a false impression that we were lovers in an attempt to make her jealous. Instead, she triggered Dee's hurt over my past indiscretion, and all the secrets and angry pain came thundering out. The catalyst we needed to finally get at the truth of what happened all those years ago. To pave the way to start again.

Not that I'm going to thank Lisa for any of that.

"Do you know if Ms. Manning is at home?" I ask.

"She left about an hour ago." George's lips twitch in a conspiratorial smile. "The coast is clear, sir."

No denying that's a relief. I can handle Lisa, but I'd rather not expend the energy.

I take the private elevator up to my penthouse suite. The floor to ceiling windows overlook the iconic skyline. A state-of-the art kitchen has every modern convenience and the bathrooms feature heated towel racks and marble floors. But despite the luxury, it never felt like home.

I grab two leather suitcases from the closet and pack. I'll keep the condo for now. Work from here when I'm in the city. Leave my desktop and some clothes. To put it on the market would only draw unwanted media attention. It would definitely reach O'Malley's radar. I can't help but wonder again what he's up to.

I log into my computer and view his blog and social media accounts. He still hasn't posted anything about our confrontation on Saturday or made reference to my "mystery woman." I should be relieved. Instead, his silence feels like the vibrating quiet that crackles the air just before the clap of a storm.

Frustration has me dragging my fingers through my hair. It has taken every ounce of restraint to standby and await his next move. But approaching O'Malley would expose him to my weakness. I won't risk that. Dee and my family—they're all that matter.

At four o'clock, the email from Nolan arrives. I read the notice of termination twice and only after I send the letter back with my approval, closing the door on that chapter of my life, do I feel somewhat better.

I pick up my phone and call Dee.

"Hi, Mick." Her voice, laced with affection, slides through me like warm honey.

"Hello, Counselor." I lean back in my swivel chair and feel myself unwind. "How has your day been?"

"Busy. But I can spare a few minutes before my conference call. How was your meeting with Pivotal?"

"Good. Top on my list is to hire an architect. I'm thinking of Jordyn."

"That's great!" Dee enthuses. "Jordyn is awesome. Not that I'm pressuring you or anything, but her garden townhouse complex won an innovation award and was written up in *Architectural Digest*."

"No pressure, huh?"

"None." She laughs. "It just so happens that Jordyn is super talented and I think you two would work well together."

"I couldn't agree more." Jordyn impressed me at Lexie's party when we briefly talked about the project. She had a number of creative ideas that aligned with my vision, and from the way she once took me on to defend Dee, she's obviously determined, ballsy, and loyal. Traits I admire in the people I work with. "I'll give her a call."

"So, what do you have planned for this evening?" she asks.

"Spending some quality time with Delayna," I say of the main character from my manuscript *Dark Angel*.

"Should I be jealous?" she teases.

"Nah. I'll be thinking about you the whole time."

"Won't that affect your ability to write?"

"It actually inspires it." I close my eyes to better picture Dee, sitting at her desk, all those curves she tries to disguise, hidden beneath navy tweed. "There's this scene I plan to create based on my fantasy of stripping Ms. Chase out of one of her serious business suits."

"Really?" This still surprises her. The depth of my desire.

"Why don't I tell you all about it." I sit back and lower my voice to a husky whisper. "I can go step by step. Layer by layer."

"Unfortunately, that's not an option at the moment."

Dee's sudden change in tone tells me someone has entered the room. It's probably her assistant, Lena.

"Are you alone?"

"Not any longer."

"That kills my plan for phone sex."

"You have the voice for it. Please be sure to reschedule that for another day."

"I can't wait to get my hands on you."

"I'll...uh...look forward to that too."

I smile, hearing the catch in her voice, liking that only I know what's going on beneath her professional composure. "Tonight, Dee."

"Yes. That time works. I have to go."

"Do me a favor," I say. "Think of me."

"Always."

"Later, beauty."

I pack my laptop, zip up my leather bags, and without a backward glance head for home.

CHAPTER FIVE

Dee

MAIN STREET IN BROCKVILLE IS one of my favorite places to stroll. There's an array of cafés, boutiques, and restaurants. In the summer, it's common to see people, old and young, enjoying iced coffees or lunch on the cobblestone terraces covered by brightly colored awnings.

Arriving early, I park a couple of blocks away from the Village Spoon. Though the days are sliding deeper into October, the weather is unseasonably mild and I welcome the walk. Makes me feel less guilty about skipping Pilates yesterday morning. I get a hot tingle when I think about the workouts I've been getting with Mick instead.

Humming to myself, I browse the windows and dally inside an independent bookstore. I select a romantic novel with a happy ending and pick up a journal with a vintage floral cover. I've never kept a diary before. Not even as a young girl. Feelings were something I mostly avoided. But I'm on this new journey so just maybe…

With a bit more time to spare, I stop at a candle shop where I buy two jasmine pillars, then poke around a new jewelry boutique with a Grand Opening sign.

"May I help you?" A young saleswoman with her hair in a fishtail braid over one shoulder approaches.

"Just looking, thanks."

I peruse the glass cases, sparkling beneath fluorescent lights. There is a pair of dangly earrings that I briefly consider and cufflinks for Mick that have typewriter keys. I'm still contemplating them as I find myself wandering over to the rings. Men's rings.

The selection ranges from classic to handcrafted designs. I glance at each one until my eyes land on a piece that strikes me as perfect. I ask to see it.

"That's from our Rebel line," the sales woman says, opening the case. "Makes a statement, doesn't it?"

"Yes," I agree. Boldly so. The wide band, sculpted in black titanium with two rows of studded black diamonds, conveys power and strength. I assess the size, gauging it will fit. Then muzzling my internal lecture on all the sane and practical reasons why I shouldn't, I insert my credit card into the machine and leave minutes later with the ring box in my purse.

I wait, expecting buyer's remorse to set in at any moment. After all, we've only been back together a mere four days, not to mention I'd just blown my carefully managed budget. Instead, feeling elated at the notion of Mick wearing my ring, I practically skip across the street and enter the Village Spoon.

A high cathedral ceiling allows the compact dining room and cocktail lounge to seem simultaneously intimate and spacious. Jordyn is already there, seated in a booth. She lifts her hand to wave me over. A smile breaks across her face as I make my way through the bar, occupied by the after-work crowd.

"Hi, Jord." I set my bags down and lean in for a hug before sliding in on the opposite side.

"Hi yourself, chickie. You are positively glowing."

I touch my cheeks, unable to contain my grin. "Relationship high."

"Looks good on you."

There's something in her voice that has me reflecting on her unexpected confession Friday night.

I'm not the kind of woman men want to settle down with. So why pursue something I'm gonna suck at.

Jordyn is selling herself short. It saddens me that she doesn't see all she has to offer. That she thinks men will find her lacking; that they won't find her soft and feminine enough. She's so wrong, but I understand what it's like to doubt your worth. Before Mick, I didn't trust another man to love me for me either.

I stare back at my pretty friend with her short, sassy haircut framing high cheekbones and prominent mossy-green eyes. "A relationship with the right man would look good on you too."

"Pfft. Are you still hung up on that? I told you it was the champagne talking. I'm not interested in sharing the remote or a bathroom. Waking up to the same man day after day, for weeks, months, God, years... uh-uh." She shakes her head for emphasis, protesting a little too much.

"I just want to see you happy, Jord."

"Please," she groans. "Don't become one of those people."

"What people?"

"Those people who want everybody to be in a relationship because *they* are. I'm happy that you're happy. But I'm good as I am, okay?"

"Okay." I let it go for the time being.

"Sooo..." She leans forward and puts her elbows on the white linen tablecloth. "Guess who just called me?"

"Who?" I ask, though I have a fairly good idea.

"I'll give you a hint. He's the hottest guy on the planet and in love with one of my best friends."

"Hmm." I put a finger to my temple and make a hard thinking face. "I'm drawing a blank."

"Shut up." She laughs. "You probably already know."

"Tell me anyway."

"Mick's considering me for his new project. We're going to meet on Wednesday. Eee!" She squeezes her fists. "We tossed around ideas at Lexie's party. We seemed in sync, you know? But I didn't want to be forward and ask him, given our friendship. Might seem like I was taking advantage or something. But holy shit, I'm psyched." Her eyes pop with excitement. "It's an awesome project. Great cause, great client, and will be fab for my portfolio. I really want this."

"You'd be great for it, Jord. I told Mick you're an amazing architect."

"Oh." She deflates.

"No," I hurry to explain, "Mick mentioned you first. I just gave a thumbs-up. Papa's Kids is too important for him to hire anyone but the best. If you get the job, it will be based on your own merits."

"You're sure?" she questions dubiously. "Because from what I've seen, Mick would do anything for you."

"Not this. He won't hire you just for me. Whatever advantage you have is because you impressed him at Lexie's party. And speaking of Lexie..."

She breezes through the restaurant with her usual stylish flair. Belted designer jacket and shiny mink bob swinging against her collar.

"Sorry. A PR planning meeting with a client ran late. What did I miss?"

"Only that Mick might hire me to design the new residence for Papa's Kids. Can you believe it?"

"Of course," Lexie says. "The man has taste."

"Aw." Jordyn bats her eyelashes, pretending to blush. "That's so sweet."

"I know you have a talent for more than just man-eating." Lexie flashes her white smile and turns to me. "Hi, Dee."

"Hey, Lex."

She shrugs out of her jacket, revealing a tapered blouse neatly tucked inside a high-waist pencil skirt, an outfit made for her long, svelte body. I often feel like a big, lumpy potato next to her, but I'm in a better place today.

I shift over and Lexie settles in beside me. We exchange a hug.

"You look wonderful." She regards my face close-up. "Radiant."

"Thanks. I feel great. How was the rest of your birthday weekend?"

"Clearly not as good as yours." She bumps my shoulder.

The server arrives with a basket of warm sourdough bread and runs through the chef's specials. We order a celebratory bottle of sparkling wine and entrees: a rare steak with crispy frites for Jord, roasted quail on a cauliflower purée for Lexie, and the grilled halibut with cilantro-lime salsa for me.

"Spill the goods, girl," Jordyn demands when the waitress is gone. "Every dirty detail."

My feelings of happiness are all so new that I'm almost afraid to jinx them. But excited to rave about my incredible weekend, I lean in and tell my friends everything. Well, almost everything. I don't mention the meltdown that happened after brunch, as that was a very private moment between Mick and me. Nor do I go into any specifics about our sex life because they're way too special to share. But I do tell them all about the time I spent with Mick and my family, and the seamless way we reconnected.

Their mouths curve up in thrilled-for-me smiles and Jordyn wags a knowing finger. "Don't think you're getting away without some sex deets. If that kiss we witnessed on Friday is any indication, Mick must be smokin' in bed."

My pulse kicks into sixth gear just thinking about the way he claims my body as if he wants me more than anything in the world...how the feel of his hands, his mouth, drive me wild, how loving him cuts to my very soul and makes me lose my mind.

"Holy shit!" She tosses her napkin at me. "You lucky bitch."

I grin and toss the linen back. "He curls my toes every time."

Both women squeal with delight. When the server brings over our wine, we raise our glasses.

"To toe-curling sex," Jordyn toasts.

"To you and Mick," Lexie adds.

"To second chances." I click my glass to theirs and take a good luck sip of bubbly wine.

"How serious are things?" Jordyn eyes me across the table.

"I feel like we're moving at warp speed. He already has drawers and closet space. And I even bought him this." A show of the black diamond band garners enthusiastic oohs and ahhs. "I keep surprising myself. You know me. I'm usually slow and cautious. I debate, think, overanalyze. But a few nights with Mick and I've lost all reason."

"I can see why," Jordyn remarks with a knowing smile. "The man is fine as wine and looks at you as if you're the only one in the room."

"And we weren't the only ones who noticed," Lexie says. "My mother assured me that she didn't call the media. But someone at the party must have. Thank goodness Mick had a bodyguard stationed outside to warn him."

Her reminder is like being roused from a glorious dream by a bucket of cold water.

"I met the bodyguard. Stiles." Jordyn licks her lips in an exaggerated motion. "Dark and delicious."

Lexie rolls her eyes and turns back to me, in full PR mode. "How have you and Mick decided to handle the media?"

"We um...we haven't talked about it."

"What?" Her defined eyebrows jerk upward. "Didn't you see the pictures of Mick coming out of the Lemon Lounge? They were in the Tribune and all over social media."

I swallow hard and shake my head.

"Really, Lexie." Jordyn's tone drips with sarcasm. "I doubt Dee and Mick were keeping up with celebrity gossip this weekend."

"My point is, Mick's a gorgeous sports star and well sought-after bachelor," she tosses back. "A significant woman in his life is going to be big news."

A big woman in his life will be even bigger news. I reach for a piece of bread.

"Lots of celebrities keep their relationships secret," Jordyn argues, knowing me well enough to know I wouldn't welcome the attention.

"That's true, but Mick and Dee were already seen together by fifty of my guests and wait staff. I know how persistent the media can be. Juicy tidbits of a public figure's private life are worth mega bucks." She gives me a sympathetic look. "I don't want to see you get blindsided by some money-grubbing photographer or ruthless reporter who sniffs out a story. Mick can get advice from his own public relations people, but my suggestion is to head off the media and tabloids with a press release."

A press release? This is exactly what I feared, that the black cloud of doom would eventually open up and rain all over my fucking parade.

"You're freaking her out," Jordyn accuses.

"No, it's okay." I manage to find my voice. "I am freaking out a little. But Lexie's right, it is something I should talk to Mick about." The thought of that conversation makes me miserable.

"Sorry, Dee," Lexie says, her expression rueful. "I didn't mean to spoil the mood or bring you down."

"You haven't spoiled anything," I add with as much of a smile as I can. "I'm out with my girls to have a fun night."

Both women eye me skeptically. "I'm fine. Really," I insist, even as the knot in my chest tightens, overcome by the inescapability of Mick's fame. I've always chosen the background, to be as inconspicuous as possible. Now I could be dragged into the spotlight. Me and my big ass body. The damn knot squeezes harder. But I breathe through my smile and reach for another piece of bread.

AT TEN O'CLOCK, I ARRIVE home with my emotions still rolling. I try to anchor them with what's familiar and secure. My bungalow. My quiet street. The brisk wind that skips off the lake. It blows against me and rustles the trees. My nose tickles with the scent of cut grass. Mick had mowed the lawn and raked the leaves. That small bit of normalcy is somehow settling.

I climb the steps to the porch and unlock the door. Mick's presence surrounds me—the faint smell of cologne, his shoes in the foyer, and his leather jacket on the coat rack.

I shrug out of my trench coat and slip off my heels before following the loud music down the hall to the spare bedroom I use as a home office. Mick is sitting behind the scarred and worn desk I'd bought in law school from a secondhand store. One I've been intending to replace. He'd suit something sleek and modern, but regardless of the old piece of furniture, Mick is in his element.

Short, defiant waves swirl around his head. Concentration pleats the space between his eyebrows and his attention is riveted to the screen. Chinese take-out cartons litter the desk. The only light in the otherwise darkened room is the glow from the laptop and shimmer of colorful jewels from my prized Tiffany lamp.

He doesn't hear me over the pulsing drum beat and sensual riff of a saxophone. I should go, I tell myself. I'm trespassing on the privacy of his work. Yet I can't tear myself away.

He'd once confided that writing was his escape, his survival. I realize just how true that is in the way it seems to consume all of him. As a teenager, I had the privilege of reading his many stories. Fantastical battles between good and evil that he waged with the vivid stroke of words. Never, though, had I the pleasure of seeing him create.

It's enthralling. Magnetic. His long, tapered fingers attack the keyboard with such passion I can feel them on my body. His focus is singular and intense like the way he makes love to me. Energy pumps out of him in electric currents, charging the air. I'm entranced by it. Utterly seduced.

I have no concept of how long I've been standing there when he stops. He flexes his fingers and looks up, catching me in his hot, dark gaze. My blood burns everywhere at once.

No greeting, no smile, Mick pushes out of the high-back chair and rounds the desk. Dressed in joggers and a black top, all six-feet-five inches of him prowls toward me with the graceful power of a panther. I quiver with each step, longing to be devoured.

Mick doesn't disappoint. He grasps the lapels of my jacket and tugs me against him an instant before he takes my mouth in a lust-filled kiss. I tunnel my hands through his hair, pulling him impossibly closer, falling impossibly deeper.

As the song changes to Miguel's soul-baring falsetto, "These lips can't wait to taste your skin…" Mick's kiss grows hungrier, edging toward savage. He dislodges my hands and yanks the jacket off. Then in one swift move, he grabs hold of my white blouse and rips it down the middle.

I gasp. Shocked and wildly turned on. *This is his fantasy.*

He absorbs the thrill in my eyes, then crushes me against the wall. No words yet spoken, the music does the talking. He slides his tongue across the tops of my breasts and between the cleavage. I fist his hair, but manacling my wrists in one hand, he brings them over my head and restrains them against the smooth plaster. With the other hand, he drags my skirt up my stocking-covered legs. His eyes blaze a fiery brown when he touches above the lace band and encounters my bare thigh. His teeth bite my stiff nipple through the satin cup as he shoves the swatch of my damp panties aside and plunges two fingers inside me, hard and fast. My breath explodes in a paroxysm. The hit to my unprepared system is jolting. His thumb circles my clit and within seconds I come.

Releases with Mick are always potent...but this one tosses me into a whirlpool of slick, stunning sensations and steals the strength in my knees.

He holds me up with his body, and whips off what's left of my blouse. Staggered, I clutch his shoulders for balance. He nips at the pulse rioting in my throat and his hand locates the zipper of my skirt. The material gives way and pools at my feet.

I stand there all but bare; my excess flesh squeezed into a champagne-colored bikini set and sheer stay-ups. Mick's gaze sweeps past the tops of my stockings to my panties. I instinctively suck in my stomach, wishing I hadn't stress-eaten all that bread. But my self-consciousness quickly evaporates beneath the branding heat of his stare.

He reaches around to unclasp my bra. His deft fingers release the two eyelets. He slides the straps down my arms and the polished cups fall away, freeing my breasts with a heavy bounce.

The air that brushes my skin is cool, the hands that cover me are not. His big, warm palms slide over my breasts and his mouth—oh God—his mouth is everywhere. On my nipples, my belly, between my legs, licking me through the satin, pressing the wet fabric into my cleft, creating a delectable friction that drives me to the barbed edge of insanity.

When he kisses his way back up my body, needing to take him to the brink with me, I lift his shirt over his head. Everywhere I'm soft and round, Mick is hard and lean. Washboard abs and that sexy V of muscle that runs from the hipbone to his pelvis, tremor under my fingertips as I seek those spots that I know make him hot and growl for me. Everything about Mick is such a turn on; from how he coaxes pleasure from me to the way he takes his pleasure in return.

Placing hungry kisses down his torso, I eagerly reach inside the waistband of his pants. Going commando, he springs warm and weighty into my hands. The thick length pulses, the wide tip already wet. I sink to my knees and lick away the shiny trail, reveling in his excitement for me.

"Dee." The rasp of my name breaks his silence and his eyelids grow heavy as if the pleasure is intoxicating.

That look alone is its own provocation. He combs his fingers through my hair, scattering the pins and freeing the curls from their hold. He binds them around his fist as I take him deep into my mouth. I love doing this for him. For me too. I love listening to his rough, erotic groans. Love the masculine smell and taste of him, the shameless way he slides in and out, glazing my tongue with his thick, salty essence. The way he grows harder until his cock is like slick iron between my lips. I moan my desire, spurred on by his.

"You suck me so good."

I trace his length with my tongue, caressing the throbbing veins, licking each one. Then with a tight, firm suction I take him to the back of my throat and out to the tip again. Swallowing the creamy evidence that tells me how close he is. I can feel the restraint vibrating off him, feel him holding back his release.

Another thrust into my mouth and he pulls out, breathing hard, his dark eyes primal. "Lose the panties. Now."

The bite of authority conveying his ruthless need fills me with a dizzying triumph. I wiggle out of my underwear while he shoves his joggers down his legs and kicks them off. With lightning speed his body is back against me, his chest hard to mine. Then his hands are on my behind, gripping tight, moving me.

My back hits the wall again. I fold my arms around his neck and wrap one leg around his hip. Mick bends slightly, his pelvis beneath me, positioning himself where I want him most. His penis hovers at the lips of my waiting sex. I make a plaintive sound and my eyelids begin to close.

"Leave them open." He stops me. "I want to see your eyes when you come. Want you to see mine when you do."

Dripping...dying... After all the intense foreplay and teasing, I am ready to be taken. "Mick, please," I beg. "Fuck me."

This side of me belongs to Mick. He releases my sexy beast, taunts it, responds to it, driving his cock into me with an inexorable thrust. The sheer power surrenders me to the frenzy. My hips rock frantically to meet his demands; a relentless mating that jars my body and jounces my breasts.

The song lyrics change to "I'm a slave to your flesh." The sexually charged music combined with our raspy groans, slapping skin, and the sounds of our bodies banging against the wall add to the carnality of our lovemaking. It's raw and base, a whippy aggression that assaults my senses and strips all self-control.

There's no vacancy in my mind to think about anything else, except Mick and his strong muscled arms holding me up, his beautiful face ravaged and beaded with sweat, his hips flexing beneath the heel of my foot as he vigorously pounds through my clenching core.

He's the only man ever capable of giving me a vaginal orgasm. With each rugged thrust, the pressure inside me builds, swells, unfurls, until it releases like liquid steam and I climax in a blinding rush. He watches me come apart, holding my gaze as my sex spasms, the muscles rippling and clasping around him.

"Fuck, fuck," he growls, digging his fingers into my hips, yanking me down harder and faster, prolonging my orgasm as he races brutally toward his own.

Through the ecstatic haze and roaring in my head, I watch him too. See the moment he goes over. His fevered eyes lose focus, his large, quaking body pins me to the wall.

I press my open mouth to his and somewhere in the midst of pulsing vibrations, torrid heat, and sweaty pleasure, I marvel at how right I'd been in allowing Mick past my defenses. In trusting that he was the one I could lose my inhibitions with. The one I could bare myself to.

LATER IN BED, WITH THE light and music gone, there is only the still darkness of the room and the low hum of our contented breaths. Mick's bristled cheek rests on my stomach and I'm running my fingers through his hair.

To me, the next best thing to making love with him is this—afterward, floating along that lazy river of satisfaction.

"Mick?"

"Hm?"

"When I arrived, were you writing the scene you told me about earlier?"

"Mm-hmm, but the reality of you is so much better." His fingers idly trace the outer curve of my breast. "I'll go back and improve it in the morning. Add those fuck-me stockings."

"I thought *Dark Angel* was a sci-fi thriller about a vigilante lawyer."

"It is. With hot scenes that you inspire. Sorry about your blouse."

"No, you're not." I rub my leg against his indolently. "But neither am I. In fact, I like knowing I'm your source of inspiration. Like a muse."

"You fit the bill. A beautiful, feminine spirit who stimulates creativity by arousing the body and brain with sensual energy."

"Sounds like a convenient description that artists invented to get laid."

"Well..." He raises his lips to mine. "We are known for our ingenuity."

"I can attest to that."

Our laughter turns into wonderful kissing before he resumes his resting position. I close my eyes, feeling sated and sleepy and happily in love. His light caress on my skin is hypnotic. I'm starting to drift off when I hear the murmur of his voice again.

"My mind being on other things, I forgot to ask about your dinner."

Lexie's advice comes crashing back through the tranquil intimacy.

"What's wrong?" he asks.

"Nothing. I'm fine." The word ricochets in my head. *Fine, fine, fine.* People left you alone when you were fine. They didn't probe and poke for the real feelings. They didn't see the secret stashes of food or the stain of tears on the inside. Childhood memories twist inside me, matted and messy.

"Dee." He stops the nervous play of my fingers in his hair and reaches over to turn on the bedside lamp. I blink against the sudden brightness and see his quizzical expression. "What just happened? You were relaxed before I asked about dinner and now you're not."

His awareness is no surprise. He knows me well. Knows from the tensile stress in my body that fine isn't fine. I could feed him pretty white lies and get the easy, post-coital mood back. But since we've reunited I've been nothing but open and honest with Mick. It's secrets that ruined us before. I won't make that mistake again.

I take a deep breath. "Lexie brought up something we haven't talked about." Something that I have the urge to escape like a deer that senses an approaching wolf.

"What's that?" The muscle ticks in his jaw. He knows.

"Your...your fame and handling reporters."

"Christ." He rolls onto his back and I mourn the loss of his body. "What did she say?"

"That we were seen together at her party, that someone alerted the media...that you're gorgeous and famous...that a woman in your life will be a big story. She suggested we head it off with a press release."

His features steel into a rigid mask. "No."

I should be relieved that he doesn't want this anymore than I do. Instead I'm taken aback by the finality of his response. "Just *no*. Didn't you hear anything I said?"

"Yes. And don't you think I hear you breathing through your anxiety? See the fear in your face?" He abruptly climbs off the bed. "I'm not putting you through a press release."

I follow him, clutching the sheet to me while he remains naked. "Because you don't think I can handle it?"

"Because you shouldn't have to!" His hands fist at his sides. There's an undertone of anger that I don't understand. "Dammit, Dee." He strides to the other end of the room. "You were the one to tell me that you couldn't live with reporters invading your privacy. What do you think a press release will bring?"

Bony wings of panic beat in my throat. I can picture the headlines, the hash tags, the comparisons that will be made between his previous line-up of supermodels and me. They won't be kind.

Mick isn't blind to my insecurities. He sees them in me every day, every time I cover up. Of course, he doesn't think I can handle the press and the things they will print. I'm not sure I can either.

He shoves his legs into a pair of sweatpants and prowls in front of the window like a caged tiger, his hand scraping through his hair, his movements restless and agitated.

"I realize it won't be easy," I say, hating that my voice shakes. "But better than me being ambushed by reporters out for a story."

He stops pacing and his head snaps up. "That won't happen."

The hard conviction tells me his comment isn't a hollow promise. "What do you mean?"

"Just trust me on that."

"No! Tell me what you mean, why you're so certain."

His stance is poised for battle and his expression doesn't yield even as he answers. "Any reporter would have to go through Stiles or one of his men to get to you. And that's not possible. They're all ex-cops or former military. Stopping reporters would be child's play to them."

My head spins as my brain clambers to assemble that I have highly trained bodyguards and that Mick hadn't said a word about it until now. Under duress.

"You're having me followed." It's not a question. "Talk about an invasion of my privacy. I thought I had to worry about the press, not the man I'm sleeping with."

"Christ, Dee. I'm not tracking your whereabouts. I'm doing what's necessary to protect you."

"Just another precaution," I retort.

"Yes."

"Unbelievable." I grab my robe off the foot of the bed and pull it on before letting go of the sheet. Furious with him, I yank the belt into a knot.

"You're mad that I'm protecting you?" he asks incredulously.

"How can you not get this?" I glare at him through the web of hair that has fallen across my face. "I'm mad that you didn't tell me. That you had no intention of telling me."

"I didn't want to alarm you."

"So, you decided what was best. Making the decisions. Taking over my life."

He crosses to me and grips my arms. "You think I want to control you, Dee? I don't. You think I want to take away your independence? You're wrong. But I have to balance that with protecting you from the very thing you told me you didn't want." He lowers his hands to my waist, and when he speaks next, his tone is gentle. "I'm not taking over, baby. I'm taking care of you."

With that, he expects me to fall into his big, strong arms and let his deep-voiced reassurances pacify me. And just like Friday night when he faced the press while Stiles took me home, and just like yesterday when he assured me that I didn't have to worry about his fame, he'll feel better for having soothed my fears, and I'll feel safe, snuggled up in my cozy bubble of blissful avoidance.

And God help me, I'm tempted to fall right into that comfortable pattern. But I know all too well as he looks at me with those dark brown eyes awaiting my surrender, that if I continue to passively go along, soon neither of us will respect me very much anymore.

"I understand that you want to shield me from the media. I've given you every reason to think that I need you to. But..." I continue on a surge of resolve. "You can't just hire bodyguards for me without my input. You can't just decide 'no' to a press release without involving me. That's not how relationships work. Your fame isn't yours to handle alone anymore. We're in this together."

He shakes his head. "I don't want it touching you, Dee."

"That's not possible." I bracket his cheeks between my palms. "You can't protect the people you love from everything. You can't protect me from this."

He recoils as if I'd struck him.

"Mick," I whisper, hurting for him that I'd spoken a truth he can't bear to hear. "I—"

His hand lifts to silence me. His expression shutters. He blocks me out and tugs open the drawer I'd given him just yesterday, and changes into running gear.

"Y-you're leaving?"

"I can't be here right now." Then turning, he stalks out of the room.

Shaken, I watch his retreating back, and minutes later hear the front door close with a resounding click. Abandonment is a powerful trigger. Even as my adult-self registers that Mick hasn't really left me, that scared little girl inside isn't quite convinced.

The last time I saw Benjamin Chase was the morning after my fourth birthday. I remember sitting at the round kitchen table, eating leftover cake from the box. It had pink flowers and white buttercream icing. Food was my mother's way of keeping me occupied and content.

They were fighting again. As a truck driver, my dad wasn't often around, but when he was, all they did was fight. I don't know what started it that time. His job, probably. But I could hear them in their bedroom. He shouted that he couldn't take it anymore. That he was sick and tired of her moods. That she needed help. She cried and screamed. Words I couldn't decipher through her sobs. I heard something crash. More yelling. Then my father stormed from the room, a duffle bag in his hand. She chased after him. Hitting his back, spitting out curses. Accusing him of always leaving her alone with me.

He stopped at the kitchen table as my mother continued her rage. I had a spoonful of cake in my mouth.

"For Christ's sake, Tess, you can't feed a child all this junk. Look at how much weight she's gaining."

I had no idea what my father meant then, but I knew from his tone that it was bad.

"It's baby fat," she yelled in my defense, or maybe her own.

"That's enough, Dee-Dee," he said, taking the box away from me and dumping it in the trash. "She shouldn't be having all this sugar."

"Why don't *you* feed her for a change if I'm such a lousy mother?"

"I have to work, Tess. God knows you can't hold down a job for longer than a minute before you quit or get fired."

"Everything's always my fault," she wailed. "Why do you hate me?"

"I don't hate you. I just can't keep doing this."

"Don't leave me, Ben. Please." Her anger abruptly turned into crying and bargaining as it usually did. "I'll do better. Get another job. Keep the house clean. Take care of you and Dee-Dee. Please..." She gripped his arm as tears streamed down her cheeks. "I'll die without you."

"Calm down, Tess." He stroked her hair. "I'll be back after this job."

"You promise?"

"I promise."

"I love you, Ben." She sniffled.

He kissed her forehead then came over to me and bent down. "Daddy has to go away for a while. You be a good girl for Mommy, okay?"

"Okay." I nodded. "When will you come back?"

"Soon."

But it was a lie. I think on some level my mother knew that too. He left and she stayed in bed while I watched TV and subsisted on ice cream and whatever else I could find that didn't require cooking. I waited and waited for her to feel better again. Keeping away from her room like she asked me to. Being quiet. Not answering the door when Miss Bridget from across the hall came to check on us. I don't know how long it was before the police were called, then Social Services. That was the first time I was taken into foster care. The first time I realized nothing would ever be fine again.

For years after, I blamed her for not being strong enough. Blamed my father for not caring enough. Blamed myself for not being the good, perfect daughter worth keeping.

I rub the stabbing tightness in my chest, reminded of a line from an old movie, *Hope Floats*. "Childhood is what you spend the rest of your life trying to overcome." A depressing thought.

I pad to the office, throw away the empty Chinese food containers, and pick up our strewn clothes, wishing I could undo the last half hour. At the front door, I switch on the porch light for Mick. Upon seeing my purse and bags in the foyer, I remove the novel, diary, candles, and ring box. A fresh wave of sorrow engulfs me as I place the ring inside my lingerie drawer.

Minutes later, I'm standing in the kitchen, my emotions in knots. The craving is there to comfort myself. To soothe the pain. Numb the emotions. Mick had stocked the fridge and pantry with groceries from Mort's Deli. Gourmet cheeses, deli meats, thick loaves of Italian bread, salads, crackers, two pints of ice cream. Enough to feed a family of six or a one-woman binge.

It's the reason I never keep this much food in the house. I know better. Though that hadn't stopped me two Saturdays ago. After learning about Papa T's death, I overdosed on a container of low-carb muffins, tub of keto ice cream, and low-carb crackers. I would have preferred pizza and brownies, but the truth is I can binge on almost anything. Because it's less about the actual food and more about the compulsion.

My chest is already tight; my breathing, rapid and overloaded with anxiety. The yearning to binge is a temptation I can barely resist. The only thing that pulls me back from that perilous edge is the knowledge of where this temporary comfort will end: with me hugging the toilet bowl and hating myself. And worse, Mick finding me that way.

The night that I'd literally flushed away twenty-one months of abstinence, I'd been too raw and vulnerable to work through the delay and distract method I'd learned in therapy. This time, I won't make any excuses. The pull is a clear and present danger. But I make myself walk away.

In the living room, I roll out my yoga mat, light the candles in the fireplace—preferring them over the hassle of logs—then lie on my back with my knees bent. Counting in tens, I breathe through a series of stretches—deep inhalation from the diaphragm that expands my rib cage, and exhale slowly navel-to-spine. I pay attention to each move and breath of air. Even as my mind wanders to negative thoughts and painful memories, I direct it back to the exercise, noticing how the anxiety starts to unwind inside me and relax some of the tightness in my chest.

Twenty minutes later, the desire to comfort-eat isn't totally gone, but it's at least diffused. I think about calling Mama T just to hear the hug in her voice. But I'd spoken to her earlier and calling twice in one day, especially at this hour, would raise concern. Instead, I open the floral journal. Now what? Biting my lip in thought, I finally write:

I will be strong and confront my fears.

I will let the past go.

I will believe I deserve happiness.

I will only say "I'm fine" when I truly am.

It's not prolific, but they are the intentions that come to mind. I put the book away, inside my night table, and go wash up for bed. I slip on one of Mick's T-shirts. It doesn't help that the top smells like him or that I can still feel the delectable ache between my legs.

I crawl into the queen-size bed. Big and empty, loneliness surrounds me. I leave the lamp on, and missing his body heat, pick up the novel—going first to the happy ending—and wait for Mick to come home.

CHAPTER SIX

Micah

YOU CAN'T PROTECT THE PEOPLE you love from everything.

I run faster, pound the pavement harder, trying to escape the truth that lances through me like a thousand serrated blades.

I hadn't been able to protect my mother from my father's abuse. Not Cayo from dying. Not Dwayde from the custody case. Or Dee from losing our baby.

I run another mile. If I just keep moving maybe I can block it all out. But the regrets and remorse chase in dogged pursuit, slashing and tearing through my guard.

Each step is fraught with snatches of the night. Dee's burst of courage and me shutting her down cold. *We're in this together,* and me, walking out. The panic on her face when she thought I could be leaving her floods me with guilt.

I'd been afraid that Dee would be the one to run scared. But here I am. Literally running, because staying and facing my fear of failing her was harder.

She accused me of wanting to take over her life. She couldn't be more wrong. I respect and admire everything she's made for herself. It's that life and the one that we're building together that I'm trying to protect. If we were to go public with a press release, reporters would hound her at home, at work, everywhere she goes. Her normal, anonymous life as she knows it would no longer be her own. I could ensure the media's physical distance—I'd hire an army of security to do it—but I couldn't prevent their presence or what they might write.

And O'Malley with his personal vendetta, coupled with his ambitions for a big story, will swoop in for the kill. If he looked hard enough, he could find out that Dee had been shuffled in and out of foster care, that her troubled mother committed suicide, that the Torreses had taken her in. From there he'd surmise that we'd had an intimate relationship as teenagers. He could learn of her miscarriage...of her battles with food that landed her in the hospital two years ago. Jesus. I can see it all exploding in the press and over social media.

My hands bunch into tight balls of fury. I would destroy O'Malley and crush whatever sources allowed the story. But for Dee, it would be too late, the damage done. Her privacy and all her vulnerabilities would be exposed. Taken in by the masses, chewed up and spit out. And she'd be left in the wreckage.

You can't protect me from this.

That makes me want to smash my fist through something. I keep running, pumping my legs and arms until my shredded lungs force me to stop. Bent at the waist, sweat drips off my face and I suck in heaving breaths.

I won't fail Dee this time. I can't.

IT'S PAST MIDNIGHT WHEN I return. Toeing off my sneakers, I enter the bungalow with the creak of hardwood beneath my feet. Dee lies curled on her side. The ambient glow of the lamp whispers over her face and curls that are spread across my pillow. Her breaths move in the rhythm of sleep and a novel limply dangles from her hand. I remember Dee telling me she always read the ending of a book first. I couldn't understand that then. But after learning about the unpredictability of her childhood—never sure of what each day would bring—I get why she welcomes certainty. It's what I'm determined to give her.

I manage to ease away the novel and turn off the lamp without waking her. I watch Dee sleep for several more minutes, then go take a shower. Ducking under the hot spray, the water rains over me, washing away the sweat if not the tension. After drying off, I quietly slip back into the bedroom. It's only when I slide beneath the covers that she stirs.

"Mick?" Her eyes blink open. Brown and generously sprinkled with flecks of gold—the sunlight that has always warmed the cold darkness in me. She traces my jaw with her fingers.

I bring them to my lips for a kiss that's steeped in love and apology.

A sad, understanding smile appears. "About earlier—"

"Ssh." I cut her off, stopping the conversation I don't want to have again. "It's late. I just want to be with you. Hold you. Sleep with you."

"K," she murmurs and cuddles into my arms. "I'm glad you're home."

"Me too, beauty." I strum my fingers down her back until her breaths are deep and even again.

Then shutting my eyes, I beg for relief from my thoughts. But shrouded in black silence, they keep striking with knifing persistence.

Everybody has a weak spot, Peters.

Our baby was a girl.

Your fame isn't yours to handle alone anymore.

You can't protect the people you love from everything.

I lie awake for hours, battling my mind and reaching for sleep. When it finally comes, my dreams take me to a dark, unforgotten place.

I'M EIGHT. IT'S AUGUST AND the pavement is hot enough to fry bacon. My T-shirt sticks to my skin and sweat stings my eyeballs. I dribble the ball up the long driveway and stop in front of the net. My throat feels like I've been eating sawdust. Gotta focus and make this shot. He'd already warned me.

I line the width of my feet with my shoulders, slightly bend my knees, and position the ball. I squint against the sun. Scared that my stance might be off, I shift over and set up again.

"What the fuck's wrong with you? Shoot the goddamn ball!"

His bark is meaner than the two Rottweilers' down at Mr. Hadley's repo lot. Better do it. I push the ball upward with my shooting hand. Jump and release. Hold my breath.

The ball hits the backboard, wobbles around the rim, teetering like a drunk. Then it spins inward, actually touching the net. I watch, my heart hammering against my ribs. Droplets of sweat trickle into the corners of my mouth. I taste the briny liquid mixed with my fear. I pray. But no one's listening.

The ball spins outward and hits the ground with an echoing thump. It bounces several times before rolling along the pavement toward my father. He stops it with the toe of his shoe. His obsidian eyes cut into me. His nostrils flare and his top lip curls up bearing his teeth. It's the evil face I give to the monsters and demons in my stories.

Like the ball, I wobble. There are no second chances after a warning. He kicks the ball away and lunges at me, grabbing my arm, calling me a useless pussy. His blasts of dragon breath reek of whiskey. He accuses me of daydreaming about my stupid writing. I wasn't at that time, but I don't talk back.

He's a big man; tall with wide shoulders, his hands are three of mine. He hauls me into the house so fast I fly through the air. My feet don't touch the ground until we reach the living room.

He yanks off my sweaty shirt. My back is still a crisscross of welts from the last time. He never hits me in the face or anywhere that would leave noticeable marks. He knows how to hide this stuff. And no one can touch him anyway, 'cause he's the sheriff.

That isn't the only reason I don't tell anyone. He said he'd kill me. He could too. He has a gun. But even though I don't think death would be much worse than this, I still would never tell. Not even my best friend Victor, or Papa or Mama T. He might hurt them if they knew.

He shoves me forward over the arm of the couch. I squeeze my eyes tight and hear the familiar sounds. The scrape of metal from undoing his buckle, the swoosh of the belt pulling through his pant loops, the thud of leather tapping across his big palm.

I flinch. Nothing. He likes to do that. Make me wait. I never cry, though. Not a single tear. No matter how bad it gets. That's the one thing he can't make me do.

When it comes, the crack of thick leather against my skin feels like a sharp whip of fire. I bite through my lip to keep from crying out. He counts them off for every missed shot, "one…two…three…four…"

"Malcolm!"

Mom. No. Please.

"Stay out of this, Luiza."

He holds me down hard at the back of my neck. He's yelling at her how I'm a fuck-up, that when he was eight he could make a hundred shots just like that and I can't make a lousy fifty.

"It's ninety-three degrees out there today, meu amor." She's being real nice, talking to him in her soft voice the way she does to try to make him stop. But she's scared. Her Portuguese accent gets thicker when she's scared. "He probably just needed a break and some water."

"You baby him too much. You're turning him into a weak-ass pussy with all that fairy-tale bullshit you let him write."

The belt cracks across my back again. My body jerks.

"Malcolm. Please...eu imploro...no more." I hear her tears. They're my fault.

"Get your ass in the kitchen," he says in a low, chilling voice. "I'm warning you, Luiza, for the last time."

He means it. But she won't leave me. She never does.

"I'll do anything, Malcolm."

He's on her in seconds with a punch to the stomach. Her face mangles in pain and she drops to her knees, the groceries spilling out of their bags. I watch in horror, wanting to fight back, wanting to kill him. But fear paralyzes me.

"Mom! Mommy!"

She's balled up on the floor, taking blow after blow for me.

"Stop!" I scream, begging, pleading, until nothing squeezes past my raw throat but useless, powerless whimpers.

Dee

I'M JOSTLED AWAKE. MICK TWISTS viciously in his sleep. Instinct warns me not to touch him. My heart tripping in my chest, I throw off the covers and lower onto the floor, kneeling beside the bed. "Mick."

He thrashes, his legs kicking at the sheets, his pleas guttural, desperate. "Stop! Please. Pleeze stop." Then he cries, hopeless, despairing cries that sound like an animal caught in a trap. I can't bear it.

"Mick! Wake up!"

His eyes fly open. Through the moonlit-dappled room I see the harsh, angry glint in them. Feel the raging violence arc into me.

"It's okay," I say softly. "You were having a bad dream."

His body depresses into the mattress, then goes still. A film of perspiration covers his skin. "Dee?" he croaks.

"Yes. It's me. I'm here."

"You're on the ground." His breaths sough. "Did I do that?"

"Of course not. I moved off the bed."

"Because you were afraid of me?"

"Not of you...of your nightmare."

"Christ..." He drags a hand up over his face and through his hair.

Painfully aware of the secrets from his childhood, I can well imagine what horrors had stolen into his dreams. I lean over and touch his shoulder. The muscle trembles like an earthquake beneath a hard layer of rock.

"Do you want to talk about it?"

No answer. Just broken breaths.

I brush the lock of hair off his damp forehead. He squeezes his eyes closed as if he's trying to fight off those cleaving demons and shove them back into the deep, black hole they'd come from.

"I'll get you some water."

"No." His hand shoots out to grab my wrist, then quickly releases it as if he doesn't trust himself to touch me. "Come back to bed. I'll sleep on the couch."

"Don't go." I wrap my arms around him when he sits up and hug him. He's still shaking. For all the times that Mick has loved me through my grief and pain, I know how good it feels to be held and wanted; to lose yourself in pleasure. With my mouth at his neck, tasting the salt on his skin, I whisper: "Stay. I want you here with me. I want *you*."

"*Dee.*" His voice is anguished, the memory of the nightmare still holding him captive.

But I won't let it. I won't let the past, with its sharp, jagged claws, tear us apart.

Whipping off my shirt, I straddle his hips and push him onto his back, covering his body with mine.

"Make love with me, Mick," I urge in a breathless whisper, rubbing my sex over his cock that hardens with pleasing quickness.

"Dee." He groans deep in his chest before rolling me under him. Our gazes hold and I see a glimmer of the man I love come back into his eyes.

Tears of relief trickle down my temples.

"Don't cry, baby. Please."

"I'm okay," I assure him, running my palms down his back. "Just be with me."

His mouth lowers to the dampness of my cheeks, then to my lips for the most heartrending kiss. In contrast to the violence of his dream, his touch is gentle, his passion subdued.

"You're beautiful," he murmurs, kneeing my legs open and easing every thick inch into me.

It's hot and smooth, and so exquisite that my soul blooms with a million velvet petals. "I love you," I gasp against his mouth.

Like the calm after a storm, Mick slowly strokes into me. His eyes watching my face in the shifting shadows of moonlight, his fingertips painting my skin, his mouth sucking my nipples with unbearable softness.

Desire is a dance as light as air. I glide to the sky on gossamer wings. My hands seek his, our fingers interlock over my head, and my heart swells from the purity of it.

I rise to meet him. Our damp bodies tremble as we climb, riding that silken crest. The tempo is unhurried, divine. I circle my legs around his hips, clinging to him. He delves deeper, harder, not gaining in speed but in force and strength. His steely strokes take us higher and higher, until we're soaring. Delicious warmth spreads inside me, holding, and then we're falling, floating. Our breaths in moans, our names in sighs as we catch each other on the slow tumble down.

I fall asleep cocooned in Mick's arms, surrounded by his scent on my skin.

But when I wake, I'm alone. I try to tell myself that the weight of my disappointment is out of proportion. Mick had said he would write in the morning, so now that the day has broken through the night, he was up doing just that.

I touch the empty space where he'd been and an icy shiver runs through my veins as if mocking my denial. I'd wanted to wake up to him—to see his face, to feel his heat, to be secure in the knowledge that we are back to being okay.

On another shudder, I lumber out of bed and take a hot shower to chase away the chills. Afterward, I dress in a slate gray suit. Its formality is a shield of composure when I am feeling anything but. The faint crescent marks beneath my eyes hadn't been there yesterday morning. Then, I'd been living in my happy bubble where nothing bad could touch us, even if that was just an illusion.

I dab on concealer and dust my cheeks with bronzer. When I'm satisfied that I look put together, I exit the bedroom in search of Mick.

He's in the office as expected. Not writing. He's standing in sweatpants and nothing else. His back is to me. He's staring at the black and white print I'd bought a few years ago. It's of a little girl with her hand raised and the only splash of color is a red heart-shaped balloon floating in the air. I used to see the picture as symbolic of loss, the balloon having escaped her grasp. Now I wonder if she's actually reaching out to grab it in a sign of hope.

"Hi," I say quietly.

Mick turns. I'm overcome by the impact. His face and body are extraordinary but it's the man inside that owns my heart.

"Hi." He steps toward me. His hair is messier than usual, the waves sporadic as if he'd been repeatedly raking his fingers through them, and the tired strain around his eyes betrays how little sleep he had gotten.

I glance at the open laptop. "Are the Muses being unkind?"

"Except for you, the others are total wenches."

We laugh, but it sounds forced. Our usual ease marred by too much left unsaid.

"How about a change of scenery?" I suggest. "Go take a shower and I'll fix us some breakfast."

"Sounds good." He cups my face and brushes his lips across mine. "I won't be long."

Watching him saunter down the hall, I grab hold of that hope. We'll talk things out and find our way back.

I shrug off my suit jacket and step into the kitchen. After setting the coffee to brew, I crack four eggs into a mixing bowl, season them with salt and pepper, and add fresh chives that I pick from the plant on my windowsill.

I'd gotten into growing my own herbs and cooking healthy food after my downward spiral landed me in the hospital. With that, I'd stopped dieting because every failed attempt only made me fatter and feel worse about myself.

The buzzing of a cell phone halts my introspection. I look for where the sound is coming from and trace it to the hallway. As I whisk smoked salmon and low-fat cream cheese into the mixture, I absently wonder who would be calling Mick at 7:00 in the morning.

The vibration stops. But almost immediately it starts up again. Another three buzzes. And another. Someone desperately wants to get hold of him. When they call a fourth time, worry pinches my chest. What if it's an emergency? Papa's Kids? The family?

I go out into the hall. Mick's phone is pocketed inside the exercise armband he must have worn to jog last night. It's lying on the foyer table beside his keys.

Buzz.

My unease over prying is outweighed by concern. I slide his phone out of the band and peer at the screen. A 305 area code and unfamiliar name flashes. *Mackie?* I should let Mick deal with it when he's out of the shower. We haven't discussed answering each other's phones.

Buzz.

I start to put the phone back when it vibrates again—just once—a text. ***Got the eat shit and die letter from your lawyer...wtf????***

I blink twice at the incensed message. Not sure what to make of it, I lay his phone on the table and re-enter the kitchen with questions peppering my mind. Who is Mackie? Why would Mick have sent him a legal letter? And why hadn't he mentioned a thing about it to me?

As much as I attempt to deflect the hurt, I can't. Not after the way he'd kept the bodyguards a secret, not after the way he shut me out then left. Not after he wouldn't tell me about his nightmare. I scramble the eggs in a pan, my eyes stinging with the threat of tears. As much as I'm trying to be open and honest with him, if he can't do the same, then what kind of future do we really have?

I turn off the stove and go set the table. Mick emerges in a long sleeve tee and jeans. As if he'd given himself a pep talk, his mood is much improved.

"It smells delicious in here." He folds his arms around me and nuzzles my neck. "You smell even better."

I take a rallying breath. "Your phone rang several times while you were in the shower."

"Thanks." His lips trace my ear. "I'll take a look later."

"I...um...in case it was an emergency or something...I checked."

He pauses. I can feel the tension roll through him like a ball of knotted wire.

"It was someone named Mackie."

His head lifts to look at me. "You answered my phone?" Disapproval hardens his voice.

"No. But obviously that would be a problem for you." Turning from him, I retrieve two plates from the cupboard, feeling too slighted to care if I'm overreacting. I mean, really...if he's not hiding anything, then what's the big deal?

"Dee," he says behind me.

I set the plates down on the counter harder than intended. They clatter against the granite as I spin around to face him. "I read the text. Maybe I shouldn't have but I did. This Mackie is extremely angry. He said you sent him an *eat shit and die letter* from your lawyer. What's that about?"

The vein pulses at his temple. "Nothing."

Going from hurt to outrage over the blatant lie, I glower at him. "Oh, I see. I'm someone to fuck, but not to trust."

"Christ." His own anger spikes. "Don't try to make what I think of what we do together sound cheap and meaningless. You know how much I love you."

"Love isn't enough. Not without trust and open communication."

"You know things about me that no one else does. How the hell can you possibly think I don't trust you?"

"That's not an answer." Our relationship hadn't survived secrets and eluding the first time around and it wouldn't survive them now. "Talk to me, Mick. Tell me what's going on."

"Dammit." He releases a harsh breath and paces away. "Mackie is my agent."

"Your agent?"

"Yes." The small kitchen allows him little room to walk off his frustration. Two long strides down the galley and back to me. "I hired Beckett MacAllister nearly eleven years ago. He saw an opportunity to take me from popular to superstar status. He got his fair share…made plenty of money representing me. Naturally when I quit the NBA, he wasn't ready to see the cash flow end.

"Since my retirement, he's been trying to entice me back with high profile opportunities. I told him that wasn't going to happen, but he chose to believe I was just taking a hiatus…that once I got past my grief and got bored of Papa's Kids, I'd return to the spotlight." Mick stops in front of me. The look on his face is a mix of anger and disgust.

"Beckett's latest prospect was for me to host a sports talk show. When he called on Friday, while I was on my way here, I told him flat out no. He went on about striking while the iron was still hot. I didn't feel like getting into it with him then. I was looking forward to being with you. So, I ignored his efforts of persuasion. Figured Monday would be soon enough to put an end to it. But Mackie had other plans. It wasn't Lexie's mother or anyone at the party who leaked my attendance at the Lemon Lounge to the press. It was him."

"What?" My hand flies to my mouth in surprise. "How do you know that?"

"He said something that gave him away. Then he admitted it. Not only did he send the press to the Lemon Lounge, he's the one responsible for them being at the community center that day. His way, he said, of keeping me relevant. Fucking unbelievable. It's my fault for hitting

O'Malley, but Beckett set that ball in motion. My own agent. Someone who I thought had my back."

"I'm so sorry."

"You live and learn," he says dismissively. And yet, I can see how stinging that betrayal was for him. "I had my lawyer draw up the paperwork to end our contract. The payout isn't as lucrative as continued work would be, but as far as I'm concerned, he's lucky I don't sue him and ruin his reputation. The fact that he's pissed now, isn't my problem."

"Why didn't you tell me any of this before?"

"It just happened yesterday, Dee."

"That's not the reason. You weren't going to tell me, were you?"

He releases a lamented sigh. "No."

"Why?"

"Because I don't want to bring that life here. This is the life I want... what we have..." He gestures between us. "You and me...untouched by my fame."

"That's not possible. You are famous. That's our reality."

He shoves a hand through his hair. "I fucked up last night, Dee. Walking out on you...I have no excuse. There isn't one to justify it. All I could think about was my need to protect you. And then you said that I couldn't." He briefly closes his eyes. "It hit me hard—my failure to protect you just like I'd failed to protect my mother."

Oh Mick. I had thought his agonized pleas were for himself. I should have known better. "Your nightmare was about your mom."

He nods as a look of shame stalks his eyes.

I slide my arms around him; my heart bleeding with sorrow for the woman and boy who lived that terror, and for the man that it still haunts. Hearing me say that he can't protect the people he loves from everything—as true as that is—for someone like Mick, it's the cruelest of blows.

"I'm sorry for saying what I did last night. That was insensitive. I didn't mean to dredge up old memories."

"I know that, Dee. You have nothing to apologize for."

"Nor do you, Mick. You were a little boy. You didn't fail your mother. And you didn't fail me either. I failed you."

He shakes his head, refusing to relinquish the blame. "I just want to make you happy. I don't want anything to get in the way of what we have."

"Then we won't let it. We'll find a way to deal with your fame. I'll find a way. Just trust me not to run scared."

He takes my hand and threads our fingers together. "When I quit the NBA, I left all that it entailed behind me. I was determined to finally have my own life—write, build out Papa's Kids, coach Dwayde's team where basketball was fun, not about fame or money, or my old man."

"You haven't said much about him."

"There's nothing to say. He's out of my life."

Which doesn't comport with the tension cording his muscles or explain why, as I'd learned from Mama T, that he'd bought the man he despises a mansion. So many questions, but given his closed demeanor on the subject, I decide to hold off when the nightmare isn't so fresh.

"What happened after you quit?" I ask.

"Reporters that had covered me for years were curious, of course. I'd made a living being in the public eye and I couldn't just drop out of sight because I'd had enough. It took a couple of months for the hype over my retirement to settle down. Asher, my PR Director, handled press releases about Papa's Kids. I didn't give many interviews unless it was related to that. Otherwise, I kept a low profile. Not the kind of normal *you* know, but as close to normal as I could get." His voice takes on a heavy tone. "Dwayde paid a heavy price for my fame."

Another guilty burden he bears.

"I'm not ready to put you...to put us out there." Mick lifts my hand to his lips in a habitual gesture that conveys how special I am to him. "For a while longer, I want to hold on to this...you and me. No media. No publicity. Don't we deserve that—after all the years we've been apart, after everything we've been through? Don't we deserve more time just for us?"

I can't deny the truth of that or the relief I feel. Our relationship is still new and more serious than either of us has ever had. We need to learn how to navigate through that uncharted territory without the added pressure of the media. I mean, it has been days since we were seen at the Lemon Lounge. If our dancing together and that kiss hadn't been reported on by now, it probably wouldn't be. There is no harm in delaying. It's actually better, I continue to rationalize.

The custody hearing is in less than five weeks. Though no conflict of interest exists—I was hired as Dwayde's lawyer, not as an impartial advisor to the courts—still, I'm aware of the optics. If the media learned of our relationship it could muddy the ethical waters and turn this case into a sideshow. Dwayde doesn't need to be caught up in any public spectacle on top of everything else he's dealing with.

"What are you thinking?" Mick asks, studying my face.

"That more time for us sounds wonderful." His double take makes me smile. "Were you expecting a different response?"

"I'm not always sure what to expect with you."

"Nice to know." I give him a smacking kiss on the lips. "That will keep you on your toes."

"You can have me on my toes, my knees…at your feet…anywhere you want me."

"That sounds promising."

"So, we're good?"

"Not about you keeping things from me. I mean it, Mick, that isn't okay."

His fingers glide down my cheek. "You are my heart and soul, Dee. I'll do anything to protect you."

I feel the depth of love in his touch, in his words, but they give me little reassurance that he won't keep shutting me out. "I need honesty, Mick."

"You're right, I should have told you about the bodyguards," he admits. "But I promise you won't even notice them."

"That's not the point."

"It is to me. I'm trying to give you normal, and keep you safe from my fame at the same time. I won't compromise on that."

"Relationships involve both communication and compromise. It has to be a partnership. 50/50."

"50/50, huh?"

"You're not taking me seriously."

"I take you very seriously." He pulls me to him. "We'll negotiate terms over dinner. I have a meeting downtown that may go late. I'll arrange for a car to pick you up at 7:00."

I squint up at him. Stunned that he would chance us being seen together after the conversation we just had. "Do you really think dinner out is a good idea?"

"I want to take you on a date."

"I'd love that but—"

"I've already made the arrangements. You're going to love this place. One of my investments. I want to show it off to you. Make it a night you won't forget. So, just say *yes, Mick*."

His tone turns playful, but I can see how much this means to him.

"We're really going to have to discuss this partnership thing," I mutter.

"Over dinner."

"You're relentless." I nip his chin. "But an unforgettable date with the restaurant's sexy investor does sound too good to refuse. Do you think he'll put out?"

With the consummate skills he'd shown on the dance floor, Mick dips me dramatically. "I'd say he's a sure bet."

I DRIVE TO WORK IN a state of renewed optimism. The thought of us being together without the imminent risk that reporters could turn up out of nowhere and catch me off guard allays my previous worries. And yet, with the sweep of relief comes the realization that in continuing to hide our relationship from the media, a bodyguard will be tailing me wherever I go. How can we operate with any kind of normalcy when someone is constantly watching my back? When I'm paying for my anonymity with the price of my valued independence?

I turn into the parking lot and exit my car, scanning the lot in search of some telltale sign. Surely, I'd notice something. But all I see is the typical flow of morning commuters. Nothing out of the ordinary. Just as Mick promised.

Of course, his security people would be trained to blend in. Which means my bodyguard could be the man in the blue suit walking beside me, or the guy in the jeans and cap that is leaning against the lamppost as if he's waiting for someone. Fact is, it could be anyone.

Okay, enough with making yourself crazy.

I enter the six-story building, looking forward to the distraction that I'll find at work. Many of my colleagues couldn't understand why I left a large, reputable family law firm with a view of Grant Park and a lucrative salary to start a child advocacy practice twenty minutes away from the popular downtown Loop. My clients are mainly kids in the system. Most of my cases come through the courts and Social Services. It's not high profile or glamorous, but I love what I do and I'm proud of what I've built.

Bypassing the elevator for the exercise, I take the stairs up the five flights to my office.

"Morning, Boss." Lena pops out from the kitchenette in greeting. Her pink Mohawk, multiple piercings, and black combat boots would be out of place in most law practices. But the avant-garde style suits Lena and her strong work ethic suits me.

"Morning." I shrug out of my coat and hang it on the hook. "How did the audition go?"

"We got the gig!" Her face lights up and the jeweled stud winks in the corner of her smile. "Next Friday at the Atomic Freeze."

"Congratulations," I say, coming forward with a hug, knowing what a big break this is for Lena and her all-girl band. "That's great news."

"We're just filling in for an opening act that had to cancel. But we're still stoked about the exposure."

"If they're smart they'll soon be booking you as the headliner." My sincere words taste bittersweet. I'll hate to lose Lena when the time comes, but I understand following your dreams.

"Thanks. I'm trying not to expect too much. Just go with it and see what happens. Appreciate all your support, Dee. Will you come?" Her palms press together in the sign of a prayer. "I really want you there."

There's no hesitation. Even though punk rock isn't my type of genre, Lena has been invaluable to me. My practice couldn't have doubled in size so quickly without her meticulous organizational skills and willingness to do whatever was asked of her beyond the tasks of an assistant. Above that, I consider Lena a friend.

"I wouldn't miss it."

"Awesome!" She throws her arms around me for an effusive hug then steps back. "Bring Mick. I'm dying to meet him."

"Uh…" *Awkward.* Lena still doesn't know that Micah Peters and my Mick are one and the same. Though she expressed her suspicions, I've evaded the complicated truth.

"Uh, what?" Her eyes widen eagerly. "Tell me."

My message to Mick about trust and honesty scratches my conscience. "You know how you've wondered about—"

"I knew it!" She shoves her fist in the air for a victory pump before I even get the words out. "You and Micah Peters."

"The thing is…" I try to temper her excitement, "with Mick being a celebrity and a witness in Dwayde's case, we're keeping our relationship low key for the time being."

"Oh yeah sure." Lena sobers. "Totally get that. I won't say a word to anyone." She makes a zipping gesture across her lips before they curve up into another animated smile.

"How are you not shocked by this?" I have to ask.

"Shocked by what?"

"Me and Micah Peters."

"Why? Because he's famous and mega hot?"

"Well, yes." It's what everyone else will wonder.

"That doesn't make him blind or dumb. I can totally see why Mick would be into you. You're smart, successful, caring, and beautiful. I could go on. You're amazing, Dee."

"Thanks, Lena." Her words mean more to me than she could ever know.

"I'm just curious as to how you happened to meet Micah Peters before the case?" She fills a mug and tops it with skim milk and fake sugar. "I got the impression you guys have history."

"We do. But that story is for another day and over lots of wine."

"You supply the date. I'll bring the booze."

"Sounds like a plan." I eye my watch. "Ready to work?"

"Yup. Files for your meetings are on your desk."

"You're the best." I take the coffee she hands me and go to my office.

It's an excellent space. Timber-beamed ceilings, distressed hardwood floors, and brick walls that might have given the loft a closed-in, cavernous feel if not for the giant slanted window panels that bring in an abundance of natural light.

Before getting started on what will be a busy day, I pull my cell phone out of my tote bag to text Jordyn and Lexie in our group chat. I lead in by telling them that no one from the party had called the media, putting Lexie's mind at ease about her mother's involvement. I explain that it was Mick's agent who has since been fired.

Given he was the leak and not anyone that saw us together, we're going to take some "us" time and keep our relationship out of the press for as long as possible. But Mick isn't taking any chances with reporters. That means I have a bodyguard. :(

Jordyn responds first: *why the frown???? I can think of worse things than having Studly Stiles guard my body ;)*

Me: *It's not Stiles. That would be too obvious. Mick is trying to give me "normal" so I don't know who it is. But it feels weird to know someone's following me around. Seems over the top.*

Lexie: *Sounds like Mick is just being careful.*

Me: *That's what he said. I'll deal. Mick is worth it.*

Jordyn: *Gagging here...*

Me: *lol. Change of subject then, Girls Night next Friday? Lena's band is playing at the Atomic Freeze.*

Jordyn: *Hot guys in leather. I'm in.*

Lexie: *Punk Rock?* I can picture her making a face.

Jordyn: *Don't get your pearls in a twist. It'll be fun.*

Me: *Plus, I promised my support. You have to come. Please.*

Lexie: *Ugh. Alright.*

Me: *Great! More details later. Gotta run.*

I silence my ringer and get to work. The day flies by with meetings, reports, and legal briefs. Stopping long enough to down a container of Greek yogurt and catch up with Lena, I excitedly tell her that Mick and I are going on a date tonight. Then I turn my attention back to my mounting caseload. It's past four when I have a chance to open Dwayde's file, specifically to review the information about the Franklins.

By all accounts, they are well-respected by the people in their hometown of Grandview, Kentucky. A small, tight community where Charles Franklin, who inherited Franklin Farms from his great grandfather, has a hospital wing in his name and is both a prominent businessman and deacon of the local church. His wife, Joan, is a generous philanthropist who sits on a number of charity boards. Without so much as a parking ticket to mar their picture-perfect image, they have been lauded as loving parents to Joyce, and devoted grandparents to Dwayde.

But just because it shines, doesn't make it gold. I met them, and my gut says all is not as they would have us believe. Beneath Franklin's Southern charm seemed a controlling man, used to getting what he wanted. And Mrs. Franklin, well...she was unnaturally thin, excessively nervous, and her mind spacey as if she might have been overmedicating. Franklin directed her every move. A Stepford Wives kind of vibe that I found odd and disturbing.

Add to that, Dwayde's reaction toward them. Not just anger, but a depth of hostility that appeared inconsistent with his claims that he doesn't remember them. I saw the flicker of recognition when they mentioned his pony, Dasher. I saw the sheer loathing on his face when they gifted him with a shirt bearing the family crest as a symbol of his legacy. He raged: "I don't care about being a Franklin...I'm a Torres and they're my only family!" Then tore from the hotel suite.

I tried to reason with Charles Franklin, to get him to drop the case, to put Dwayde's best interests first. Wasted breath. He told me he would "win" Dwayde back as if his grandson was some trophy to be prized.

We've had one court hearing since then. During the preliminary review of evidence, opposing counsel, Thomas Jackson, produced a document. One that Joyce allegedly signed when Dwayde was four years old, giving custody to her parents. A document that suddenly surfaced after Dwayde outright rejected them. I'd called that a little more than convenient.

I pick up one of the pictures of Franklin's daughter, then fifteen. She'd been featured in *Equestrian News*. Joyce is holding her first-place ribbons. I study the shy, dimpled grin and those big Franklin eyes so much like Dwayde's and her father's. Then I look at the photo of her months later, after the fatal poisoning of her horse. She appears ghostly, her face sunken, her skin sallow. Her smile flat-lined.

"What happened to you?" I ask aloud.

According to Dwayde: *She said a lot of stuff while she was high and running at the mouth, but I didn't pay no attention to it.*

Dwayde is a sharp kid. He'd paid attention. But he's not talking.

Not to me. Or to Mick. Or to his foster parents. Not to his psychologist either.

In my meeting with Dr. Rachel Sass, she could not conclude with certainty that Dwayde remembers more than he's saying. I, on the other hand, have no doubts. I'm all too aware of what secrets look and feel like.

She'd advised me to be patient. Not to push too hard and risk him shutting down completely. But patience is a luxury I don't have when time isn't on our side, and I still have more questions than answers.

"Hey, Boss," Lena's lighthearted intrusion pulls me from my heavy thoughts. "It's 5:15."

"Oh." I look up at the corner of my computer screen then over at her standing in the doorway. "Lost track of time."

"I figured. You don't want to be late for your hot date with Mick."

"I never said *hot* date."

"No." She grins. "But your eyes did."

CHAPTER SEVEN

Dee

THE FORTY-MINUTE COMMUTE GIVES my work brain a chance to slowly shut off.

Anxious for the night ahead, I arrive home and search my wardrobe. The black slacks and tunic I had planned to wear now feel too uninspired. Too in my comfort zone. I have this opportunity to reinvent myself, or rather to discover who I really am behind the cloak of insecurities.

I retrieve the floral covered book from the end table. I can't really call it a diary. It's more like a list of manifestations and self-improvement goals. Sitting on the bed, I open the cover to the first page and read what I've written so far:

I will be strong and confront my fears.

I will let the past go.

I will believe I deserve happiness.

I will only say "I'm fine" when I truly am.

I pick up the pen and after several minutes of thought, decide on a title. **Dee's Personal Aspirations Journey.** Then I add two more to the list:

I will be less critical of my body.

I will be bold and confident.

I read the full list. Repeating the words out loud like a mantra, hoping that my psyche will absorb them. With that, I put the book away and walk back to the closet. I select a dress, the color of midnight. An impulse purchase I made on a night when I'd been home alone, online shopping, and feeling ambitious. The dress has a Bardot neckline that exposes the shoulders and snugly fits from chest to knee. All the reasons why it's been hanging in my maybe-one-day section for the last six months.

But I think about what attracted me to the dress in the first place. It had been the model. She owned her curves. Staring back at the camera with a hand on one voluptuous hip, a vivacious smile on her lips. Sexy and fearless.

The woman I want to be.

Laying the dress out on the bed, I go shower, shave my legs, and smooth on fragrant lotion. Then tramping down the niggling second thoughts, I wiggle into my undergarments and step into the dress. While the bathroom mirror is not full-length, it's long enough for me to see all the relevant parts.

Even with the strapless body-shaping slip beneath that's supposed to smooth and minimize, there's no disguising my big boobs or round, thick hips. If only I were long and lean like Lexie or athletic like Jordyn. If only...the tapes start playing.

Stop! I give my head a shake, willing the negative noise away. *I will be less critical of my body.* I repeat that several times again and slap my palms on the vanity, looking sternly into the mirror as if daring my reflection to mess with me.

Okay. Deep breaths. I straighten. I define my curls with a lightweight gel, apply shimmery taupe to my eyelids, dust on bronzer, and finish off the look with a pop of red smudge-proof lipstick. Pleased with my hair and makeup, I exit the bathroom and slide on a pair of black heels, add simple hoops to my ears, and fasten on the stunning diamond necklace from Mick.

At 7:00, the doorbell chimes. I toss a long shawl around me—because insecurity is a dogged beast—and grab my clutch with the ring box inside.

"Mademoiselle Chase," greets a well-dressed gentleman in his late forties, complete with a cultured French accent. "I'm Bernard, your driver this evening."

"Nice to meet you, Bernard."

"Tout le plaisir est pour moi."

I think in translation it means, it's his pleasure or something like that, but anything said in French sounds pretty awesome.

"Where are you from?" I ask.

"Belgium." He cups my elbow and leads me down the stairs to the driveway.

I try not to gawk, and fail. When Mick had said he was sending a car, I hadn't expected a stretch limousine.

Bernard holds the backdoor open and I slide across the long bench seat. "There is a button on the armrest if you need me for anything."

"Thank you."

After a polite nod, he closes the door and I'm engulfed in pure extravagance. Plush warmed seats with massage options and two touch-screen plasma TVs are built into the walls. Subtle blue lighting offers a serene atmosphere and classical strings play from a hidden surround system. On top of the marble bar sits a silver ice bucket with a bottle of wine the color of pale sunshine. Beside it, I find one stemless glass and a small pearlescent card that bears my name in Mick's fluid handwriting. I lift the flap.

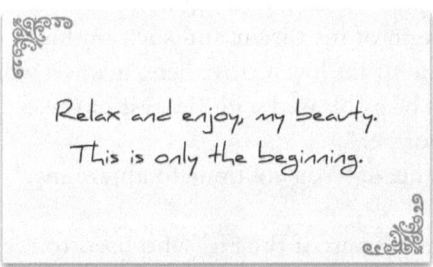

My heart twists and my emotions spin. An apt response, considering the way I've felt since Mick stormed back into my life. As though I've been hit by a cyclone that has whipped me up in its force and taken me to an alluring and seductive world I've never known before.

I twist the crystal stopper out of the bottle and pour myself half a glass. The aromatic notes please my nose and the fresh autumn taste brimming with pears and apples add a crisp, sweet element to my palate. I'm not much of a connoisseur, but I recognize it as delicious.

"Cheers," I toast myself and sit back and enjoy the ride.

WHEN BERNARD TURNS OFF THE interstate and pulls into an open field, I peer through the tinted windows. Against the backdrop of a violet sunset waits a white helicopter and Mick.

He walks toward the limo with long, graceful strides and cool confidence. Watching him is eroticism in motion. He shakes hands with Bernard then approaches the rear door.

It opens and the soft light spills over him. Casually elegant, he's wearing all black too—dress slacks with a tailored suit jacket, and the shirt beneath is left unbuttoned at the collar and one below. His short waves are carelessly tossed and a dusting of dark stubble coats his cheeks and jaw.

Before I can get my wrap, he holds out his hand. Our palms touch; his warm and sure, bring me to my feet. He checks me out from my glossy curls to the pointy tips of my shoes, then reverses the tour, leisurely letting his gaze glide upward. Pausing on my dress, the pendant, my red lips, and finally my eyes, where his gaze stays. He turns my hand over and presses a kiss to my wrist. "You take my breath, Deeana Rae."

I smile up at him, wanting nothing more than to bury my face into the exposed column of his throat and suck on his skin. But we're not alone. "Thank you for the lovely drive here. It was a wonderful surprise."

"I hope you'll be as pleased with the rest of the evening."

"How can I not be?"

He shakes his head. "You continue to amaze me."

"Why?"

"Because I wasn't sure if the girl who used to read the endings of books first would welcome surprises."

"I still read the endings first," I admit. "But lately I've found myself open to new adventures."

His movement is swift, making my breath catch and release an instant before his mouth is on mine. Desire sparks fast, a forest catching fire. Tongues tangle, the kiss ravenous, urgent; a need that befits weeks spent apart rather than hours. No matter how many times, it's never enough. I constantly want him...crave him with a hunger so fierce it shakes me.

"Christ, Dee," he groans, breaking the kiss. But doesn't go far. With his hands flexing at my hips, he rests his forehead on mine as he exhales quick, hard breaths. "It's impossible not to get carried away with you."

"I know the feeling." My fingers brush over his lapels. "Maybe we should climb inside the limo and finish this."

"I can lay you out and have my way with you."

"Please." I shiver.

"Don't tempt me, baby. We have reservations and what I want to do to you takes time." He kisses me again. This one brief, but the passion between us lingers as his hands fall away. "Let's get your things before I change my mind."

I wouldn't complain, but I also appreciate the merits of delayed gratification.

Mick drapes the shawl around my shoulders and hands me my purse. I think of the ring tucked inside and hold the clutch against me.

"Shall we?" He secures my arm through the bend of his elbow. "We'll see you on the other side, Bernard."

I'd forgotten about our audience of one. But the fact that Mick hadn't suggests that despite Bernard's refined appearance he is as much a bodyguard as he is a driver. I should have known Mick would take all the necessary precautions. But I appreciate that he'd done it in a way to give me a nice experience rather than make it feel like security detail.

I manage a sheepish glance in Bernard's direction. "Thank you again."

"Mademoiselle Chase." He nods.

"Where's the other side?" I ask turning back to Mick.

"You'll see."

"No hints?"

"Nope. Have you ever flown in one of these before?"

"First time," I admit with nervous excitement. "Have you?"

"A few times on business and I've taken Dwayde up for fun."

Meaning, no other woman has shared this experience with him. That makes it all the more special.

We board the luxury three-seater and Mick introduces me to our pilot, Finn. But I notice he doesn't give my name, only trusting so much in Finn's professional discretion. The pilot goes over the safety rules and equips us with earphones and mikes. Within minutes we are buckled in and taking off.

The front windshield and wide windows allow for a panoramic view. Below, Chicago unfurls in a symphony of dazzling lights reflecting off the skyscrapers. Mick is an excellent tour guide, pointing out the John Hancock building, Wrigley Field, and the Lincoln Park Zoo. I watch as veins of traffic circulate through the knot of downtown and the river glints like a golden ribbon winding far beneath us.

Mick links our fingers, our grins huge. I feel weightless. Giddy.

When we land, Bernard is there to whisk us off to where the next surprise awaits. Fusion—a swanky Asian-inspired restaurant that I'd read about in *Wine and Dine* magazine but had no idea Mick was one of the silent partners.

As soon as we're escorted through a concealed side entrance and ushered up via private elevator to the exclusive VIP dining room on the rooftop, we are treated to five-star service. Ownership definitely has its privileges. The waiter is expert, never allowing our glasses to empty. Mick drinks sparkling water, while the wines I receive are paired to complement the dishes on the tasting menu. From succulent tempura lobster, savory leg of lamb slow cooked in sake-infused soy sauce, to pan-seared ahi tuna topped with wasabi pesto—every bite is divine.

Mick eats with gusto, whereas it's second nature for me to battle myself. I've lived so long categorizing foods as good and bad, using them as comfort or denying myself as punishment, that I haven't often allowed myself to eat just for the sake of pleasure. Tonight, I do. It's hard not to around Mick. He's such a foodie, his delight evident and contagious.

Aside from the meal, Mick is a charming, attentive companion. I like the way he listens, the way he makes me laugh. I like learning anything about him to add to what I already have stored. I like that he's a coffee snob and thinks no self-respecting caffeine drinker would settle for instant. I like that despite his wealth he prefers the simple things in life, except for fast cars, good food, and expensive watches. I like that he still remembers the first story he ever wrote at age six about a superhero boy and his magic dog.

I like the way he looks at me, touches me—drawing circles on the nape of my neck, keeping the intimate connection throughout dinner.

Just when I can't imagine the experience could get any better, acclaimed Executive Chef Kit Nakamura appears with a portable cooking table. She and Mick share a business-friendly exchange and she is professional and courteous to me. Once we get through the pleasantries, it's fascinating to watch a gifted artisan at work. She flambés the dark cherries with a healthy dose of liqueur, making an impressive show of flames. Next, she pours the warm sauce over a gold-dusted chocolate dome for a lava-melting effect. The reveal is an elevated sundae, this one she tells us is made of ganache brownies and candied-ginger ice cream. Every indulgence I usually try to avoid.

She takes a reverent bow at our applause before she departs with the cooking table and server.

I really shouldn't, I think, when Mick scoops up a spoonful and brings the dessert dripping to my lips. But impossible to resist, I open for him and let the decadent taste of rich dark chocolate and sweet cream slide over my tongue. Leaning in, he brushes his mouth across mine.

"Mm. Delicious."

Though heat throbs between my legs, a shiver moves through me as I imagine Mick licking chocolate off my body.

"Such a response," he teases and looks into my eyes.

"Eating with you is sexy. It's never been that way for me before. I can't help my reaction"

"I don't want you to help it." Under the table his palm caresses my knee and starts to inch up.

"Behave." I cover his hand, pausing its ascent and smile at the wicked flash in his grin. We feed each other a few more bites before I force myself to stop and let Mick finish. "I have something for you," I say when he puts his spoon down.

"Oh yeah?"

"Close your eyes."

He obliges. "When I open them will you be naked?"

"Not yet," I playfully taunt, feeling brazen and happy. I get the ring from my purse and set it down in front of him before I eagerly lift the lid. "Now open."

My excited reaction wanes at his sharp intake of breath. He doesn't move. Hardly blinks. The moment is still except for the compulsive ticking in his clenched jaw.

I twist my napkin, kicking myself for ruining our light, flirty mood with my impetuous gift. "I...um...wanted to give you something meaningful, but if it's too much—"

"It's not too much. It's perfect." He slides the black diamond band on his right finger and cups my cheeks, the metal of the ring is cool on my skin. "You're perfect." He kisses my lips, my nose, and my eyes when they close. "Dance with me."

Pleasantly buzzing on wine, Mick, and the wealth of emotion spiraling between us, I rise with him and he leads me onto the glass-enclosed balcony. Stars illuminate the sky like twinkling snowflakes and sultry jazz music floats through ceiling speakers.

Pulling me close, he aligns our bodies and we move together. Our dance is slow and sensual. As if a prelude of what's to come. And I can't wait.

LATER, WHEN WE EXIT THE restaurant, the limo is parked at the side entrance. Mick settles in beside me, shutting the door and locking us in. The partition behind Bernard is closed. There's a bottle of champagne in the ice bucket and a silver platter of strawberries. I appreciate the thoughtful gesture, but I'm too amped up to eat or drink anything else.

As we pull away from the curb, Mick takes my hand and holds it on his thigh. The simple act makes me achingly aware of just how much I want him. I meet his gaze in the powdery blue light. "I remember the first time we were alone in your Mustang."

Affectionate amusement glitters in his eyes. "We drove out to the lake. You were wearing this long skirt with a blouse buttoned all the way up to your neck. And over that a sweater with another million buttons. You were locked up tighter than Fort Knox."

I laugh at his analogy, which isn't far off. "I was nervous."

"There was no reason to be."

"I know. You were so careful with me. So patient."

"Patient?" He scoffs. "I was desperate for you. I still am."

"That's handy since I'm feeling pretty desperate myself."

"Come here." He draws me onto his lap and slides his fingers into my hair, holding my head to kiss me deeply.

I suck on his tongue, tasting espresso and chocolate. He groans low. A need that matches my own. Craving more, my breasts swell and peak, my core pulses along with the rapid pounding of my heart. I feel the prod of his erection against my hip. I shift—the stretchy material allowing me to easily straddle his thighs—and rock over his thick bulge.

He makes a dark, primitive sound that drives me crazy. His phenomenal scent, lusher now with arousal is drugging. The heat of his powerful body wraps around me like a blanket of lust. I want to feel that heat against my skin. The burn under my fingers. His strength and fire pitted against my own. I frantically yank at his shirt, tugging it out of the waistband of his pants. My hands shoot under, kneading rock-hard pecs, nails scraping warm skin.

"Slow down, baby." He traps my wrists.

"Let go." I nip his chin, not trying to be gentle.

"You're testing my will," he says through gritted teeth. "I love having your hands on me. But I have something else planned."

My breath quickens as my head swirls with possibilities.

Mick removes my hands and places them around his neck before pressing a button on the armrest. "Drive around until you hear otherwise."

I should be embarrassed that Bernard will assume we're getting busy in the back of his limo, but at the moment I'm too high on pheromones and Mick to care.

Still straddling him, my fingers play with the tapered hair just above the nape of his collar and I resume our kiss. Licking into my mouth, he runs his hands over my back, searching. I laugh, a breathless puff of air, and whisper against his lips. "There's no zipper. You have to… um…peel it off."

"*Daaammmmnnn!*" He tugs the material down both arms and lowers it to my waist. His eyes of smoked coffee streak over the flesh pushed above the bra cups of the slip.

My body quivers when he lays me back onto the seat and slithers the dress over my hips and drags it down my legs and off. The slip disappears next and I'm left in thigh-high stockings, heels, and no panties.

For one dreaded second, I hope to heaven that I don't look like some plus-size, centerfold-wannabe. But those tapes that prey on my self-doubts don't have their usual galvanizing effect. Part of that is I don't let them and the other part is Mick and the way his avid eyes are devouring me.

"You are full of surprises yourself, Ms. Chase."

"Panties seemed impractical."

"Prudent and sexy." He traces the band of one stocking, leaving goose bumps behind. "Are there any limits, Dee?"

"Not with you."

"I treasure that." His eyes are that familiar blend of hot and tender. "I'd never hurt you. Pain's not a turn on to me. I only want your pleasure."

"You have it."

He nuzzles my nose then moves to sit. Eager and curious, I watch him slide off his jacket and retrieve a long, crimson scarf from the inside pocket. "It reminded me of your red dress," he says with a wolfish grin as he tightens the length of the material between his two fists. The act so carnal it has me squirming.

"Don't be afraid." He levers over me, all broad shoulders, narrow hips, and solid, hard thighs.

"I'm too turned on to be afraid."

"That's the idea." Mick loops the silk through a handle on the door and raises my arms above my head, massaging my wrists before he tethers them together with the soft fabric.

I've never been restrained before. Wouldn't have thought that something that renders me utterly helpless could feel so tantalizing. I'm not the submissive type, at least not my notion of what submissive means. I value an equal exchange of power in relationships. Yet when it comes to sex with Mick, I'm thoroughly aroused by a shift in the balance. Because I know that his brand of dominance is tempered by love, affection, and respect.

"Spread your legs."

Responding to the erotic demand, I do as he says, letting them fall open to expose my fleshy inner thighs and the evidence of my desire between them.

Mick draws a shuddering breath. "You're so wet and I've barely touched you."

"I've been this way for hours."

"Then I better make it worth the wait." He lifts the clear dome off the tray and plucks a big, ripe strawberry between his thumb and forefinger. Holding it by the stem, a dark fire brews in his eyes. And when he touches the cold berry to my exposed sex, I gasp on a hard shiver.

In that moment, I know that whatever he has planned is going to undo me. He circles the entrance of my body and thrusts the tip inside, filling the air with a fruity, provocative scent. The feel of cool pressure against wet heat is sinful.

"Mick," I whimper in protest when he stops.

Smiling, he withdraws the glistening berry and brings it to his mouth, deliberately teasing me with the touch he withholds.

"Is it your plan to torture me to death?"

"No." He takes a bite and sweeps the soft, juicy end across my lips. "I want you very much alive and coming all over my mouth."

Rapid spasms tighten my core. "That's not going to take long."

"Yes, it will," he whispers, sucking the fruit from my lips.

"No fair," I moan.

"I never said I play fair." With that, he drags the fragrant berry over my skin and his hot mouth follows—sipping at the hollow of my throat, licking the juice with the swirl of his tongue, moving to my shoulders, down my arms, and back up across my chest.

I'm swamped in sensation. Drowning in it. He rotates the strawberry around one stiff nipple then…I'm surrounded by hot, wet suction. The delicate pulls of his mouth are excruciatingly tender. I cry out, yanking on the restraint, trying to get free to touch him, to grab those wavy strands of hair and urge him to bite, to suck harder, anything to relieve this piercing ache.

"Easy, beauty," he soothes, kissing his way over to my other straining nipple, and treating it to the same lavish attention.

I can hardly breathe to moan by the time he slides down into a prone position. My legs widen readily, my body so aroused that I feel flushed and fevered.

"You're beautiful here too." His gaze blatantly scans every fold and crevice, every drop of need. "Pink and creamy."

Anticipation sizzles my nerve endings.

He swallows the last bite of strawberry, before his dewy mouth goes to the bare skin above the lace band of my stockings. He works his way up to the crease of one inner thigh, then the other, his tongue flicking slowly upward until he reaches the apex.

Headlights beam through the darkened glass. I blink against the glare, a reminder that I'm in the middle of Chicago—in the back of a limo—with my wrists bound, my legs wide open, and Mick between them.

He kisses my pubis, down the trimmed landing strip to my lips. My lower lips. He nibbles them gently. I'm already coming undone and he's only kissing.

"*Mick.*"

"Right here, beauty."

He brings his thumbs to my labia and I feel him carefully part them as if he's separating the petals of a flower to expose its center heartbeat. His mouth lowers again, hovering over tender tissues, bathing me in a warm, moist cloud. He licks my cleft with the flat of his tongue, slow swipes, picking up my essence, sliding over and around my clit.

Pleasure slams into me. With the skill of a man who knows my body well, his maddening laps and diabolical tongue lure me to the cusp of orgasm. Over and over and over again.

"Please..." I beg, twisting against the hold. "Please, let me come."

"Soon." He hums, teasing me with feather light strokes, making me grind mindlessly into his coaxing mouth until I can't take it another minute, until I'm sure I'll die if he doesn't get me off.

Only when my moans are keening cries, and I'm thrashing, my head tossing from side to side, does his tongue work that singular spot in quick, firm circles.

All the buildup, the teasing, the waiting coalesces into a firestorm. I sob his name and lock my legs around his back. My hips churning, my body shaking as sensation blazes through me, surging, annihilating everything in its path.

And still he doesn't stop. His mouth is tireless, staying with me through the violent tremors, sucking and licking with a steady, unending rhythm, goading my orgasm to roll on and on, making it impossible to tell where one eruption ends and another begins.

The pleasure is so intense, my toes curl inside the tips of my shoes. I'm suspended in a dark vortex with Mick at its primary center. I hear the sounds of his ardent mouth mingling with my cries, see his broad shoulders, the back of his head moving, feel the velvet tip of his tongue massaging me outside and in.

I buck against the restraints, coming again on a thready cry, rising and falling until he finally stops and I go limp and boneless. My mind is still dazed when I feel Mick's lips brush against my inner thighs. My legs still sprawled when I hear the metal rasp of his zipper. My eyes drift open. The juxtaposition of him being fully clothed, while I'm virtually naked with my hands tied only adds to the allure.

Mick rises over me. Balancing his weight on one arm, he reaches inside his pants to grasp his erection. I can see it, thick and pulsing in his hand.

"I'm so hard for you." He strokes himself from the wide base to the glistening head, demonstrating how desperately close he is to the edge. How much he had reigned in his own needs to take care of mine. "I can't wait any longer, baby."

With a harsh groan, he grips the backs of my thighs, roughly yanking me to him, and lifts my legs so that they rest vertically along his chest, my ankles over his shoulders. I can feel his jutting cock, hot and stiff against my slit. He lowers his gaze and rumbles low in his throat as he shoves forward, watching the slick, fierce entry into my body. The connection is searing. It's where he belongs. Where I belong. Us. Together.

He grinds his hips, and one minute he's buried deep, hard and huge, and the next he's pulling almost out, and back in again, all the time watching, groaning, rasping heated words that make me hotter, wetter. *I love watching my cock move in and out of you. The way you open and close, sucking me in deep, squeezing me.*

He lets my ankles slip off his shoulders and gathers me beneath him, confining me, kissing me voraciously. His chest vibrates with gruff, primal noises, his breaths do the same, gusting into my mouth. His body is tight against mine, his arms steel bands around my open thighs, his cock claims me. Possesses me.

I glory in the way he fucks me, as if he has to, as if his next breath depends on it. This part of myself that I didn't know existed before him has found its equal. I was made for this volatile mix of pleasure-pain, for this sweet, savage rhythm. I was made for him.

My lungs heaving for air, I pull wildly on the restraints and struggle against the muscular weight of his body to rock into his pivoting lunges. But like a tugboat fighting a tidal wave, I'm helpless to do anything. All I can do is feel that thick column of muscle hitting every inch of me, the incessant pressure at the mouth of my womb, the perfect angle of his shaft rubbing against my clit. Ecstasy shatters.

I climax in a silent scream, clenching tightly around him. The pleasure heightened and magnified by my bound wrists and the way he has my entire body confined.

"That's it, baby." He stills, his muscles cording. "Squeeze me. Make me come. Ah, Dee." He turns his cheek into the curve of my neck and slams into me for several hammering seconds. "Yes! Oh fuck, yes." His open mouth bats against my skin as he grips my behind, and pumps his warm seed deep inside of me.

I lie beneath him, sated, drunk on his heat and musky scent. Mick had totally controlled my pleasure, aroused it beyond anything I've ever known, and it had been the hottest and most erotic experience of my life.

Micah

IT'S A WHILE BEFORE I can move. Before I even want to. There's no place I'd rather be than over Dee's soft curves, with my face buried in her hair. Only the awareness I must be heavy has me shifting my weight to the side. Looking down at her in the hushed light, with her skin a misty gold and her eyes still closed, I release the knot that had pulled tighter every time she yanked in passion, and massage her wrists.

"You were unbelievable."

"Me?" Her eyes flutter half-open. "You did all the work."

"Hardly work." I lick each of her still puckered nipples and she moans for me. "There are so many things I want to do to you."

"Well then..." her hand curls around my neck when I incline my head to kiss her lips. "I guess you'll just have to put all those fantasies to good use."

"No fears?"

"None. I trust you with my heart and my body."

Her words, given so freely, so sincerely, hit like a sledgehammer. Not for the first time am I struck by the magnitude of her trust. Her openness. By the way she holds nothing back this time. Baring herself physically and emotionally in the most defenseless ways. Gifting me with a ring as a symbol of her love. Allowing me to restrain her, no questions asked.

I can't believe how lucky I am to have her. Can't believe that this beautiful, incredible woman is all mine. I can't screw it up. And yet, I keep risking it all.

She'd been angry that I hadn't been forthright about the bodyguards, and again when she'd inadvertently found out about Mackie. Despite my reluctance, I'd partially opened the door on my fame when I didn't want her anywhere near it. But I still haven't told her about O'Malley... haven't told her all there is to tell about my old man either.

There is no easy way to untangle myself from this web I've made of secrets and omissions.

Except for the truth.

Something I'm not ready to reveal. Not on the night I promised to make special for her.

"What are you thinking about so intently?" she asks, trailing kisses along my jaw.

"You."

"Oh?" I feel her grin and shove the nagging thoughts into that corner of my mind where all the dark things live. "What about me?"

"I want you again." My hand slides between her thighs. "Any objections?"

"No. Just one request."

"Anything."

"Take me home first. I want you naked this time."

STEAM, MIXED WITH THE SCENT of jasmine, fills the enclosed bathroom. Though I don't need any additional aphrodisiac other than Dee, the flickering glow of candles and the misty air provide an intimate, seductive haven.

The water cascades down her like a waterfall, slicking back her curls and spilling over every salacious curve. I move in close until our bodies touch.

"Thank you." She sips at the drops rolling off my chin. "For the entire evening...every romantic detail. You went to so much trouble for me."

"It was no trouble, Dee. I just did what I hoped would please you."

"*You* please me." Her mouth slides over mine, opening, kissing. "You attended to my every need. Now it's my turn."

Dee shifts around to come up behind me, and reaches for my shampoo. With the water streaming over me, I plant my palms on the cool tile for balance and close my eyes, anticipating the feel of her magical fingers. When it comes, my sigh bounces off the wet walls.

She tips my head back and lathers my hair, her fingers like soft tentacles massage my scalp, temples, and behind my ears. She takes her time, drawing blissful sounds from me before guiding my head under the shower spray to rinse. Next, I hear the snap of plastic opening, smell my body gel, then—

Her soap-covered hands rub across my shoulders. She digs her thumbs and fingers into the spots where I carry my tension—dissolving the knots with a deep, firm pressure.

"Mm..."

"Good?" she asks, using her knuckles in a counter-clockwise roll.

"Mm-hmm." Too good for words.

Dee adds more soap and dances her sudsy hands over my back, working down my spine...my ass...my legs. She glides back up my thighs and urges me to turn around, unabashedly eyeing my erection as she strokes her hand down my shaft and gently palms my heavy sac.

I've never known a sexier woman. No one has ever had such carnal control over my body. That literally has me by the balls.

She presses her mouth to my pecs, to the flat disks, bringing them stiff with her agile tongue, creating rings of fire with the jerk of her fist. It's ecstasy and agony all rolled into one. But as much as I want to bend her over and take control, my feet are glued in place, not one cell in my body is willing to end this playful torment.

"I love how you feel." Her hand tightens on my twitching cock. "How hard you get. And I really love this." Before I can respond, she descends to the floor of the tub, and kisses the head with tiny, fleeting pecks.

"You're killing me."

Those crystal amber eyes look up and her smile is that of an angel's. Though with my cock this near to her lips, she looks more the sinful kind, sent to Earth to grant my every erotic fantasy.

"I love having my mouth on you," she murmurs. "Love the way you taste. The sounds you make when you're about to come."

Her explicit words, throaty voice, and the sight of her wet breasts send me into a full boil. "Suck me, Dee."

"I plan to." Her lips widen then close around the tip.

"Ah...your mouth." I snake my fingers through her hair to stay afoot as she takes me past the groove, and deeper.

Dee isn't tentative. With the billowy steam pluming between us, she sucks me into a sexual vortex that leaves my mind oblivious to anything but her warm, soft hands and hot, silken mouth. Stripped to the basest level, my restraint collapses under the extreme pleasure. I thrust between her lips and she takes it all, sucking me harder and faster, moaning little feral purrs that vibrate from her throat and skitter up my spine.

There is no way to stop the avalanche of sharp-edged need, the storm force that rips free and spins out with the untamed power of release. I come; an intense, breath-stealing climax that squeezes my chest and reaches down into my gut with a hard, wrenching fist. Dee swallows, watching me lose control, drawing out every groan, every shudder until I'm tapped. Depleted. Wiped out.

"Damn, baby." I catch my breath. "You destroy me."

She smiles and licks her lips, as if still tasting me there. I pull her up for a kiss, her tongue a tangle of flavors—hers and mine. The lust that she had thoroughly drained from me only moments ago comes flooding back. But I force myself to go slow, to let the urgency build again.

"My turn." I slide Dee around and settle her back against my chest.

She leans into me with a husky murmur. I massage a liberal amount of vanilla body wash over her shoulders and down her arms. My mouth seeks her neck as I run my hands around her lush breasts, reveling in the elongated peak of her nipples.

Dee's body is a treasure grove of curves and dips, an unlimited array of sensual discoveries. My hand slides down the groove of her waist to the womanly mound of her stomach, and the smooth satin between her legs.

"Ohh." She widens her stance in welcome and I press two fingers inside.

The bath wash mixed with her own moisture makes for wet, slippery strokes. Her hips buck to the tempo of my fingers and the acoustics in our small cocoon amplify her sweet, breathy noises.

I reach up with my other hand to remove the shower head from its cradle and spray off the front of her, letting the water hit her nipples, then aim the nozzle lower. I spread open her pussy lips, and direct the jet stream over her clit. Within seconds, she slaps her palms onto the tiles and cries out in the throes of orgasm, her body quaking so hard she can barely stand.

I catch her to me. The nozzle drops in a spiral, spraying erratically before it straightens and calms.

Dee, panting in the aftermath, goes liquid in my arms. "What do you do to me?"

"Same thing you do to me." We own each other's pleasure. Finding total ecstasy in every kiss, in every touch, in every second we spend loving each other.

I turn her around and back her up against the wall.

"Put your foot on the edge."

She does as I say, raising one leg to the lip of the tub while she clutches my shoulders.

I press against her and watch her dreamy eyes go dark, midnight over amber. The blood rushes in my head, in my heart, in my loins. *Now.* I drive into her with one unstoppable thrust.

Our breaths explode...then hold. We remain still for one quivering moment, joined, mated, completing the link. Then we begin to move. Slowly. Deliberately. Creating sensation over sensation, building layer upon layer of passion. With one hand braced against the tiles for balance and the other caressing her ass, my palm squeezes the gift of generous flesh.

Wanting to watch her take more, to see those gorgeous eyes go wild then dazed again, I slide my fingers between her well-rounded cheeks, flirting along the seam, pausing at her rosebud.

"*Mick.*" She stutters a moan and the pulse in her throat jumps madly.

I keep my touch light. "Only your pleasure, Dee. And only if you want it."

"I've never...oh...oh..."

"Do you like that?" I circle the sensitive spot packed with dozens of nerve endings. "Does it feel good?"

"Sooo good."

Desire is white hot. I increase the pressure of my middle finger. Dee groans long and trembles all over as I ease past the puckered ring. She's warm and soft. And so fucking tight. I pause to let her adjust. Then withdrawing a little, I push back in, a fraction deeper.

"Am I hurting you?"

"No," she whispers, her muscles clenching greedily around that single digit. "More."

And I give it to her in incremental degrees, hearing her gratifying sounds escalate with every slide.

"Dee," I groan. "I'm so deep inside of you."

"I feel it. I feel you filling me everywhere."

Our mouths touch, not kissing, just sharing pleasured breaths. Our wet skin slicks together, our hips rock back and forth, my cock stroking into her snug pussy, my finger thrusting into her tight rear. We're not moving fast, but with no less abandon. I know she's close. I can tell by her hitching moans and the blind opaque of her eyes, by the way her inner muscles spasm like warm pockets of suction. I'm swearing in my head because I can't even speak, and then we're coming.

Pleasure is vast and fluid, a sea of rolling waves, crashing, peaking, a summit of ecstasy as two explosions collide at once, and nothing, I mean nothing has ever felt this good. This perfect. This right.

Our mouths cling as that last sweeping wave claims us. Our gazes lock, our hearts and souls bind. We say each other's names in a quiet susurrus of breaths. Then silence. Kissing softly, tenderly, until the water runs cold.

I dry us off and take Dee to bed. Drawing her close, possessively close, exhausted, happy, my mind close to empty. I crash.

CHAPTER EIGHT

Dee

THE BLANKET IS A COZY tent, warm from Mick's body and the sensual kisses moving across my belly.

I lift the covers and gaze down at his face—strong masculine planes and angles offset by his dark hooded eyes and thick lashes.

"Morning," I sigh on a half breath, my system already wide awake and on hot alert.

"Morning, beauty." Mick shifts lower to bury his face between my open legs and slide his tongue inside my core.

Wanting to give him the same awesome pleasure, I readjust my position and slide down to his impressively hard cock. I take him deep into my mouth while his agile tongue slowly and expertly devours me. I detonate seconds before he comes at the back of my throat all salty and warm.

Our raw, raspy moans still echo in my mind as I rush to get dressed for work.

I don't have much time to fight with my hair. Not that I'm complaining. After pulling my curls back into a quick ponytail, I find Mick in the kitchen filling the blender with fruits and spinach. He's wearing jogging shorts and a heart-stopping grin. But best of all, with no nightmares to disturb his sleep, there aren't any haunting shadows beneath his eyes. If mind-blowing sex is the sedative Mick needs to keep his demons at bay, I am all too willing to be his drug.

"Smoothie okay?" he asks. "It's fast and I know you're running late because of me."

My blood thickens with the heated memory. I have barely come down from the high of my climax and I'm still wanting more.

"A smoothie sounds great. And for the record, you can make me run late any time."

"Keep looking at me like that, Counselor, and you may not make it to work at all."

"And what would I do here all day while you write, be your sex muse?"

"You're reading my mind."

"It's not that difficult. Kind of follows one path."

"Yep." He catches me around the waist. "Straight to you."

FRIDAY IS GAME DAY. MICK had arranged for more security than seems necessary, but I can understand his caution considering what happened here with that reporter several weeks ago.

If he's nervous about the game, it doesn't show. Coach Mick, looking mighty fine in his signature red Nike ball cap and Lions T-shirt, is relaxed and all smiles. He'd once told me that coaching Dwayde was the first time he truly enjoyed basketball.

As the game progresses, Victor gives me a running commentary, explaining the positions and the plays. I follow along, paying most of my attention to Dwayde, who is constantly on the move, looking for openings to pass the ball or take his shot. The game is entertaining and the fledgling Lions team is holding their own against players that look bigger and more experienced than they are. I watch Mick shout out praise encouraging his players, debate several calls with the ref, and lift his team when they fall behind.

The opponents continue a decent lead until the final quarter. Making several good shots, the Lions close in. Tension mounts. I sit with Victor and Isabelle at the edges of our seats. Mick calls a time-out with less than a minute on the clock.

Located behind the Lion's bench, close to the court, I'm able to hear most of what he says to them. "You're playing good ball out there. Defense is strong and you're taking smart shots. Whether you win this or not, I'm already proud of you. Just have fun and don't forget what matters."

"Smarts, hearts, and guts!" they chant in unison, all hands pumping in the center of their circle before they run back to the floor.

The Lions don't win. But Dwayde scores a three-point shot in the final moments that ties up the game and sends them into overtime. I've nearly chewed a hole in my bottom lip when the opponents score the winning point as the buzzer sounds. Mick high-fives his team, and looking up, blows me a kiss.

It's a bit reckless considering we are in hiding, but at that moment, it's the most natural thing in the world.

MICK GIVES THE TEAM SATURDAY off. We spend a lazy morning lounging in bed, making love, and eating breakfast among the tangled sheets.

Much later, I work for a couple of hours and get some laundry done while Mick writes. For dinner, we prepare a stir fry together in domestic harmony. Afterward, we're chilling in the living room when Mick disappears for a few minutes and returns with a slim velvet box.

"What's this?"

"Just a little something." He takes a seat on the couch and lifts my feet onto his lap. "I hope you like it."

Excited to see what's inside, I flip up the lid.

"Those are some of the things that remind me of you."

I remove the linked bracelet from the box to look more closely at the charms, running my fingertip over each one, touched by the thought that he'd put into selecting them. The scales of justice, a diamond-encrusted heart, two interlinked circles, one engraved with "family," the other "friends," one black crystal, and a female sculpture.

"What are these?" I ask of the stone and woman.

"That's a spinel crystal," he explains. "From the Latin word, 'spina' meaning spine, it represents strength. And the woman is Aphrodite, the goddess of love and beauty. That's how I see you."

Okay...wow! "This is the best gift I've ever received. It's so personal and thoughtful. I love it!"

"I'm glad. Let me put it on you."

I hand him the bracelet and lean over to give him a big, appreciative kiss. "I love you."

Smiling, he opens the clasp and places it on my outstretched wrist.

"It's beautiful." I lean back admiring the little charms. "I think I'm just going to stare at it all night."

"Sorry to spoil your plans, but there's something else that I really want to do."

"Well…" I wiggle my brows. "We can fit *that* in too."

"I always want *that* with you." He traces the arch of my foot. "But first, I want to take you to a movie."

"Like going out?"

"I've never taken you on a movie date. I'd like to."

I'm not sure how we'll manage that, but a date with Mick is too tempting to refuse. "What do you want to see?"

"You pick."

My brows lift. "That's a risky move."

"Proof of my love."

"No kidding." I laugh. We have vastly different tastes in movies. He's a shoot 'em up, action packed guy all the way. While my taste runs toward old movies, documentaries, and artistic indie films. Checking listings on my iPad, I decide not to make him suffer through a coming-of-age piece set in the scenic countryside of Ireland and choose a rom-com I figure he can tolerate. The added benefit is I'm ensured a few laughs and a happy ending.

Mick orders the tickets online and drops me off at the front of the theater, instructing me to find a seat in the back row. I shrug out of my jacket that I'd layered over a long, loose sweater and leggings.

The movie stars Amy Schumer, who I think is hysterical. I also admire the way she totally owns her body despite the pressure in Hollywood to be thin. It's been out a while now, so the theater is fairly empty. Only a dearth of patrons is scattered throughout, none of them in the back row.

When the lights dim, I see Mick walking up the aisle with a large popcorn container and a drink. His cap is pulled down low and he's still wearing his shades. Even without recognition, just the man himself would cause a stir.

"Hi, beauty."

"Hi."

After settling in beside me, he takes off his *disguise*, and puts the drink in the holder between us, and the popcorn on his lap. We share the same straw and our fingers brush as we reach inside the carton. He's sitting close, our shoulders and outer legs touching. I'm fully dressed yet I can feel his touch on my skin.

The contact in the dark cinema is innocent, but the sensations going on inside me are like an exposed live wire. Mick slips one arm around my shoulder, his eyes sliding over to mine. The heavy-lidded desire in them lets me know that he can feel what I'm feeling, and is feeling it too.

He moves the popcorn aside and his mouth lowers, softly caressing my lips. His buttery tongue is a delicious invasion. I'm distantly aware of the audience chuckling as my hands pull on the wavy strands of hair to intensify the kiss, my tongue stroking with his lush slides, my whispered moans mingling with his heavy breaths.

Now I know why my movie choice didn't matter to him. It doesn't matter to me either. We make out, working each other into a frenzy, only taking it as far as a public venue will allow. The forced restraint makes the foreplay all the more intense.

I'm gasping and wet when he murmurs against my mouth, "I gotta go, baby."

"Go?"

"The movie's over."

"Already?"

He smiles and tweaks my nipple before he slides his hand from under my bra. "We'll finish this at home. Meet me out front in ten."

"Okay." I touch his cheek, finding it both sexy and sweet that Mick had chosen to give me an experience I had missed with him in our teens. "Thanks for the awesome date."

He brings my hand to his mouth. His lips kiss my palm, then my wrist from where the bracelet dangles. "I'm sorry to have to leave you. There's nothing more I want than to walk out of here holding your hand."

"It's fine, Mick."

He doesn't look like he believes me, but with the credits rolling, he shoves back on his cap. Then he's gone.

SUNDAY I'M UP EARLY. WAKING before Mick is rare, but I'm too wound up to sleep. Victor and Isabelle agreed to forfeit their turn to let me host brunch. It seemed like a good idea at the time. Now I'm a nervous wreck.

I shower and dress comfortably in an open flannel shirt over a tank top paired with boyfriend jeans. On the menu is a breakfast casserole. I got the recipe off Pinterest. Kid friendly; nothing too ambitious. But what if it doesn't turn out? What if the children hate it? What if brunch is a big freaking flop? I've never hosted a brunch before. The most I've hosted is dinner for my friends. Two people, not twelve! What was I thinking? I'm no Martha Stewart, not even close.

Counting my breaths, I redirect my thoughts to the recipe rather than on the potential disasters. My to-do list also helps. Aside from keeping me organized, the structure gives me something concrete and practical to focus on. When Mick awakens, he allows me a wide berth, sensing I need it, and sets up the table and chairs that we rented for the occasion.

Upon seeing the crammed fit in the living room, I snap at him. "How is anyone supposed to eat when they can't even move?"

"It's not that bad."

"Not bad?" I glare at him, infuriated by his nonchalance. "It's terrible."

"What would you like me to do?"

"Nothing!"

I storm into the kitchen and fling open the cupboard to get a punch bowl. I toss in mixed berries and quickly cut up apple cubes and orange slices, managing not to chop off a finger in my hurry. But when I go to open the bottle of cranberry cocktail, it slips out of my hands, spilling onto the kitchen floor, and splattering up on the cupboard doors and all over the front of my clothes.

"Shit!"

Mick rushes into the kitchen, taking in the scene, his concerned eyes scan over me. "You okay?"

"I just made a big mess. I am a mess."

"Baby." His eyes move over me in understanding. "You are stressing yourself out."

"I know. I'm sorry for snapping at you before."

"Don't worry about it. Go change and I'll clean this up."

"You sure?"

"Yep." He kisses the tip of my nose and ushers me out.

I throw my clothes into the washer and go find something else to wear. I'm standing inside the closet in my robe when Mick comes in.

"Kitchen's cleaned up and we had another bottle of juice, so all good. Anything else to be done?"

"Not for now, thanks." I take deep breaths, trying to calm myself down.

"I know a way to help you relax."

"Don't you dare." I elbow his ribs when he comes up behind me. "Our family will be here any minute and I still have to find something to wear."

"I'll pick out something."

"Uh...no."

"You don't think I have good taste?"

"I think your taste is excellent. But...*Mick!*" I protest when he moves around me and starts perusing the contents of my side of the closet. Embarrassed, I wince at the idea of him seeing the tags advertising my size. I'm sure the only double-digits his supermodels had worn were two zeroes.

As he gets to the back and hones in on my maybe-one-day section, he pauses and his brow furrows. I imagine it would be like stepping out of a black and white movie into technicolor. But he doesn't say anything. Instead, he selects slim-fit jeans and a raspberry-colored knit pullover with a drawstring hem that ties at the waist and slips off one shoulder.

"How about this? You look great in red."

"The sweater's too short to wear with those jeans."

"Why's that?"

I roll my eyes as if he really needs to ask. "It won't cover my butt."

"Why do you think I chose it?"

"I'm serious, Mick."

"So am I. I've seen you break out of your comfort zone before."

"That was different."

"How?"

When I can't come up with a good reason, he pushes on. "It seems to me you bought these clothes for a reason. But..." He gives me a brief peck. "I'll leave it to you. You'll look beautiful in whatever you choose."

Oh, he's good, using that reverse psychology on me. He basically issued a challenge then walked away as if it didn't matter to him one way or the other. But I know he'll be disappointed if I go with my usual long tops, and more than that, I'll be disappointed in myself.

Mick gawks when I walk out. "Daaammmmnnn, baby. Can we cancel brunch?"

"No." I shove him back when he approaches. "Serves you right for picking this."

"I'll take blue balls any day to see you owning your sexy body. You have no reason to cover it up, Dee. None."

The doorbell rings. As he goes to answer it, I hear him humming a line from an Ed Sheeran song, "I'm in love with the shape of you."

My heart turns to goo. "Mick?"

"Yeah?" He turns around.

"Thank you." I smile. "You always make me feel like a million bucks."

"A mil doesn't even come close to your worth." He sends me an air kiss and opens the door.

It's Jordyn and Lexie. They've been my family for nearly two years and including them felt right. They take one look at my outfit and shriek with excited praise. Mick's wink carries an *I told you so*.

He recognizes that inner conflict in me, the tug-of-war I battle between covering up and stripping off those layers. Not just in terms of the clothes but the negative tapes in my head. He encourages me to accept myself. To accept the beauty that he sees in me.

I get my friends coffee. Lexie has only met Mick twice, the first was not a pleasant encounter and the second was at her birthday party. A bit like me, she's initially reserved until she gets to know someone. But with Mick's easy-going manner, it doesn't take long for them to hit it off.

Meanwhile, Jordyn and Mick are already besties. After one interview, he'd hired her on the spot to design the new facility for Papa's Kids. I'm not surprised that they get along so well. Both are charismatic, outgoing, direct, and confident. They make me laugh, and their best quality is that they give with all their hearts.

James and Maria arrive soon after with the kids and Mama T. My foster mom greets my friends with hugs and kisses. She immediately loves them for loving me.

Dani and Justin are restless from the long drive. Mick and James take them out back for a game of tag, while I catch up with Mama T and Maria, and they get to know Lexie and Jord. When Mason starts to fuss, I offer to take him from Maria.

"He's teething," she explains.

Poor little guy. I put ice cubes inside a soft towel and rub it gently against his gums. "Better?" I coo, cuddling him to me, kissing his head and breathing in his powdery baby scent.

Mick re-enters the house, cheeks flushed from exertion. He stops. His face fills with awe. It's the way he looked at me last Sunday when I rocked Mason in my arms. As if he had fallen in love with me all over again.

"You okay?" he asks.

"I'm fine," I tell him. And I truly am.

Victor and his family are the last to arrive. Dwayde hangs back. But Mick coaxes him out with some good-natured ribbing. Lexie and Jordyn fit right in, assisting with the fruit torte. Mama T issues orders, taking over. I smile and hug her, happy that she seems just as at-home here as she had at Maria's.

While the casserole cooks, Dani and Justin watch a show on my iPad and I attempt to nurture the budding connection with Dwayde. I don't talk about the case. This isn't the time or place. Instead, I try to engage his interest in art. In anything, really. He's still standoffish, but I accept, despite the time constraints, that gaining his trust is more a marathon than a sprint.

The women are clustered together in the living room, Jordyn regaling them with a story that has them all laughing. The men discuss the upcoming college basketball season. When Dwayde joins them, I go check on the casserole. Since it needs more time to brown, I crank up the heat.

Gabi comes into the kitchen to show me selfies of three dresses that she's considering for a party. Truly, she looks gorgeous in all of them, but I pick the gold strapless mini. The style suits her slight curves and the color works well with her tan skin and new caramel highlights.

"Isabelle picked that one too."

Mick pokes his head inside. "Everything good in here?"

"Yep. Just giving the casserole a few more minutes while I help Gabi pick out a dress."

"A dress for what?"

"A party next weekend," she answers with a dismissive shrug. "It's no big deal."

Suggesting otherwise, he steps to her, his inquisition face firmly in place. "Where will this party be held?"

"A girl from school is having it at her house."

"Will there be alcohol?"

"Probably. It's a party. That doesn't mean I'm going to drink."

"I'd rather you didn't. But if you do, stick to a cooler that you open yourself and never, I mean never, leave your drink unattended. You can call me any time, understand? I'll come get you, no questions asked. Just be safe."

"Okay, okay." Her exasperated breath flutters her parted bangs. "I already got this lecture from Cop Boy," she says of Victor. "You can take it down a few notches. I'm not stupid."

"I know that, Gab, but it bears repeating. Let me see the dress."

"You're not gonna like it."

"Unless it covers you from head to toe, that goes without saying. Show me anyway."

She hands him her phone and Mick's jaw clenches so hard I think he's going to break a molar. "Where's the rest?"

"It covers my bits."

"Jesus, Gabi." He drags a hand over his hair. "Don't even say bits."

"I'm almost eighteen."

"You're still eight to me."

Gabi is handling herself so I don't intervene, enjoying Mick in his role of big brother. It gives me a glimpse into what he would be like as a father. What he would have been like if we hadn't lost our baby. She'd be fourteen now. A teenage girl. I touch my stomach feeling a wave of sadness for what could have been. But the wave doesn't swallow me under as it has before. Because of the beautiful man in front of me that got me to open up, to finally talk. For the first time, I feel like I'm driving forward, with my past getting farther behind me in the rearview mirror.

"Protective much?" I hear Gabi say and tune back into their exchange.

"Yes. And so is Victor. He's not going to let you out in that dress."

"Sure he will. I have my secret weapon."

"What's that? You gonna blindfold him?"

"Haha." She punches his arm. "I have Bells. She'll convince him. She's got Victor wrapped around her finger. Seems to run in the family, right Dee?"

She winks at me and saunters away.

"What the hell just happened?" Mick asks.

"Gabi's growing up." I put the casserole under the broiler to hurry it along.

"Yeah, I see that."

"Do I have you wrapped around my finger?" I tease.

"Absolutely." He squeezes my butt and whispers in my ear. "But it's fair play, since I get to have you wrapped around my cock."

"You are so bad."

"You like me bad." His mouth travels across my cheek to my lips.

"True." I grin into his kiss, and soon forget where we are and that the casserole is still on broil.

Only the smoke alarm jerks us apart. The dish is unsalvageable. I order pizza and we all squeeze around the dining table. It's tight and we're bumping elbows.

Not the brunch I had envisioned. But my place is noisy, full of laughter, and I'm surrounded by the people I love.

It's perfect.

And so are Mondays when they start with Mick. A quickie in the shower saves me time for my hair, but I decide to leave it down. Lena's eyes almost bug out of her head. It's part of the new me. I'm not exactly sure who that is yet, but I like who I'm becoming.

The day is long and productive. Since Mick is out for the evening, after hitting the gym for an hour, I make myself a salad and enjoy a glass of chilled wine before soaking in a bubble bath. That's where Mick finds me.

He strips out of his business attire, making my nipples harden, and slides in behind me, cradling my back against his chest.

"Are there bullets in the water or are you just happy to see me?"

Laughing, I splash him then lean back into him. "How was your meeting at Pivotal?"

"Good. Jordyn should have a preliminary design for me by next week."

"That's exciting."

"Yeah. I'm pumped to break ground." He scoops warm, frothy water over my shoulders. "Sorry, I missed having dinner with you tonight."

"Don't be. This project is important. We'll have lots of dinners together. Did you at least get something to eat?" I ask, noting that it must be 9:00ish.

"I grabbed a bite with my lawyer after the meeting."

"Oh, the one working on the project?"

"No, my personal attorney, Nolan. He handles most of my financial affairs. Now he'll handle ours."

"But we don't have money together."

"I fixed that."

"You what?" I angle my head to look up at him over my shoulder.

"It's no big thing. I opened up a joint checking account, included you on some investments, and started the paperwork to pay off your mortgage. All the documents are on your desk for you to look over and sign. Don't worry, the house will stay in your name."

"I can't accept any of that."

"Why not?" His tone is defensive.

"Because I'm not comfortable taking your money."

"It's not charity, Dee. I'm living here. Wouldn't you expect me to share the costs?"

"Sharing the cost is chipping in for bills and groceries, not opening a joint account and investments with your money or buying my house. You should have talked to me about this first," I say, feeling justified on one hand and like an ungracious brat on the other. "I don't like having decisions made for me. I thought you understood that."

"And I thought we were making a life together."

"We are."

"Then my money is yours," he says smoothly as if it's settled and brushes aside the tendrils that have fallen from my topknot to place kisses on my neck. "There was no intention to undermine your independence."

What he's doing feels so good, but I won't be placated. "For me, independence is having a fair exchange. You come into this relationship with way more than I do."

"Financially, yes. But what you give me is priceless, Dee. This is only money. At least spending it on Papa's Kids and the people I love gives it purpose. I didn't do much to earn it."

I hear the bitterness behind his words. Since the morning after our fight, Mick hasn't talked about his fame or much about any of his life that spanned our separation. But nor had I asked. Cautious about upsetting our easy rhythm, I'd stayed away from delving into sensitive areas. But I'd be lying if I said I wasn't anxious to know all there was to know about Mick. It's that need for more that has me tiptoeing into murky waters.

"Why do you think there was something wrong with making money through playing basketball?"

"I don't think that. But it wasn't right for me. I didn't love the game like I should have. I didn't play with my heart. Most times it was a chore. But I faked it. Did what was expected. What they paid me a shitload of money to do. What did I have to complain about, right?"

"Money doesn't buy happiness. It's trite, but true."

"The NBA would be a dream for anyone in my position."

"It was never your dream, Mick." I lace our fingers together and toy with the ring he hasn't taken off since I'd given it to him. "Why did you choose it?"

"Sometimes there is no choice."

"You mean pressure from your father?"

His fingers tighten on mine. "I wasn't exactly a victim. I took advantage of the perks. Took on the image of the famous sports star. And for a while it was heady. All the attention, the money. I played the part. Over time it became harder and harder to distinguish between who I was and the persona that I created."

"Your wealth and fame are a part of you, Mick. But they don't define you."

"I'm not sure about that."

"Well, I am. I see how committed you are to Papa's Kids. I see the way you are with me, and your family. Down-to-earth. Kind and generous. You're still the boy next door that I fell in love with."

His chest lifts and falls on a weighty exhale. "I wish it could be simple. Then I could take you on dates without sneaking around or needing bodyguards. We could just be together. The bank account, the investments, buying your house, those are just symbols of my commitment. Because what I really want is for us to have a normal life."

Frustration burns in his tone that he's somehow failing me. I turn to face him. "Maybe I haven't made it clear what I want and value most."

"What?"

That's an easy one. From the moment we met, and he looked at me with those espresso-brown eyes, simmering with magnetic energy, I knew then that Mick would become vital to me. That the essence of him would be imprinted on my skin, in my bones, in my very soul. I knew he would mark me in ways more permanent than time.

"The answer is you." My knees straddle his hips and my palms cup his whiskered cheeks. "That's all I want, Mick. Rich or poor. Famous or not. I don't care as long as I have you."

"Yeah?"

"Yeah."

"Good." He draws me closer. "Because I have no intention of ever letting you go."

"You couldn't shake me loose, babe. I'm like your ball and chain."

"A beautiful anchor."

"You say the most amazing things." I rub against him. "Wanna play with my bullets?"

He laughs before taking my mouth in a fierce kiss, and soon the water is sloshing all over the floor.

CHAPTER NINE

Micah

TUESDAY MORNING, BEFORE THE SUN even yawns into the sky, I celebrate another peaceful sleep by kissing my way up Dee's supple body—my favorite way to wake her up.

"*Mm.*" She stirs. "Didn't you get enough last night?"

"It's never enough with you." I nuzzle her breasts. "You're soft and warm. Fuckable."

On a sound caught between amusement and arousal, Dee shoves at my shoulders, rolling until she's bestriding me. Lust fires my blood. She looks good up there—drowsy eyes, hair, a tangle of curls, chocolaty hard nipples that beg to be sucked. I grasp her hips and guide her down until she's sheathing me like a glove.

"Ohh." She leans forward, bracing her hands on either side of my head, her breath hot on my mouth. "I love waking up to you."

THERE'S NOTHING LIKE TOSSING THE sheets with Dee to kick off the day. After she drifts back to sleep, I put on my jogging clothes and head out for a run.

The fallen leaves crunch beneath my feet as the crisp autumn breeze sings in the air. I feel good—loose and energized. Charged by the burning passion between us. It's addictive the way Dee loses her insecurities with me, how trusting she is. How uninhibited. I can't get enough of watching her arousal, of getting her off, or feeling the spellbinding strength of my own desire—all the more staggering because it's attached to deep and profound emotions.

I run ten miles, along the waterfront and then back through our neighborhood. I slide my cap back on and lower the bill. Day-to-day activities surround me—a woman walks her dog, a couple loads two toddlers into car seats, another jogger passes me with a wave. I see a man get into a van as the cozy bungalow we now share comes into view.

It had taken an abundance of persuasion, but Dee had finally signed the papers, only agreeing to the purchase agreement if it was amended to have us as co-owners.

Eventually we'll need something bigger. Perhaps on the lake with a huge backyard, like we talked about all those years ago when we would lie under the stars, dreaming of our future together. I want to give Dee that and more. I want to give her everything.

I'm still smiling as I jog up the stairs, whistling when I reach the top. Then shocked panic slams into my chest. An envelope waits on the welcome mat addressed to **M. Peters**. Recalling the van from moments ago, my gaze swings back to the street. It's gone. And Hilton, Dee's bodyguard, isn't set to arrive for another fifteen minutes.

I stare at the familiar handwriting with a vicious sense of foreboding. My breaths rush. I rip open the envelope and pull out a square piece of white note paper—like rat poison, toxic in its impact.

FRIDAY NIGHT, 11:00.
YOUR CONDO.
TIME TO TALK.

No name. None needed.

Rage swamps me. My old man had this delivered here. To *Dee's house*. Deliberately taunting me with the knowledge that he knows about her. Knows where she lives. Knows about us.

Shit, shit, shit. Worse than any fucking nightmare.

I haven't seen Malcolm Peters in years. Haven't spoken to him either. I'd made my deal with the devil long ago. He was to stay out of my life and away from what's mine.

Now he's back.

I should have anticipated this. People could have seen Dee in Springvale, certainly Mama T would have gladly told her friends about her foster daughter's return. Although my family knows not to discuss our relationship, Malcolm, aware of our past, had obviously put one plus one together and came up with Dee and me.

Son of a bitch. Pacing, the violence chasing me, I drag a hand through my hair, feeling the weight of Dee's ring on my scalp, trying to keep calm, trying to keep my head on straight.

If I thought all he wanted was more money, I wouldn't give a damn. But it's never just money with Malcolm. He wanted to gouge at me, to bleed me of every drop of happiness for his own sick revenge.

Balling the note in my fist, I go inside the garage and bury it, and the envelope, in the trash can, battling anger and that sense of powerlessness that I hate the most.

I should have killed him. Every time he passed out with his loaded revolver dropped carelessly on the table or nightstand, I eyed the black metal. Imagined the weight in my hand...lifting...aiming...

That's not who you are, meu bem. You have too much good in you.

I wasn't sure my mother was right. But I never picked up that gun. Not even after she died. Maybe I was afraid of disappointing her. Or maybe I was just too damned gutless.

But dwelling on regret isn't going to change a fucking thing. Malcolm is alive and kicking, and as usual, has an agenda. I grab my phone from out of the armband, my fingers quick on the buttons.

"Stiles," he answers.

"It's Mick. I need 24/7 security for Dee."

"Consider it done. But it helps to know why."

"Someone was here. At Dee's. Left a note in an envelope on the doorstep for me."

"What kind of note?"

"The note doesn't matter. What matters is that someone got this close."

"A reporter?"

"My father." I have no choice but to tell him that much. "There's no love lost between us. I don't know what he wants, but he's not to get within five miles of Dee."

"He won't. Hilton is on route. I'll brief him."

Too enraged to go in the house, I grab the toolbox off the garage shelf and follow the flagstones to the gate that opens onto the tidy backyard. Lethal thoughts circle my head like vultures. I locate the loose fence boards I'd noticed while mowing. Insert a nail. Pound. Insert. Pound. One after the other. Swinging the hammer fueled by adrenaline and fury, striking the wood with a loud, resounding thwack.

"Mick?"

Darkness edges my vision. I pull my gaze to the sliding glass doors. Dee is standing there in one of my sweatshirts, and nothing else. The first hints of sunlight dance over her loose hair, a waft of wind blows a few strands across her cheek.

I should tell her about Malcolm. But looking into those golden eyes staring at me with such love and affection, I just can't get the words out. Another excuse, more prevarication. I set down the hammer and stride across the grass, eating up the short distance, and skim my knuckles down her cheek, forcing my tone to stay even, my hand not to shake. "Thought I'd fix the boards before the weather gets too cold."

"You don't have to do that. I can call a handyman."

"It's no problem. I'm good with my hands."

"Yes, you are. In fact, you'd look great in a tool belt."

"I'll buy one."

"Will you wear it with nothing else on?"

"A fantasy of yours, Counselor?" I walk her back inside the living room and gather her close as if to prove I can hold on to this, hold on to her. Dee's grin melts into a moan. I cup her face, kissing her, losing myself in the slick, minty warmth of her mouth and the quick whip of passion that snaps between us.

Dee shoves off my cap and pushes her fingers through my hair, her tongue tasting mine in hot, provocative strokes, our chests crushed together, her heart thundering so hard, I don't just feel it against me, but inside of me.

My senses seduced, I lower my hands to fill them with her. The only woman to ever make me *need* so desperately, so completely, to the exclusion of all else.

We'd made love just over an hour ago and still she responds with urgency, rolling her hips, feeding me her raspy moans before I let us up for air.

"Wow." Her laugh is breathless. "What was that?"

"You," I say at her throat. "Stay home with me."

"I wish," she murmurs. "You make it hard to go."

"Then don't." I kiss my way back up to her lips, before resting my forehead against hers and binding my arms around her tightly.

"Tempting, but I have meetings and deadlines."

My muscles flex with every protective instinct to make her stay. Though a bodyguard will keep Dee safe, I still don't want to let her out of my sight, which is a biting paradox since being with me poses the greatest danger to her.

"Mick?"

She tries to incline her head to see my expression. I hold her still. Can't have her looking at me right at this moment.

Dee leans into me and runs her hands over my tight shoulders and back. "You okay?" she whispers.

"Yeah, I'm good." I swallow another guilty lie, and without relaxing my hold, keep her close for as long as I can.

AT 6:00 THAT EVENING, STILES buzzes me into the office space he occupies in downtown Chicago. One of my former teammates recommended JDS Security after the shit went down at the community center, and introduced me to its operating owner, J.D. Stiles. I was impressed upon meeting him. His size alone would put the fear of God in anyone with an ounce of sense, especially when you added the scowl and black emotionless eyes, the alert body language that suggested he could just as soon shake your hand as shoot you.

To say Stiles isn't a friendly guy would be a vast understatement, but I'm not looking for friendship. He's known for being discreet and getting the job done.

I push open the door and step inside. It's as sparse as I remember. A grid of state-of-the-art computer monitors line the wall of his office and a long rectangular table serving as a desk sits in the center with two guest chairs across from the one he occupies. No family photos, no artwork. Practical and without fuss, much like the man himself. It doesn't boast of the dozens of bodyguards and security experts he has out in the field, nor that a majority of his clients are business executives, government officials, and celebrities.

"Mr. Peters." He stands in greeting.

"Cut the Mr. Peters crap. You damn well protect Dee and my family, you can call me Mick."

His eyebrows arch into his cleanly shaven head as I take my mood out on him. "No offense, but I don't call clients by their first name."

"I thought the customer was always right."

Stiles grunts a sound that's as close to a laugh as I've ever heard from him. "How about some coffee?"

"Sure." Running on fumes, I could use the caffeine hit, preferably delivered straight into my veins. I'd been a useless ball of garbage since getting Malcolm's note. I couldn't think. Couldn't write. Couldn't sit still. Every time I picked up the phone to call Dee, I copped out, knowing she'd hear the trouble in my voice. I thought about texting her, but I couldn't fake that either. A message from Stiles saying he wanted to meet only amped up my angst. I suggested his office over the bungalow where Dee could come home.

"Try this," Stiles says, returning with a cup of black java that's strong as fuck.

"Damn!" I grimace at the taste. "What is it?"

"Killer brew."

"No shit." Prepared, the second sip goes down smoother. "You said you found something on O'Malley." I drop into the guest chair.

"You knew he was fired a year ago from the *Tribune* for making up sources to get a story published."

"Yeah. He was a pushy sports reporter, not well liked, so the news got around. One minute top of his field, now writing some small-time tabloid shit. Lost his job and credibility. That's why he's jonesing for an exclusive. I smell his desperation every time he comes at me."

"Why the hard-on for you?"

"I've been private about my personal life. I keep the media away from my family. I don't do many interviews...guess that caught his interest. He seems to think I have something to hide."

"Do you?"

"What the fuck is this, Stiles?" I jerk forward. "Are you working for O'Malley or me?"

"Didn't mean to cross a line." His tone is conciliatory, but unapologetic. "Digging into the details when they seem relevant is part of the job."

"How is this relevant to protecting Dee?"

"Don't know that yet. But I pulled O'Malley's cell phone records and traced a repeated number back to your father."

"What?" The word leaves me in a shocked and angry breath.

"Most of the calls lasted mere seconds. I assume O'Malley was gunning for a story or comment and didn't get one."

I breathe a little better. Malcolm had nothing to gain by talking to O'Malley and everything to lose. Except... "You said most."

"That's right." He slides a printout of O'Malley's phone records, with one date highlighted in yellow. "This call lasted over fifteen minutes. It doesn't take that long to blow someone off. Recognize the date?"

I look at it closely. Freeze.

"I take it you do. The same day O'Malley followed you to Mort's Deli. Not long after, he placed that call to your father and obviously got his attention."

My brain only takes a moment to process the significance before my throat squeezes again, the air struggling to find an outlet.

"Got any thoughts on that?" he asks.

Only one. *Dee.* O'Malley must have repeated what his source told him about my "mystery woman."

A woman you couldn't seem to keep your hands off of.

Intimate dances...passionate kiss.

And most importantly, she's said not to be your unusual type.

Ah...that got a reaction. Protective. Proprietary. It's written all over your face, Peters.

Malcolm would have immediately recognized my soft underbelly, ripe for him to slice wide open. But he hadn't shared anything about Dee's identity with O'Malley. Otherwise, the sleazy mother fucker would have been all over it. Somehow, Malcolm had gotten O'Malley to back off. That's the only logical explanation for why O'Malley hasn't blogged about me or tried to reach me since.

And yet, I take no comfort in the possibility that Malcolm may have taken care of my O'Malley problem. Not when he must have done so for his own nefarious purposes.

When I think of Malcolm plotting and planning, finding out where Dee lives, sending a note to her house, feet away from where she slept, I want to put my hand through his fucking chest.

Shoving out of the chair, I stalk to the door without answering the question Stiles posed. Telling him about my screwed-up relationship with Malcolm won't make a difference. "Take care of Dee. Do not let her out of your sight. She's going to a club with her friends. Atomic Freeze. Friday night." The same night I'm meeting Malcolm. "Send Bernard to drive them. And I want you inside the club with her. Stick to Dee like glue. And if anyone even tries so much as to get near her—"

"No one will…you have my word on that. But Mr. Peters, the more I know—"

"You know all you need to. Just keep Dee safe."

Outside, the east horizon has turned a gloomy shade of gray. I walk to the lot, nearly empty at this hour, pulling in breaths of the cool evening air, and face the gutting realization that I'm sinking deep in quicksand with no clear way out of this mess.

I yank open the car door just as my phone vibrates. I check the screen. It's Dee. I hit the Decline button. Can't talk to her now. Can't go home to her either. I put my phone away and drive—hoping the faster I go, the farther away I'll get from my problems. I leave the city…find a lone stretch of country road and open the throttle. The Porsche flies.

I could justify my lies and omissions in the beginning. *It was too soon. I didn't want to scare her away.* That no longer works. I've since come to recognize an inner fibrous strength that even Dee doesn't give herself nearly enough credit for having. I don't harbor any reservations that she won't stick this out with me. I can't stand the thought that she would. How jacked up is that?

After driving an hour through the back roads with my phone buzzing and my guilt riding shotgun, I finally stop at a dive. The type of watering hole that's faceless—where several of the letters in the flashing sign are burned out, the drinks are strong, and getting drunk is a solitary pursuit. I amble in, tugging my cap down low. The stale stench of cigarettes and sweaty bodies hovers in the grimy air and the dim lighting gives me cover. Not that anyone here would recognize me or even care if they did.

Two men sit at the bar, one slumped over. I choose the stool located at the other end. A woman with big hair and a bored expression takes my order.

"Rum, ice, splash of Coke."

Just one glass, maybe two, I tell myself. Not enough to get smashed, just enough to dull the edge, to blur the anger, to shade the guilt.

She slides the glass in front of me. I crave it badly, but I'd be a fool if I weren't scared to death of what it would do to me. Twelve years was a long time to be sober. Yet not long enough to forget what it had been like when I wasn't.

My hand closes around the glass. I stare at it so long, the bartender asks, "You gonna drink that, honey, or just look at it all night?"

I'm still contemplating that perilous decision when my phone vibrates again. Unwrapping my fingers around the glass, I fish it from my pocket and see half a dozen missed calls from Dee and a text: *Where are you? Please let me know you're ok.*

CHAPTER TEN

Dee

I WATCH MICK THROUGH THE front window. I watch and worry. My relief upon first hearing his car pull into the garage port has slowly seeped out of me like tiny grains through an hourglass.

He hadn't contacted me all day. It's not that I expect Mick to check in. We both have busy careers, and I respect the need for separate interests and to spend time apart. But this is the first time since we've been together that he hadn't informed me that he'd be late or had other plans. So, when 9:00 p.m. rolled around and I still hadn't heard from him, my earlier concerns were renewed.

I sensed something was off this morning. Not at first. Mick had awakened at the crack of dawn, ready to start the day, beginning with me. He'd gripped my hips, thrusting beneath me, whispering raunchy, dirty words as I rode his gorgeous body to exhaustion.

My exhaustion, that is. Afterward, while I dozed, curled up like a contented cat, Mick in all his athletic glory still had the energy to go out for a jog, then fix the fence. Which come to think of it, is one of his tells. Pacing, needing to move, nose to the grindstone; doing, fixing, that's how Mick copes when he's troubled.

I hadn't noticed the signs right away—diverted by the sight of those well-trained muscles flexing as I watched him swing the hammer, then his rousing kiss that wiped my thoughts clean. It wasn't until the fire banked between us that I became aware of the change in him; an undercurrent of tension that hadn't been there before.

I asked him several times before I left for the office if he was okay, and each time, he offered assurances that he was. I wanted to believe him—ached to—because the alternative meant he was shutting me out. Again.

As the hours ticked away this evening without a call or a text, without him answering my messages, I knew something was seriously wrong. Felt it in the pit of my stomach. I busied myself with an online Pilates class, showered, tried to do some work, and avoided the kitchen. I was this close to contacting Victor when Mick finally arrived.

But he hasn't ventured inside. Cloaked by the night, he stands under the hardy leaves of a tall, green ash, head down, hands shoved into his jacket pockets.

It's unusual to see him so still when he's troubled. No pacing. No movement. This doesn't look like the fixer, the fighter I know him to be. This looks like defeat. Unable to continue watching whatever's nagging at him, I pull open the door.

Mick's head comes up. I can feel his stare for several moments before he steps out of the dark and into the light from the porch. He removes his hands from his pockets and walks toward me. The confident swagger I've come to expect is diminished by the slouch of his shoulders and the hesitant pace of his gait. He climbs the three stairs, one slow step at a time, until he's right there. Face-to-face. His brim is pulled down low; his full mouth set in a tight, grim line. What looks like conflict and apology adds to the burden in his eyes.

I don't speak. I don't ask him what's wrong. I just reach up for him and tug his mouth down to mine.

"Dee," he rasps as our lips crash with turbulent force.

My mouth opens, his tongue thrusts inside, tasting me in lush, aggressive strokes. His hands grab my hips, slamming me against his body; his heart pounds, a raging drum beat against my chest.

Yes! I could weep. Not just fire, but an inferno. He eats up my moans. His foot kicks the door closed and I feel him moving us into the house. Pressed up against him, I jockey off his hat and then my hands are in his hair, holding him close. He growls, kissing me back, roughly. The feral desperation in him is as much a red flag as it is a turn on.

"Love me," I plead, my sex throbbing, my heart aching.

"I do love you." He drags his mouth from my lips to my neck, nipping and sucking hard. "I more than love you. That word isn't powerful enough...no word could ever be."

129

"Then show me."

"I won't be gentle."

A warning or a promise? I don't care. "Do it, Mick. I want it." I need it.

In swift, impatient moves, he yanks open my robe, divests me of it, and shoves off his jacket, sailing it across the floor. My breath snags as he spins me around. My fingers clutch the hallway table.

Mick isn't always tender, but this is more intense, more urgent. A rapid succession of moans escapes my throat as his hands reach between us. The erotic sound of his zipper renders the air, the immediate brush of his cock against the bare cheek of my ass tells me he hasn't bothered to pull down his jeans, another sign of impatience that I find thrilling.

He bends me over. There's little time to brace for the impact when he takes hold of my hips and plunges into my drenched sex. His decadent groan cascades over my senses. His shaft fills me to the root with sleek, brutal drives that shake my body.

"Sooo good," I pant from the searing heat that burns my skin, my core, that blisters me all over.

Mick removes one hand from my hip and slides his forefinger and middle finger into my open mouth. I suck them in deep, milking them the way I would his cock.

It feels naughty and sexy. My climax mounts, my moans spilling out when his fingers leave my mouth. Then I feel his hand at the top of my bottom, feel his wet fingers glide between the seam, feel the incessant pressure coaxing me to flower open for him.

A novice to anal play, I would never have explored that curiosity with any other man. But with Mick, there are no limits. No reservations. With him, I've been downright uninhibited. Even raw.

Not as tentative as he was the first time, he pumps ecstasy into me. My fists grip the table, consumed by the dual stimulation, by the slick sounds of saturation, by him finger-fucking my ass while taking me doggy-style in the middle of the foyer.

All self-consciousness abandoned, my hips rock back and forth, racing toward orgasm. And Mick, knowing just what I like, what I need, slides his other hand to my sex; the pads of his fingers parting me to rub his thumb over my clit, exerting an exquisite pressure. The effect is devastating.

I climax. A volcano, liquid hot, spreads through me. My moans are guttural, throaty wails. My limbs tremor as I clamp down, writhing in the throes of one of the most intense orgasms I've ever had.

"Fuck, Dee." Mick grabs my hips with both hands, his fingers imprinting my flesh, and pounds into me.

LEIGH CARRON

My body, wet and greedy for each stroke, offers no resistance to his ruthless appetite. I quicken to his rhythm, loving the feel of him riding me hard, reveling in my own power of being masterfully serviced. It's primal—base—an untamed animalistic mating that rips a sob from my throat and makes me come again; a series of quick, pulsing contractions that tighten my core and make me quake from head to toe.

Mick tenses. Then erupts. A soul-wrenching growl trembles the air as he pumps against my behind, flooding me with his hot, thick semen.

I can feel it dripping down my thighs when he finally pulls out and pivots me into his arms, clinging to me, catching his breath in my hair.

We stay that way through the aftershocks. My mouth against his damp throat, soothing him with kisses, my arms wrapped around him, hoarding the closeness—afraid that the moment will end all too soon.

And it does.

Mick eases back. The way he looks at me pinches my chest. The fire is gone. The only fight I see in his tormented eyes is the one he's having with himself.

"Baby...I'm..."

"Don't." I stop him. "I can't bear to hear you apologize for loving me like that."

"I wasn't going to." He softly kisses my lips. "I was going to apologize for the way I handled things. I was selfish. Cowardly. I avoided you. I made you worry. I am sorry for that, Dee. But I'm not sorry about loving you. I could never be."

His words don't settle me. Rather they shove me further off-center. "Why were you avoiding me?"

His muscles tense, his body an unmalleable block of steel.

"I sensed there was something wrong when you returned from your jog this morning. Will you tell me what happened?"

"No."

That hurts. "Is it because you don't think I can handle it?"

"I think you're one of the strongest women I know. It's not that. It's my shit."

"Then that makes it mine too."

"Not this."

"I don't understand."

"I know."

The contrast is not lost on me that I'm fully exposed while Mick is clothed and covered like his secrets.

I slide my hands to the back of his neck and look into his eyes. "I have no idea what you think you can't tell me, but there is nothing that could ever drive or scare me away this time. I will face anything with you, Mick. That's my truth. I hope you'll give me yours."

He crushes me to him, his breaths heavy and burdened. "I went to a bar tonight."

I swallow my shock and try not to reveal my alarm. "Did you drink?"

"No. But I wanted to. Badly. I hadn't come that close since Cayo died."

"You were strong."

"I wasn't. The only thing that stopped me was seeing your text. It was like being pulled out of a deep hole that was about to close me in."

"I'm glad you found a reason." This time. I find it hard to imagine the Mick I know—dominant, in control, a force to be reckoned with—giving in to self-destruction. But he is an alcoholic. "Have you thought about seeing anyone?"

"A therapist, you mean?"

"Yes."

"I did during rehab and for a while after."

"Was it helpful?"

"Some." He shrugs. "Didn't give it much of a chance. Too much talking and prodding."

"That's how I felt about that kind of treatment too. That's why I chose behavioral therapy. I didn't want to get into the messy stuff of my past or my childhood. I'd always found it too painful to open up that Pandora's box...until a wise man convinced me that it actually helps to talk instead of keeping the pain locked inside."

The mood shifts. "Don't go there, Dee," he warns, closing off again. "This isn't the same thing."

I have no idea what it is or how we're going to find our way back if he won't talk to me. But pushing the issue now will only drive him away.

WE WASH UP AND CRAWL into bed, saying very little. Mick pulls me into his warmth. Tears pool in my eyes, but he can't see them.

"It's late." He spoons against my back, hugging my waist, softly caressing my skin. "Try to sleep," he murmurs.

I doubt I will. But I must have dozed off at some point because I wake in the wee hours with a start. Anxious. Disoriented. It takes me a moment to register that Mick is still lying behind me, his arm draped over my hip. When relief rushes through me, I realize it was the fear of losing him that had yanked me out of sleep.

Through the still darkness, I absorb the feel of his body heat and listen to his breathing. It's too fast for him to be at rest. Dreading he might be on the verge of another nightmare, I carefully turn with my heart in my throat. He's wide awake and looking at me. His eyes are haunted in the shadows. How long had he lay like this, giving me comfort to make sure I slept while he couldn't?

My fingers brush over the arch of his brow. "I want you so much, but it feels like you're slipping away."

"I'm right here, beauty. You have me."

"Not all of you."

"You own me." He takes my mouth in a deep, passionate kiss. "Can't you see that?" He puts my hand flat on his chest, right over his pounding heart. "Can't you feel that?" He lays me on my back and nudges my legs open. "I'm yours."

The next couple of hours pass in a sensual blur. I'm insatiable. Gluttonous. I grab at him with greedy hands, my nails raking across his damp skin, my mouth working tirelessly over his hard body.

And Mick's need for me is just as ravenous. Love bites to my neck and breasts, relentless sucking of my nipples, constantly fucking me with his cock or his fingers or his tongue. Still it's not enough.

Our lovemaking is frantic, tinged with an anguished despair as if each time could be our last. It's nearly 3:00 a.m. when—sweaty, exhausted, and sore—I finally collapse onto his chest.

He closes his arms arounds me and kisses my temple. "Sleep now, beauty."

Micah

FOURTEEN YEARS EARLIER...

There's pounding in my ears and it feels like my head's been hit by a sledgehammer, then run over by a Mack truck just for fun. I can't open my eyes. But there's a weight on my chest and something soft tickles my nose. I'm not even sure where I am. I manage to pry one eyelid half open.

Daylight streams through the window of my apartment. I squint against the sun's cruel glare and look down. Sable curls? Disbelief, amazement, and happiness rush through me at once. Dee. It's Dee. I'm in bed with Dee. But how? My fuzzy brain grapples to compute. If it's a dream, I don't want to ever wake up. I want to lock it up in a magical bottle, so that I can conjure her up and feel her light on my darkest days.

"Micah! Open this door. Now!"

Papa T? What was he doing here—in my dream? Dee murmurs beside me, then shifts, her hair falling away from her face.

What the fuck? A nightmare unfolds in front of me. I shove away from this girl who's not Dee and jump off the bed. My heart breaks all over again.

"Who's at the door?" she asks groggily, pulling up the comforter that Mama T had picked out for me.

Disgusted with myself, I gather her clothes strewn near mine on the floor and toss them to her. "Get dressed."

"Hey." She huffs. "What's your deal?"

Ignoring her question, I pull on the jeans and top I'd been wearing last night. My memory returns through the heavy cloud of alcohol. I'd been at a teammate's party when I should have been here studying to get my ass off academic probation. My student advisor warned that they could pull my scholarship. Most days I wished they would. Let someone else decide my fate for me. I was doing a lousy job of it myself.

The party was in full swing when I arrived alone. I greeted the guys, went through the motions of high fives, and played my role of the carefree freshman out for a good time. The usual groupies were there along with some unfamiliar faces, including a clique of sorority girls that were probably taking a break from the frat boys to scratch their jock itch. If so, they'd come to the right place. New girls were like throwing fresh meat into a cage of hungry lions. My teammates were all over them. But tired of the usual scene, I wasn't looking to hook up. I'd just come for the free booze.

There was plenty of it on a table in the living room, but then I'd have to socialize. Rejecting that option, I'd made my way to the kitchen. Jackpot! I'd already had a few drinks before I arrived, courtesy of my neighbor. As long as I paid, he supplied the goods since I'd gotten caught trying to pass off a phony ID at the nearby liquor store and couldn't go back.

I filled a red plastic cup with rum and a splash of Coke. Chugging the dark liquid down, it burned like a bitch, but added to my buzz to take the edge off. I wiped my mouth on my sleeve and filled the cup again, belting it back in two big gulps, seeking the numbness I craved. After another, I switched to beer to pace out the night.

As I was crouched down to grab a bottle of Miller from the cooler, I heard the clicking of heels on the tiled floor. I looked up to find a pair of long, shapely legs saran-wrapped in blue jeans that stretched to Heaven or Hell, depending on your perspective.

I straightened to full height. Her face was unfamiliar. But attractive with a nice smile. I might have tried to smile back if not for the hair. It was a lighter brown than the rich sable I hadn't forgotten, but it curled like spirals past her shoulders. No way! I didn't need any more reminders.

"Excuse me." I brushed past her, but she circled my bicep with her hand causing me to stop.

"Are you leaving?"

"Yep. Not my scene tonight."

"Mine either. I'll go with you."

"Why?"

"You're Micah Peters," she said, as if that were reason enough. "I've watched you play. You're like so amazing and the hottest guy at school."

I was a hot mess, but this girl wasn't interested in my mental state. She took the beer from me and placed her mouth over the tip, sucking back a long drink. She licked her lips when she handed it back. Message clear.

If only she didn't have those curls that made me think too damn much.

"Come on," she urged. "Let's get out of here."

It was a bad idea. But lately my life has been one bad idea after another. Why change the pattern? I filched a case of beer and we snuck out the back door deciding to walk to my on-campus apartment because it was closer than her residence. Besides, she had roommates and a strict dorm mom, I didn't have either.

She wasn't much of a drinker, but I got shit-faced and stopped noticing her curls. By the time she put her hand on the zipper of my jeans, I didn't notice anything except her willing body and my hard-on.

She wrapped those legs from Hell around me and I pushed up her shirt to feel her tits. After that we must have fucked. It's a blurred memory, but the proof is in the used condom on the floor. Even when I'm drunk I don't break that rule. I'd only ever with *her*. Bare inside of Dee, that had been pure Heaven.

The thumping on my door comes again. "Micah Anthony! I know you're in there. Open up!"

"Who's that?" she asks, reminding me that she's still here.

Shame slaps at me as I fasten my jeans and look over at the girl buttoning up her shirt. There was only one exit route: through the front door. Unless I make her climb out the three-story window. I'm not that much of an asshole yet, though I'm working on it.

Why the hell should I care if Cayo Torres finds a girl in my room? I'm nearly nineteen. Single. His daughter bailed on me. I'm free to screw whomever I want. I walk to the door then remember the condom. I turn back to throw it in the toilet and flush the bowl. Who was I kidding? There's no one whose opinion of me matters more than his. No man I respect more or want to be like. But I've failed on that score time and time again.

Damn, I wish this girl with her tangled hair and crusted mascara didn't look like she just crawled out of my bed. Or that I didn't look like I'd been drinking for the last five days straight.

My mouth tastes like I have paste for spit and my head is still a punching bag, but I'm stone cold sober and scared as shit when I open the door. Papa T is six inches shorter than me, and I probably outweigh him by over fifty pounds, yet he's a giant of a man in every way that counts.

His eyebrows shoot up and he doesn't mince words. "You look like crap and smell like a brewery."

"Uh...I wasn't expecting you."

"I can see that." He steps into my studio apartment.

I picture it through his eyes and cringe. Piles of dirty clothes, empty liquor and beer bottles, the rumpled bed, the girl with the curls. I'm sure he doesn't miss that detail and figures she's some kind of substitute.

"Who's your friend?"

I don't even remember her name, which is pretty low of me. When seconds pass without my answer, Papa T shakes his head and I feel his disappointment down to my bones.

"I'm Phoebe." Christ, it even rhymes with Dee. She grabs her shoes, looking embarrassed. "It's...um...nice to meet you, Mr. Peters."

He doesn't correct her. "Nice to meet you too, Phoebe."

"Bye, Mick."

"Yeah, bye." I know I should say more. She's probably expecting it. But what is there to say? I'll call you, when I know I won't.

"You've really gotten yourself into a jam, son," he says, closing the door.

There's no place clear of dirty clothes to sit except the bed of shame, so I choose the floor, pressing my back against the wall.

Papa T takes a seat next to me. I bring my knees to my chest and rest my chin on top. "Are you being safe...responsible?"

I nod, unable to meet his eyes.

"Rita and Victor have been worried about you," he says gently rather than scolding. "We know it's been hard, struggling with your loss. We thought you needed time to heal, but you're not doing that. You're keeping it all inside. You don't return our calls. We haven't seen you in months." He puts a hand on my shoulder. "We're concerned, Mick. And now I see we have every reason to be. Drinking and sleeping with girls you don't even know the names of isn't going to make you feel better."

I clench my hands, fighting the urge to ram a fist through the wall. "This is all I know how to do. I'm just like *him*."

"You're not!" He gives me a firm shake. "You are not your father. You don't have to drink to cope and you don't have to follow his dreams. You can be your own man. Choose a different path, one that's right for you. Don't give up on your gift and passion for writing or stay stuck in the past nursing your anger and grief. You're young. You don't realize it, but time is short. Precious. Don't waste this life."

I couldn't know then how poignant those words would be, but they still affected me. Seeped into that place that I had closed off after she left. "I want to stop. The drinking doesn't make me forget. The girls don't make me forget. Nothing does. I want to be better than this. I don't want you and Mama T to keep worrying about me. But I don't know how to do anything else."

"Wanting to stop is the first step." His hopeful smile is like a beacon guiding my dark and broken soul. "Let me help you with the rest."

I TAKE A TWO-WEEK leave. Only my student advisor and coach know the reason. I don't tell my old man. I can't deal with him on top of everything else.

Papa T found this place out in the boonies that looks more like a retreat than a place for young male drunks to dry out. It must cost a fortune, but he says he has insurance. I don't believe it will cover all this.

My roommate is a thin, pale dude with dirty-blonde hair he wears in a long ponytail. He plays the guitar and doesn't talk much. That's fine by me. I have to talk enough in therapy. That's the absolute worst part about being here, even more than the night sweats and shakes. I seriously hate that shit. I don't talk about Malcolm. Ever. Only Dee holds those secrets and she's gone. I don't want to talk about her either. What's the point when it won't change anything? But Papa T tells me it's an important part of the process. He says I should participate to get the most out of my time here. I'll start the outpatient program after that. Guess what I'll be doing there? More talking.

Victor and Mama T call every night and Papa T visits every day. He's staying at a nearby hotel. I feel bad that he's missing work and missing time with his family.

"You are family. This is where I want to be."

I don't take his words lightly. He's bound and determined to see me healthy and living again. I won't let him down.

On the last day, Papa T drives me back to the apartment. It's stripped clean, no liquor bottles. New sheets on the bed, clothes washed. Smells of Lysol and laundry detergent. A fresh start.

"Thank you for this." I hug him hard. "Thank you for everything."

"I'm proud of you, Mick."

"I want you to be. I promise no more drinking. No more nameless girls. And I'm going to talk to Coach. Tell him I'm not coming back next season."

"That's a big step."

"I'm ready for it."

"Have you spoken to your father?"

"It's none of his business."

"He's going to find out."

"So, what? He can't stop me."

IT'S ALMOST TWO MONTHS BEFORE I finally sit down with my coach to tell him I'll finish out the season, but won't be back. I avoided telling him this long because it also means telling my old man. But I get it done and it's a relief. Like shedding a thousand pounds off my shoulders. The coach was livid; he said I was making a huge mistake, one that I'll live to regret. He doesn't know me. He doesn't know that basketball was the mistake.

It's funny how I start playing even better as the end of the season draws near. I'm still busted up over Dee, but I'm breathing again. My grades have improved. I haven't had a drink in more than ten weeks and I don't wake up with strange girls in my bed.

Therapy still blows. Maybe because the counselor says I'm putting the blame on Dee for my drinking when I really need to look at myself, at my addiction. I ignore his advice and find a constructive outlet.

Whenever I'm tempted to take a drink, I jog. Whenever I think of Dee, I jog. Suffice it to say I jog a lot. But on the plus side, I'm in the best physical shape ever. And my head's clearer. I've even started hanging out with some of my teammates that are a good influence on me.

Friday, after last class, we make plans to meet up at the gym to lift weights. Hurrying to my apartment to change and grab a bite first, I walk in to discover Malcolm Peters.

I'd expected a confrontation. I'd rehearsed it over and over, what I would say and how I would say it. But I wasn't expecting to do that today.

He takes a swig of whiskey from the bottle he's holding and stares me down with those steely, black eyes. At nine, I would have been shaking in my Air Jordans. At nineteen, I meet his gaze and don't feel anything but contempt.

"How did you get in here?" I ask, dropping my backpack onto the floor.

"Did you think a flimsy lock would keep me out?"

I don't back up when he steps forward.

"You and Cayo come up with this lamebrain plan?"

"I make my own decisions. I'm quitting at the end of the season and going to NYU."

"Oh, so you're a big fucking man now."

"I'm old enough to do what I want."

"Yeah." He looks me over. "Your balls aren't too big for me to break."

"Try it, old man."

His whiskey-laugh sprays in my face. "You want to fight me, son?"

"I'm not your son."

"Fuck Cayo. He's not your father."

I'm tempted to tell him otherwise, but something about his venomous focus on Papa T prevents me from egging him on. "This has nothing to do with Cayo. I've made up my mind and you can't change it."

"Sure I will. With the right incentive."

I stand on alert, my fists clenched, ready to fight back.

"If I was going to lay hands on you, you'd already be out flat." He takes another swig of whiskey. "What I got is better. You see, you can talk a good game, son, but one thing I know about you that you never learned to hide was your pussy ass weakness. You let people matter and that's a major fucking flaw. So, have a drink..." he extends the bottle, "and let me tell you exactly how this is going to play out. And it sure as shit won't be you going to NYU."

CHAPTER ELEVEN

Dee

MICK'S SHOUTS HAVE ME JACKKNIFING out of bed, my heart racing like crazy. I stare at the man I love snarling vile curses, his hands balled tight, his fists striking air. I move farther away, afraid that he might accidentally hit me. Mick would never forgive himself.

He curses again and takes another swing, hitting the table lamp and sending it crashing to the floor. I scramble for the light switch on the wall. The room illuminates. Hatred and rage contort his face and a layer of sweat coats his juddering body.

"Mick!" I scream several times before it punctures through his nightmare.

He startles awake, searching wild-eyed. "What?" He grapples for air, his chest rising and falling rapidly.

"You were having another nightmare." I pull the throw blanket off the window seat and wrap it around my chilled body.

He looks down at the cracked lamp on the floor. Shame and mortification cut across his expression.

"I don't care about the lamp, Mick." I move to the foot of the bed, facing him. "What were you dreaming about?"

"I don't remember."

"You're lying. It was about your father again. You were in a rage, fighting…"

"I have to go." He swings his legs over the side of the bed.

"Go where?"

"Home."

"I thought you were home."

"Christ, Dee." He picks up the damaged lamp and sets it back on the nightstand. "I should never have come here."

"You don't mean that." Yet the stark bleakness in his eyes tells me he does. "*Mick*."

He moves past me and quickly dresses.

"You can't keep walking out or avoiding me every time there's a hurdle."

"A hurdle?" He spews. "This is a fucking mountain."

"Then we'll climb it together."

Mick looks at me as if I'm insane. "Why the hell would you want to?"

"How can you ask that?"

"Because I'm fucked up. Because I could have hit you in my sleep. Because you don't deserve any of this."

"You are not fucked up. You need to deal with what's in your dreams. With whatever is tormenting you. Let me help you do that. I love you."

I step toward him, but he puts up a hand to stave me off.

"You love who you think I am."

"I know who you are."

"You don't know what's inside me, Dee."

"If you mean your father, then you're wrong. Do you think Dwayde is anything like his mother? Do you think those kids you pour all your heart into helping have tainted blood or don't deserve love because of where they come from?" His unyielding demeanor remains closed. "You are not your father, Mick. Don't make excuses to run."

"I can't stay." His voice carries a sad resignation. "Don't ask me to."

"I'm not asking…I'm begging."

"*Stop.*"

"No." I block his path. "Do you know how hard it was for me to open myself up to you? To let you see every flaw, every shame, every hurt? I let you in, Mick. I was terrified to give so much. To risk myself that way. But I did it. Because I trusted in our love. I trusted you."

"I know you did and I'm sorry," he says thickly, averting his eyes.

"I don't want you to be sorry. I want you to talk to me. To fight for us. Please."

"I can't."

A slap couldn't hurt more. Tears sting my eyes. I cross my arms around my waist, trying to hold myself together, and step away. Because as much as I love him, I know the road for a healthy, enduring relationship between us is paved with honesty and truth, not secrets and denial.

AS IF IN MOURNING, I dress in all black. A high-collar blouse beneath my suit hides the hickies on my neck and concealer disguises the circles under my eyes. But nothing can hide the sorrow. I feel it in every pore. In every joint.

The possibility that Mick and I might really be over is just too much. But even if he were to come back, I won't live with only the bits and pieces he chooses to share. I want it all or nothing. And yet, that nothing is killing me.

"Dee?" I glance up to see Lena in the doorway. She looks concerned. "You alright?"

"Just tired." It's a struggle, but I force the corners of my mouth to lift. "What's up?"

"Calista Sanchez is on line one. She says it's important."

Engrossed in my relationship woes, I hadn't even heard the phone ring. "Thanks."

I pick up the receiver and put my composure in place. "Hi, Calista."

"Got the lab report." She jumps in unceremoniously. "The signature on the custody document is a high match to Joyce Franklin's."

I'd expected as much. "Thomas Jackson wouldn't have put forward a document he hadn't tested himself first."

"You're probably right. He's an arrogant ass, but he's not a stupid man."

"He may have miscalculated on this one," I say. "His clients can't have it both ways, claim their daughter was too hopped up on drugs to care for her son, yet have been of sound mind to sign a legal and binding document that would give them custody."

"I'm with you on that," she confirms. "I'm having my team work on a response to have the judge toss it."

"Have you spoken to your clients yet?" I ask about Victor and Isabelle.

"No. Not yet. I was about to call them when you-know-who came crawling out of the woodwork."

"Jackson of course."

"None other. He has a copy of the results too and couldn't wait to use it to his advantage."

"What does he want this time?"

"A visit alone between his clients and Dwayde."

"That's out of the question."

"That's exactly what I told him. But heads-up, I expect you're next on his hit list. Just sent over the lab results."

"Got them," I say, opening her email.

"We'll chat later. Gotta reach my clients and fill them in. Not looking forward to that."

Neither was I. But because Calista doesn't know about my personal ties to the Torreses, I bend to protocol and allow her to inform them before I make contact.

"Let me know if you hear from Jackson," she adds.

"Will do."

I've barely finished reading through the report when he calls, waving his victory flag.

"Yes, Ms. Sanchez informed me," I acknowledge. "A visit alone with Dwayde is a non-starter. I shouldn't have to remind you of how badly it went when he saw your clients at their hotel, and I was with him."

"Precisely. My clients believe it was your presence that brought about his reaction."

"Excuse me?"

"Nothing personal. Mr. Franklin commended you on being a consummate professional. But a professional nevertheless. It made the situation awkward and fraught with tension. A supervised visit is unwarranted. My clients have done nothing wrong, they don't need to be chaperoned. It's insulting."

"Their sore feelings are not my concern. To Dwayde, they are strangers."

"They are his grandparents," he counters. "And as evidenced by the signed document, his rightful guardians."

"A signature that's worth less than the paper it's written on."

"Yet another point on which we disagree."

"The only point that matters under State law is that Detective and Ms. Torres are Dwayde's legal guardians."

"A mere oversight," he blusters. "Joyce Franklin abandoned her son, giving the courts latitude to assign guardianship to the Torreses. That would not have occurred had my clients known where their grandson was."

"But it did occur. Three years ago. And now Dwayde has a happy and stable life here in Chicago."

"My clients are his *biological* relatives, Ms. Chase. A fact that the judge evinced would be significant in her ruling for custody and I purport would easily extend to visitation."

"Biology is not the sole consideration in either proceeding and you know it."

"Oh yes." His drawl gets under my skin. "Those so-called familial bonds you alluded to."

"The attachment is real, Mr. Jackson."

"A starving dog will always bond with the hand that feeds him."

"Your analogy is disgustingly offensive." I bristle.

"Let's look at the obvious. When Detective Torres found the boy, he had run away from his drug-addicted mother who couldn't care for him then, any more than she could when she took him from the security of his grandparents' home in Kentucky. He was malnourished and homeless. It's understandable that he would develop a phantom attachment to the people who took him in. But change the hand—"

"Dwayde's feelings aren't fickle nor are they transferable. Mr. Franklin already insinuated that he could *win* Dwayde as if he were some derby prize. I can tell you that these callous references don't speak well for your clients. Nor does attempting to push and bully their way back into Dwayde's life."

"My clients kept their distance for over two weeks to give him time and space. I'd hardly call that bullying."

"It is when they waited to use the lab results as another intimidation tactic."

"The timing is purely coincidental. My clients are anxious to see their grandson again. Alone."

"That, Mr. Jackson, is not going to happen."

"Based on what grounds?"

"Based on the expressed wishes of Dwayde's legal guardians. Detective and Ms. Torres had generously agreed to allow your clients to visit with Dwayde as long as I was present. They were under no obligation to do so."

"I didn't realize you were also representing the Torreses."

"Make no mistake, I represent Dwayde only, and his best interests."

"Rebuilding a relationship with his grandparents goes to the very heart of the boy's best interests. My clients will be in town next weekend. They've suggested lunch on Saturday after attending his practice, then Sunday brunch and tickets to see an NBA game. All very public and geared toward the boy's interests. Surely you don't take issue with that."

"I very much have an issue with this transparent maneuver to get Dwayde alone. If your clients are serious about getting to know him, they could start with dropping the pursuit of custody."

"Nice try, Ms. Chase. But that, as you say, is a *non-starter*. It floors me that a reasonable request to spend a little time alone with their grandson would be denied by foster parents overstepping their role as temporary caregivers. I'd wager any judge would grant this request by virtue of my clients' stellar reputations, their past relationship with the boy, and the legal document that assigned them custody."

"On the contrary, Mr. Jackson. I'd wager any judge would throw that baseless document out of court and recognize that your tactics are to pressure a scared twelve-year-old into a visit with strangers who are also trying to take him away from the only family he's known."

"You're good, Ms. Chase." His tone is smug and condescending. "I'll give you that. But beneath your charming bravado, you know you'll lose. My advice: let's not waste cycles on this and put the boy through a needless court appearance when the outcome is inevitable. A couple of meals and a basketball game. Who's going to deny the boy that?"

"Consider it denied and this conversation over."

"Then to quote a famous line, *I'll see you in court.* Have yourself a nice day."

He disconnects and I slam the phone down, getting no satisfaction from the act.

This news is going to crush my family. And I worry what the added guilt will do to Mick.

THE MOOD INSIDE THE KITCHEN is taut with stress. Isabelle would already have been at home after letting her kindergarten class out at 2:00 p.m., but Victor had left the precinct early on personal time, and Mick, I suppose, must have heard the news from Victor and come rushing over.

I wasn't expecting to find him here. Hadn't prepared myself to see him again so soon. When I noticed his car parked in the driveway, it wrecked complete havoc on my vulnerable defenses. But that was nothing compared to coming face-to-face with him.

At first, I stood there as if in a daze. My attempt at composure was eclipsed by distress. Unsure of how to respond, I'd waited for some sort of cue. The ring still on his finger gave me a modicum of hope. As did his eyes that moved over me with a gentle touch conveying his love. Or maybe pity. Either way, it was brief—a flash of a moment before he donned an impenetrable mask and stepped behind an invisible wall where I could see him, but couldn't reach him.

Now seated at the kitchen table, I tug at the lapels of my suit jacket while he paces the ceramic floor behind me in intermittent bursts. Isabelle makes coffee, not that it will calm her nerves, but it gives her something to do. Even Rufus, lying under the table at Victor's feet, senses the tension filling the room and lets out a whine.

"What the fuck is wrong with these people?" My foster brother's temper is rare, but when it brews, it boils and bubbles over. "They had no desire to meet with us from the beginning to discuss Dwayde. Instead they sicced their lawyer on us with letters and threats. But for Dwayde's sake, we made excuses for their insensitive behavior and heavy-handed methods. We encouraged him to see them. We tried to give them the benefit of the doubt. But that visit was hell on him.

"We're through, Dee." His hand slices the air for emphasis. "I'm sick of their games. Sick of their threats. Using some bullshit custody document to pull this crap. We are not going to force another visit on Dwayde, unsupervised or otherwise. Let them take us to court. I welcome the fight."

"Then we'll fight." I look at Victor, empathizing with his anger and frustration, and work to steady my own rocky emotions. "But let's be clear on what that will entail."

"Calista already warned it won't be easy," he says, resisting any objection. "That doesn't mean we cave to their demands because it's hard."

"I agree with that. We just need to be prepared for what's involved. I'm sure Calista explained that the standard for visitation is much lower than it is for custody. Jackson will argue that your denial is unreasonable, and will push for visitation on the grounds of their past relationship with Dwayde. Specifically, being his primary caregivers until he was taken from them at age four by a mother unfit to care for him. He will assert that losing Dwayde has been hell on them and has deprived Dwayde of his loving grandparents. So, now that they've found him after eight long years, they should be given the opportunity to re-establish their bond."

"Shit!" Victor shakes his head. "You make it sound like we don't stand a chance."

"I'm not trying to discourage you. I'm just presenting the reality of what we are up against...of what Dwayde will be up against."

"What about how he feels?" Isabelle anxiously searches my face. "That must count for something."

"It absolutely does," I assure her. "That's the other side of the argument, what Dwayde wants. He's twelve, old enough to have a say.

But for the judge to take that into consideration, Dwayde will need to explain why he is so vehemently opposed to having anything to do with his grandparents."

"Dwayde still maintains that he doesn't remember them." Isabelle sighs, and sets a mug of coffee down in front of me.

"I'd like to try to get more from him." I shift my gaze between Isabelle and Victor. "If we're going to court, Dwayde will need to know what's going on. He will need to know that his continued silence won't work in his favor."

"You can't tell him this." I turn to see Mick stop pacing. He looks at Isabelle and Victor, pointedly ignoring me. "All that's going to do is shake Dwayde's foundation when he's just started to feel settled again. For all we know, the Franklins are calling your bluff. Let's wait to see what they do before involving Dwayde in these legal matters."

I'm not surprised by Mick's overprotective response. After all, hiding the unpleasant things is the way he operates. But I won't go along with keeping Dwayde in the dark any more than I will accept it for myself.

"Whether the Franklins file a petition for visitation or not, there is still the custody case. Pretending that everything is fine and back to normal is not going to do Dwayde any good. In addition to my personal relationship, I'm also his lawyer, and my responsibility is to be honest and straight with him. He has the right to know what's happening. This isn't something we should keep from him. There shouldn't be any secrets."

Mick flinches. My intended aim, hitting home. But that doesn't stop his argument. "Do you really think telling Dwayde this is going to make him talk?"

"I'm not expecting miracles, but I will give it my best shot."

He turns to Victor. "You're going along with this?"

"I think Dee's right. Even though Dwayde has seemed more like himself in the last couple of weeks, he jumps whenever the phone rings, and there's an edginess to him as if he's waiting for the other shoe to drop. As much as we all want to protect him and make him feel secure again, he doesn't. And he's not going to until this is over. We have to tell him. I don't know if that will make him talk. I hope it does, for his own sake, as much as for the case."

Victor takes his wife's hand that she had laid on his shoulder. "What do you think, Bells?"

"I wish there was another way. I wish we could just make it all disappear, but we can't. He should know."

They exchange a withered look, but remain convicted. Victor's gaze travels back to mine. "We trust you to tell him, Dee. But we want to be here as support."

"Of course." I can feel the heat of Mick's disapproval. "I'll be careful with him."

"We know you will." Isabelle's voice carries an audible tremor. "I'm sorry." She waves a hand in front of her eyes welling with tears. "I promised myself I wouldn't do this. I try to stay positive and hopeful, but sometimes it just comes over me. The thought of losing him…"

Victor stands and pulls his wife into his arms. "We're not going to let that happen, Bells."

She buries her face into Victor's chest and quietly cries. My heart breaking, I slide my gaze away, giving them privacy, and risk looking back at Mick. What I see there shreds me. Self-blame is etched in his features, guilt beating in the clench of his jaw. Instinctively, I start to go to him, but upon catching my intent, his arms lock over his chest in a gesture that couldn't be any clearer than a bright orange *No Trespassing* sign.

I ease back down into my chair. Shaken. More than the remoteness, it's his rejection that wounds the deepest. This Mick resembles none of the warm, loving man that I'm used to. Instead it's as if a cold, angry stranger has invaded his body.

Rufus starts barking then, breaking through my confused hurt. The excited bulldog-mix waddles on his squat body toward the back door, his stubby tail wagging.

"It's going to be okay," Victor consoles as Isabelle dries her tears with a napkin.

Moments later, I hear Dwayde bound through the door that opens onto a mudroom beside the kitchen. He laughs as he greets Rufus. "Did you miss me, boy? Yeah, I missed you too."

Then he enters the kitchen in his gray and burgundy uniform, backpack hanging off one shoulder. His cheery smile abruptly falls and he pulls up short. "How come you're all here?"

"We need to talk to you," Victor explains.

"Something bad's happened." His big eyes go bigger, rounder with fear.

"We just need to talk, sweetie." Isabelle overcompensates her angst with an upbeat lilt and pats the cushion of the chair. "Come sit down."

"I don't want to sit down. Just tell me."

"Dwayde…" I say softly because I'm about to deliver a blow. "Mr. and Mrs. Franklin's lawyer contacted me today."

"They want to see me again?"

A NAKED BEAUTY

"Yes."

Fresh and bright panic explodes across his face. "I have to get out of here. I have to go where they'll never find me." He takes a quick step back and Mick reaches him first, puts a hand on his shoulder, staying him in place.

Dwayde lives in a nice, middle-class neighborhood and goes to private school, but he grew up on the streets. Running at the sign of trouble is second nature.

"You're not going anywhere." Mick crouches to bring himself at eye level with Dwayde. "This is where you belong. Understand?" When Dwayde doesn't respond, he takes his chin, and firmly repeats: "Understand?"

Dwayde nods.

"Good, then let's sit and talk this out," Mick says despite his antipathy toward our plan.

Dwayde drops his backpack and slowly, mechanically, takes a seat. Victor and Isabelle flank his side and Mick pulls out a chair next to me. I inhale a hitch of breath, affected by his nearness, my body innately reacting to his scent, to the memory of him loving me all night long.

But my priority is the boy staring down at his lap.

"Dwayde?" I pause and wait for him to lift his head.

"I'm not going," he asserts defiantly, his eyes bouncing from Victor to Isabelle. "I won't see them ever again. And you can't make me."

"We're not going to make you, sweetie." Isabelle puts a hand on his forearm. "Dee and Ms. Sanchez have already told their lawyer that."

"But the lawyer can try to make me, right?" He turns back to me. "That's what you said before."

"Their lawyer can go to court to try to get a judge to agree that the Franklins should be able to see you."

"I don't care what any dumb judge says, I still won't go."

His insolence is understandable. He has every right to be surly when his life keeps getting turned upside down. But I have to break through the defiance to make progress.

"The judges in these cases aren't dumb, Dwayde. They are actually very smart and care about making the best decision. That's why they need all the facts. That means we will have to explain in some detail why you don't want to see the Franklins."

"I told you I don't know them."

"You could get to know them."

"I don't want to."

"Why is that?"

150

"Because I don't like them."

"What makes you not like them?"

"I met them and they sucked ass."

Isabelle winces, but under the circumstances doesn't scold him for his language.

"I got the impression you didn't like them even before the visit."

His sullen gaze drops, and he starts drawing patterns on the table with his fingers.

"It would really help if you could tell me anything," I cautiously probe. "Like even things Joyce may have said about living in Kentucky."

"She just liked to run her mouth." He grows more agitated. "Who cares what she said?"

"I care if Joyce said anything about her life there, about her parents—about what kind of relationship she had with them or what kind of people they were."

"Why?"

"Because it could be important to our case. Right now, we only have what their friends and people in their community have said about them."

His head snaps up. "What did they say?"

"That the Franklins are kind and generous, and were loving and devoted parents."

A flush of anger burns along his light mocha cheeks and his voice raises. "Those are lies!"

I startle at his outburst. "What makes them lies?"

As if catching himself, he shakes his head fast, from side to side.

"Did they ever hurt you, Dwayde?"

No answer.

"Did they hurt Joyce?"

More silence.

"*Dwayde,*" Victor implores, "if there's something you know about the Franklins, you need to tell us. We will protect you, keep you safe, but we need to know."

"I keep telling you the same thing over and over again. I don't remember them...I don't know nuthing about them!" He wails, his eyes bright with tears. "So, stop asking me and just make them go away!"

Dwayde lurches from his chair with such force it topples over. He runs from the kitchen with Rufus on his heels, thumping footsteps and skittering paws sounding on the hardwood, up the stairs, then the slam of a door.

"Well, shit." Victor exhales.

"We're wasting time." Mick's voice is a low throb. "We have to find her."

"Who?" It takes Victor a moment to process. "Joyce?"

"Yes." Mick doesn't waver.

"Are you out of your mind? You want to bring the woman who beat the hell out of my son back into his life?"

"I'm not suggesting that. But..." Mick leans in, keeping his volume to a harsh whisper. "She has the answers, Victor. We have a month before the judge hears the custody case, never mind visitation. You saw how Dwayde was, do you really think he's going to give it up by then?"

The vein in Victor's neck bulges. "Even if I agreed with you, which I don't, what makes you think we can find her when Franklin couldn't?"

"We don't know jack shit about what Franklin did. You've said so yourself that it's suspicious that they never reported their daughter and grandson missing. No calls to the police. If they had, the Franklins would have been notified when Dwayde went into the system. But for some reason, they didn't do that. So, for all we know they didn't hire private investigators either. Joyce was in Chicago when Dwayde ran. She could still be here."

"I'm aware that their behavior raises a number of red flags, but..." Victor challenges, "on the long shot that we could even find her, why would she want to help us or Dwayde?"

"For money."

"Mick!" Isabelle says aghast. "You're not really suggesting that we should pay her."

"She's not going to do it out of the goodness of her heart, Bells. I'd make the arrangements through Stiles. He'll broker the deal in exchange for useful information. And your names, the custody case, and anything to do with Dwayde and his whereabouts will be kept out of it."

This isn't the first time Mick has mentioned something similar. He had initially proposed that I offer the Franklins money to drop the case. His penchant to buy away problems doesn't sit well with me.

"It's not that simple." I meet his foreboding stare. "Assuming Joyce can even be found, we can't just pay her for any relevant information and present it as evidence to the courts. It wouldn't stand without her testimony. For that, she'd not only have to be credible and agree to be a witness, she'd have to know where Dwayde is. All that to say, trying to find Joyce is a bad idea."

"Sure, when you put it that way." He clenches and unclenches his hand. "But I'm not talking about rules and procedures. If we get something damaging on them, we'll take it directly to the Franklins. Fuck the courts. We'll settle this ourselves."

152

I stare at Mick, flabbergasted. "You can't just take matters into your own hands when we're in the middle of a court case. This isn't one of your stories. This is real life, and it doesn't work that way."

"Your way isn't working either," he blasts back.

I take a calming breath, rankled by his criticism on top of everything else he's been dishing out, and rein in my temper. "There are rules and procedures for a reason. Just as there is case strategy. We are not relying solely on the potential bad acts of the Franklins to win. Admittedly, that would work to our advantage if we could prove it, but in the absence of that, we will still build a strong custody case."

"That by your own admission would be stronger with evidence against the Franklins."

"Yes, but I don't see finding Joyce as a viable option."

"I do."

"And you always know what's best for everyone, right?" Lines between personal and professional blur as I let him see my angry hurt.

"I take care of what's mine."

"That you do. No matter the cost."

His eyes blaze. Mad as hell, Mick pushes to his feet and storms out the back door.

"I'll go talk to him," Victor says. "Mick thinks he has to be the one to fix this."

I could cry. Mick thinks he has to be the one to fix everything.

CHAPTER TWELVE

Micah

"WOULD YOU QUIT WEARING A hole in my grass?"

I spare a side glance over at Victor as he strides across the back lawn with an indignant scowl.

"For God's sake," he mutters and clutches my arm, halting my pace mid-stride. "Stay!"

I tug loose. "What am I, a fucking dog?"

"Hey..." he gets in my face. "If it growls like a dog and snaps like one."

"Back off, Victor."

He inches away, but his expression remains severe and astute. "What was with that bullshit in there?"

"Since when is looking out for Dwayde bullshit?"

"When it's wrapped up in something else and not making you think straight."

"I don't know what the fuck you're talking about. But what I do know is that we need to find out what these people did to their daughter because all the judge is going to see is a wealthy couple that has reputation and biology on their side."

"And we have family. That's what counts."

"It should, but the system doesn't always work for the good."

"I work in the system, Mick. I'm not blind to its faults. But I still believe in it to be just and fair."

Even as a kid, Victor played by the rules, his strong moral compass ingrained by two good and decent parents. For him, there are no shades between right and wrong, while for me it's all too easy to play in the gray areas when I think I have to.

"If Joyce is still in Chicago, there's a chance Stiles could find her. Then we'd be armed to take them on."

He shakes his head. "She's a hard-core druggie. Her information probably isn't worth a dime."

"It's worth trying to find out."

"Have you thought about Dwayde?" Victor changes his tactic. "If he got wind that we were even thinking about looking for her, he'd bolt."

"He won't get wind of it." I glance toward the house.

"Still…Dwayde could give us something."

"It's not gonna happen."

Victor eyes me critically. "What makes you so sure?"

"Because he hasn't budged an inch." And because I've been there as a kid. I'm still there. Sheltering my secrets. After all these years. Every ugly piece sealed and guarded from the people they would hurt the most.

"He did budge today," Victor argues.

"Yeah, then he caught himself and clammed right back up."

"Regardless, we will do this the right way. No shady deals. No Joyce. I mean it. You will not try to find her."

"Fuck!" I pace away, splintered by that sense of powerlessness that tears at me like hot-tipped talons.

"What the hell is up with you, man?" Victor follows, giving me a once over that's trained by thirty years of being as much brothers as friends. "This isn't just about the case. What's going on with you and Dee?"

"Nothing." The lie rasps out of my throat and I work to get a grip. But Victor isn't buying it.

"Try again."

"I'm handling it."

"Doesn't look that way to me."

"Then stop looking."

"You were rough on her in there. Cold. Seems like all is not copacetic."

I drag a hand through my hair, hating myself for what I'm doing to her. But if I soften one bit, I'll weaken completely. And weakening is not an option in keeping her safe from Malcolm.

"What is it, Mick?"

"Go be with your family, Victor. They need you."

He lays a hand on my shoulder. "You're family too."

What am I supposed to tell him—about O'Malley when he's dealing with his own problems? About Malcolm? There is too much he doesn't know, that he can't ever know.

"It's for me to deal with."

"Funny how that works. You want to fix everybody else's problems, but no one can help you with yours."

"It's not like that."

"Sure. Whatever you say."

"Look, I'm doing what's best for Dee." I choke on the words.

"Acting like a Class A dick is best for Dee?"

Shame layers onto guilt. "You think I want to hurt her? It's gutting me, but keeping my distance is for her own good."

"How?"

"There's some shit in my life that I don't want her anywhere close to."

Victor's look could drill holes. "Dee doesn't strike me as the kind of woman who wants some damn martyr protecting her."

"I'm not trying to be a martyr."

"Yeah, you keep telling yourself that."

"I'm done talking, Victor."

"You're done talking?" His laugh is mirthless. "You haven't said a goddamn thing."

"I have my reasons."

"You're a real case." He shoves me back. "I shouldn't have to remind you after everything you and Dee went through that making the choice for someone else will come back and bite you in your dumb ass."

His words slam into me with nuclear force.

But I can't heed them.

$\mathcal{D}ee$

THOUGH I'M PROBABLY THE LAST person Dwayde wants to see, I knock on his door. When there's no answer, I turn the knob and peek inside. Dwayde is sitting on the double bed, clumsily made, but attempted. He balances an open sketchbook on his bent knees, making short strokes with a pencil. Rufus is curled up into a plump ball, sleeping.

"May I come in?"

He spares me an unwelcoming glance. "I don't want to talk about them anymore."

"Then we won't."

"What do you want then?" His eyes narrow as if he thinks it's a trick.

"Just to check in before I go."

"I guess that's your job."

I would sigh over his cynicism if I didn't understand that he sees me as a lawyer in a suit trying to get information he doesn't want to give, rather than the woman in jeans that had played video games with him on Sunday.

"This is more than just a job to me." It had been from the start. "You're precious to the people I love. And we're family now."

For a moment, I have the pleasure of seeing his guard slip. "I guess you can come in."

"Thank you." I step inside and take a survey of his room. White California shutters contrast cobalt blue walls covered in basketball posters and a few hip-hop artists I vaguely recognize. A wooden dresser sits in one corner, cluttered on top with clothes, game consoles, and wires; a book shelf beside it holds more knickknacks and gadgets than books, and across from the bed is a drawing table with paints, drawing pencils, and the charcoal set I bought him.

"I like your space." It's bright and lived-in. Not impersonal and bare the way I'd kept mine at his age, wherever I happened to be. This is home.

Overlapping sketches are tacked onto a corkboard above his desk. I stroll over to get a closer look, awed by the talented finesse of such a young hand. Most are of Rufus and family members.

"These are great, Dwayde." I move the edge of one drawing to study a sketch of Papa T, lounging on the porch swing, a cigar in one hand, the laugh lines and peaceful expression captured perfectly. "When did you do this one?"

"Before he got sick."

"You must miss him," I say through a pang of grief.

"Yeah."

"It's so life-like. All the details."

"It came out okay." He shrugs, staying on the cautious route.

"It reminds me of the times I'd sit out there with him after dinner when the kitchen was cleaned and the dishes put away. Mama T couldn't stand the smell of cigars, but I didn't mind. I just liked being with him, you know? Hearing him talk...laugh. He had a great laugh. Loud and infectious."

Dwayde doesn't say anything, but when I turn back, I see the memories of the grandfather he loved reflected in his eyes. We have that bond in common. I walk over to the bed, sit on the edge of the mattress, and hold his gaze.

"When I ran away from Springvale, I thought that in time I would be able to put it all behind me. Start a new life and pretend the one I left never existed. I fought my mind to do it. But I couldn't, no matter how hard I tried. My past...my secrets...were always there like a poison spreading inside me." Driving me to binge, to seek comfort from the pain. "I didn't tell anyone. Not Jordyn or Lexie. Not any of the psychologists that tried to help. No one.

"And then when your Uncle Mick showed up wanting answers, even after all those years, I still wouldn't talk about it. I thought it would hurt too much to let all that poison out. But I was wrong. When I finally did—even though telling Mick and my family why I left was one of the hardest things I've ever done—I felt better for it. Free. The secrets couldn't hurt me anymore."

He stares back, his expression blocked and guarded. I hadn't expected him to spill his secrets. My intention was to plant the seed. "Well, I'll let you get back to your sketching." I pat the dog's head and rise. "You can call or text me anytime. Not just about the case. But for anything."

"Yeah, okay."

"Okay." I turn and walk to the door.

"Um...wait!"

I pause and pivot back around to see him climb to his feet. He takes the sketch of Papa T off the wall. "You can have this if you want."

"Really? I'd love that." I accept the drawing from him, then acting on impulse, lean in and kiss his cheek. "Thank you. It means so much to me."

"Yeah, aw'right." He shifts awkwardly. "See ya."

I hug the picture to my chest and exit the room. At the bottom of the stairs, Victor and Isabelle stand in the hallway, talking close, their voices hushed. Mick is nowhere to be seen, which means he's likely gone. I tuck away my feelings to deal with later.

At the sound of my footsteps, the couple turn their heads in my direction.

"How is Dwayde?" Isabelle asks when I reach them.

"He didn't want to talk, and I didn't want to push him again this soon."

"Better to give him some time," Victor agrees, even though that probably goes against his cop instincts to press for more; to get the confession. "What do you have there?" His chin lifts to indicate the paper I'm holding.

"Oh." I smile and show them the sketch. "I was admiring this and Dwayde gave it to me. It really captures Papa T, doesn't it?"

Victor looks at the drawing wistfully. "Every night after dinner, Papa had to have his cigar on that swing. Rain or shine. Remember when you tried a puff and almost choked to death?" He laughs then.

I join him, glad that we can find humor around the pain to enjoy the good and funny memories.

"Dwayde only shares his art with family," Isabelle says when our laughter fizzles. "He may not admit it, Dee, but he knows you're looking out for him. Thank you for being here." She gives me a heartfelt hug. "I'm going to take him up a snack. I'll leave you two to talk."

"I'll be up to see him shortly." Victor kisses his wife's forehead and walks me to the door. "So, what now?"

"We'll see if Jackson follows through on his threat. He'll have to act soon to get an emergency court date for their petition to be heard before the custody hearing. Meanwhile, we keep building our case. It's obvious that Dwayde knows more about the Franklins than he says. And it seems that whatever he remembers or whatever Joyce may have told him wouldn't present them in the best light."

"That's for damn sure. I think we've seen plenty that supports it."

"But you know that's not evidence." I carefully put the sketch inside my tote bag, sliding it between a notebook to keep the paper from getting wrinkled. "We can't accuse them of bad parenting or anything else without proof."

"The PI firm Calista hired hasn't turned up squat," he laments. "Not much of a surprise, I guess. The Franklins wield a lot of power in their community. People might be afraid to say anything that could cost them their status or livelihood."

"Or they really don't know anything." I think about Malcolm Peters and his abuse. How no one, not even Victor who was closest to Mick, had any idea about what was happening in that house. "People can be very good at keeping up a pretense."

"That's the truth. But what could these people have done or what could Joyce have told Dwayde they did that would make him afraid to tell us?"

"That's what we'll have to keep working through with Dwayde to find out."

"Yeah," he says, but there's a heaviness in his voice. Victor is tough and sturdy, the kind of person you can rely on, but this case has been hard on him.

"How are you holding up? Honestly."

He combs a hand over his spiked crew cut in a gesture that reminds me of Mick. "Most days I firmly believe no judge would take Dwayde away from us. But..." The stress lines around his dark eyes deepen. "There are times when I think, what if the system fails and these people that I don't trust for a minute get custody of my son? You heard Dwayde, he'll run. He'd be back on the streets before the ink dried on the paperwork."

"Stop." I put my hand on his forearm. "Don't even go there. The strength of our case is you and Isabelle, and the life you are giving him. He has a wonderful extended family. Friends. He's healthy, safe. Loved. He's thriving. Dr. Sass will confirm that. His teachers will confirm that. Your character witnesses will as well. While a judge will factor in the biological relationship with the Franklins, we will keep coming back to what Dwayde wants, and what's best for him. And that's clearly you."

"We work in the system, Dee. We know it's not perfect."

"It isn't always," I concede. "But I have confidence and faith in our case."

"That's not a guarantee."

I can't argue that, so I don't.

"Sometimes I wish I were more like Mick, "Victor says. "He's not constrained by rules and boundaries. Don't get me wrong, he's a good man, one of the best I know, but to him, the end justifies any means."

"That doesn't make it right, Victor."

"No, it doesn't. But he thinks it does."

"And that's all that matters to him." My voice catches.

"Hey..."

"I'm sorry. You don't need this right now."

He frowns at me. "You sound like Mick. I can deal with more than one thing at a time. What's going on?"

"I wish I knew."

Victor nods slightly. "He left to clear his head, but said he'd be back to see Dwayde. You got any ideas on what's got him all screwed up?"

"No. I really don't. His behavior changed yesterday morning between the time he went out for a jog and returned home."

"Did he get a call or text?"

"Your guess is as good as mine. But whatever it is, he's convinced himself that it's his problem to deal with alone."

"That's pretty much the same BS I got from him today."

"I don't know what to do. I told him I could handle anything. He doesn't have to shield me. But he's chosen to anyway."

"Mick will come around." His arms envelope me in a supportive embrace. "He loves you, Dee."

I wish I could believe that love would be enough. That it would conquer all. Because there's no doubt that Mick loves me madly... endlessly. The same way I love him. That's never been our issue. It was my secrets that had broken us before. And now I fear it will be his.

CHAPTER THIRTEEN

Micah

I GET BACK TO MY condo, pissed at life. Pissed at myself. I change into shorts, and going shirtless, take to my home gym. The first crack of leather sends the punching bag swinging on its chained hinges. Rapid jabs and uppercuts work me into a blistering sweat. Down my back, my chest, my face, burning my eyes. Can't stop.

I shouldn't have gone to Victor's today knowing she'd be there. I should never have gone to her house last night, either. I should have ignored her message and drank myself into a blind stupor. I knew what would happen. As soon as I walked up those steps and saw her beautiful face—eyes like spun gold, her sultry curves...

One kiss was all it had taken. Feeling selfish, greedy, out of control, without any thought to gentleness, I plunged inside her, hard and raw. The feeling was indescribable. Desperately reckless, I immersed myself in her scent, in the creamy give of her body, going as deep as I could get. I put my fingers in her mouth, watching her suck and roll them with her tongue. I had to claim her everywhere. Her ripe, round ass, her tight clenching pussy, that little pink kernel of flesh. I marked them all until she exploded around me. Her muscles contracting, her moans throaty and sexy, I'd come with all my might. Emptying myself, giving everything I had to give.

Except the truth.

She'd given me hers.

Nothing could ever drive or scare me away this time. I will face anything with you, Mick.

Lost, guilty, bursting with despair, I'd made love to her again and again. Each time more impassioned than the time before. I wanted to bury myself in her and stay there forever.

Hours later, Dee fell asleep draped over me. Her hair across my chest, her honey-colored skin soft and glistening; my golden angel. I tried to stay awake, but my body betrayed me. And then my mind. Malcolm's note, the memories—both manifested into another nightmare. I came out swinging. Broke Dee's lamp. It scared the hell out of me that my fists could have connected with her. No further warning required. I had to leave. I was too fucked up. The situation with Malcolm was too fucked up. I couldn't involve her. I couldn't stay.

I walked away from the woman who brings me so much joy, who gives me so much love.

Christ. Seeing her today, still bearing that sad confusion in her eyes burned through my chest. I could feel her pain radiating through me along with my own.

I'd been so stupid...so naïve to think the deal I'd made with Malcolm would be the end of it. Instead, he's like a vampire, sniffing out blood and coming back for more.

If there's one thing Malcolm preys on, it's weakness. My weakness. If he believes Dee matters to me, he will use her as a tool and a weapon. Knowing what he's capable of, I have to convince him that Dee means nothing to me. That my motivation is payback. It's ruthless, callous, it's what Malcolm understands.

Gasping for air, I stop and hug the punching bag until I can get hold of my breaths. As long as Malcolm thinks Dee isn't important to me, she'll be safe. Protecting her...protecting the people I love...that comes first. I pick up my phone and call Stiles.

"I need you to find someone."

"A missing person?"

"You could say that." I drag a towel over my face and neck.

"Whatcha got?"

"Her last known whereabouts are over three years old and even with that they're sketchy."

"What's the name?"

I might care about going to Hell for breaking Victor's trust if I weren't already there. "Elizabeth Joyce Franklin is her legal name. But she goes by Joyce. Though she could have aliases."

"Who is she?"

"Dwayde's biological mother. I think she might have information relevant to the custody case."

"What do you know about her?"

"She'd be twenty-eight now. Originally from Kentucky. Might have a Southern accent. Dwayde said they moved around a lot before coming to Chicago. She seemed to settle here the longest. She's an addict. From what Dwayde has described, she sold her body for money and drugs. The last place they were living at before Dwayde ran away from her was an apartment building near a tunnel. That's all I have."

"Not much. Got a description or any pictures?"

"Nothing current. Sending what I have." I pull up the photos on my phone that I'd saved from an earlier search.

"She was a kid," he says moments later.

"Fifteen. Into competitive horseback riding," I say, explaining the pictures from a local newspaper featuring the smiling girl with her ribbons and trophies. "At least she was before her horse died and she quit. She had Dwayde less than a year later. No listed father on the birth certificate. Her parents say they don't know who he is. But it's hard to know if that's the truth."

"What happened to her? Why did she leave Kentucky with Dwayde?"

"That's what I need to find out."

"So, what's the plan?"

"To locate her. But I don't want her tipped off about any info on Dwayde, my family, or the case." That's my one concession. "Just tell me where she is."

"If she's alive. If she can be found. If she's in any shape to give information. Those are big *ifs*," he echoes Victor's and Dee's warnings. "Are you sure you want to do this?"

I don't hesitate. "I'm sure."

CHAPTER FOURTEEN

Dee

DAY TWO WITHOUT MICK IS like trudging through a fog. Nothing seems clear. My movements are slow and labored. My heartbeat, dull and heavy. I have to push myself to get out the door.

At least at the office, I can escape the misery to concentrate on work. When I call Calista to update her, she says I sound as if I'm coming down with a cold. I wish it were something that liquids and Tylenol could cure.

By 6:00 p.m. I'm dragging. Lena clocks out and I should do the same. But I really don't want to go home to an empty house. I could call my friends, but then I'd have to tell them about Mick. I think of going to the gym, but it requires too much energy. I think of food, of greasy carbs and gobs of sugar.

Mostly, though, I think of Mick.

An hour later, when my mind can't process another report, I call to check up on Dwayde. Victor answers.

"Hey, Brat." He uses the old nickname he had for me. "How ya doing?"

"I'm…" I start to say *fine* because old habits die hard. The truth isn't always pleasant, but at least it's real. "I'm still at work trying to distract myself and not fall apart."

"You shouldn't be alone. Why don't you come by? We'll fix you something to eat."

"Thanks. But rain check, okay? I'm just not up for that tonight."

"We're here if you change your mind."

"Okay. How's Dwayde?"

"He's been unusually quiet. Withdrawn. But he perked up when Mick stopped by to lift his spirits with a marathon of sword fighting. Mick left not long ago."

"How did he seem?"

"Lost. And he looked like hell."

Hearing that fills me with a mix of emotions. On the one hand, it feeds my hope that Mick is struggling with our separation, yet on the other hand, I hate knowing he's as miserable as I am.

"I'm worried about him, Victor."

"I am too. He's not himself and still won't talk about what's eating him. He got agitated when I mentioned you. That's when he left."

Concern has me revealing a confidence Mick wouldn't appreciate me sharing. "He went to a bar."

"No, he wouldn't."

"He did. He told me. Two nights ago. He didn't drink, though," I assure him. "He walked away. But I'm afraid he might not the next time."

"I saw what he went through before he got sober. I don't believe he'll go there again."

Victor doesn't know about the abuse or the depth of Mick's guilt. He hasn't witnessed the nightmares. He hadn't seen that hopeless defeat in Mick's eyes. "I don't want to believe it's possible either. But he's an alcoholic, Victor. And his defenses are low right now."

"I'll talk to him, Dee. Keep an eye out."

"Thank you."

"I know I have no right to ask you this, but please don't give up on him. I still have faith that Mick will come to his senses."

The conversation with Victor leaves me drained. I pack up and shut off my emotions for a while as a matter of preserving my own recovery, and urge myself to the gym.

When I arrive home, it fills me with bittersweet relief to find that Mick's clothes still hang in the closet. His laptop still sits on the desk. The extra key card to his condo is still in a catchall tray on my dresser. It's painful to be around his things, but it would have been worse to find them gone.

I skip dinner, afraid that if I start eating, I won't stop. I shower and stay under the hot spray for a good half hour. I watch the news, without really listening, and I'm in bed before 11:00. Wearing one of Mick's

T-shirts, I curl up on his side of the sheets with my arms around his pillow and fall into a short, restless sleep.

DAY THREE BLOWS IN LIKE a chilly draft. Despite the mild October weather, I can't get warm. Through the layers of a turtleneck and blazer, I feel the cold in my bones.

Concentration is a painstaking endeavor. The lulls engulf me in sadness, but I fake composure and keep going.

Somehow, I make it through the hours, consuming more caffeine than I should. Arriving home that evening, I muster up the energy to dress for Lena's big night when what I really want is to collapse on my bed and sleep for a week. Maybe I'd wake up to find this was all a bad dream.

"HOLY SHIT!" JORDYN EXCLAIMS WHEN she peeks out the door.

Bernard tips his hat. The limo is visible at the curb.

"Bonjour, Mademoiselle Chase. Mr. Peters asked that I be at your service this evening."

Somewhere along the way, my gloom had morphed into anger. I have half a mind to send Bernard away. My friends and I already made plans to take an Uber after having wine and appetizers at my place. But spite won't make me feel any better, nor would it be fair to put Bernard in that position or deny Jordyn the excitement over our fancy ride.

"Thank you, Bernard. We'll be ready to leave in a few minutes."

"Take your time." He tips his hat again and returns to the limo to wait.

"Aw...that's so sweet of Mick," Lexie gushes with a smile that's covered in sugar and sprinkles. "What a thoughtful surprise."

I stifle the bitter snort rising in my throat. On the surface, Mick does look the part of a thoughtful boyfriend. Only I'm not even sure he's my boyfriend anymore. But I do know that the limo is merely a prettied up bodyguard detail. That adds to my anger. Mick won't talk to me and yet he's still protecting me. I don't get it. But I'm not going to let that ruin our evening.

My friends got all dressed up for a fun night out. Lexie in a black tulle miniskirt and platform ankle boots. Jordyn in tight leather pants, her short hair fashioned into a faux mohawk that looks great on her. The least I can do is keep a smile painted on my face. I'll tell them. Just not right now.

"Bernard is dashing in an ooh-la-la sort of way," Jordyn says with a bad French accent.

"Oh, please don't tell me you're going after him," Lexie says. "He's practically your father's age."

"Not quite." She laughs. "Besides, I have nothing against older men. But I much prefer a certain ex-military man. Must be all that badass testosterone 'cause just the thought of Stiles makes my thong wet."

"Ew." Lexie's nose wrinkles. "Can you not?"

"Just speaking the truth." Jord pops a cube of cheese into her mouth. "I want to do him sooo bad."

"Really, Jordyn. You've only seen the man once and barely exchanged more than a few words with him."

"I don't need words, Lex." She makes a sshing signal with her finger against her lips. "In fact, the less spoken the better...I just need his hard body."

"That's reverse sexism."

Jordyn rolls her eyes. "You seriously need to get laid by someone other than Dr. Missionary, then maybe you'd get that stick out of your ass. Unless you're into anal."

Lexie spits out her wine, choking on a gasp.

"I'm guessing not." Jord waggles her brows and grins. "Don't know what you're missing, chickie."

That's my cue to usher us out the door. The last thing I need is to think about what I'm missing with Mick. But avoiding those thoughts isn't possible. As soon as we slide into the limo, I'm right back to that night. I'm even wearing the same black dress. The one Mick peeled off to ravish my body. I grip the door handle where he'd bound my wrists and squirm against the heat of arousal pooling between my legs. I'm so angry with him and yet I can't stop wanting him with every aching beat of my heart.

THE ATOMIC FREEZE IS HOPPING when we arrive. Loud music blares through a sound system. Piercings, colorful hair, and tats are the norm. I'd paired my dress with knee-high boots and a silver choker, but in comparison to this crowd, my attire is super conservative.

People mill around the tables drinking, others are rocking out on the dance floor. Most of them, I'd say, are in their twenties to early thirties. It's not all that different from other clubs I've been to; people dancing, drinking, and having a good time. Despite the hollow pain in my chest, I plan to do the same.

While Lexie secures a spot for us near the stage, Jordyn and I fight our way to the bar. I place an order for three Crantinis and send a quick text to Lena.

Me: *Break a leg!*

Lena: *I'm terrified.*

Me: *Deep breaths. You've got this.*

Lena: *Glad you're here.*

Me: *Me too. Can't wait.*

As I put my phone away, Jordyn tugs on my arm.

"What?" I lean close and yell over the music.

"My hormones might have me hallucinating..." she speaks loudly next to my ear, "but I think I see the man of my wet dreams behind you."

"Who?"

"Stiles. Who else?"

No! My head spins in that direction. My blood rages. Damn Mick. It is Stiles. We hold eye contact. His stare is indecipherable. I'm sure he can read in mine that I'm pissed.

"Oooh." Jordyn jostles me. "He's looking at us." She sends him a rolling finger wave.

Stiles doesn't respond.

"Did you see his reaction?" she asks with more enthusiasm than is warranted.

"He ignored you."

"No, he *pretended* to ignore me."

"Lay off," I snap. "He's on duty so just leave him alone."

"Whoa." Her eyes are probing and full of concern. "What just happened?"

I'm incensed that Mick would send Stiles inside to watch over me— by him exerting his control while still keeping his distance. But that's not on Jordyn.

"Sorry, that was uncalled for. I'll tell you about it later. I want to enjoy the rest of the night without thinking about bodyguards or anything else."

She quickly sets aside her own confusion and slings an arm around me. "I'm your girl for that. We'll party hard and forget all about Tall and Tempting."

A nearly impossible task, but I appreciate the sentiment. Since Lexie hasn't met Stiles she's oblivious to the man sticking close like a guardian shadow, his demeanor markedly vigilant.

When Frankie's Brides take to the stage, my mind disengages and I scream for Lena. Punk rock isn't my kind of music, but their energy is on fire and the crowd's frenzy is contagious. The lead singer in a dark veil has a great raspy voice and her interactive style is entertaining. But it's Lena with her extra spiky mohawk, dressed in a grunge satin gown and long fingerless gloves who steals the show. Her drum solo is mind-blowing. She's seriously badass and the audience eats it up. I couldn't be happier for her.

We stay until after the band completes their set to have a celebratory drink. Lena's sailing on a high. I give her hugs and praise. She introduces us to all four of the female members of Frankie's Brides and to her partner of six months, Adam. I'd briefly met him once when he'd picked her up at work but she talks about him a lot. They are adorable together. Affectionate and really into each other. I'd be lying if I said I wasn't feeling a little envious.

Before the headliner comes on, we say our good-byes and we're back in the limo by ten-thirty. Without much food absorption, that last Crantini hits my system with more impact than it should. The interior of the limo sways briefly then stops, my world comes back into focus. My problems, still there.

"That was actually fun," Lexie says as Bernard pulls away from the club. "It's still early. We could stop off at a bar or another club, if you two feel up to it."

"Sorry. Count me out." I uncap a bottle of water for a sip. "But you guys go for it. Use the limo."

"You're not feeling well?" Lexie looks at me. "You didn't have that much to drink."

"It's not that."

"It was seeing Stiles at the club," Jordyn puts in.

"That was Stiles?!" Lexie exclaims. "The big, bald guy with the goatee that I saw near you the entire night?"

"Yes." I nod.

"Why would you be upset about seeing Stiles?"

"Because…" My frustration mounting once again, I blurt out: "I don't get why Mick is still protecting me from the press if he's dumped me."

Jordyn's face contorts into a what-the-hell-are-you talking-about expression and Lexie's tone is equally incredulous.

"What do you mean Mick dumped you?" Lexie asks.

"I mean he ended things, kicked me to the curb, ripped out my heart... whatever euphemism you want to use. He walked out on me."

"That bastard!" Jordyn fumes. "I'm going to kick his ass sideways."

I don't doubt her, which has me saying: "Please don't say anything to Mick. Papa's Kids is a great opportunity for your career."

"You think a project is more important to me than our friendship?"

"Of course not. It's just that I don't want you going off on him and jeopardizing the work."

"Hold on..." Lexie interjects, visibly struggling to comprehend. "This is Mick we're talking about. I've never seen a man more in love. This doesn't make sense, Dee."

"No, it doesn't." I slump against the seat, exhausted from it all. "On Monday, we were planning a future and on Tuesday night he just walks out. Something happened that he won't tell me about. He won't tell Victor either."

Jordyn's hazel eyes spark and she raises one hand, her palm facing outward. "Wait...he walked out and wouldn't tell you why?"

"Pretty much. He said it was his problem to deal with and that I don't deserve any of it."

"Aw, babe..." Jordyn consoles and scoots over to slide an arm around me. "Why didn't you tell us this before?"

"I didn't want to say the words out loud. I didn't want to openly deal with the hurt or talk about it. I didn't want to ruin our night."

"You don't have to do this alone." Lexie draws closer too and puts her hand in mine. "We're always here for you."

"I know. He hasn't picked up any of his stuff. So, I just keep waiting... hoping he'll call or show up. That he'll decide to let me in."

"Why are you waiting?" Jordyn tilts her head up at me.

"He left, Jord."

"Yeah, 'cause he's being a protective jerk. He said you don't deserve this. That's not an I-don't-want-you-anymore breakup. That's some I'm-Tarzan-you-Jane crap."

"I know that. But it doesn't change the fact that he's chosen to shut me out."

"So..." She shrugs. "Don't let him."

Jordyn's words, given simply, smack me like a two-by-four. I've been so caught up in feeling rejected, in being afraid to risk my heart further, that I'd crawled back into my shell.

Mick is a protector, a fixer. He tries to control everything, including what he thinks is best for me. And I've been letting him. We're supposed to be in a relationship. We're supposed to be in this together. How can he believe me when I say I can face anything with him when I haven't shown any attempt to do that? I let him walk out the other night. I haven't tried to contact him. I told him to fight for us, but I haven't fought for him.

My resolve gathering steam, I sit up straighter, taller, surer.

"You're right, Jord." I need to do this for Mick as much as for myself. "I'm going to see him tonight and demand answers."

CHAPTER FIFTEEN

Micah

11:09 P.M. IT'S FITTING I SUPPOSE that he's late. Malcolm had made me sweat it out often enough when I was a kid. Rarely had he lost his cool or got stinking drunk and started beating on me. His brand of punishment was calculated, controlled...the slow removal of his belt...the tap of leather on his palm. He got off on building up the anticipation, the fear. He got off on the power. That had to be why he'd chosen to become a cop. Unlike Victor, he wasn't driven to serve and protect.

I long ago stopped wondering what was inside him that drove him to hate, to violence, to destroy anything good or decent. His thwarted dreams and the alcohol didn't cause it. They were just poor excuses. I know because I'd used them to justify my own behavior. Drinking, worrying my family, screwing girls I didn't know or care to know. Acting like a self-indulgent prick, blaming Dee, blaming it on not going to NYU—because I depended on a bottle of Jack to get me through each day.

At 11:23 my cell phone rings. Connected to the security system, I'm alerted that the call is coming from the lobby.

"Mr. Peters, it's Simon from the front desk. Your father is here."

My *father*. What a joke. He wasn't that in any meaningful way. Yet he liked to boast about it. The consolation prize for not making the NBA himself was being the father of someone who had. He'd made sure of that.

"Send him up."

Minutes later there's a knock on my door. I unlock the clench of my back teeth and answer with calm intent. "Malcolm."

"Hello, *son*." He drags out the taunt with a drawl, and removes his baseball cap marked Sheriff across the front.

At fifty-two, he's still commanding with his large brawny frame. A few sprinkles of gray are threaded through his straight brown hair and faint spidery lines fan out the callous slate of his eyes.

Other than our comparable heights, there's not much physical resemblance between us. I got my bronze complexion and black wavy hair from my Brazilian mother, who came from a mix of European and African ancestries. She was proud of her rich heritage, but he would tear her down by calling her a mongrel. Hatred heats my insides. I can't stand that he's here. Can't stand that I have to spend one second in his presence.

Upon entering the penthouse, he sweeps the area with hard, piercing eyes, trained to scope out an unfamiliar situation. Then another slower study as if taking in the details of the soaring ceilings, the bamboo flooring, the vast expanse of space.

"Must be hard to hate me when you've got all this."

"Not hard at all."

"Humph." He walks into the living room where the view of the city spreads out in front of him. The paper bag in his hand makes me leery. "How much did this place set you back?"

"What do you want, Malcolm?"

"What's the rush?" He turns to me with a conniving grin.

"You've got five minutes."

"Relax, *son*. Let's have a drink."

"I don't drink."

"Kept that up, did you?" He waltzes into the kitchen as if he owns the place, drops his cap on the counter, and brandishes a bottle of Irish whiskey from the paper bag. Then removing his jacket, he drapes it around the back of a stool—revealing his gun strapped into a waist holster—and starts pulling open my cupboards in search of glasses.

I don't give him the satisfaction of seeing my inner rage.

He selects two tumblers, screws off the bottle cap, and generously fills each one. "A toast." He hands me a glass.

The urge is there, but I breathe the liquor in and cross my arms over my chest.

Amused by my refusal, he smirks and lifts the tumbler into the air. "To new deals."

"You want more money, is that it?"

"The money's been okay." He shrugs as if a two million-dollar house and the monthly installments that my lawyer funnels into his bank account are chump change. "Got me a new Cadillac. Not as fancy as your cars, but it'll do. What a waste that you pissed all your opportunity away to help street trash. But you always were too sensitive. Too much of a pussy. That was your mother's fault."

"Don't say another fucking word about her."

He leans his face into mine. "Or what, son?"

"Try me and you'll find out."

"Still a protective son of bitch." He laughs, but backs away and takes a seat on one of the stools.

I remain standing.

"Heard the Chase girl was back in Springvale."

When I don't react, he provokes some more. "Dropped you and the Torreses like a sack of rotten potatoes and here you are welcoming her back. Pitiful. The whole town's talking about her return like she's the second coming."

"What do you care that she's back?"

"Stupid question." His top lip curls. "You care."

"Not particularly."

"Right," he mocks. "You couldn't even sell that shit to O'Malley."

I keep my face neutral, not giving away that I'm privy to their contact.

"Been calling me ever since you quit the NBA. Thinks he's onto some story. Wanted to know why you really left, how did I feel about it, he asked shit about our relationship, wanted to know why you don't ever talk about me, why you act like I don't exist. Why you treated Cayo like he was your fucking father." Revved up, he lifts the glass to his mouth in triple time, sucking back the liquor.

"He kept sniffing around. I blew him off but then you fueled him. Starting up that piece of garbage, Papa's Kids. All for Cayo when he was dead and buried. Like he was some fucking hero. Then using your fists on O'Malley. In public. He wasn't going to let up after that. You poured gasoline on a burning flame, boy. But your stupidity turned into a prize for me.

"When he last called, I was about to give him the brush-off again. Then he started talking about you being at this party, slobbering over some woman that went against your type. He asked if I knew her, and why you were being so damn secretive and protective. 'Course he couldn't know why you would choose *her* when you had models sucking your dick. But I knew. Knew you never got over her."

I strive for control.

"I figured when you quit the Heat and left Miami it was because you found out she was here. Checked it out and realized you had no clue, otherwise you never would have stayed away."

That catches my attention and something in my face must betray me.

"You didn't think I knew she was here before now? Shit, boy, I've known for years." He revels in the confession. "You and Cayo going to Amherst looking for her, hiring a private investigator...made me laugh. Cayo thought I could help, being the sheriff and all. Like hell I would. I found her myself within a few weeks of her dumping your sorry ass and leaving town. She was right here in Chicago. But I sent your guy on a wild goose chase with phony leads. 'Course he never turned up anything. Meanwhile she was only a couple of hours away the whole time. Easy to keep my eye on her.

"But I couldn't figure out why she ran off to live in some shitbox, working a couple of jobs. Didn't make a scrap of sense. Not at first. But as time went on, oh, it became clear as day."

His fingers clutch the glass as he tilts it back for another drink. "Guess you didn't know she was knocked up."

I feel my jaw muscle pulsing like a ticking bomb.

"Ah, but you know now. That's why she ran. Belly was out to here." He gestures with his hand several inches from his stomach. "Must have been about five, six months along. Her running was the best thing. A baby was not in my plans, son. You would have thrown it all away for a fat ass and big tits...to be some two-bit writer and have a house full of idiot rugrats."

His insults of Dee are bad enough, but hearing that he had known where she was right from the start, I have to lock my arms at my sides to keep from wrapping my bare hands around his throat. He had watched Dee trying to make ends meet, holding down two jobs. He let her struggle alone, all while carrying my child. I can barely keep my emotions quiet, barely contain my utter urge to kill him.

"Guess she didn't want the goody-two-shoes Torreses to find out she was fucking their golden boy. So, she took off without telling anyone. While you were drinking and crying yourself to sleep, she was going to have your kid. Then she must have lost it 'cause when I saw her again about a month later, no more baby belly. Poof. Gone."

Scalding fury boils in my chest.

"Am I upsetting you, boy?" He studies me. "You look a little piqued."

"Where is this going, Malcolm?"

"I'm getting there. Tell me…" one hand spins his glass in a slow circle. "Did she give you some sob story when you found her? Or maybe she's the one who came to you. *I was pregnant and scared. I'm so sorry for leaving, but I didn't know what to do,*" he imitates in a high voice. "Did she tell you she never got over you either? I bet she did. You're worth millions. She's a smart cookie. I bet you ate it out of her hand like a good little lap dog.

"You see, I know you so well, son." He drains the tumbler, his eyes glittering with evil glee. "I figure I have a few more years before I'm ready to retire. My 401k and pension aren't going to cut it for me. I might want to get me one of these highfalutin places, travel, live the good life I could have had if not for you. I'm thinking five mil for now. That's a drop in the bucket. You're rolling in it, thanks to me."

"You expect me to give you five million dollars?"

"Plus, any extras I might need here and there."

"Why would I do that?"

"For her."

A cold blade slices down my spine. "You're playing with a losing hand. I'm done with Dee."

"No way in hell." He starts in on the other glass.

"Payback is a bitch." I force my mouth into a self-satisfied smile. "I used her and now it's over."

"Nah. You don't have it in you. Whatever your game, it's only to protect her."

"You're wasting my time. Dee isn't my problem. We're through here."

"We're not through by a long shot." He lifts the tumbler to his mouth again and I fist my hands to stop myself from smashing it into his face.

"Did you think I'd buy that load of shit? Christ, boy, you are dumb. After O'Malley gave me the goods, I drove by her house a few times. Thought I'd find your car in the driveway. Thought I'd make my move when I did. But I got better. You were mowing her fucking lawn, raking her leaves. No man does that for revenge pussy.

"Catching you play house, I decided to bide my time. Let you believe there was a real future between you two. That only makes this sweeter 'cause I'll never let you have her. I'll destroy her before that ever happens.

"You see, I got the 4-1-1 on Deeana Rae Chase. A father who didn't stick around, a mother that sent her away to foster homes before she finally offed herself. Imagine what O'Malley could do with all that? I'm sure you have, that's why you've been keeping her hidden.

"But I got O'Malley just where I want him. He won't be printing anything more about you, unless I say so. And I got lots I could say. Like about her screwed up life, her pregnancy, the way she left you and her own foster family without a fucking care. Now she's back with dollar signs in her eyes. I could play up the gold-digging angle. The public would love that. Of course, you'd be out there denying it, defending her, which will only amp up the story's value and make you look more like a lovesick fool. Hell, I could make five mil off this alone. It would be a best seller. Better than any drivel you could ever write."

My restraint breaks. I'm on him before I can think. Bringing both of us and the stool crashing to the kitchen floor, my fist connects with his face. He grunts. I hit him again, like a hammer to his jaw; feel my knuckles explode. He strikes back, missing. I lay another one into his gut and scramble to my feet. He jumps up swinging, but quicker, I duck and retaliate with an uppercut to the chin that has his head snapping back. He recovers and rushes me, his fists ramming into my ribs. The hits steal my breaths, but he's no match for my strength, fury, or adrenaline.

I shove him hard and land a roundoff kick to his gut that has him doubling over. Rage pumps off me and my mind stays in that dark place where I don't care about the consequences. With the advantage, I smash him into the wall, bringing my knee up and into his balls with sharp, rapid force. He wheezes in pain and my hands go around his throat, my grip tight. His face reddens, his eyes water and bulge in their sockets.

"You go near Dee...you go to O'Malley, you do anything to hurt her, and I will finish you." Slowly, reluctantly, I release my grip and pull away from him.

His windpipe clearing, he slumps against the wall, hacking out coughs. His jaw is marked with the promise of a large bruise, and blood seeps out of a gash across his cheek. He withdraws the gun and aims at my chest.

It's not the first time. But I'm not afraid.

"Walk away, Malcolm, before one of us ends up dead." I give him my back and go to the door, bearing the ache in my ribs. I yank it open and turn to him.

He eyes me like a wolf readying for another attack. A combination of pride and fury must have him burning to pull the trigger. But killing me in my own condo, when I'm too far away for it to be self-defense, would be a messy business even for Sheriff Peters to explain.

Common sense rules. He finally lowers the gun and holsters it again. Then ambling over to the counter, he takes a long swallow of whiskey, grabs his jacket and hat—leaving the bottle behind—and walks toward the door. He stops in front of me, his eyes like black lances, his sneer vicious. He slides on his cap, lowering the brim to cover his injured face.

"That little stunt just cost you another five. I want ten mil in my account by next Friday. And stay away from the girl or I will ruin her. And if either of us ends up dead, it will be fucking worth it."

CHAPTER SIXTEEN

Dee

WHEN BERNARD PULLS UP TO my house, my friends see me off with good luck hugs. On a mission, I go inside and straight to the bedroom. I retrieve the extra key card to Mick's condo.

While a surprise visit isn't exactly fair, that's too bad. If he'd just been open and honest with me in the first place, I wouldn't be about to head back to the city in the middle of the night like some clichéd version of a ditched girlfriend who can't take a hint.

The talk with Lex and Jord had sobered me right up. Still, to be on the safe side, I call an Uber. Minutes later I see on my phone that the blue Honda has arrived.

In a rush, I pull open the door and hit a wall. That's what running into Stiles feels like. I stumble and he catches my arm. What the hell? I hadn't counted on him still being here after Bernard dropped me home for the evening.

"There's a man parked outside. He says he's your Uber driver."

I prickle at his intrusion. "You spoke to him?"

"That's my job."

"Well, your job sucks."

"Sometimes it does."

If he's making a joke, it doesn't show in his one-note expression.

"As you can see there's no press around, I don't need a bodyguard."

"You'll have to take that up with Mr. Peters."

"Oh, I intend to."

I lock up and step around him. He doesn't try to stop me. I get into the Honda, irritated that he will probably call Mick to head me off at the pass. But the key card in my purse is insurance that Mick can't avoid me. I stew the entire drive to the Gold Coast address.

When the driver pulls up to the front, I thank him and turn to find someone opening the back door. Stiles. I ignore the hand he extends. I get that he's just doing his job, but I'm not in any mood to be gracious to someone aiding and abetting Mick's protection of me.

Securing the clutch beneath my arm, I climb out and notice the doorman from the night of the storm.

"Good evening." He smiles, recognition dawning on him as well. "It's nice to see you again. Better weather this time."

"Yes, it is." I return his smile.

"I'm George."

"I'm Dee."

Stiles glowers as if I had just divulged national secrets.

"I'll ring Mr. Peters for you."

"That won't be necessary, George." I flash the card from my purse. "I'll show myself up," I add before Stiles tries to accompany me.

Micah

WHISKEY WAS NEVER MY DRINK. Yet sitting in my darkened living room, slouched on the couch with the bottle in my hand, I intend to get drunk enough for the taste not to matter.

I know better. I know it's nothing more than an escape, a crutch, a one-way trip to Hell. And I don't give a damn.

Malcolm had given me my first glass of whiskey before I was Dwayde's age. I remember the fast burn down my throat and the way I'd gagged and my eyes teared up. He'd called me a pussy and made me drink the whole thing. I remember that the harsh bitterness eventually mellowed out and warmed my belly. Mostly, I remember the gratifying sense of numbness.

Nevertheless, when I began drinking in my teens, I stayed away from whiskey and most of the hard stuff at first, thinking that would make me less like my old man. I believed in tainted blood and the sins of the father. But could never quite reconcile that when I met Dwayde and started up Papa's Kids. Those boys had come through horrors worse than mine, yet they had so much good in them.

I rationalized that all the bad I had gotten from Malcolm must have been diluted by the decency and compassion of my mother for the first eight years of my life and by the Torreses after that. But it didn't change what was in me.

I flex my knuckles where the skin is split and swollen. It's the first time I'd ever hit him. Wasn't nearly as satisfying as I'd expected it to be. I contemplate the alcohol. Studying it like a fucking book when what I want is to get drunk enough for the thoughts to stop. I'd already made my decision. There is no price I wouldn't pay to protect Dee. Money's the easy part. Living without her...Christ! But that was a problem for tomorrow. As for tonight, I'm going to drown out my bleak future in the rest of this Jameson.

CHAPTER SEVENTEEN

Dee

AS SOON AS I GET off the elevator, my determined steps slow to a halt. My momentum lost to stunned surprise. There's a woman outside Mick's door. I recall her immediately as the same strawberry-blonde who had shown up at his place the last time I was here. Lisa. She's not easy to forget.

Her attire then had been a tight, cropped tank with jean cutoffs. Tonight, it's a silk kimono that stops short at her crotch, showing off tanned, toned legs. Her toes, encased in high-heeled slippers, are painted to match her boosted lips. Glossy bloodred.

She stares a moment longer before she slips on her bitch face and regards me in the way of a high school mean girl. A look I remember well. My instinct is to flee as my teenage self had done many times. But I refuse to give in to the feeling of being that scared, fat girl hiding in the back stairwell.

Proving I'm past that, I make the walk forward under the scrutiny of her judgey blue eyes.

"Mick's neighbor, right?" I resist tugging at my dress. "Liza."

"It's Lisa." She smirks. "And you are?"

"Here to see Mick."

"Oh, this is awkward."

When I don't take the bait, Lisa gives her hair a little flick and leans in, giving me a whiff of cloyingly sweet perfume. "I'm not usually one to kiss and tell, but woman-to-woman, I'm lucky I can still walk."

My smile is indulgent. "I don't know which is sadder, your repeated attempts to get Mick's attention or your ridiculous effort to make me jealous."

"No, honey…" Her tone turns nasty. "What's sad is you coming here in that cheap dress thinking Micky could really be into someone like you."

Her insult lands a perfect blow to my psyche. I struggle for composure and search for something to say, but I've never been good in these situations with witty comebacks. All I can manage in hanging on to my dignity is to move around her and wave the card in front of the key pad. The indicator turns green and I open the door. Thankfully the alarm isn't set.

I step inside and turn back to her. "Good night, Lisa," I say sweetly and have the supreme pleasure of closing the door on her shocked red pout.

Ohmigod. I lean against the door. I'd actually toppled a mean girl for the first time in my life. And it feels freaking amazing. I would do a happy dance except I'm well aware of why I'm here. Mick and his secrets.

I step out of the foyer, activating the motion lighting. An open-concept boasts a spacious living room and an impressive view of the skyline all lit up and sparkling. The condo is quiet, but I sense he's home.

My heels click-click forward on the hardwood. I peer into the kitchen. My eyes widen, my pulse jumps. A bar stool lies on its side as if it had been knocked over. Two tumblers sit on the kitchen counter. One empty, the other nearly the same. My anxiety picks up speed. I look for the bottle and find it in the trash. Jameson Irish Whiskey. Also empty.

Panic whacks at my chest. I hasten down the hallway until I reach Mick's bedroom. His bed is neatly made but his discarded clothes lay on the floor outside the en suite bathroom. I catch a glimpse of red on his light-colored shirt. Like a big smear of lipstick. The shower is running. I feel like I'm going to be sick.

With the door to the bathroom open, I see Mick through the walk-in glass enclosure. His eyes are closed, his head is tilted back under the spray. Water cascades over him, running down his face and throat to the defined muscles of his pecs, gliding along his washboard abs and the thick heaviness of his cock.

My emotions riot against my body's instinctual response to seeing him so intimately after nearly a week apart. It brings home how insanely

I love him, miss him, need him, want him. But the red on his shirt, the whiskey, the two glasses, Lisa…

I'd assumed she was coming over with plans of seduction. Maybe she really had been leaving. Visions of them flash through my head—drinking, flirting, Mick fucking her picture-perfect body on the kitchen counter. Her lipstick staining his shirt, the stool getting knocked over as he drives into her hard, the way he likes it.

I'm lucky I can still walk.

No. No. No. I shake off the images. Shake off her words. Lisa had to be lying. There has to be another explanation.

Mick turns around, giving me his broad back and muscular ass. He shuts off the water. I watch him slide his hand over his wet hair, slicking back the waves before he opens the shower door.

Steam follows his exit. He reaches for a towel, then facing where I stand on the threshold, his eyes do a double take. Then darken with anger.

"How did you get in here?"

"I used your spare key."

"You shouldn't have." His drying motions are quick and agitated. But he looks stone-cold sober.

"There are two glasses in the kitchen and I found an empty bottle of whiskey in the trash. A bar stool is lying on your kitchen floor and there's a red stain on your sweater. Explain that to me."

"No," he snaps and wraps the towel around his waist, tucking in the end.

"Have you been drinking?"

"What I do is no longer your concern."

The flash of my ring still on his finger says otherwise.

"Lisa was outside your door when I got here. She insinuated that you two had sex."

His eyes shoot fire, but his response remains cool and indifferent. "Again, not your concern."

Dismissing the words, I pay attention to my gut, to what it tells me about the man I know beneath this coarsened stranger. "I don't believe Lisa. I don't believe you would or could have done that. And you know why?" I rush on before he can respond with another slap of apathy. "Because I trust you. As stupid and gullible as that sounds, I do. You have lied to me, kept secrets, evaded, avoided, pushed me away…and still my trust in you hasn't shaken."

Micah

I'D SPENT THE LAST HALF hour resisting the urge to drink. I tossed the whiskey down the sink and tried to wash the stench of Malcolm and the guilt off me. I tried to put Dee out of my mind. Now here she is. My voluptuous beauty in that sexy black dress, her wild curls a perfect frame for her dazzling eyes. I want so badly to run my fingers through her hair, to wrap the spiral strands around my fist and angle her head back. Kiss those lush pink lips, taste the delicate skin on her neck, feel the trip of her pulse.

All the willpower I had built up earlier is cracking under her nearness, her love, her unwavering faith. After everything she's witnessed, after everything I've said and haven't said, Dee still believes in me. But I have to be strong. Selfless. For once, I have to do the right thing for her.

Get this over and done. Quickly with total detachment—like ripping off a Band-Aid. The pain is a serious fucker, but at least the wound is freed, out in the open to eventually heal.

I take a deep breath, swallow, and look into her eyes. Big mistake. I battle to leash my emotions and make my voice clipped and controlled. "There is no us. Not anymore."

"Is that right?" Her sarcasm tells me she doesn't buy it for a second. "You want me to believe that you entangled us all up into owning a house together and into sharing a bank account, only to dump me a day later."

"Poor timing, I admit. But things change. I don't care about the money or the house. They're yours."

"I don't want your guilt money. I want answers."

"The reasons are my own. You'll have to accept that."

"Well, I don't. I saw Stiles at the club and at my house tonight. That's not in keeping with the usual low-key security discretion. What's changed?"

"That's not your concern either."

"Screw you." Her chin lifts in stubborn defiance.

God, I love that spunk, but not right now.

"What happened on Tuesday morning while you were out jogging? Did you get a call...a text...an email? Who contacted you?"

"Jesus, will you stop?" She was getting too damned close. "Just go home, Dee."

"Not until you talk to me. I know you, Mick. This isn't you."

"You don't know me."

"Maybe part of that is true because you only share pieces of yourself. But what I do know without an ounce of doubt is that you still want me."

Like an asshole, I drag my eyes up and down her body. "Is that what you came here for? To get fucked?"

"You're deliberately trying to hurt me."

"I'm pointing out the reality. I could be inside of you in two seconds flat, but it won't change the outcome. We did this dance the other night and we're still in the same place."

Livid—I can see the flames in her eyes, feel the anger like steam scorching off her. She abruptly pivots on her high-heeled boots. Both relief and dread fill me that she's going. Only Dee had come here with too much fire and grit for that. She stops at my discarded clothes, picks up my shirt, flicking it out and inspects the stain. "This looks like blood."

"Goddammit." I reach her and snatch the garment away.

Her anger turns to alarm. She runs her hands over my chest, my sore ribs. "Where are you hurt?"

The feel of her hands on my bare skin is too much. I grip her wrists, but in doing so, she notices my torn knuckles.

"You were in a fight. That's someone else's blood."

"Enough!"

"Who was here?"

"Christ." I shake her shoulders. "Leave it alone. I'm not hurt. I wasn't in a fight. There's nothing here for you to concern yourself with. Just go." I release her while I still can.

"I'm not leaving." She wraps her arms around my waist. Her breath, soft warm puffs on my skin. "Talk to me. Whatever it is, we can deal with it together. But I can't take the secrets."

If I tell her, she'll risk Malcolm. Then what? He'd follow through on this threat. Maybe worse. His wrath is unpredictable. We wouldn't see its full extent until it blew up in our faces. I hadn't protected my mother from him. But I sure as hell can protect Dee. *Rip the Band-Aid off.*

I put my hands on her arms and lift them away from me. "It's over, Dee. We. Are. Over."

"After all we've been through." Her eyes go glassy with tears. "You're just going to throw it away because of some misguided sense of protection? I did that to you, Mick. I took away your choice to decide about me and the baby. We both paid for that. Don't make my mistakes. Don't make the decision for me."

A bullet couldn't land with deadlier force. But I absorb the explosion in my chest and stick with the plan. Not just ripping off the Band-Aid, I remove the ring she'd given me and extend it to her, slicing open a new wound and tearing us apart.

"The decision is made, Dee. Don't come here again."

The raw pain on her face is excruciating to witness. But I don't deserve to look away. Dee breaks eye contact first. On a tragic sniffle, she turns, and without taking the ring, walks out of my bedroom. Out of my life.

I listen to the staccato click of her heels resound through the condo. When she gets to the front door, the alarm sensor beeps as it opens then closes. Finally, silence. The quiet is haunting. I have to grab the edge of the dresser to keep myself from going after her.

As I stand there in a towel, holding her ring in my palm, with all the shit of the night whirling through my head, there's one jarring question that reverberates the loudest: if I'd just done the right thing, why does it feel so fucking wrong?

CHAPTER EIGHTEEN

Dee

THE TEARS FALL, SPILLING DOWN my cheeks, running off my chin. I know some of how Mick must feel. As if he's drowning; the secret a lead weight, pulling him further underwater, the truth a lifeline that seems too far, too daunting to reach.

I also know, it's not an excuse for hurting someone you love.

When the elevator glides to a stop, I swipe at my wet face and exit into the lobby. I lower my head past the front desk staff and make it to the door.

"Ms. Chase?"

I look up to see Stiles, broad and looming. He can't miss what surely must be my reddened eyes and the mascara tracks staining my cheeks. For a moment, I think his gaze softens with compassion. But it's gone just as fast, returning him to Robocop.

"Mr. Peters asked that I see to getting you home safely."

Of course he did. That's what Mick does, takes care of everything. But I don't have the energy to argue or any desire to wait for an Uber.

George holds the door. Trained to be discreet, he pretends not to notice my state and bids me a goodnight. I manage a faint smile as Stiles ushers me by. I get into the back seat of his SUV, and don't attempt any conversation. To be expected, neither does he.

I mumble a thank you after we reach my house and Stiles walks me to the porch. Jordyn's car is in the driveway behind mine, and she's waiting for me at the door, which can only mean one thing.

"Mick called you?"

"Yes." She hugs me tight, her oversize sweatshirt smells of men's cologne.

"Sorry. He shouldn't have interrupted your night."

"Don't be silly." She actually blows a kiss to Stiles over my shoulder before she closes and locks the door. "It was skanky of me to hook up with Eduardo," she says of her long-time friend with benefits. "I was thinking about someone else the entire time. But enough about me. How are you?"

"About as good as I look."

"For what it's worth, Mick sounded wrecked. I didn't even have the heart to blast him. Though I did manage to get in a few choice words."

"You didn't?"

"Never mind that." She air-flaps her hand. "He asked me to check on you. I would have called, but I knew you'd just say you were fine."

"Love you, Jord." I hug her again.

"Love you too, chickie. Wanna talk about it?"

I set my purse down on the foyer table and pull off my boots. "It couldn't have gone any worse. When I arrived, Lisa—the neighbor I told you about—was outside his door."

"What?" Jordyn follows me into the kitchen.

"Yep. Want some tea? I'm going to make chamomile. Hopefully it will help me sleep."

"Sure. I'll make it, though. You sit."

"Thanks. Let me get out of this dress first. Lisa called it cheap."

"Jealous be-atch."

I laugh for the first time in what seems like forever. Jordyn can always do that for me. "I'll be right back."

I go into my bedroom and text a message to Mick.

I know you didn't mean the things you said. You're hurting too. Please don't let whatever it is make you start drinking again. You have worked too long and hard on your sobriety to give it up for anything or anyone. I love you. Always.

I power off the phone and toss it onto the dresser. Otherwise, I'll check it every minute awaiting a response that isn't about to come. I change into pajama bottoms and one of his shirts. I'll have to stop doing that—eventually. After I wash my face, I go back into the kitchen and take a seat across the table from Jordyn.

"So, what happened tonight?" she asks as I nestle the warm mug between my palms. "You said the neighbor was there. What did she want?"

"Mick," I say wryly. "She pretended to be embarrassed for me while she eagerly confided to having sex with him."

Jordyn's eyes round. "Did you believe her?"

"No. I mean, yes, for one brief moment after I got inside. There were two glasses on the counter and an empty bottle of whiskey in the trash. Mick's clothes were on the floor outside the bathroom. His shirt had a red stain that looked like lipstick and he was in the shower."

"Holy shit! I would have struck first and asked questions later."

"I might have too. But I jumped to conclusions when I saw Mick with a girl all those years ago. That had devastating consequences. I wasn't going to do that again, no matter how damning the picture appeared. I just couldn't see Mick doing that. I had to give him an opportunity to explain."

"Sure, I get that. What did he say?"

"Nothing."

"Are you kidding me?"

"I laid it all out and his only response was that it wasn't my concern."

"Was he drunk?"

"Not from what I could tell."

"Maybe Mick is good at covering up the signs."

"Anything's possible, but I'm 99.9% sure Mick hadn't been drinking."

"Well, I doubt that Lisa woman could drink off a bottle of whiskey by herself and still be standing."

"I don't think Lisa ever got inside. Someone else was there before I arrived. A kitchen stool was knocked over and what I first thought was lipstick on Mick's shirt turned out to be blood. Not Mick's. I got a good look at him, only his knuckles were scuffed up."

"Mick punched somebody *again*?"

"He's not violent, Jord." I leap to his defense. "I've only known Mick to ever use his fists twice. Once on my high school bully and his minions, and the other was that aggressive tabloid reporter."

"And tonight," she points out.

"Yes, and tonight, which must mean whoever was there was a threat to someone he cares about."

"Which by his recent behavior we can assume must be you."

"It would seem that way. He couldn't get me out of his place fast enough. He was hurtful and insulting, when he is neither of those things. Whatever's going on, he doesn't want me anywhere near it."

"That might be good advice for your own safety."

"I'm not in danger, Jord. I have bodyguards."

"Exactly." She makes a face.

"Well, I'm protected then. I'm more worried for Mick than for myself. I can't let him handle this alone." The way he has been doing since he was a child. "Whatever it is, I'm going to find a way to be there for him."

"Look, I know I encouraged you not to let him shut you out. But Mick seems adamant."

"He's not the only determined one."

"I can see there's no talking you out of this."

"I love him, Jord."

"I know you do, babe." One of her hands covers mine. "Let's crash before the sun comes up and look at this with fresh eyes when we wake up."

Grateful for her, I finish my tea and stand, linking our arms. I turn off the kitchen light and grab an extra toothbrush from the linen closet. "So, Stiles, huh?"

"He is sexy."

"He's robotic."

"That's just the outer layer. You know what they say about still waters…"

The fact that Jordyn is even considering how deep Stiles might run says a lot. But if I point that out to her, she'll just shrug it off with a sexual innuendo. Stiles probably isn't all that bad, it's the circumstances. I'd love for Jord to fall for a good guy who treats her like gold.

I'd love it if we all got our happy endings.

THE MORNING AFTER DAWNS WITH a frenetic beat in my chest. I hadn't slept much. Drifting in and out of consciousness, I kept seeing Mick's face, the bottle of whiskey. His abraded knuckles, the blood on his shirt.

At six, I give up and climb quietly out of bed so I don't wake Jordyn. Feeling groggy, I brush my teeth and splash water on my face. I look awful, and could use a shower, but I need caffeine first.

Pulling on a terry-cloth robe and tube socks for warmth, I tiptoe out of the room. In the foyer, I pause to peer through the front window. The Hummer is gone, but the now familiar black sedan is back. Sighing, I let the curtain fall back in place and put on the new coffee machine with all the bells and whistles that would be a barista's dream. Mick had recently ordered it and specialty beans from Italy. I teased him for being a coffee snob until I had my first cup and swore it was my new obsession.

I look around at the touches that Mick has added. Family photos in the living room. A Vitamix blender for the morning smoothies he often makes me before work. In such a short space of time, our lives have melded together. I could see the picture of our future forming, day after day. Year after year. I could barely make out the shape and texture of my life before him. It's not that my previous life was bad—I had my career, my friends; I was working on my recovery. But it was missing color and vibrancy. It was missing him.

I rub at the knot beneath my left breastbone. I can't let myself accept that this is the end. Hanging on to a kernel of hope, I shake off the morose, and douse my coffee with skim milk and three sweeteners. It smells delicious and tastes even better. I enjoy a few sips, then take the mug to my office. I stop on the threshold, remembering the way Mick looked writing in here, the time we'd made love up against the wall.

A shiver runs through me. I would give anything to be with Mick again. Anything to help take away his troubles and have him back. That has me doing the unthinkable. I sit behind my desk and open Mick's laptop. Shaking off the twinge of guilt, I enter his password, Beauty<3. He'd confided it in me: Beauty with a heart. Mick trusted me with that but not his secrets.

The screen opens on his manuscript. As tempting as it is, I don't read one word. Mick had said he'd share it with me as soon as it was to his satisfaction. I still hope I'll get that chance. I minimize the document and go to his email. It seems like the best place to start.

I scroll through his in-box, glancing at the work-related messages from Nadia at Pivotal about the expansion project and Jordyn in regards to the design. I skip a couple that look investment related. All of them are opened and flagged. I look for Tuesday's date, hoping to discover something telling, but it's just more of the same. Of course, Mick could have deleted any message he might have received or maybe he'd received a text. Still, I continue my search and stop on an email from Stiles. The Subject box reads: Weekly Invoice.

I double click on the attached PDF. It opens onto JDS Security letterhead with a one-page summary of costs. I draw in a breath at how much Mick is spending. I scroll down to the second page to view the details, not surprised to find my name and Dwayde's listed under security services. But what nearly knocks me off my chair is the last item: *P. O'Malley*.

"Morning."

I jump at the sound of Jordyn's voice. "*God!*" My hand flies to my throat. "I didn't hear you."

"Sorry." She lounges against the doorjamb, eyeing me then the open laptop. "Whatcha doing?"

"Something bad."

"That much I got from the hand-caught-in-the-cookie-jar reaction. Tell me."

"I'm creeping Mick's laptop."

"Ooh, that is bad." She grins. "I like it."

"It's awful, Jord."

"It's not as if he's given you much choice."

"That's what I'm telling myself."

"Did you find anything?" she asks, hitching a hip on the edge of my desk.

"I found an invoice. From Stiles." I turn the laptop toward her.

"JDS." She squints at the logo. "I wonder what the JD stands for? John Douglas, Jack Donovan..."

"Focus, Jord." I tap my finger on O'Malley's name.

Her brows scrunch up. "Wait...isn't that the tabloid dude Mick punched?"

"Yes. It just has his name. Nothing about the service Stiles provided."

"So?"

"So, that's weird. The other services are listed. O'Malley could be the problem that Mick is hiding from me. That could be who he heard from on Tuesday. O'Malley's had it in for Mick. Maybe he found out something to threaten him with. His past, me...oh my God, that makes sense, right?"

"I mean, it's possible, I guess. But you're extrapolating a lot from a name on an invoice."

"I know." I shake my head, my brain racing. "But what if I'm right and O'Malley was at Mick's last night?"

"You really think Mick would invite O'Malley into his condo?"

"If he had a good reason to. Say, if O'Malley made a threat that could affect me, Mick would probably agree to meet him. Given their history, it could have gotten heated. Add alcohol to the mix and boom." I mimic an explosion with my hands, while Jordyn looks at me as if I've lost my mind.

"I know Mick is an aspiring writer...didn't know you were."

I ignore her sarcasm. "I'm onto something, Jord. I can feel it."

Micah

"SHE WHAT?" I GAPE AT Victor and continue pacing. After practice, the boys had headed to the locker room, leaving us alone in the gym. I could tell Victor had something on his mind, but I wasn't expecting this bombshell.

"You heard me. She asked if I could find out if O'Malley looked like he had taken a punch to the face."

"Don't tell me you went along with this."

"I promised to look into it. Otherwise, trust me, bruh, she would have done it herself."

Just the thought of Dee getting anywhere near O'Malley has my skin crawling and my hands fisting. "Why would she think O'Malley would be at my condo?"

"She found an invoice from Stiles with his name. It seemed suspicious to her and she thought the two might be connected."

The floor squeaks with the abrupt halt of my sneakers. "Dee went into my laptop?"

"I told you she's determined. So, why was O'Malley a line item?"

"It's standard security protocol. Stiles suggested I look into him after he threatened to sue me."

"That's your story?"

"It's not a story."

"Right." He snorts. "Was O'Malley at your place last night?"

"*Hell no.*"

"Hm." He peers at me closely. "Think I believe you on that."

"You'll stop Dee from going down this road then?"

"You could do that yourself by telling her the truth."

"That's not an option." My gut churns. "Just see to her for me. Don't let Dee go off on some wild goose chase and tangle with O'Malley."

"Don't worry, I won't. But this is some bullshit, Mick. Someone obviously ran into your fist last night." His eyes drop to my bandaged knuckles.

"I ripped them on the punching bag."

"Oh yeah," he scoffs. "And the blood Dee saw on your shirt?"

"It came from my knuckles." The lies keep rolling. "Dee is looking for things that aren't there."

"She didn't imagine the two glasses and bottle of whiskey."

"A couple of former teammates stopped by. They had whiskey, I didn't. Are we done now?"

"You're lying, man. Your right eye twitches ever so slightly when you do. Right now, it's twitching like a motherfucker."

"Is that what they taught you in detective school?"

"Ah...classic. Sarcasm as a defense."

"Give it a rest, Victor. I'm good."

"Good, you're not. You were off your game at practice. You've got circles around your eyes darker than a raccoon's and you look like hell. When did you last sleep or have a decent meal?"

"I don't need mothering."

"What you need is a good kick in your ass. But it's no fun kicking a man when he's already down. I'll feed you instead."

"I'm not hungry."

"Too bad. Bells is preparing lunch and Dwayde has a joystick with your name on it."

"I won't be good company."

"No shit. But we'll have you anyway."

"I'm not drinking, Victor."

"I didn't say you were."

"That's what this is about. Did Dee send you here to babysit me?"

"Call it what you like, but I'm not leaving you on your own."

"Christ, you're annoying."

"I ooze charm and you know it."

Lacking the energy to argue, and frankly being alone with my own miserable company isn't appealing, I pick up my jacket and pull it on.

"She loves you, man."

I know that with everything inside me. I must have read her text message a thousand times. But it's her love for me that puts her at greatest risk. "Dee needs to move on."

"That's what you want her to do?"

"Yes." Another lie that almost strangles me.

"I applaud your altruism." He slowly claps his hands in a mocking gesture. "Very generous of you not to stand in the way of Dee getting on with her life and eventually meeting someone else."

My jaw clenches so hard I can feel it grinding.

"All those Sunday brunches and family events with Dee and her new partner. A man you'll know she goes home with at night filling in the space that used to be yours. A man she'll fall in love with. Marriage. Kids. You'll be Uncle Mick."

"Fuck you."

"No, fuck you, Mick." He nails me hard in the eyes. "Because that's what moving on looks like. So, if that's not what you want, you better figure out if this precious secret of yours is worth holding on to...and you better figure it out fast."

CHAPTER NINETEEN

Dee

DAY FIVE WITHOUT MICK BRINGS a dull ache throughout my body. Like a heartsick flu. I lie in bed—another restless night spent here— listening to the solemn tattoo of morning rain hitting the roof.

I'd been wrong about O'Malley. Victor had assured me of that. But we both know Mick is lying. He didn't have former teammates over, and he didn't tear his knuckles on a punching bag. So, what happened? Ugh. My mind's been in constant go-mode, and I'm still no closer to figuring it out.

If not for Lexie and Jord, I might have spiraled. Yesterday, they kept me distracted with an afternoon pedicure, and an evening of take-out sushi, Netflix, and lots of wine.

While on my own, though, I struggle not to binge. Afraid of being yanked back into that vicious cycle of stuffing each comfort-drenched bite into my mouth, followed by guilt, self-loathing, and empty promises never to do it again. I lived that way until two years ago. Until my answer to a lengthy binge and weight gain was to subsist on water, coffee, and diet pills for weeks. Until it landed me in the hospital. My rock-bottom that finally kicked me out of denial and forced me to see that I needed help.

But last week, I canceled my monthly appointment with Dr. Roland because I was on an awesome high. I should have known better. Should have anticipated the potential for a fall. After all, I'm an addict, a compulsive overeater. Food is my drug and negative emotion is my trigger. It sounds so weak. It sounds like an excuse to pig out. But only someone who's been there can truly understand.

Before I plunge deeper into my morose, I crawl out of bed to get ready for brunch at Mama T's. It's doubtful that Mick will show. That has me torn between hoping he doesn't and wishing he does. To see him and not be with him would be sheer torture, but I also don't want him cutting himself off from the family we share. Especially when that kind of isolation could lure him back to drinking.

I strip out of my pajamas and turn on the water as hot as I can stand it. Beneath the spray, with the persistent heat on my pebbled flesh, thoughts of Mick engulf me. I pick up his body wash and pour a liberal amount into the palm of my hand. The woodsy aroma permeates the small space.

I spread the gel over me, rubbing his scent down my neck, across my chest to the curves of my breasts. Responding to the ache of my tightened nipples, I cup my boobs and squeeze. Feel his touch on me.

I stroke the tips and my breaths turn to pants. I keep plucking with one hand, and slide the other down my torso, imagining they're his. Big, slightly rough, arousing every inch of skin. My legs part and I feel his fingers slide between them. *Ohhh.* I close my eyes and see Mick. See us making love in the shower, my back pressed against the wet wall, his pleasured groans rasping into my mouth, his thick, hard cock, expertly gliding in and out of me, his deep, sexy voice telling me how good I feel, that my tight pussy is his, that I'm going to make him come so hard. Gasping, my sudsy fingertips massage my clit in short, rapid circles, my hips grinding into his imagined touch. Faster. "Yes. Oh, God. *Mick*," I cry out his name and come on a quick, shuddering orgasm.

THE RAIN HAS STOPPED. AND because the temperature is still relatively mild, I dress in fitted black jeans and a lightweight pullover that doesn't quite cover my hips. I debate the bracelet Mick had given me that dangles from my wrist, and decide to leave it on. With my hair still wet, I scrunch the curls with product, brush on bronzer to boost my pale olive skin, and lightly dab white eye shadow into the corners of my eyes to camouflage the tiredness. A trick Lexie taught me.

I haven't told Mama T or Maria about the…no, not breakup, that sounds so final. I settle for separation, though that is only marginally better. Neither has Mick, obviously. My family would have come running if they knew. Victor and Isabelle check in on me every day. But out of respect that it's our situation to reveal, or maybe staying hopeful too, they haven't shared our story. But I'll have to say something today when I arrive for brunch alone.

Before I leave, I tidy the kitchen and take the empty wine bottles and sushi containers out to the garage. It looks odd without Mick's Porsche taking up the space. My entire house feels that way. Technically, with the papers signed, it's our house. That only makes me more sad.

Walking across the concrete floor, I throw the bottles in with the recycling and lift the lid off the large green bin to toss the plastic containers inside. That's when I notice the edge of a manila envelope. I always recycle paper. I'm anal about it. I remove the envelope.

It's addressed to **M. Peters**. I feel my brow furrow. There's only his name handwritten on the front. No address or sender information, which means it hadn't been received by mail or courier. And that Mick likely tossed it sometime between the last garbage pick-up on Monday morning and when he left Tuesday night.

I check inside. Nothing. In hot pursuit, I remove the two garbage bags already in the bin, and untie the first one. Yesterday, snooping through Mick's laptop, today the trash…

In my haste to check the bags, I almost miss a lone crumpled piece of paper at the bottom of the bin. I stop what I'm doing to dive my hand inside. The paper had been crushed so hard that it resembles a crinkled ball. I work to flatten out the wrinkles and see that it's a note, also handwritten with a thin, black, felt-tip pen. Short, terse, and to the point.

My chest tightens and my knees feel weak. All this time I thought Mick must have received a disturbing call, text, or email. It had to have been this—an unsigned note, delivered here. Someone who would know where to find him. Someone familiar. Someone whose handwriting Mick would recognize.

Time to talk.

Could it be? The nightmare. Mick distancing himself from me. The heightened security. The bottle of Jameson. *Ohmigod.* My breathing goes shallow. Whiskey was his father's drink of choice. Mick had told me that long ago. It's Malcolm who was at Mick's on Friday night. It was his blood on Mick's shirt.

He's protecting me from his father.

TWO HOURS LATER, I REACH Whitley's Farm. Papa T used to bring us here at Thanksgiving for their hayrides, corn maze, and the best pumpkin pie ever. In the winters, Victor and Mick would toboggan and tube down the steep hills. I was always too scared and self-conscious to try.

According to Mama T, the Whitleys retired years ago and put the property up for sale. Now Malcolm lives here in a house he had built and Mick paid for.

I pull up to the black iron gates. I haven't seen Malcolm Peters in fifteen years. I used to think I saw glimpses of him when I first ran away to Chicago. It was odd that my mind would have conjured him up because I hated the man. He had a snake-oil salesman type of charm. But beneath the gleam of his fake pearly white smile was a violent alcoholic and a brutal cruelty. Good sense warns me to be careful. Assuming he's even home.

As I lower my window to press the intercom, I hear a car pull up behind me. Through the side mirror, I see an unfamiliar gray sedan. The door on the driver's side opens and out steps Stiles. His emotionless mask is in place as he approaches.

Was the man ever off duty? And where was his Hummer? He locks on me with unsmiling eyes as his big frame blocks my access to the call button.

"What are you doing here, Ms. Chase?"

"That's my business."

"Mr. Peters won't like it."

"I don't report to Mick."

"I do."

We stare at each other in a battle of wills, neither of us prepared to yield. I'm about ready to go off on him when the gate suddenly opens.

"Don't!" Stiles warns as I hit the gas. He leaps forward in an attempt to stop me.

I floor it; swerve, narrowly missing him and drive through. *Sorry Stiles*, I wince, leaving him in my dust. He likely won't have time to get to his car and make it inside before the gate closes. And, if he follows on foot, I'll have a decent head start.

The driveway is a long, winding stretch; a distant memory of the snow-covered joy ride it used to be. At the top, set among a bevy of trees, sits a Tudor-style mansion with three steeple roofs and two lion statues framing the entranceway. But my eyes are immediately drawn to the front porch where underneath the cobblestone arch, stands the King of the Castle. Older, grayer, a slight paunch, but no less intimidating.

I don't have time to settle my hyper bouncing heart, assuming a physically-fit Stiles is on my tail. Adrenaline pumping hard, I leave the engine running and exit the car.

"Well, well, well, if it isn't Deeana Rae Chase," Malcolm greets with his patented smile. "This is quite a surprise."

"You don't look surprised." But his face does look like it had taken a few good punches. His jaw is bruised, his left eye swollen, and there are three butterfly bandages on his cheek.

"Technology is amazing these days." He holds up his phone. "I get a ding whenever someone arrives at the gate and I can see who it is. Seemed like your bodyguard was giving you a hard time."

"What made you think he was my bodyguard?"

"Ah…" He taps his temple. "I know a lot, Deeana. You must have really wanted to see me."

"Don't be flattered. It's not a social call."

"I see you developed some moxie over the years. You used to be a shy, frightened rabbit, scared of your own shadow."

"I didn't come here to talk about me." I walk to the edge of the steps and stay there.

"Come inside and have a drink."

"Of whiskey? Like you brought to Mick's."

"Is that what he told you?"

"He didn't tell me anything about Friday night. But I know you were there. And from the look of your face, it wasn't a friendly father-son chat."

"You don't know anything."

"Oh, I do. I know about the abuse, Malcolm."

His fake smile loses its shine. His mouth thins.

"Mick told me years ago. I kept it a secret when I never should have. I thought...hoped...once he got away from you, he'd be free. But I've witnessed his nightmares. Horrible and vicious, filled with violence where he's fighting back. Looks like he finally did."

"I'd be very careful about levying unfounded accusations."

"They're not unfounded." My voice trembles with anger. It takes every ounce of prudence not to lunge at him as he stands there all indignant and self-righteous. "You got what you wanted. He played ball. He became the superstar you were grooming him for. He gave you bragging rights. He bought you this house. But it's still not enough, is it? What do you want from him now?"

"I gave him the life most can only dream of. More than he deserved."

"He didn't deserve to pay for your wrongdoings. It was your reckless decision to drink and drive. You are the one that wrapped your motorcycle around a pole and ruined your shot at basketball. That was all on you. Not Mick's mother and certainly not Mick. But you took it out on them; beat your wife and a defenseless boy. That doesn't make you a man. That makes you a sick, fucking coward."

"Watch your mouth." He bares his teeth, coming forward. "You don't want to push me, Deeana."

"Step away from her." The harsh voice sounds from behind me. Even winded, Stiles is formidable.

"Get the hell off my property."

Stiles ignores the warning and gets between us. He's doing his job, but technically he's trespassing and Malcolm is the sheriff.

"Let's go, Stiles. I've said my piece. I'm done."

"Well, lookie here." Malcolm gazes demonically down at his phone. "Seems your Knight in Shining Armor has arrived to save the day. This should be interesting."

It happens fast. The loud roar of an engine, the burn of tires on the hill, the blur of Mick's Porsche. He breaks with a halting screech and is out of the car in seconds.

"Mick!" I scream, tearing away from Stiles and rushing to him. "Don't do anything. Please." I grab the front of his sweater. Panicked. "Please."

He's vibrating with rage. "Get in the car, Dee."

"I'll go, but not without you."

Malcolm laughs, a sound filled with malice, enjoying the scene before him. "I wasn't expecting this turn of events."

"Stay the fuck away from her." Mick pushes me behind him and I struggle against his grip. But he's too strong. Too furious.

"She came to see me."

"If you ever see her coming again, you better run in the other fucking direction."

"Or what?"

"Or I will kill you."

"Threatening a law enforcement officer in front of witnesses. Not very smart." He crosses his arms across his wide chest. "I could haul you in for that and your lackey here for trespassing. But I'm enjoying my Sunday too much for the headache of all that paperwork. Instead, I'm going to let you off easy with ten little reminders." He holds up ten fingers, then backs up and enters the house, slamming the door on us.

Mick turns to glare at me, his jaw tight, the muscle ticking out of control. "Get Dee's car home," he instructs Stiles, then tugging my arm, he leads me to his Porsche and opens the passenger door, practically shoving me inside.

Relieved that the confrontation is over without anyone physically harmed, I don't argue. Truth is, despite the terrible circumstances, I'm dying to be with him. Inside the confined interior, I soak up every stormy inch.

The stress of the week shows in the purplish crescents beneath his eyes and in the angles of his face that are sharper than before. But nothing detracts from the beauty of him.

While I feast on all the details, Mick's fiery gaze points straight ahead. He drives fast as if the devil is on his heels. His scraped knuckles grip the gearshift and I notice that the black diamond band is back on his finger. My heart rejoices at the sight. But I caution myself against too much optimism. Mick had only come here to protect me and I'm only in his car because he doesn't trust me on my own. A fact that has him scowling in silence.

He doesn't speak, not a single word until he pulls onto Mama T's street and parks behind Maria's minivan. Only then does he whirl on me.

"What the hell is wrong with you?"

"Me?" I huff. "You brought this on with your lies and your secrets."

"Malcolm is not someone to toy with."

"I wasn't toying. I found the note and put together that Malcolm sent it. That he was the one at your condo Friday night. His face confirmed it."

"First O'Malley...now this."

"I wasn't right about O'Malley. But I'm right about Malcolm."

"Do you think that matters?"

"Of course, it matters. You matter, Mick."

"Christ!" He thumps the steering wheel.

"What did Malcolm mean by ten little reminders?"

"Don't you ever stop? We've dealt with enough for one day. And we still have to get to brunch."

"I wasn't sure you'd come."

"I wasn't sure either. But good thing I did otherwise I would have missed this vigilante stunt of yours."

"I am your inspiration for *Dark Angel*."

"This isn't funny."

"True. I'd call it poignant. After all, the stories you write involve tough, kick-ass heroines. You like a strong woman even if you do want to control and dominate."

"Shut up, Dee." He lays his head back against the rest. The anger in him dissipates. But the worry is still there. "When Stiles called to tell me where you were headed, I went out of my goddamn mind. If I hadn't already been in Springvale…if I hadn't been close…I don't know what I would have done."

"I'm fine, Mick. Look at me." When he does, I angle in my seat to face the fear lingering in his eyes. "I'm sorry. Not for what I did. But that you were scared for me and that I could have put Stiles or you in jeopardy. I didn't consider the consequences. All I cared about was getting to Malcolm."

"Why?"

"To call him on the abuse. He never should have been allowed to get away with hurting you and your mother. I wanted him to know that it wasn't a dirty family secret anymore. I wanted him to know that you are not alone in this."

"Jesus, Dee. This isn't some crusade. You don't go poking the dragon."

"I'm not afraid of Malcolm."

"You have no idea what he's capable of."

I lean in closer and reach out to brace his bearded cheeks between my palms. Our eyes fix on each other. "Don't you know that I would fight dragons for you, Micah Anthony? Slay them one by one. That's how much I love you."

With a curse, his mouth is on mine in an instant. His hands in my hair, his tongue sliding between my lips, kissing me long, deep, and passionately.

"I've missed your taste," he whispers, nibbling my bottom lip. "Missed your smell." His nose traces the curve of my neck. "I've been in hell, Dee. And I've taken you there with me."

"Then free us both."

"Beauty," he exhales and presses his forehead to mine, our noses touching, our lips a breath apart. "Staying away from you was the lesser of two evils."

"I don't believe that. Nothing can be worse than us not being together."

"It's killing me, too," he says hoarsely. "It's killing me to stay away. Killing me to hurt you. I can't sleep, I can't eat. I'm barely surviving. But our separation is the price."

"The price for what?"

"I love you so damn much." His words are pained whispers. "Everything I've done is because I love you."

"I know that. But you can't keep hiding your secrets behind your love for me. It's not fair."

"I can't risk you being involved."

"You'd rather lose me?"

"I can't stand that either. Victor painted an unbearable picture of you with another man. I wanted to tear the head off of someone that I don't even know."

"There's no one for me, but you." My hands tighten on his face. "No one. But you have to give me something. You have to be honest with me."

He smooths back my hair, his fingers moving with a restless edge. "After brunch. We'll talk then."

"You'll tell me everything?"

"I won't make that promise, Dee. I haven't thought it all through yet. But we'll talk, okay?"

"Okay." I hug him desperately.

It's at least a start.

CHAPTER TWENTY

Micah

"BAH, YOU'RE LATE," MAMA T scolds affectionately as she hugs us both. "What were you two doing in the car for so long?"

"Making out," Gabi offers, all so helpfully, and grins at my predicament when Dani asks me what that means.

"Um..." I lift her into my arms. "It's grownup kissing." An answer that makes Dee blush. Damn, I love her. Our *breakup*—despise that term—was a week of utter hell.

But no one other than Victor and Isabelle appear the wiser. I hadn't wanted to make the end real or final by putting it out there and it seems Dee hadn't wanted to either. I hedge more of Dani's questions on the topic of making out until Maria has had enough fun watching me squirm, and steps in to save me by distracting her daughter.

Welcoming the chaos of my family, I slide Justin a few bucks for another lost tooth; kiss Mason who is strapped in his booster seat, drooling all over a rubber toy; and give Dwayde a fist bump, gauging his mood.

"How you doing?"

"Aw'right." He shrugs, but the last few days I've spent with him say otherwise.

The custody case and whatever he's hiding have got to be overwhelming. I know what the hiding part feels like.

Mama T had chosen a traditional American breakfast. With brunch preparations already underway, she assigns me to the waffle station with Victor.

"Finally got your head out of your ass?" he says while stirring the mix.

"We're going to talk later."

"That's good, man. Don't break her heart again."

"I don't want to."

"Then don't." I hear the clip in his warning. Victor's on the right side of this—Dee's side.

I steal a glance at her working the eggs and bacon griddle with Maria and Bells. Her curls bounce as she moves. She's so pretty. So fucking brave.

The call from Stiles had scared me spitless. I'd been getting off the highway, still debating whether attending brunch and being around her was a smart move. But all second thoughts fled the instant I heard she was approaching Malcolm's. I raced over like a bat out of hell. Luckily, it's Sunday and the streets were empty. With the iron grip of panic twisting my chest, I'd made the trip in record time.

Stiles had caught up with her by then, but just knowing Dee had been alone with Malcolm… and seeing her merely feet away from him was like waving a red cloth in front of a bull. I was ready to charge when Dee got in my way, gripping my sweater. As savage and protective as I felt, the frightened look on her face, the pleading in her voice, stopped me from breaking Malcolm in two. All I wanted then was to get her away from there. But…

If my motive had solely been Dee's welfare, I would have sent her off with Stiles. It's what a noble man would have done. Instead, I'd whisked her off in my car with no real plan except to torment myself with her nearness. She looked so good. Smelled so good. I felt like a desperate man in need of water after a week-long drought.

I burned in silence the entire drive. By the time we reached Mama T's, I'd worked myself up into a combustible mix of fear, anger, and desire. I railed on her, leading with my temper. Going to see Malcolm, what the hell had she been thinking?

That's when Dee told me about finding the note. She'd pieced it together, not everything but enough. She'd seen my knuckles, she'd seen Malcolm's face, she knew he'd been at my condo and that we'd fought. She just didn't know why. But that hadn't stopped her from confronting him. She'd gone there to stand up for me. To let him know I wasn't alone.

Jesus. Hearing what she'd done…hearing her say she'd slay dragons for me, the darkness faded. And there in the light was Dee—my beautiful, avenging angel. I could no longer resist her. Truth is, I didn't even try. I kissed her, touched her, and still I couldn't quench my rapacious thirst. I wanted her back, I wanted what we had, I wanted to remove the pain from her eyes. I said we would talk.

But what can I tell Dee without getting her caught in the crossfire?

That's the damning dilemma I contemplate all through brunch. As usual it's a boisterous affair with lots of loud chatter and good-natured ribbing. I try my best to relax and engage. But the closer it gets to *talk-time*, the more I question the wisdom of divulging my secrets.

I'M STILL IN MY HEAD on the drive back to Brockville. My unease worsening when I feel Dee studying my profile.

"Having second thoughts?" she asks, attuned to my disquiet.

"Yeah," I admit, keeping my eyes on the road. "I know you need answers, Dee."

"I do. But I want you to want to tell me."

"It's not that I haven't wanted to tell you. It's that protecting you comes first."

"Keeping me in the dark doesn't actually protect me, you know?"

"So I discovered."

"You're not the only one that feels protective, Mick. I want to look out for you too. I want to be there through the good and the bad. You can trust me."

"Beauty." I look over at her. "There's no one I trust more than you."

She reaches for my hand balled around the gearshift. Brushes her thumb over my ring then lifts my hand to entwine our fingers in a silken link that inextricably binds us. And in that moment—for better or for worse—I decide to tell Dee everything.

"Where do I even start?" My pulse accelerates.

"At the beginning." Her voice is patient and those big luminous eyes give me every bit of her attention. "Start there."

I take a breath and ease in from a familiar launching pad.

"My mom met Malcolm soon after she immigrated from Brazil. She'd lost her parents at an early age and was taken in by an aunt who had five other mouths to feed. She fended for herself mostly, and set her sights on moving to the US. It seemed so big and glamorous to her. The Land of Opportunity."

"I remember you telling me that she wanted to be a teacher and write children's books."

"Yeah. She had so many plans and dreams for herself. But she never got the chance." Guilt eats at me like acid. "She was in awe of Malcolm at first. This cool, good-looking guy. A basketball player. Rode a motorcycle. My mom had never even gone on a date before. She fell hard for him. Even when she began to see glimpses of his mean streak, she made excuses for him. That was my mom, she saw the good in everyone."

"He exploited that."

Dee's understanding makes it easier for me to continue. "All Malcolm cared about was basketball. Not just the sport, but that it meant money and fame. Power and prestige. He was obsessed with it. A wife wasn't in his plans, certainly not a baby.

"He blamed her for trapping him, then he blamed her for crashing his motorcycle and ending his basketball future. But through it all she romanticized that he would eventually come to love us." I shake my head at her wistful naïvety. "I'm sure he only married her because he'd lost the only thing he cared about and wanted to make her life a living hell. And he did."

A cauldron of hate and fury boils inside of me. "After he recovered, he went into the police academy. It wouldn't give him the money and fame he craved, but I think he chose it for the power. Beyond that, it shielded him. No one saw the real him behind the sheen of his badge. Except us."

I stare out at the road but it's not just the stretch of highway that fills my vision, it's the memories. "As much as he hated me for being born, he needed me to fulfill his dreams and that made him hate and resent me all the more."

My chest heaves and I feel Dee's hand tighten on mine. "I knew when a beating was coming. He'd get this look on his face. Cold. Icy. Then he'd slowly remove his belt, getting off on my fear. Making me anticipate every fucking action that would lead up to that first hit. But I could take that. I didn't cry. I made my mind go elsewhere. Escaped into another world until it was over. But what I couldn't take, what I could never escape from was him hurting my mom."

I try to swallow past the dry knot in my throat. When my voice comes next, it's sandpapery rough. "She always intervened, trying to stop him. But that only made it worse for her. One night he looped the belt around her throat and dragged her from my room like she was a fucking dog, calling her a mongrel." The memory of it still slicks my skin with sweat.

"I just stood there as I always did. Shaking like a fucking coward. She gave up everything for me. She took those hits that should have been mine. And I never, not once, fought back for her."

The dark pain of the past blurs my vision. Too fucked up to keep driving, I withdraw my hand from Dee's and pull over to the shoulder. I put the car in park. My hands grip the wheel. My breathing is ragged.

Mick." Dee unbuckles her seat belt and, coming up on her knees, leans across to pull me in for a hug.

I hug her back, a grip brutal in its intensity. My body trembles as if I'm sobbing. But I don't shed any tears. Dee sheds them for me. Sad, heart-aching rivulets.

"I never wanted you to hear those details," I choke. "I never wanted you to know how badly I'd failed her."

"You didn't fail her, Mick. You were a child. There was nothing you could have done to stop him."

"She stayed because of me."

"She stayed out of fear." Dee eases away, revealing those golden eyes, wet and anguished for me. "That kind of abuse takes a psychological toll. Your mom was scared, she was alone. She didn't have any family or money of her own. Her husband was an esteemed police officer, popular with the department and the community. That can make a woman not see options to leave or get help the way others might."

"I used to wonder if she drove her car into that guardrail on purpose... to get away. But deep down I know she would never have left me."

"No, she wouldn't have left you, especially not that way. She loved you so much, Mick. She wouldn't want you blaming yourself for any of this." Dee places her palms on my cheeks. "There is no one to blame but Malcolm. He tried to break you. To make you think you were weak. You are not. You are a survivor. And you are one of the strongest men I know."

"I wanted to be strong. Good. I wanted to make Cayo and Rita proud of me."

"Of course they were proud of you."

"I didn't deserve it. I turned down the NYU offer. I went off to NC State and made a total mess of it all."

"Because I left."

"No!" My refusal is swift and steadfast. I remove her hands from my face and place them in mine. "I can't deny that I was busted up over losing you. But in hindsight, that was an excuse, not the reason. The truth is, basketball was the easier choice. I didn't have to face a confron-

211

tation with Malcolm. I didn't have to take on a new challenge or put my creativity out there and possibly fail. I could just drink, play ball, and go along. It was a cop-out."

"That's unfair criticism."

"It's not. I'm being real, Dee. You didn't see me back then."

"What were you like?" She sits back on her seat but keeps her face and body angled toward me.

"Apathetic. Indifferent. I shut down. I didn't write. I ignored my family, the people who looked out for me, who loved me even at my lowest. I got drunk on the daily, skipped classes, and started flunking."

"I can't imagine you like that."

"I wouldn't want you to. One day, after weeks of not returning their calls, Cayo showed up at my apartment." I avert my gaze. "I'll spare you the details, but he caught me in a bad way. Still, he didn't judge or give up on me. He convinced me to get help."

"Is that when you went into rehab?"

"The first time." I look back over at her. "Papa and Mama T footed the bill for the entire thing and Cayo stayed in a hotel until I got out of the in-residence portion of the program. They did all that for me."

"You were their son, Mick."

"I know. Cayo and Rita never made me feel like I was anything less than theirs. I wanted to be worthy of all they had done for me. I wanted to stay sober. To do better. To be better. I actually thought I would."

"What happened?"

"After rehab, I started hanging out with a good group of guys. I got my grades up. I went to the therapy sessions. I even told my coach that I was quitting at the end of the season. I was planning to reapply to NYU. But then Malcolm showed up." I can feel the hate in the blasted heat of my breaths. "I knew he wasn't just going to let me quit like that. But what could he really do, I figured? I was nineteen. I could make my own choices. I stood up to him. I told him my plans. He laughed in my face and threatened to tell Cayo and Rita about the abuse."

Dee blinks, perplexed. She would expect threats to hurt them—to somehow ruin them. But for Malcolm to threaten to reveal his own despicable secret... "I don't understand," she says.

"You couldn't. You can't fathom how his twisted mind works. Play ball or destroy my family. There was no choice. Not to me. What could they do about the past? I was an adult, in college. Knowing then would have been worse."

"You thought they'd blame themselves?"

"It would have plagued them, Dee. They would have picked through every memory looking for signs or inventing them to fit with the knowledge. Rita and Cayo were my salvation, but they wouldn't see that. They wouldn't see how adept I was at hiding the abuse. They would only see what they missed. And they would never have forgiven themselves. I was not going to do that to them. Not after all they'd done for me. I wasn't going to let them live with something that wasn't their fault."

"So, you stayed and started drinking again?" she asks gently and without judgment.

"It got me through the days. Mostly. And when it didn't, I just drank more and more until it finally landed me in the hospital—alcohol poisoning. But I still wouldn't have quit drinking. Not on my own. It took Cayo, Rita, and Victor to pull me out of that hell again. That's when I knew no matter what I had to endure with Malcolm, I wasn't going to keep doing that to them. Thanks to my family, I stayed sober."

"You did the work."

"I just found a way to cope. Fame, money, women. Everything he wanted and I promised not to be."

"You didn't abuse people, Mick. You didn't hurt anyone. You can't compare yourself to Malcolm."

"I did exactly what he would have done. Mackie put me out there and I seized the opportunity. Took advantage of it all until Cayo got sick. That was one hell of a wake-up call. The man I considered my real father was looking death in the eye and I was doing the bidding of the man I hated. I couldn't do it anymore. I quit."

"How did Malcolm take that news?"

"Money has a way of easing things."

"You paid him off?"

"Cayo was dying. I didn't want him taking knowledge of the abuse to his grave. And Mama T and Victor were still alive. If more money was what it would take, it was a small price."

"You said more money...you'd been paying him all along? Is that why you bought him the house?"

"Cars, whatever. It was all part of the deal. I know that offends you, but you wanted the truth and here it is."

"Yes, I'm offended...disgusted, but not by you, Mick. Never by you. I detest your father."

"Welcome to the club."

"You still pay him?"

"Indirectly through my lawyer. Doesn't matter. It gave me the freedom to quit and start up Papa's Kids."

"Papa T would have been honored by how you chose to celebrate his memory. And something else, Mick. He would not have wanted you to choose basketball or pay off Malcolm to protect him."

"Maybe not. But the alternative wasn't an option. The money worked to keep Malcolm away."

"Not really," she points out. "How did you get the note?"

"He had it delivered to the house. He wanted me to know that he had found out about us."

"That's what you received Tuesday morning?"

"I found it on the doorstep after my run."

"That's why you pushed me away. To protect me from Malcolm."

"I couldn't let him hurt you."

"Hurt me how?"

"Christ. I never wanted you involved in any of this, Dee."

"I'm already involved. Just tell me."

"Your instincts were right about O'Malley. He's part of this."

"How?"

I tell her about O'Malley confronting me at Mort's Deli. "He's long believed that there was a story. Quitting at the height of my career and fading into the background only armed those suspicions. And punching him in the face didn't help quiet them any. He tried to entice me into giving him an exclusive in exchange for dropping his plans of a lawsuit. When I didn't bite, he goaded me with information he had acquired from a source that was working at the Lemon Lounge the night of Lexie's party."

"Information about us?" Her breaths quicken.

"Not specifically. He didn't know who you were, but he'd heard enough to assume the woman I was with wasn't a casual date. I tried to play it cool, disinterested. But O'Malley picked up on my defenses. I could tell he wasn't going to let it go until he found out your identity."

"That's why you hired bodyguards for me?"

"Yes."

"How would that stop him from finding out?"

"It wouldn't. But I wanted you protected in case he did."

"Why didn't you tell me?"

"We had just gotten back together and I knew how you felt about staying out of the public eye. I told myself at first that I didn't want to scare you off. But as more time passed, the truth is I just didn't want you to know."

I can tell she doesn't like that answer. "What happened after the confrontation?"

"O'Malley went silent. After making me a habit for months, he abruptly stopped. Nothing on his blog. No contact. Made me nervous as hell. I couldn't figure out his angle. Then Stiles discovered a call between Malcolm and O'Malley from the same day he came into the deli."

"That explains his name on the invoice," she says, assembling the pieces. "Do you know what they talked about?"

"I assumed O'Malley was looking for information on my mystery woman. Malcolm confirmed it. He knew by the way that O'Malley described my protective and proprietary reaction that it was you. That's when he came up with a plan to somehow get O'Malley to back off so he could use the information himself."

"He wants more money?"

"$10 million."

Her jaw drops.

"I don't give a damn about the money, Dee. What he wants is way more than that."

"What else could he possibly want?"

A shudder of rage rocks through my frame. "Malcolm gladly confessed to knowing everything. He knew where you were the entire time. While Cayo and I were looking for you, he found you and watched you struggle. He knew you were pregnant. He knew later that you'd lost our...our baby. I could have been there. I should have been. But he kept us apart."

"Oh, Mick." She leans across to hug me again. "I can't imagine what hearing that must have done to you. But it's not your fault."

She wants so badly for me to believe that. But I can't. "He's trying to keep us apart again."

"How?"

"He threatened to expose the private, intimate details of your life...your past and childhood. He threatened to tell it all to O'Malley and make you look like a ruthless gold digger that wants me back because of my money. He threatened to ruin your reputation if I continue our relationship."

"More emotional blackmail." She releases me, her temper flaring. "The money is just sport to him. He's using your feelings for me to squeeze you dry."

"I'll fix it, Dee."

"Not this time," she says firmly. "You have to stop trying to fix everything. You have to stop seeing me as someone you need to protect at all costs. I'm not fragile."

"There's nothing I wouldn't do for you."

"I don't want you to do anything except promise we'll be together." My heart bleeds at the look of love on her face. I'd missed it so much. "Don't let Malcolm keep us apart," she pleads. "Come home to me."

CHAPTER TWENTY-ONE

Dee

IT'S THE MIDDLE OF THE night when I awaken. My head's a little muddled but my first clear thought is that Mick's not beside me. I shove off the blankets and make my way down the darkened hall. It's quiet, no sound or movement. The inside bolt on the front door is still in place and his shoes are still on the mat. I sigh with relief and search for him.

When the office proves futile, I find him in the living room. He's asleep, lying face-up in his sweatpants. The throw blanket is draped over him, his head rests on a toss cushion, and his legs, too long for the length of the couch, hang partway off the arm.

I'd hoped that after our earlier talk and him coming home that he was ready to let me all the way in; ready to let us be in this together. We hadn't talked about Malcolm again. He was emotionally exhausted, I could see that. And truthfully, I was just so happy to have him back that I didn't push him.

After an excruciating week apart, we spent most of the evening and into the night having wild, jungle sex. In the bed, on the sofa, the floor, the shower, breaking only to have a late dinner before we resumed our marathon of untamed, animalistic fucking.

Now, finding him out here withers any optimism that we had turned the corner. Either he'd snuck out to the sofa because he'd had a nightmare or because he was afraid of having one. Either way, it's a problem.

I refuse to go back to secrets, evasions, or being shut out. I refuse to be treated as if I'm made of glass. His nightmares and Malcolm are not for him to handle alone. Not anymore. That's a talk we'll be having first thing in the morning.

Letting him sleep, I gently brush a hand over his hair, adjust the blanket across his bare shoulder, and return to bed.

The next time I awaken, it's with a jolt. My pulse races. I lie still for a moment, trying to gather my bearings. Trying to shake off the lingering sense that something is wrong. Then I hear it. The noise that must have woke me. I sit up. My ears, straining. A distinct whimper, followed by another. The sound of a wounded body and soul. Goose-bumps sweep over my skin as I hear Mick cry out. "*Stop,*" he begs. "*Please stop.*"

Everything inside me aches for his torment. Rushing to the living room, I kneel beside him. "Mick! Wake up!"

He recoils, rolling into a fetal position, shaking. His eyes still closed, a sob escapes him. I climb onto the sofa and cradle his trembling body.

"Ssh, baby, I've got you," I whisper to that little boy. My tears mingling with his, I hold him close, praying in some way it helps him heal, that he finds strength in my love to exorcise his demons.

I HAVE NO IDEA WHAT time it is when I vaguely become aware of movement and the feel of Mick's arms around me. I rest my head against his chest, snuggling into the warmth of his skin.

"Where are you taking me?" I murmur.

"To bed."

I try to make out his features, but I'm still slipping out of sleep, my senses are dull. Yet I recall enough of why I'd been on the couch that when he lowers me onto the mattress, I grip his shoulders. "Stay."

"I'm not going anywhere." He settles the covers over us and spoons me from behind. "Go back to sleep."

I know we need to talk but betrayed by an insufficient amount of rest, my body shuts down and my mind quickly follows.

THE SCENT OF MICK AND the touch of his lips along my jaw hit my senses before I even open my eyes. When I do, Mick's there. Warm, bronze skin against the pure white sheets. I slowly stretch, feeling the kinks from spending some of the night on the couch. "Mick…"

He takes my mouth, hushing me with a kiss. His hands push up my T-shirt to cup my breasts and roll my nipples, swiftly making them tight and achy.

I curve a hand around his neck, drawing him closer. He moves one hand down to my cleft. A thousand sensations collide. I reach for the loose waistband of his sweatpants and shove the front down. He's hot and stone-hard in my palm. I stroke him the way he likes it. Slow, my fist tight.

"Take me inside you."

"Yes," I moan as he levers over me. I circle my fingers around the thick girth of his erection and take all of him.

The rough, ragged hiss of his breath clenches my sex. Mick gathers me beneath him, buries his face in my neck, and plunges deep. The powerful friction whips up my never-sated appetite to be loved and ravaged by him. My arms and legs cage his strong body, my hips meet his inexorable drives.

Our passion for each other is always ferocious. I slide my arms around his waist and lower my hands to grip the flexing muscles of his ass, squeezing, urging him on. I bask in the exquisite feel of the wide crown of his penis hitting that tender spot in me, the motion causing his pelvis to rasp along my clit.

The surge of release is arrow-sharp. I bite into the curve of his shoulder, buffering the screams that want out of me.

Mick holds my hips, rubbing out the rest of my orgasm with hard, fast thrusts.

"Ah, Christ. Dee." He pins me down and erupts with a deep, rumbling groan against my throat.

I'M DRESSED FOR WORK WHEN the aroma of freshly made brew beckons me to the kitchen. Mick is at the counter outfitted in a thermal shirt and joggers that sheaths his body. He turns and hands me a steaming cup of sweetened milky coffee.

"Thank you." I take a cautious sip and study him. Without the haze of lust, I search his face for any signs that he remembers his nightmare. What I see beyond the striking features is the stress back in his dark, troubled eyes. My heart breaks for him. I press a loving kiss to his lips.

He cups my face, holding me there before pulling back. He drops his hands and picks up his own mug. Seeming deep in thought, he leans against the counter and stares down into his black coffee.

I count the silence. Five beats. Then: "I want to talk to you about Malcolm."

"Okay." I'm on board with that.

"What I told you yesterday was a lot to absorb." He looks up at me. "You needed…deserved answers to explain my behavior…to explain the pain I put you through. No apology or excuse can ever make that up to you."

"Mick…"

"Just let me finish." There's an edge to him, a sense of focus that suggests he'd been preparing. "I told myself it was better to shove you out of my life before you got dragged through the gutter. I tried to let you go. Tried to do what I thought was right. But I couldn't. That makes me selfish. Reckless even."

"It's not selfish or reckless," I rush to alleviate his guilt. "I don't want you to let me go."

"Malcolm's threats are real, Dee. I got a text from him."

"What did he say?" Dread pounds like a wooden bat inside my chest.

"*Great show yesterday.*" He stabs out the words. "*Makes the deal sweeter.*"

"My God. He's really enjoying this."

"Every fucking minute of it."

"Okay." I take a breath to calm, to think. "Let's talk about how we should handle him."

"No." He rejects that outright. "Malcolm isn't your problem. He's mine."

"How can you say that?" My voice raises, dismayed that we had taken ten steps forward only to end right back in the same place. "It's my past or some sullied version of it that Malcolm is lording over us. This concerns me too."

"I won't have you involved any further. It's better for now that I go back to the condo."

I stutter backwards as if being hit. It hurts that much.

"Dee, I'm—"

"Don't!" I set my mug down on the counter with enough force that the coffee sloshes over the sides. "I don't want to hear any more apologies. Or excuses. We don't work through what's difficult. What's messy. What's unpleasant. Not when it comes to you. That's off limits. But pleasure you give me in spades. Sex is the one thing that you can totally control."

Temper flashes in his eyes. "You think I fuck you to control you?"

"To control the situation sometimes."

"That's bullshit!" He bangs down his own mug and glares at me.

"We didn't finish resolving anything. But we made love, didn't we? All night long and again this morning."

"So, what's your point?"

"That sometimes sex is a way of avoiding the difficult things. Like talking about why you slept on the sofa."

"The reason is obvious. I could have hit you in my sleep the last time. I wasn't going to chance that again."

"Why didn't we talk about it then? Why did you sneak out in the middle of the night?"

"I didn't sneak out. You were sleeping."

"That's not why," I scoff. "You knew you were going to leave. You planned to. Don't lie to me. I can't stand that."

"I'm not lying," he snaps. "It was on my mind and I couldn't fall asleep. But I wasn't going to wake you to say I was going on the couch. You would have been upset and I'd already dumped enough on you."

His admission adds to the festering hurt. "You just proved my point."

"What point?"

"That you didn't want to upset me. That's difficult. You can't control my feelings or reaction. But sex between us is easy. Emotionally and otherwise. You know exactly how to please me. We get lost in it...at least I know I do. You make me so crazy with wanting you that nothing else matters."

"It's the same for me. So why is our great sex life a sudden problem?"

"Because as amazing as the sex is, it's not the only important part of our relationship. Everything else matters too. Open communication being at the top of the list, even when things are hard to talk about. You can't control it all, Mick. Sometimes bad things happen."

"You think I don't know that?"

"I think you blame yourself for too much of it. Your mother. Papa T's death. The custody case. Not being there for me when I was pregnant. You blame yourself for things that aren't your fault."

"It is my fault that I didn't use a condom. I got you pregnant. You were scared. You saw me with another girl. That's why you left."

"I could have used birth control. I could have told you about my pregnancy instead of making you think I was having doubts about us. I could have confronted you about Tamara. I had other options besides leaving. But you won't let me take any of the responsibility."

"I should have been there."

"And you would have been if I'd let you."

"Malcolm knew. If he didn't want to punish me—"

"That's Malcolm's fault. Not yours."

"We lost our baby." His voice breaks, filling me with a wrenching ache.

"Miscarriages happen, Mick. There is no guarantee you being there would have changed the outcome. But you don't believe that because you filter everything bad that happens to the people you love through your guilt over your mother. You've convinced yourself that you should have been able to protect her when there was no way that you or any child could have. And you wear that falsehood like it's a scarlet letter."

"I don't need you psychoanalyzing me."

"I'm not." I struggle to reason with him as he paces angrily to the window over the sink. "It doesn't take a psychologist to see the hard-edged guilt you battle."

"I'm handling it, Dee."

"If that were true, you would not have had another nightmare last night."

He stills. All the color drains from his face. "I…" He rakes a hand through his hair. "I don't remember."

Tears flood my throat. "I woke up to noises and found you crying, begging your father to stop. I assumed it was about your mother. And when you wouldn't wake up, I held you and rocked you."

"Christ. That's why I found you asleep with me on the couch?"

"Yes."

He looks at me with something that resembles disgust and shame. "I'm sorry you saw me like that."

"Mick." I go over to him. Touch his arm bunched with tension. "There's no embarrassment or apology needed because I was there for you in a vulnerable moment. You've held me when I've cried."

"It's not the same."

"Because you're a man?"

"Because I don't want you dealing with my shit."

I inhale sharply and turn on my stocking feet.

222

"*Wait*." he calls.

I walk faster down the hall. Needing to get far from him before I say something I'll truly regret.

He catches up with me inside the bedroom. "Will you wait a damn minute?" He grabs my wrist, spinning me around.

My hair whips across my face. "I have waited and I'm sick of it. You give bits and pieces, but you don't give me all of you. You won't let me share your pain. You won't let me help. You won't let me in."

"I've told you everything."

"That's not enough! Telling isn't the same as making me a part of your life. Relationships aren't only filled with sunny days, Mick. We have to be able to weather the storms."

"Maybe my storms are too much."

"*No*." My arms go around him. The need to give him reassurance is more important than hanging on to my hurt and anger. "I used to think my baggage was too much. I thought I didn't deserve love or happiness. I thought I wasn't worthy. That's why my mother and father didn't want me."

"That's not true, baby," Mick rebuts strongly, hugging me tight.

"I know that. Or at least I'm starting to. You've helped me. You make me feel loved and wanted. You encourage me to let go of those self-deprecating tapes that tell me I'm not good enough. You've supported me through my sadness and grief...through my insecurities and doubts.

"I know I have to do the work for myself. But you being there helps. That's the point, Mick. Growing, getting better, moving beyond our pasts so that we're at our best together. It's about being each other's safe space."

"I've always wanted to make you feel safe," he says quietly. "I know your parents never gave you the security you needed. I wanted to do that for you. And it kills me that I haven't."

His admission scrapes my soul raw. "I do feel safe with you. I love that you are strong and protective. But sometimes you're too strong, too protective."

"I make you feel fragile." He remembered. He listened. He cares. He just doesn't know how to deal with it.

"You challenge me to be sure of myself, to be more confident, but then you won't let me face the tough things with you."

"I know you're not fragile, Dee. But Malcolm is outside of the realm of tough things. I don't want you getting hurt."

"He can't hurt me, Mick. And he can't hurt our family either. Not if we don't let him."

"I'm not going to let him."

"You think more money is going to fix this?" When he doesn't respond, I continue. "It won't. It might afford you more time as he strings you along, playing his sick games. But it will still chain you to him and to your past. You have to tell the family. You have to let us help you."

I can feel the tension coursing through him; every muscle in his body deflecting my words. "That's never going to happen." He releases me and steps away. "I won't risk you. And I won't have Mama T and Victor blaming themselves."

I ache for him that his own experience makes him believe that. "You don't have to keep protecting them, Mick. Mama T and Victor will put the blame where it belongs. On Malcolm."

"And take plenty for themselves."

"What about Dwayde then?" It's fighting dirty, but I'm desperate. "Have you considered what this could mean to him?"

"This has nothing to do with Dwayde."

"He respects and admires you. Can you imagine how inspiring it would be for him to hear how you survived your abuse too and grew up to be this amazing man? It's even possible that you telling the family your long-kept secrets could be the catalyst Dwayde needs to tell us his."

"You don't know when to quit." He stalks away.

"Mick." I follow.

"Let it go, Dee. Stop pushing me."

But I stand my ground. After a lifetime of doubting myself, of never truly feeling planted or rooted, it finally feels firm beneath my feet. Because I'm changing. Because I know that facing my demons is the only way to conquer them. Mick needs to do the same, even if he isn't ready to acknowledge that yet.

"You're not that nineteen-year-old boy anymore." I put my hand over his heart. Feel it thumping hard and fast against my palm. "You may not have thought you had a choice when Malcolm gave you that ultimatum then. But you do now. You can choose not to be shackled to him anymore. You have the key to free yourself, Mick. You only have to use it."

CHAPTER TWENTY-TWO

Micah

AFTER RUNNING FOR TEN MILES, I return to the house. Dee has left for work, which saves me from another unwanted argument. I power wash and seal the patio stones out back. She had made her point. Knocked me over the head with it. But how do I make this need to protect her from everything bad just go away? I know it's unrealistic. Just as I know she's right that it all comes back to failing my mother. I see that—I'm not blind to my issues—but guilt isn't a light switch I can just turn off.

I guzzle down a glass of water. My thoughts won't stop. I pull out my phone. Malcolm's text is still there. Obnoxious and mocking. I could call Nolan and have the money ready by tomorrow. I could add on another $10 million, but it still wouldn't be enough. No amount is ever going to satisfy him. Not when what he really wants is to cut Dee out of my life, to make me bleed, to make me suffer. That has me wanting to punch the fucking wall. Instead, I put the phone away and finish securing the fence boards.

When I'm done, I come inside the house to shower. As I go to get my clothes from the drawer, I notice a book on top of the dresser. I haven't seen it before. The cover is off-white and made of some kind of crinkly aged or vintage-looking paper with dried flowers.

Curious, I pick it up. There's nothing written on the front. Nothing to indicate what it is or what it's for. I flip open the cover. Across the top of the first page is a title penned in Dee's flowy cursive: ***Dee's Personal Aspirations Journey***.

Realizing I have stumbled onto something private, I should stop. Dee hadn't given me permission to read this. But neither had she hidden it. She'd left it right here in plain sight, unless she'd left it out by accident. Either way, I really shouldn't, even though I know there's nothing that I'm telling myself that's going to stop me.

Deflecting a stab of conscience, I let my gaze slide down to read what she's written.

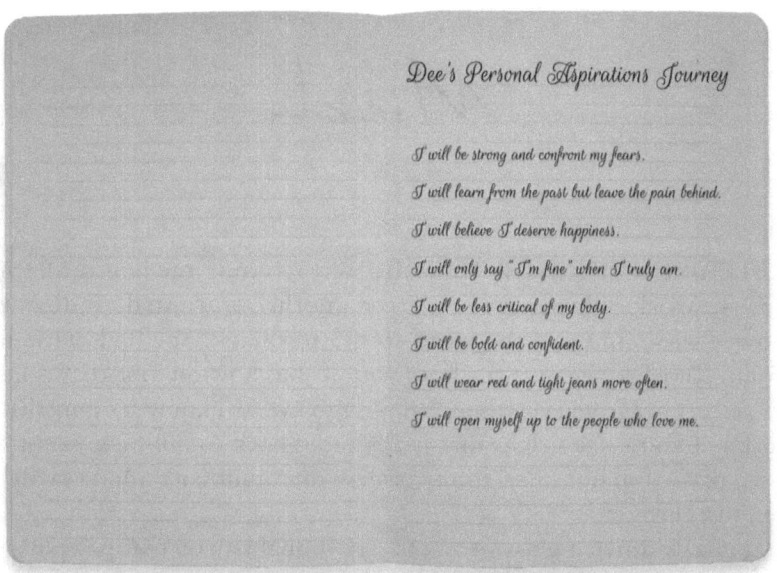

Emotion crowds my throat. This is what Dee must have meant about *doing the work*. Bravely taking on her fears and insecurities, shedding her baggage. I skim my fingers over the words. Feel her blossoming in each one.

That's the point, Mick. Growing...getting better...so that we can be at our best together.

And here I am, stuck. The contrast couldn't be more clear. I'm the one still living in darkness. Shaded by the past. Burrowed deep. Cultivating my guilt with the pathetic need to protect and rescue everyone else, to fix everything—but me.

226

A White Knight complex, a damned martyr as Victor had said.

All because I carry the sins of my father.

I have handcuffed myself to his threats, his demands, his bad deeds. I've let Malcolm use my family against me. I've let him take advantage of my love for them. I've let him play me, own me, manipulate me. As long as Malcolm can pop into my life at any time with the guilt card, I'll never be free.

I stare back at her list, recalling what she'd said to me earlier. *You have the key…you only have to use it.*

There have been very few things in life that I've been sure of. Loving Dee was my one true certainty. Right from the beginning, I knew we were meant to be together. I knew the love we shared would shine as bright as the stars, no matter how dark the nights became. I know that still.

And I'll be damned if I'm going to let Malcolm take that away from me.

I'M IN THE OFFICE WHEN Dee gets home. She stands at the threshold, her suit jacket removed, her shoes off, her toes curling into the floor. The look in her eyes is hesitant. Because I'd put it there.

"I wasn't sure you'd be here," she says.

"It's where I want to be. Where I want to stay, if you'll still have me."

Her whole face seems to brighten with a flare of hope.

"Come here, beauty."

I roll back the chair and she settles sideways on my lap. She presses her smooth cheek against mine and loops an arm around my neck. I hug her waist, drawing her close, and breathe in the warm scent of vanilla and Dee.

"I have a confession to make."

"Oh?" She tilts her head, regarding me.

"I read your *Personal Aspirations*. I know I shouldn't have. But the book was there and…no excuses, I looked. I'm sorry."

"That's okay." She smiles with relief as if she'd been expecting worse. "I wasn't keeping it from you. It's just something I started about a month ago. Goals I could strive toward in being the woman I want to be. Not hindered by my fears and insecurities, you know?"

"You are an incredible woman, Dee. I see how courageous you are. How strong. You continue to push yourself to overcome your past. I haven't done the same. But I'm going to take a page out of your book."

"In what way?" Her eyebrows arch.

"After you left this morning, I did what I always do—jog and busy work to outrun my problems. I wanted to get away from all you'd said. Because I knew you were right and I wasn't ready to deal with it.

"I've been in denial for so long. But after I read what you'd written...it...it just clicked. I finally forced myself to face some difficult truths. Not just that I feel guilty, but how much that guilt has shaped and warped my thinking, my actions, everything that matters. It made me obsessed with protecting the people I love. It made me want to live by some noble code that was the exact opposite of my father. I needed to prove to myself that no matter the DNA we share, I could be as different from him as night from day."

"You are nothing like him, Mick."

"Maybe not. But in trying to do what I thought was right, I was anything but noble. I've made so many mistakes with you, Dee. I've lied. Said awful things. I've shut you out and I've hurt you. I'm sorry, baby."

"I don't care about what's been. We've both made mistakes. I only care about how we move forward."

I stare at her. Eyes like brown sugar, the fan of long lashes, the curve of her cheekbones and the pretty bow of her full pink lips. Details I cherished from the moment we met. Our long and complicated history—filled with both great joy and regret—flashes through my mind. But what falls into place is our future.

"Together. That's how we move forward."

"I want that more than anything. You know I do. But I can't go back to the way it was."

"I'm not expecting you to. I mean together as in sharing the good and the bad. In letting you be there for me through it all. But I need you to give me some leeway to still look out for you and protect you. Not because you need saving. You don't, Dee. But because I love you."

"It's the same for me, Mick. Taking care of each other, that's what I want."

"I can do that."

"That means your problems are my problems."

"I get it."

"Including Malcolm," she says resolutely.

"Everything. I'm through with letting him call the shots. He's not getting another cent from me."

"Wow!" She shakes her head. "Give me a minute to process this."

"I'll make it quicker by getting to the bottomline. I'm going to meet with Malcolm and tell him I'm done with his blackmail. It's over."

Relief and panic wash over her face in equal measure. "I want that for you, Mick. But meeting with him, no. Please don't do that. It got physical last time. It could get worse."

"It won't," I say to calm her fears. "Last time he caught me off guard. I wasn't prepared. I let him get to me. This time I'll be in control. I'll be laying out the conditions."

"What conditions?"

"I'll explain the details later. But Malcolm isn't going to be able to use you or my family as ammunition. Not now or ever again."

"You really have had a revelation today."

"My head's hard, but you kicked it pretty good."

"I did it with love." She kisses my temple. "So, does this mean you're going to tell Mama T and Victor?"

I swallow hard. "Yes. And Dwayde. The whole family."

"That's good, Mick." Tears well in her eyes. "I'm so proud of you."

I lean into Dee. Though there's a sense of trepidation about revealing my secrets, there's also a deep sense of relief. It's the feeling that after all this time I'm finally getting it right.

Dee

OUR FAMILY IS ALL HERE. They came, no questions asked. They simply responded to Mick's call and made the necessary arrangements to gather at Maria's after dinner.

The kids have been put to bed. Mama T brought a bag to stay over rather than drive the hour back home later tonight. Victor brought Gabi and Dwayde at Mick's request.

I imagine there had been much speculation circulating before we arrived. Victor and Isabelle would likely assume it had something to do with the secret Mick's been harboring. But this was going to be a shock to everyone.

Once water, pop, and coffee are served, we assemble around the large rustic dining table. Mama T and I sit on either side of Mick. I can feel the nerves bouncing off him. I put a hand on his leg in support.

"Thank you all for being here," he begins. "I apologize for the urgency and being so cryptic."

"Spit it out," Victor says from across the table. "If we gotta dispose of a body before the sun comes up, we need to get started."

Mick gives a short laugh. Victor's attempt at humor temporarily lightens the mood, but even more than that, his message conveys the sentiment that he would do anything for his brother.

"Go ahead, *mi'jo*." Mama T pats his hand. "You wanted us here. Must be for a good reason."

He takes a breath and lets it out. "Malcolm's been blackmailing me."

The room goes shocked silent. For a moment, the ticking of the wall clock is the only sound. But the tension is loud. Mick looks over at Victor as if predicting he'd take it the hardest.

"I've been dealing with it on my own but that's not really working anymore."

"How long?" Victor snaps out, his voice matching the fury in his eyes.

"Since college."

"Son of a bitch." Victor slaps the table making Gabi jump.

"Getting mad isn't going to help." Isabelle tries to defuse her husband. "Let Mick explain."

Victor is still boiling, but he stays quiet to listen.

"It started after I told the coach at NC State that I was quitting. I had gotten out of rehab, I'd stopped drinking, I was planning to reapply to NYU. I wanted to make you proud." Mick turns to Mama T. "I wanted you to see that all you'd done for me hadn't been a waste."

"Micah." Her brow puckers in the making of a sad frown. "We were always proud of you. Even when you faltered, it didn't change how much we loved you. It was never a waste."

"I know you felt that way. But I wanted to be worthy of it. I was determined to stay sober after my first stint in rehab. I hadn't touched a drink in ten weeks until Malcolm showed up at my apartment with a bottle of whiskey and an ultimatum."

"What ultimatum?" Victor demands impatiently. "What could he possibly have over you?"

"My family."

"Us?" Mama T says, mirroring the confused look of all the eyes around the table.

"I never wanted you to know." Mick's gaze shifts between Mama T and Victor. "I never wanted you to have to hear this."

"Jesus, Mick," Victor says in pure frustration. "Stop taking care of us and just get it said."

Mick's left hand reaches under the table, seeking mine. A telling gesture that touches me deeply. I give it an encouraging squeeze.

"I've been keeping this secret for a very long time. Since I was a kid. I kept it then because Malcolm would have hurt you if you knew. But he later used that silence against me."

"I'm not following, Micah." Mama T searches his face. "What secret?"

"That he...he used to beat me and my mother."

"¡Dios mío!" Tears spring into her eyes.

"I'm sorry," he says hoarsely. "So sorry you ever had to find out."

"You don't apologize for telling me." She reaches over to hug him. "My precious boy. My heart hurts for you and your darling mother."

I wipe at my own watering eyes. Gabi and Maria do the same. Dwayde looks shell-shocked and Victor looks fit to kill.

"Did you tell anyone?" Mama T asks when she finally releases him.

"Only Dee. But I made her promise me she wouldn't tell you," he says in my defense. "She wanted to. Begged me to. But I was eighteen when I told her. I was about to go to college. There was nothing you could have done then. I thought it was better that you never know."

"It wasn't better." Victor seethes. "We would have gotten you out of there no matter how old you were. Jesus, I can't believe I didn't know. That you wouldn't tell me. We're closer than brothers."

"Victor—" Isabelle tries to interject.

"If you are going to tell me to calm down, don't bother. How didn't I know?"

"Because I hid it. He rarely left marks where you could see them. They were under my clothes and I made sure to keep covered up until they healed."

"All those times..." Victor shakes his head as if the memories are bombarding him. "When you made excuses not to go swimming...when you suddenly got modest and changed in the bathroom...when I asked you about the welt on your leg and you said you got it climbing the tree out back...and the cut under your eye that you said happened from falling on the ice...and—"

"Victor, stop," Mick pleads. "I would have said and done anything to keep you from knowing. And Malcolm knew that. He blackmailed me with it. He said if I didn't keep playing ball, he'd tell you."

"Christ." Victor is uncontainable. "After he abused you for years, you played ball for him, you bought him a goddamn house...cars...you did all that because you didn't want us to know?"

"I couldn't let him hurt you after all you had done for me." Emotion swells in Mick's voice. "You gave me everything that was good and decent. That was normal. You took me in after my mother died and treated me like I was yours. You made me family. You saved me. I owed you."

"I don't want to hear that crap." Victor shoots up from the table. "We're not keeping score, Mick. We never have. You don't owe us a damn thing."

"Hush up," Mama T directs her son. "That's not what Micah means. Now sit down and stop yelling."

Victor drops back in his seat, peeved and helpless, arms across his chest.

She takes the hand that Mick has bunched on the table. "Cayo and I knew your home life wasn't easy. We didn't know then how bad it was, but we knew you and your mother suffered because of Malcolm's drinking. We took care of you at first because you were a child in need. Then we did it because we loved you. If you weren't grateful for that, you wouldn't be the kind man you grew up to be. I understand gratitude, Micah. But Vittorio is right. You don't owe us anything. Least of all the sacrifices you made."

"I just wanted to protect you from him. He would say things like it would be a shame if you were to lose your job at the hospital or if people were to stop taking their cars to Cayo's shop. He said he would ruin Victor's chances of ever getting into the police academy. I knew you'd step in if I ever told you. I couldn't risk that."

"He counted on it," Maria says angrily, speaking for the first time. "He knew how much your family meant to you and he used us against you."

"He realized I would never want you to find out about the abuse when there was nothing you could do about it. He knew I'd never want you to blame yourselves. But it's not your fault. You have to believe that."

"What I believe is that Malcolm is a parasite," Victor spits out with repulsion. "His blackmail didn't stop with that, did it?"

"No."

"Of course not, it never does. So, what, he's demanding more money?"

"I never cared about that part. I did what I thought I had to. Whatever it took to keep him out of my life and away from you."

"But he didn't stay out of your life, did he?"

"No." Mick's tone hollows. "I'd done his bidding. Played ball. Set him up to live well. He couldn't take anything more from me. Nothing that mattered, or so I thought. Until I heard from him last week."

Victor's eyes go to Mick's scabbed knuckles, putting that piece together. "You met with him?"

"Yeah."

"What did he want?"

"He knew about me being back with Dee."

"Did he threaten her?"

"No, not physically," I answer. "But he's added me to the mix, using me as another weapon to hurt Mick with. From all I've heard, it's not just about the money, it's about making Mick pay for a debt he doesn't owe. Malcolm blames him for ruining his chances at playing ball; he has turned that into a cruel and ruthless vendetta. He knows how Mick feels about me, how he's always felt. He's trying to keep us apart again."

"What do you mean by again?" Maria asks.

Mick's eyes go hot and sharp like a flaming sword. "Malcolm told me he knew where Dee was the whole time we were looking for her. He knew she was pregnant with my baby. He laughed about it. Took glee in the fact that he kept her from me."

"¡Dios mío!" Mama T cries. "He kept you apart on purpose. He kept Dee from us. He's not just cruel, he's evil."

Victor snarls in agreement. "What's he got over you on Dee?"

"He's threatening to expose personal details about her. Nothing she has any reason to be ashamed of. But he threatened to put a spin on it. To tell that tabloid reporter, O'Malley, lies about Dee going after me for my money; things to bring out the press in droves and try to hurt Dee's reputation and career. He threatened to ruin her if I didn't pay him $10 million dollars by Friday and break off our relationship."

"*Jesus.*" Victor chokes on his Coke.

"I'm not giving in to him," Mick confirms as Isabelle pats her husband's back. "I'm done. He's not keeping us apart or using this family anymore."

"Bueno." Mama T puts a hand on Mick's shoulder. "I don't agree with what you did. But I understand why. Because you loved us all too much to do otherwise. And Malcolm took advantage of that. He is the only one to blame. You hear me?"

Mick nods.

"I mean it, Micah," she stresses sternly, giving him that familiar don't-mess-with-me look that can still make her adult children squirm.

"I hear you, Mama T."

Her face goes soft again, but her voice invites no debate. "Now Malcolm must face the consequences of his actions."

"What consequences?" Mick asks warily.

"He should be arrested."

"For what? There are no charges."

"No charges," she balks. "Malcolm committed crimes, no? Abuse... blackmail."

"Yes, but—"

"Criminals belong in jail, Micah. Being Sheriff doesn't make him above the law."

"I don't have any evidence to make charges stick, and even if I did, that would only bring a media circus."

"*Bah!* Let the press come. We have not done wrong. Only Malcolm bears the shame."

Understanding the tug-of-war between the kind of justice Mama T wants and the kind of justice Mick needs, I intercede. "You're right, Mama T. Malcolm should be held accountable. But the criminal system has limitations. It is not going to work in our favor. Malcolm can't be criminally prosecuted for abuse after all this time, and I imagine blackmail and extortion are hard to prove without concrete evidence. So, as much as I agree that Malcolm should face legal charges, he won't."

"Then there's no justice for Micah," she says woefully.

"Freedom is justice for me." Mick holds her gaze before he looks over to Dwayde. "Whether Malcolm was present in my life or not, the secret was always there. Showing up in nightmares. Clouding my judgment. Chasing my thoughts. Dee gave me the push I needed to finally tell you. To finally get free."

Dwayde shifts in his seat, then looks away.

Mick turns back to Mama T. "Justice for me is telling Malcolm it's over. It's getting him out of my life...out of our lives. For good."

"Alright, *mi'jo*. You're entitled to handle it your way. But just because you don't intend to bring extortion charges against Malcolm doesn't mean he needs to know that."

"True," I heartily agree. "And the statute on abuse for civil action is twenty years after your eighteenth birthday. So, even if you don't intend to file a lawsuit, he doesn't need to know that either."

"Two smart women." Victor winks at us. "Time to turn the tables. Let Malcolm feel the heat for a change."

The idea catches momentum. Mick, who's used to going it alone, allows his family to help—expanding on his plan. No one seems to care that it's fast approaching midnight. Maria and James whip up a bowl of guacamole and we sit around the table eating chips and dip while we flesh out the details to give Malcolm the comeuppance that Mick needs but is far less than the one Malcolm deserves.

It strikes me that despite the circumstances, laughter and the usual ribbing returns. I'm sure there will be more difficult conversations ahead that Mick will have with Mama T and especially with Victor, but at this moment the only thing that matters is we're family and we're there for each other.

I glance up at Mick and smile.

He brackets my face between his large palms and with everyone looking on, kisses me with more passion than is appropriate for a public display.

I blush a little. But my heart is full.

CHAPTER TWENTY-THREE

Micah

I DIDN'T THINK I'D SLEEP. I was so wound up from telling the family. I'd spent all those years trying to protect them, trying to protect myself from more guilt. But it had gone so much better than I could have imagined. And I have to admit the plan was much improved, more solid with their input.

When we'd gotten home after two in the morning, I'd only meant to lie with Dee for a while. To hold her before going to the couch. But as soon as my head hit the pillow, I dropped off like a log.

Now awake, I watch her curled up beside me. The woman who had made this all possible. Both her hands are cushioned beneath her cheek, her feet are wedged between my calves. Her breathing is slow and rhythmic. The shadows of the room caress her face and neck.

I lightly trace the bend of one arm from the underside of her elbow to her wrist. Her skin is soft as water. I watch her sleep for another twenty minutes; touching her, not to wake or to arouse, just because.

Before long, she stirs. Her dark lashes flutter up to reveal those sunbeam eyes that strike me right in the heart.

"Morning, beauty."

"Morning," she murmurs with a lazy smile and reaches out to slide her hand in my hair.

"Was everything okay?" I have to ask.

"Yes." Dee catches my meaning. "You were out cold for the night." My entire body eases with that knowledge.

"I don't want you to be afraid of sharing a bed with me because of your nightmares."

"Hard not to be."

"Have you always had them?"

I hesitate. This isn't what I want to talk about. But I promised not to shut down. I promised to try.

"When I was little, yeah." I press up onto one elbow. "But they lessened over time. The violence was just routine. I'd come to expect it. I couldn't control what he did to me physically, but at least I could escape from him through my stories."

"That makes me so sad." She gives me a hug and pulls back. "Did you ever talk to anyone about your nightmares?"

"Is that your subtle way of suggesting I need counseling?"

"No." Her fingers trace the curve of my bicep. "Counseling isn't the solution for everyone or everything. But I think it can do some good. It's helped me. In fact, I'm seeing Dr. Roland this afternoon."

"Is everything okay?"

"Yes. Better than okay." She smiles. "I missed our appointment last week and I rebooked for today. That's all."

"I'm glad it helps you, Dee. I'm just not sure therapy is for me."

"I don't want us to sleep apart."

"I don't want that either. Until lately, I hadn't had a nightmare since I was a kid."

Dee watches me with keen perception. "When did they start up again?"

"The day I showed up at your office," I confess; I don't want to lie to her.

"I'm sorry."

"Hey." I run my knuckles down her cheek. "You're not the cause. I know that's what you're thinking, but you're not."

"They came back when you saw me."

"They came back, because as you pointed out, I hadn't dealt with my guilt or with Malcolm. Now that I'm dealing with both, they may go away for good. But if not, I promise to consider counseling as an option. Okay?"

"Okay." But I can see in her eyes that she's still thinking she had some part in their return.

"I want you to know something," I say, twining one of her curls around my finger. "The dream I had when I saw you after all those years wasn't like the others."

"How was it different?"

"It was more like a flashback to the day Malcolm caught me writing my entrance essay to NYU. He was enraged. I'd rarely seen him like that. He was usually controlled. But this time he lost it. Hit me in the face when he'd never done that before. It happened so fast." The memory roars in my head. "I didn't see it coming. That first hit knocked me to the floor. Then a blur of kicks to my ribs. I must have been losing consciousness because I remember thinking that I might actually die.

"That's when I saw visions of my family—Victor, little Gabi, everyone. I heard my mom telling me it was too soon, but it was you...your voice, your face, your smile that was the light that drew me back."

I wipe her fallen tears with the pad of my thumb. "You were the beauty amongst all the ugliness. You gave me that. You still do."

"Mick," she breathes.

"I love you, Deeana Rae. Then..." I let my lips journey across the angle of her jaw. "Now..." They trace her cheekbone. "Forever."

She sighs sweetly and I capture the sound with my mouth. Slipping my tongue inside, I feel her toes curl against my legs and take the kiss deeper. And deeper until I'm sinking in it. A tender joining but with no less passion. The kind of kiss that I have only ever known with Dee. Where it grabs you by the soul and doesn't let go. Where time seems to still and the world stops spinning.

There is no rush. No race. Just slow. Endlessly slow to savor every minute, every move, every moan.

"I love kissing you." My mouth lingers on her lips before I ease back and move the sheet out of the way. "I love looking at you." My hands slide up the hem of her short nightie. "All of you. Even when you're not around. I still have a vivid picture of you in my head."

When the satin clears her head and her curls fall around the tops of her shoulders like ribbons of sable, I take her in my arms. Feel her tremble. I lay her back on the bed. But rather than devour all those luscious curves, I gentle my hands over them. Feeling her moan softly under my touch, her move fluidly beneath my palms. I explore her as if it's the first time. Though I know every inch of her body, it feels new. Different. As if a reawakening.

I lean in to sample all the tastes of Dee. The sleek honey of her mouth. The vanilla warmth of her breasts, chocolate swirls of her nipples. The creamy satin of her belly and the sweet heat between her thighs. I sip instead of gulp. Glide instead of dive.

I feel her heart pounding everywhere. A primal beat, pumping under my lips, my hands. Her throaty moans sprint through my blood. Her eyelids flutter, her muscles quiver, her hands tangle in my hair, pulling me closer until she's gasping and shaking all over.

The pleasure of loving Dee is clear like morning dew, vast like the bluest ocean. When her palms slide over my back, her touch is a desire that I feel more than skin deep. I slide up her body to seal the connection. She closes around me. Velvety soft and silky wet. We remain poised for a blissful moment, joined, mated. I seek her hands, locking our fingers together over her head. Then we begin to move. Together, taking and giving; a lover's dance. The music between us builds to a crescendo. I watch her eyes go smoky as she crests, feel her fingers gripping mine, her body going taut, tighter; a drawn bow of trembling need.

My vision grays, my strokes hasten, and it's Dee's cries of release that I swallow as I let myself fall.

WHILE DEE SHOWERS AND GETS dressed for work, I go into the kitchen to start the coffee. It feels good to be back home. To be back with Dee. It feels good to be building a life with her. One that will be free of Malcolm.

Putting the plan in motion, I grab my phone off the counter and scroll to his message from yesterday. *Great show. Makes the deal sweeter.*

I unclench my fist and type: *I've got a sweeter deal to offer. Tomorrow. 9 p.m. Meet me at The Grinder off Interstate 70.*

He doesn't respond right away even when my phone indicates that he's read the message. Fucking bastard. He waits ten minutes to text. *Call me.*

He's too shrewd to take my message at face value or to chance a longer text exchange that could incriminate him. I tap the audio button and make the call.

"Hello, *son*. Let's hear this so-called deal to see if it's worth my while."

"I'm not doing this over the phone." I keep my voice cool.

"Seems you've forgotten who's in control here."

"I know exactly who's in control."

"Then you know I'm the one with the story."

"You want to take your chances that you're playing with a full house, go ahead. But I think a smart man would want to know what cards are on the table before he plays his final hand."

"I don't know what the fuck you're up to, but don't think you can screw me over."

"Tomorrow, Malcolm." I hang up.

Several minutes later, Dee walks in like a summer breeze, thawing my icy emotions. Her smile is adorably crooked and teasing.

"How lucky am I?" she says as I pour the coffee. "My very own sexy barista."

"I'm the lucky one." I extend my arms out to her and she walks into them.

"You okay?" Dee asks, attuned to me.

"I will be. Just spoke to Malcolm."

"Oh." Her face lifts to mine. "What happened?"

I repeat the gist of the phone call.

Anger fires in her eyes. "He's such a dick."

I manage a grin because rarely does Dee talk like that. "He is. But he'll show. Backing down from my challenge would show weakness. That's his Achilles' heel."

"How are you feeling about the plan?"

"I think it's good and will get the job done. Until then, I don't want to think about Malcolm. I don't want him in our heads or in our house." I pull her to me, holding her close. And for a while it's just us. Exactly as it should be.

We fall back into our morning routine with ease. I pour the coffee. Dee, having time for more than a smoothie-to-go, makes a frittata. We talk and enjoy each other's company, exchanging casual touches with an intimacy reserved for lovers.

After breakfast, we tidy up and Dee leaves for the office. I answer emails and attend a video call with Nadia. The project is slightly ahead of schedule thanks to her meticulous attention to detail and Jordyn's design that only requires minor tweaks.

I pour another cup of coffee and head to the home office. I put on music, selecting the song track from *The Dark Knight Rises*. Although storytelling had started as an escape into the fantastical worlds of my making, it was also an essential creative outlet for my imagination. A driving force that could be intense, all-consuming, and often rewarding on a deep gut level.

There were, of course, frustrating times when the words in my mind wouldn't harmonize on the page and my writing fell flat. I cursed the muses then. But there were other times when the gods of inspiration gave me wings and my writing soared so high I had to race to keep up.

After hours of my fingers flying across the keyboard, I realize this is one of those times when it had soared. The music blares and I feel a line of sweat riding down the center of my spine. I hadn't ever had to suffer for my art, but it still came from pain.

I take a sip of coffee, wince that it's cold, and look back over my chapters. At night, District Attorney Delayna sheds her conservative suits and law-abiding pursuits for justice to don leather and a black mask as she tracks down guilty assailants that the court had wrongly set free. Dubbed Dark Angel, this time her manhunt results in finding the wife beater, who had nearly killed his spouse and gotten off on a technicality. The scene is as vivid as the blood she spills. His pleas for mercy scream off the page. The terror he'd inflicted on his wife thrown back at him in savage reflection. It's the image I want, the brutality I need. His pain, his suffering.

Dee has her therapy. I have mine.

Channeling the dark thoughts into my writing is as exhausting as it is energizing. I push back from the desk and flex my hands, open and closed. It's not uncommon for them to cramp when I'm at it non-stop. Knowing I've given all I've got for today, I go shower and drive over to Victor's. He's working the late shift so he's home this afternoon.

At the sound of the doorbell, Rufus starts barking and I can hear Victor try to quiet him down. When he answers, there isn't a sting in his gaze, but there's an implication of one.

I bend down to pat Rufus who is nudging my leg.

"Hungry?" he asks.

"I could eat."

"Get the mustard and roast beef."

For the next few minutes we work together assembling two behemoth sandwiches with a side of potato chips and pickles.

"How's Dwayde?" I ask, grabbing a couple of Cokes from the fridge.

"We talked a bit last night, but he was hard to gauge."

"Dwayde thinks you walk on water, nothing you said has changed that. If anything, he feels more akin to you now that he knows you have this common bond."

"Dee was hoping it would encourage him to talk."

"Is that why you wanted him there?"

"In part. But I also didn't want him to hear it from anyone but me."

"Now I know why you were so sure that Dwayde wouldn't reveal his secrets. You'd been keeping yours for thirty years."

Guilt comes rocketing back. "I fucked up, Victor."

"Just shut up and sit. I've got some things I want to say."

He pulls up a seat opposite me. His temper is on a slow simmer, but threatens to gain more heat.

"You seriously pissed me off," he begins after a few bites. "I'll get over it. But I'm gonna make something very clear—and I'm speaking for Mama and Papa too. You got that?"

"Yeah, I got it."

"You were never a burden or a charity case or anything but family."

"You took me in—"

"I told you to shut up," he snaps out. "We did what we were meant to do. What we wanted to do. We didn't expect you to make sacrifices for us or to feel some goddamn obligation, and it makes me mad as fuck that you actually did."

"It wasn't like that."

"Jesus Christ." He glares. "Can't you follow a simple order?"

"Not my strongest suit."

"No shit. Always were too stubborn. Always had to be in charge, in control."

Because he's right, I don't say anything.

"You always thought you had to give back to us because of all you'd gotten. I didn't understand the extent of it then, guess I do now. But did you ever stop and think for a moment how fortunate we are that you came into our lives? I don't just mean the ranch and business you bought for Maria and James. Or this house that gave us a start or the college funds you set up for all the kids. Way before you had money, you made our lives better just by being you. You're the brother I used to wish for. The other son my parents always wanted. You gave us as much as we gave you. More. It's time you wake the fuck up and realize that."

My mouth is bone dry. "Can I say something now?"

"Yeah, I'm through."

"I admit that I've felt I owed you all, but it wasn't out of a sense of obligation. Never that. It was always out of gratitude and love. But I realize now that's not an excuse for lying and keeping secrets. I messed up, Victor. I should have told you years ago. I'm sorry, man. I don't know what else to say. What else to do."

"What's done is done. Now we move on and deal with Malcolm. I got the piece." He gets up and disappears from the kitchen, returning a few moments later with a black device in his palm that's not much bigger than a paperclip.

"That's it?"

"Yep. One of the smallest recording devices available. It's got good range too, and a transmitter that will allow for a backup. Let's try it out."

Victor gives me a quick lesson and I tuck it inside the front pocket of my jeans.

"Testing, testing," he says from several feet away.

When I play it back, his voice comes through clear as a bell. "Cool."

"Yeah. I get to try all kinds of gadgets doing surveillance and sting operations. I'm looking forward to this one."

"Thanks for helping me out. This meeting's been a long time coming."

"Tomorrow night."

"Yep. It's set. He'll be there." I stick the device back inside my pocket. "So, we're good?"

Without answering, he raises his hand to his mouth, spits into his palm, and extends it out to me.

"Jesus." I grimace.

"You weaseling out?"

"Nope." Respectful of the pledge we made at six, I spit into my own hand and grip his firmly. "Brothers forever."

And just like that, we're okay again.

CHAPTER TWENTY-FOUR

Dee

DR. PATRICE ROLAND'S OFFICE IS decorated in subtle pastels that are both professional and calming. The good doctor conveys the same—an attractive woman in her mid-fifties with a salted afro and earthy brown eyes that are warm and intelligent behind plastic frames.

"How are you, Dee?"

"I'm great," I say, settling into my usual spot on the light peach sofa across from her. She takes a seat in the matching armchair and places a tablet on her lap, crosses her legs, and gives me a pleasant smile.

"It shows. Tell me what's great."

I feel myself grin like a teenage girl writing her boyfriend's name in big loopy letters. "I'm in love and I'm really embracing it."

"Oh." Aware of my trust issues and the insecurities that have hounded my every relationship, Dr. Roland doesn't contain her surprise. "That certainly is a new and exciting development."

"Exciting, yes. But not all that new. The man is Mick. Micah Peters."

I see recognition dawn in her expression. Not just because she's familiar with his NBA fame, but because she knows some of our complicated history. In the nearly two years that I've been coming here, I haven't shared all the details about my past. But Dr. Roland knows that my father bailed. She knows about the ten foster homes before my mother's suicide and the Torreses taking me in. She knows about my fears of letting them love me. She knows about me falling for Mick and it all falling apart. But she doesn't know about my pregnancy or about losing our baby.

I couldn't tell her before. I couldn't tell anyone. The grief and pain I had sealed inside felt too overwhelming to unlock. But I tell her now. All of it. How Mick found me again, the custody case, and learning of Papa T's death. I tell her of finally confiding my painful secrets and confronting all the hurt I caused. But I also tell her of the joy of reconnecting with my family and Mick.

Dr. Roland listens without judgment, her questions seek clarification, and her responses are compassionate. "Thank you for sharing that with me," she says when I'm done. "That is a lot to have gone through. But I'm so pleased about these positive turns in your life and with your progress. You've made some huge strides, Dee. I hope you see that."

"I do. In large part because of Mick. He's helped me with my grief and insecurities."

"In what way?"

"By encouraging me to open up. By accepting me and loving me, unconditionally. He makes me feel good about myself. Beautiful. Sexy. Desirable." A flush of heat breaks out across my face. "He knows everything about me and has never made me feel less than whole. He thinks I'm strong and resilient. I'm starting to think that maybe I am."

"In what way have you seen yourself be strong?" she asks, picking up her stylus to make a note.

"Pushing past my fears of trust and intimacy. Breaking out of my comfort zone, so to speak. I just feel myself changing…improving. I've even been dressing differently. Lingerie and wearing clothes that I wouldn't have dared before. Clothes that Mick likes me in and that make me feel good when I build up the nerve to wear them."

"Sounds as if Mick has had quite an influence in your life."

"He has."

"Hm." She makes another note.

I recognize the question in her *hm*. "You think I'm being too reliant on him for my self-worth?"

"Is that what you think?"

"No. I mean yes at first," I admit. "He's so adoring, seductive, so everything that it's hard not to be absorbed by him. I like the way Mick makes me feel. I like the way I feel about myself when I'm with him. But I also recognize that I have to keep my own sense of self that's separate from Mick. I can take all the good things he offers and still develop on my own."

"That's an insightful perspective."

"It's taken time for me to figure some of that out. But I'm getting there. Mick's been good for me and I think I've been good for him too. We both come into this relationship with baggage, jointly and separately. We're dealing with it together and that has made our bond stronger. I want to be at my best for him and for myself."

"What does your best mean?"

"More confident and self-assured."

"What do you think might be holding you back from feeling that way now?"

"My body, mostly." I glance down at myself. "I used to think that if I could just lose weight, I'd feel good. But I've done that and discovered that no matter what the scale says, I still find faults with myself. I just want to feel comfortable in my skin."

"We briefly touched on body image before," Dr. Roland recalls. "I got the impression that wasn't an area you wanted to explore."

"You're right. I wasn't in the right headspace for that then. I think I am now."

"That's good, Dee." She makes another note. "Often, body image doesn't come from what we see outside. It comes from how we feel inside."

"That makes sense. I have these negative tapes that play that tell me I'm not good enough, skinny enough, perfect enough."

"Where do you think those come from?"

"My past, I suppose. My childhood. And they're manifested in what I see when I look at myself."

"What do you see?"

"My physical flaws."

"What are those in your mind?"

That's an easy one to answer. "My hips and behind are too big. My thighs are too thick. I have stretchmarks on my stomach, and while I know lots of women want big breasts, I wish mine were small and perky. I also wish I didn't feel this way. I wish I didn't care."

"But you do?"

"Yes. I want to be able to bounce out of bed naked without pulling the sheet around me. I want to look at myself in a full-length mirror and feel about my body the way Mick feels about it. I want to see the beauty he sees."

"Do you think Mick only sees your body as beautiful?"

"No." I shake my head. "It's the whole package. Inside and out. But it's my body that I struggle with the most. I developed an unhealthy relationship with food and my body early on. I would eat to self-soothe when my parents would fight or when my mom would get depressed and withdraw from me. I remember my father saying that I was gaining weight right before he left us, and soon after that my mother sent me into foster care. I think I equated the two. That they didn't want me because I was fat. That's where the negative tapes come into play."

"They've had years to become ingrained. The good news is you can undo them," she says encouragingly.

"How?"

"There are a number of different behavioral and exposure therapy exercises. I have a client that confronted her anxiety about her body by posing nude for an art class."

"Oh God, no. If that's the assignment, you might as well ask me to jump off a cliff."

"I wasn't going to suggest that." Her smile carries humor. "Maybe one day. But for now, we'll start with reframing those messages."

"Okay, that sounds more like my speed."

She sets aside her tablet and leans forward. "Let's look at a few things that make up body image. Perception—the way you see yourself. It may not be accurate, but it's your view. Affect—the way you feel about yourself based on your perception. And behavioral—how you behave in relation to how you feel about your body.

"We're going to start with perception. What you tell yourself and what you believe. Does it stand to reason that big thighs make you unworthy?"

"No, of course not." I get her point. "But I still think that way."

"Right. That's why we work on changing those negative messages. Just because you believe them doesn't make them true."

"So, how do I stop believing them?"

"By countering any of the thoughts that perpetuate your current body image. Your homework is to make two columns. One will have the negative tapes and the other will have the kinder and healthier messages that you can give yourself. That way whenever you think your thighs are too big, challenge that thought with: there's nothing wrong with my thighs or my thighs aren't too big at all, they are strong and sexy. Find the right messages for you. And over time those will become your truths."

"And this will have me bouncing out of bed naked?" I ask.

"That will be up to you, Dee. But this will help you along that path. With continuous effort, you can feel good about your body, good about yourself. It really sounds like you want that."

"I do." Because I know as much as Mick loves and desires me, there is nothing more empowering than self-love and acceptance.

THAT EVENING, FRESH FROM THE gym, I start dinner, light the candles in the fireplace, and put on a romantic playlist. While Marvin Gaye croons about getting it on, I cut up tomatoes and basil.

The meeting with Dr. Roland left me with a new challenge I'm ready to tackle. And my relationship with Mick is on a nice, smooth path. Humming, I add the wine to the sauce and wait for it to boil. My plan is to let the sauce simmer and the flavors develop, while I take a shower and get dressed in something sexy. I want to be primped and perfumed for Mick's arrival.

Only he gets home earlier than expected. The front door opens and I hear him in the foyer. That awareness alone makes my heart sing. But it does a full-on musical when he steps into the kitchen dressed in jeans and a charcoal sweater, scrunched up to reveal his muscular forearms.

He looks entirely edible. Meanwhile, my ponytail is coming undone, sweat-damp tendrils curl around my face, and I'm still wearing the black leggings and baggy T-shirt I'd worked out in.

But the dark gaze that does a heated sweep from my messy hair to my bare feet makes me forget all about my rumpled appearance. As tangible as a touch, it's a look that rains shivers through my body and hardens my nipples.

"I wasn't expecting you for another half hour."

"I'm here now." He prowls forward with a take-no-prisoner swagger and lays a kiss on me that goes straight to my head.

Fortunately, I have a couple of wits left to remember the brunch fire-alarm disaster. "The sauce," I murmur before he relaxes his hold enough for me to turn around. I lower the flame and give the ingredients a stir while he keeps his arms around me from behind. Between the stove and Mick's body heat, I'm melting.

"What's for dinner?" His warm breath is in my ear.

"Sun-dried tomato pesto. Want a taste?"

"Mm-hmm." His teeth sink gently into a spot on my neck.

"I meant the sauce."

"I'm having an appetizer first."

I laugh, but the sound catches on a breath when his hand slips under the hem of my top and I feel his large palm splay wide against my bare midriff. "Mick."

"Hm?"

"I haven't showered yet."

"You don't need a shower. Your skin tastes salty and you smell good. Sweaty, lusty, like when I'm fucking you."

I'm helpless to the rawness of his words and he knows it. In a nanosecond, my need goes from a slow simmer to an incessant boil. I turn off the burner and twist around.

Mick cups my behind and brings me flush against him in one hard jerk before his mouth comes crashing down on mine. The kiss is quickly heady, quickly fervent. We move together, backing up and out of the kitchen. Tongues tangling, I rush my hands under his sweater. Hot flesh and flexing muscle. I knead and stroke his broad chest, my fingers tracing down the happy trail that disappears into his jeans. I open the top snap as we stumble toward the living room.

Our moans slide to raspy laughs when we bump into a wall, then slide back to moans again. Through the sound system, Ella Mai and John Legend harmonize on "Everything," their sultry voices floating in the air. Mick toes off his socks and breaks the kiss to rid me of my T-shirt.

"I want you right here." He moves us in a primal dance over to the fireplace I'd set up earlier for ambiance. "I want to see the candlelight glimmer over your sexy curves, see them in your eyes when I'm buried deep inside of you."

God, yes, the wanting is fierce. Our lips grow hungrier, racing over skin, a relentless craving that has us tumbling onto the area rug. Our breaths are quick and labored. The instinct to mate is dark, turbulent, and thrilling.

Mick tugs me out of the snug sports bra, groaning at the sight of my bare breasts. His tongue lashes over my nipples, coaxing and tasting, taking me to the edge of insanity.

We roll on the floor, our hands grappling, groping to remove the rest of each other's clothes. I can see him above me in the flickering flames. See his gorgeous face as he drives deep inside me. Our hips pump together like pistons. Riding each other hard and fast. I quiver and tense, moaning shamelessly, loving the feel of taking and being taken.

He flips me over and I scramble to get onto my hands and knees. When the negative message plays about how big my ass must appear in this position, I counterpunch with how erotic it must look with Mick kneeling behind me, holding on to the lush curves of my cheeks as he strokes his big cock in and out of my wet pussy. The image in my mind makes me crazed.

I lower my elbows to the floor, my nipples grazing the carpet as my body rocks back and forth into his feral lunges. Serrated gasps from the pleasure/pain shoot from my throat. I'm so turned on, I think I'll burst from the orgasm building in me like a pressure cooker. It boils and bubbles, blowing the lid off and then I'm coming on breathy cries of his name, my sex pulling and releasing, clenching around him.

"Ah fuck, Dee," he rumbles and flips me onto my back again. He holds me down, his damp chest hard to mine, his frenzied heartbeat thumping against my own. His tongue thrusting into my mouth, his cock thrusting into my core. He watches me avidly as I reach for it, beg for it, urged on by his sounds of pleasure, by how good he tells me I feel. Claimed by his stare, another orgasm hits, tearing through my body.

Mick's eyes on me are wild and intense. His breaths choppy, his face ravaged as he powers into me three more times before he pulls out, and kneeling between my open legs, jacks his cock.

Despite my two orgasms, I'm aroused all over again watching the slick, rapid movement of his hand, the tensing of his muscles before he comes, spurting repeatedly over my torso and belly.

"God, Mick."

"You like that?" His eyes are drugged from his orgasm, but his smile is wicked and provocative.

"Everything you do is a turn on."

He rubs his sperm over my breasts and nipples, making me throb all over. Then his hand slides down my belly and between my legs. I writhe, keening to get off again. Still he teases me, softly running his skilled fingers over the lips of my sex. I buck my hips and he pushes his fingers into me.

"I love making you come." His voice is rough. "You get so greedy for it. So hot."

"Ohh...Mick...please."

"I got you, baby. Watch."

I look at him down the length of my body, not noticing anything except the pleasure he's giving me. I watch as he withdraws his fingers, wet from our combined orgasms. He brings those fingers to my clit, massaging me in erotic circles.

"Mick!" I gasp, coming again. My body quakes so hard it leaves me breathless and my limbs like water.

"Beautiful." He lowers on top of me and treats my mouth to the most tender kiss. I wrap my arms around him feeling sated and loved to the very center of my soul.

THE SUN IS SLOWLY CREEPING in when I wake. Mick had spent the night with me nightmare-free. We'd both been exhausted, using what energy we had left to shower, eat, and crawl into bed. It's still rare to wake before my trusty sex-alarm clock that is Mick, but I take advantage of the early hour and gingerly slip from his arms. Reaching over to the nightstand, I pull out my journal and prop myself up against the pillows. I turn to a clean page and make a line down the middle. One side I label Bullshit, the other I label Truth. I complete the BS list in no time at all. The Truth list has me biting the end of my pen.

"What's got you thinking so hard?" Mick's voice, raspy from sleep, breaks my concentration.

I look over at him. He's tousled and drowsy, and very appealing.

"My homework from Dr. Roland," I say, having told him about it over dinner. "I'm working on my positive messages list."

"That's easy." Beneath the covers, where I sit with my knees bent, he skims a hand along the underside of my thigh. "I could fill up the whole book. Want me to give you the rundown?"

"No." But I smile to show my appreciation. "I have to do this myself. And stop that."

"What?"

"Distracting me," I say of the tingles radiating from my left quad and spreading to my center.

He slides his hand away. "I know this is important to you. I just hate to see you struggle with something that's so obvious to me."

"It's okay for me to struggle through it. That's part of the work. I'll get there and then watch out, I'm gonna want to be naked all the time."

"God help me when you do." He laughs. "You're already wearing me out."

"Yeah right." I roll my eyes. "You're like a machine."

"Trust me, baby, it's all you."

"Aw…" I lean over to press my lips to his. "I love you."

"Love you too, beauty. I'll go put on the coffee." He pushes out of

251

bed and I take a moment to admire the muscular lines of his naked back as he pulls on a pair of joggers.

Mick has never had a self-conscious minute in his life. Not about his body. But he has his own cross to bear that makes coming up with positive body messages pale in comparison. I'm painfully aware of what this day holds in store for him.

Tonight he's going to face Malcolm again.

I put down my pen as a shiver of another kind runs through me.

CHAPTER TWENTY-FIVE

Micah

AT 9:00, I ENTER THE bar with the bill of my cap pulled low. It's Wednesday night, less than a handful of patrons occupy the grungy place. Likely regulars. I order a Coke to prevent being hassled for taking up space without paying. I drop a $20 bill on the sticky surface. "Keep the change."

The bearded barkeep grabs the money without a thank you and slides across a filmy glass. This isn't the kind of place you come to for cleanliness or customer service.

I take a seat in a booth where the fake brown leather has foam poking through the cracks and the scuffed table has seen better days.

I casually glance out the window at Victor's rental car, and test the device, "Can you hear me?" The brake lights flash twice for yes.

Then I wait for Malcolm, staring into my untouched drink. I'd expected that hard knot in the pit of my stomach. He always put it there.

I need to be free of him. Free to move forward. When this is over, I intend to walk out of here, leaving the fury and the guilt behind. To let the memory of my mother rest in peace and to find some for myself.

Malcolm is nearly thirty minutes late when he finally strolls in. He's wearing a cap too. This one not identifying him as Sheriff. He goes straight to the bar. When he has a tumbler of whiskey in hand, he saunters past the two pool players and slides into the booth across from me. His face still carries the marks from Friday.

"This better be good."

"Wouldn't be here otherwise."

"Turn your phone off and put it on the table."

"Paranoid, old man?"

"Do it or I walk."

I make a production of taking my phone out of my jacket pocket, turning it off, and setting it on the tabletop. "Satisfied?"

"We'll see." He lifts his whiskey and drinks deep. "You seem a little tense, son."

"Yeah, well, I've been sitting here for the last half hour reflecting on the past. Do you know how much money I've given you over the years?"

"Not nearly enough."

"Because I owe you."

"Damn right you do. Look at your life, boy. Look at all you got 'cause of me."

"It wasn't the life I wanted."

"Save your bitching and whining for someone who gives a fuck, that sure ain't me. You got nothing to complain about. Cars. A condo that's worth a fortune. Fame. Anything you want, any time. Yeah, I'm really crying for you."

"None of that ever mattered to me. I wanted to go to NYU. I wanted to write, not play ball. But you threatened to tell Cayo and Rita about the way you belted me around. About the welts you left all over my chest and back."

"You're still whining about that too? My man knocked me around and you don't hear me complaining. It made me tougher. But you…" He spares me a look of disgust before he tosses back more whiskey. "Didn't make you tough or much of a man. Sure, you stopped crying after the first few times I beat your skinny little ass. You tried to take it. Didn't want to give in, didn't want to break. But I broke you anyway. You did what I wanted. What I told you to do."

"To protect Cayo and Rita."

"Because you're weak. Because you gave a fuck about those mealy-ass do-gooders who thought discipline was timeouts and taking away privileges. Fuck that. I would love to have told them about how I knocked you around while they were sitting pretty, right next door without a fucking clue. To see the pathetic look on their faces. Helpless and horrified that they hadn't looked out for their golden boy nearly as well as they thought they had. Yeah, that would have been real sweet."

"You weren't concerned that if you were to tell them they might have exposed you?"

"Fuck, no," he answers with a smug sneer that I itch to knock off his face. "My word against theirs. I'm the Sheriff. Who do you think people would have believed?"

"Guess you're right." I play along. "You had the power."

"Fucking right I do. Power is everything, boy."

"You had it over my mother."

"She deserved what she got for trapping me."

"She was so afraid of you. She took your beatings standing up for me. I wish I'd done the same for her."

"Boo-hoo. Get yourself a shrink and work out your daddy issues. I'm through with this trip down memory lane. What's the deal?"

"I'm getting to that. Over the years I've paid you millions to keep you from telling Rita and Cayo."

"And you'll keep paying as long as Rita is alive and if you want to protect the girl. Gotta say, Deeana Rae surprised me. She's not half bad looking if you're into that. I prefer my women small and tight, know what I mean? But she's got a nice rack on her that I never noticed before under those baggy clothes, and she's gotten fiery. No wonder you're so stupid for her pussy. She must be hot in bed."

I work to keep my cool. Can't let him get to me.

"It's a shame," he continues, "that you have to call it quits."

"What guarantee do I have that you'll keep your word if I do?"

"None," he says with relish. "But I can guarantee you this, if you don't pay up and dump the girl, I will ruin Deeana Rae Chase. I will sing loud about all the things I know. And embellish at my whim. Trust me on that, boy. O'Malley will get the story of his career. How's it going to look that the supposed bleeding-heart child advocate for foster children fucked over her own foster parents and is using her famous ex for his millions?"

"All I have to do to ensure this tale of fiction never sees the light of day is to stop seeing Dee and give you $10 million?"

"Has a nice ring to it." He tips his glass toward me in a mocking toast. "Have to get something out of you for the shit you and your mother made of my life."

"Now who's whining? You've been working that for ages. The beatings...the blackmail. I've paid you to protect my family. And now you want more."

"I'm just taking my due."

Having all I need, I push my glass aside and lean in. "You're not due a fucking thing."

I have the pleasure of watching that smug look collapse. He lowers his glass to the table, his face hard and mean. "Don't try screwing with me, boy. You won't like the outcome."

"Save it, old man." My words slice the air, ready to end this. "The monthly payments stop now. The blackmail stops now. You don't come to me for another cent. Not one fucking penny."

"Fuck you," he snarls. "You try cutting me off and see what I do."

"Your days of calling the shots are over. I have a one-time offer. You retire now. Go out in all your glory as the long-term respected sheriff. You'll sell the house and the property to me for $5 million, more than double the value. Move far away from Illinois. And Dee, my family, and I will never see or hear from you again."

He laughs. "In what fantasy world is that happening?"

"No fantasy. Take the deal or leave it." I shrug. "But taking it is the only way you get any more money and I get to have you gone. Win-win."

"I'm not going anywhere except straight to Rita and O'Malley if you attempt to pull this shit."

"That wouldn't be a smart move. You see I got the 4-1-1 on you," I say, mimicking his words when threatening me with Dee's story. "A wife and child abuser. A drunk. A blackmailer.

"The scandal of the Springvale Sheriff who happens to have a famous son would make for national headlines. The mayor and city council will kick you out on your ass. You'll lose your pension. Your reputation. You'll be investigated for extortion and abuse of power. On top of that, I'll file a lawsuit for damages that will bleed you dry in legal fees alone. Did you know that the statute of limitations to bring a civil suit against you for abuse isn't up for another five years? I still have time."

"You don't have shit. You'd never tell this story."

"Try me."

"Think I will." He finishes off his whiskey and sits back like he doesn't have a care in the world. Underestimating me. "Not only don't you have the balls, who would even believe you?"

"Anyone I let hear this." I reach inside the front pocket of my jeans and pull out the tiny recorder.

"What the fuck?" He lunges forward to grab for the device, but I keep it out of reach.

"Taking this one won't do you any good," I say mildly, my composure unflappable. "Everything you've said has already been backed up to the main unit. A little extra insurance. So, if you even think about doing anything to harm Dee or anyone else that I love, consider this:

"As soon as you do, a copy of this recording gets sent to Mayor Griffin. Another to the press. And one I'll gladly keep to use in my lawsuit."

"Fuck you."

I laugh. "You're the one that's fucked, Malcolm. Take the deal and start over. But know this, either way, I'm done."

DEE GREETS ME AT THE door. I'd called her on my way to assure her that I was fine. Yet those perceptive amber eyes still search mine with tenderness and worry. I long to pull her into my arms, to bask in the comfort I know she wants to give. But the sweet, clean smell of her makes me achingly aware that I still have the bar grime and the stench of Malcolm on me.

"Going to grab a shower," I say, eager to wash away the night.

Dee, seeming to understand, gets me a towel and turns on the water.

"Need anything else?" she asks.

Just you. But I don't say that. "I'm good for now."

"Okay." Dee lingers a moment, then leaves me in the bathroom.

I brush my teeth and strip off my clothes, tossing them in the hamper. When the water is hot enough and the small bathroom starts to fill with steam, I step beneath the spray. I let it pour over my head and body before I pick up my wash and clean myself with economical quickness. Then I just stand there letting the water hit my stiff muscles. Watching it swirl and twist down the drain.

That's when I feel the waft of cool air. I turn my head. See a flash of Dee's nakedness before she steps in behind me. She winds her arms beneath mine, her hands at my chest. I shift restlessly, growing hard. As if I could be anything else when Dee's soft body is pressed against me so close that there is no end to her and no beginning of me. But if I take her now, it will be out of selfishness. I'm too raw. The meeting, too fresh.

"Dee." My hands circle her wrists, stopping the fingers from strumming any farther down my torso. "I thought I'd feel more relieved…more settled. But I just feel messed up from seeing him."

"I think that's normal, Mick." Her lips move across my back. "You've been tied to him for years. Feeling free isn't going to happen just like that. It's going to take time. But you will get there. For tonight, just acknowledge that you confronted him. You let him know that you're done, that he doesn't have control anymore. You conquered. And that's pretty amazing."

"Baby—"

"I'm here," she whispers. "I love you. Let go of my hands. Let me take care of you."

Giving in to the need for her that's more than sexual, I release her wrists on a thick groan.

Dee plants kisses between my shoulder blades, licks at the skin, all the while one hand slowly slides down my abs—a hot languid trail that stokes the fire brewing in me. I want to turn and see her face, but lucid thought is fading as I watch those long, elegant fingers close around my cock. So blatantly sexual. Yet so loving and selfless.

No other single touch has ever made me ready to come in seconds. I pulsate in her grip, a seductive hold I never want to escape from.

She slides her other hand up to tease the flat of my nipple, still jerking my shaft at the same time. I'm overloaded with sensation—the water pounding at my chest, Dee's pillowy breasts against my back, her hands on me. Feels so fucking good.

I plant my feet wide and brace my palms against the tiles. Letting Dee take care of me, I let myself go and power into the wet clamp of her fist.

"Dee," I rasp as the first of my climax hits. All the tension seems to loosen. It's as if the years of matted guilt and snarled anger that had bound me to my past open up and release me. I come hard and Dee keeps stroking, whispering words of love, a soothing balm for my body and soul.

I turn to pull her into my arms and kiss her. "Thank you, beauty, for being everything I need."

I WAKE WITH A KICK of energy. I'd spent another nightmare-less sleep with Dee. I kiss my way up her body, reaching her mouth with an aroused smile. We make love under the warmth of the sheets and share a leisurely breakfast.

I tell her of my plans to donate Malcolm's property to the city of Springvale if he takes the deal. It's a big if. But one thing I know is that he won't take any chance of that recording coming out.

After Dee leaves for work, I write for a while, then go for a jog. A mild breeze skips off the lake. I breathe the fresh air into my lungs. It's only been a few hours since Dee left but I'm already thinking about the evening ahead. We made plans to have a celebratory dinner at Arturo's, a discreet, intimate restaurant just on the outskirts of the city. I haven't seen Art since the last time I was there with her—the fateful night of the storm. Now we'll go back as a couple. Solid and stronger for all we've gone through.

I return home and shower. I'm in the kitchen making a protein shake when the doorbell rings. I check the app on my phone. Yesterday, I installed an alarm system and cameras as a precaution. On the screen, I see Stiles. I'm not expecting him.

I open the door to his usual stony expression.

"Mr. Peters, sorry to drop in without calling," he says, "but I have news about Joyce Franklin that I thought you'd want to hear in person."

I still, bracing for it. I know what's coming. The last of my secrets revealed. One that's going to rock Victor and blow Dee's renewed trust in me.

CHAPTER TWENTY-SIX

Dee

I HAVE THE MUSIC BLARING in the car. Lizzo is wailing about feeling good as hell and I'm wailing along with her.

Last night I went to Mick naked. Baring my body to him as much as my heart. Sensing he really didn't want to be alone, I'd worked through those negative tapes—my self-consciousness overshadowed by my bright and blinding love for him.

That doesn't mean I'm ready to bounce out of bed in the raw just yet, but it feels like another step forward. One of many that Mick and I are continuing to take. He'd confronted his father. I was confronting my insecurities. And together we are building a relationship on a sturdy foundation of openness and trust.

I'm so proud of him. So proud of us.

I turn onto our street. Anxious to see Mick. To kiss him. Hug him. To celebrate this evening at Arturo's. But upon finding Victor's car parked out front, my good feelings slip.

Of course, my brother being here, unexpectedly, doesn't have to indicate a problem. Only there's this sudden sinking feeling in my stomach. Mick had texted me before I'd left the office to confirm that I'd be home by six. I'd assumed it was his eagerness for our date. Now I'm worried that Victor being here was the reason.

An overreaction, perhaps, but my alarm is validated when I enter the house. Thundering voices vibrate across the foyer. I drop my tote bag and hurry to the kitchen. Isabelle stands in the middle of the room between the two men with one hand on each of their heaving chests.

"What's going on?" I shout to be heard.

The argument abruptly stops and all eyes swerve to me. Mick's expression fills with that familiar look of guilt but it's Victor who answers.

"He found Joyce!"

"What?"

"He didn't give a damn about anything we said, about any of our warnings—"

"That's bullshit!" Mick's defense punches the thick air. "If you had calmed the fuck down I would have explained things to you."

"And if you had told me in the first place, I wouldn't need calming."

"Right. You would have gone ballistic."

"So, you just did whatever the hell you wanted."

"Enough!" Exasperated, Isabelle cuts them off. "Both of you need to take a breath, stop yelling, and start listening to each other."

They separate like boxers after going a round; exhaling roughly and taking to opposite ends. In that moment of hostile reprieve, I process their fight and home in on the most crucial piece of information.

He found Joyce. Beyond the shock of that news is the disillusionment and hurt. "Why didn't you tell me?"

Mick meets my gaze with apology. "I should have. But I knew you all were against the idea, and saw no point in upsetting everyone if nothing was going to come from it."

"But something did come from it."

"That's why I'm telling you now. Despite what you and Victor may think, I did not go about this recklessly. I was clear with Stiles on one thing—he was not to make any contact if he found her. And I was not planning to pay Joyce for evidence or take it any further without your involvement."

"At least that's something," Victor grants, though the anger still winds through him. "Where is she?"

Mick shifts his gaze from my mutinous stare to Victor. "In jail."

"Guess that figures. What's her story?"

"Up until recently, she'd been outrunning the law. Skipping out on court appearances for repeat offenses of assault and prostitution in Ohio, Indiana, South Carolina, and Georgia. It finally caught up with her in Louisiana. She was arrested on three counts of luring men to a motel room and robbing them at knifepoint. One guy got cut pretty bad. Her lawyer pleaded it down to two counts of aggravated robbery. She's currently serving four years."

Victor makes a pithy sound of disapproval.

"The point is she's in jail," Mick emphasizes. "Now that we know where she is, locked up and far away from Dwayde, we have the opportunity to talk to her."

"Like she's going to give a shit about helping us." Victor shoves a hand through his hair. "Look, I want to know what Dwayde's hiding too. I want to find out what the hell the Franklins have done as badly as you do. But I dealt with people like Joyce when I worked in Vice. It's dog-eat-dog survival on the streets…it makes them hardened; they only care about serving their own interests."

A frown broaches Mick's face. "You might be right. But shouldn't we at least try?"

Victor shakes his head and Isabelle's hand goes to his shoulder. Her voice is gentle yet no less imploring. "*Mi cielo*. If there's any chance at all that we can get information that could help us keep Dwayde, no matter how small, no matter how offensive or distasteful asking her for help is, we have to take it."

"Isabelle, we are talking about pinning our hopes on a violent offender who abused her son."

"I understand that. I do." She shudders. "It makes me sick to think of what she did to Dwayde. But I'm desperate."

"I know, Bells…I know." He puts his arm around her and looks over at me. "Is there any possibility at all that Joyce could reassert her parental rights and lay claim to Dwayde? She might try that if she thinks there's money in it for her."

"No," I allay that fear. "The court terminated her rights. In or out of jail, there is no provision for her to have them reinstated."

He breathes a sigh of relief but his brow remains furrowed in pleated lines of conflict. "Tangling with Joyce just seems like a no-win situation."

"Like you, I was not in support of finding her either," I say. "It seemed too far-fetched to believe it was possible. And even allowing for the chance, the risk of bringing her back into Dwayde's life was just too big. But that risk is now mitigated by her being in jail for the next four years."

"So, you're on board with this?" Victor asks with visible consternation.

"Yes, under these circumstances." And despite Mick's deception. "To Isabelle's point, if there's any chance at all that Joyce could give us something useful, we should take it. But, legally speaking," I add with caution. "Jackson will have a field day shredding whatever she might say based on her history of drugs, child abuse, and now being a convicted felon."

"Meaning we could go through all this and not be able to use it." Victor's mouth twists with uncertainty.

"That's possible. And of course, there's Dwayde to consider and how he'll react to Joyce being found, let alone me talking to her. It's a delicate situation. I don't have to tell you that. The choice is yours. He's your son and I will respect whatever decision you make."

Mick remains quiet and still, which is unusual for him. I gather it's out of respect for Victor's inner turmoil—a thoughtful and careful man who prefers things to be black or white, he deals in absolutes rather than shades. There is nothing about seeing Joyce that is absolute.

"I'm skeptical, Bells," he says, grimly. "This could blow up in our faces."

"No outcome can be any worse than losing Dwayde."

"He might not forgive us for talking to her."

"He will," Isabelle insists. "He knows our hearts. Please, mi cielo. We have to do this."

"Alright, Bells." His acquiesce doesn't disguise the weight of his reluctance. "But we are not saying a word about it to Dwayde." Victor looks from his wife to me. "Not until you meet with Joyce and we know what we're dealing with. I'm not going to cause him more distress when this might be a total bust."

Although his reason for not telling Dwayde echoes Mick's excuse, the difference is Dwayde is a child and our job is to protect him. "Agreed. We'll wait to see what comes of it. In the meantime, I'll fill in Calista and book a flight to Louisiana for as soon as possible."

"This better be it." Victor pivots to Mick. "I know you did it from a good place. But so help me," he warns, "if there's anything else..."

"There's not. You have my solemn word," he says gravely. "I'm sorry for the way I sprung it on you, then getting defensive. I was an ass."

"Yeah, you were." But there's a hint of softening in Victor's tone.

I, however, am not as forgiving. Nevertheless, my cold shoulder doesn't stop Mick from making plans to come with me. Given the custody hearing is three weeks away, I don't expend the energy fighting him on it. Especially when he arranges for a private jet tomorrow evening.

FRIDAY, SHORTLY AFTER TAKE-OFF, the attendant brings sparkling water for me and Coke for Mick. I sip from my glass, staring out the window, cruising above the clouds. We haven't really spoken since yesterday. Mick had made several attempts but my responses had been about as warm as an arctic storm. Eventually, he stopped and just gave me space.

It was the first time that we'd shared a bed and hadn't touched, kissed, or made love. I slept with my back to him and got up early to go to the office. I hadn't seen Mick again until I boarded the airplane and sat next to him in chilly silence.

I nurse my indignation, long and strong. After all, we'd promised each other honesty, even as he hid another of his secrets. Okay, so he'd told us as soon as Stiles had alerted him to Joyce's whereabouts. He'd arranged to meet at our place, away from any possibility of Dwayde overhearing. But that doesn't excuse him keeping it from me.

And yet, here I am, on my way to get information that could potentially help the case. Because, damn the consequences, Mick is protective, stubborn, and follows his heart at full speed. Except this time, he'd put on the brakes when it counted.

He hadn't gone off on his own rogue mission. That, at the very least, meant he was trying. But instead of recognizing his efforts, I got caught up in my injured feelings and held him to some rigid standard, when I wasn't exactly holding up my end.

I turn to Mick. Dark and broody, he stares down at his glass. "I'm sorry for being such a jerk."

His head comes up in surprise. "You weren't."

"I was." I set my water down and squarely meet his gaze. "I'm always preaching about open communication but I didn't give you that. Instead, I reverted back to closing myself off. We're still figuring all this out. You and me. We are going to make mistakes, have disagreements, mess up... that's a given in any relationship. I don't want to act like this. I want us to talk things out."

"I want that too." He takes my hand and threads our fingers. "I'm sorry for not telling you sooner. You had every reason to be angry, Dee. This week has been all kinds of fucked up drama. Hell...the last couple of weeks have been. You've put up with more than I had any right to expect."

I shake my head. "I didn't put up with anything. Being there for each other is part of the deal. These weeks have been hard on you too. I lost sight of that."

"We haven't had a dull moment, have we?" He huffs out a short breath.

"Nope. But we've gotten through those tough times together."

"Yeah, we have."

I lean my head against the solid strength of his shoulder and feel our connection lock back into place.

TWO HOURS LATER, THE PLANE lands at a private airport just outside of New Orleans. The evening is clear and the weather is balmy. Mick slips on his cap and leads us to a black town car. The driver, that I recognize as a bodyguard by his marked demeanor, introduces himself as Paxton. He loads our overnight bags and takes us to a luxury hotel that's located close to the French Quarter.

Mick checks in under his pseudonym, Anthony Michaels. We're shown to the Grand Penthouse suite that encompasses the entire 18th floor. Panoramic windows boast a view of the city. A marble fireplace serves as the focal point in the living room that's stylishly decorated in all white art deco furniture. I peer through the French doors, which open onto a balcony that has a fully stocked bar.

In awe, I follow Mick up the winding staircase that leads to the master bedroom. Decorated in white too, there's a sprawling king-size bed with a tall upholstered headboard. In the bathroom is a deep Jacuzzi tub and glass shower that's insanely large, big enough to hold six people. I'm not used to this extravagance. Mick isn't showy with his wealth. Humbly down-to-earth, I often forget how rich he is until moments like this.

"The suite is gorgeous." I slide my hand along the feather-soft bed cover.

"I'm glad you like it. I know we're not here under the best circumstances but it's our first trip together and your first time to New Orleans, I wanted it to be special for you."

"I appreciate that," I say, touched by his thoughtfulness. "We can order up room service and eat dinner on the balcony. The view's great."

"Or we could go out," he proposes, setting our bags down. "Put everything aside for a while and just have some fun."

"Really?" I ask because unlike his wealth, I am very conscious of his fame. The ever-present Nike cap and bodyguards don't allow me to forget. "I'd love to go out but are you sure we should?"

"Not a problem. It's Halloween night. The streets will be busy and crowded. No one will even notice me."

Mick being eye-grabbing is not limited to his celebrity. "I find that hard to believe."

"I've gone incognito here a few times."

"Hm..." I give him a sideways glance. "And during those few times, did you avail yourself of the provocative nightlife?"

He pauses from unzipping his duffle bag. "Anything before you is a blur."

"Very smooth." I smile.

Because we settled on doing something casual, I change out of my suit and put on the lightweight dress I'd packed. The style is flattering on me with its billowy sleeves, deep V-neck, and shirred torso that gradually flares out and swings around my calves. Mick blows a soft whistle of approval when I exit the bathroom.

He's looking mighty good himself—simplicity at its finest. Dark-washed blue jeans and an untucked white T-shirt against his caramel skin—pushes all my hot buttons. I debate whether to jump his bones first or see New Orleans. In the end, I choose the city now and save the best for later.

I slip on a pair of flats for our walk and Mick dons a black ball cap. When we reach the hub of the city, my senses are hit all at once. The French Quarter is even more vibrant than I'd imagined. The blare of live music spills onto the sidewalks, bars lure in customers with flashing signs, and spicy aromas tease the senses. I love window browsing the eclectic shops, sharing a po-boy from a food truck, watching the array of people—many of whom are dressed in wild and outrageous costumes. But what I love most is that camouflaged by the vivacity, we're able to stroll hand-in-hand for the first time in public.

Talking and enjoying each other's company, we lose track of the distance we travel. By the time we reach Jackson Square, the gates around the park are closed but the scent of fried doughnuts draws us to a café. At the take-out window, we order two espressos and a bag of beignets covered with powdered sugar.

"Let's go up on the levee," Mick suggests.

Linking hands again, we walk through the tunnel that leads to a boardwalk along the embankment. Lighting from the lampposts shimmers over the Mississippi River and washes the area in a golden blush. We find a bench with a view of the city. It's a perfect spot. With the fragrant bag on my lap, Mick opens it up and we dig in. Each bite sends dusts of sugar into a white cloud. It's messy, delicious, and wonderful.

When the bag is empty and our coffees finished, Mick tosses them into the trash. We brush off our clothes, laughing at the futile effort. As we start our walk back, Mick stops and pulls me to him. There's poetry in the way he kisses me.

I bring my arms around his neck, captivated by the ethereal veil of the water misting over us, the sultry breeze fluttering my dress, and Mick's sensuous mouth sliding over mine. If the paparazzi were to show up now with cameras flashing, I doubt I'd even notice.

It's a while before we come up for air to a smattering of applause. Mick playfully takes a bow for the two older couples and grins at me.

Feeling overjoyed, I loop my arm through his. We take our time walking back to the hotel. It's after midnight when we reach our room and kick off our shoes.

I open the French doors and step barefoot out onto the balcony. Eighteen stories below, the street still bustles with the sounds of music and people.

"Want something?" Mick indicates the outdoor bar.

"Yes." I turn and lean my back against the railing. My gaze glides over him. He's all masculine virility—bearded jaw, hair a sexy mess from raking his hands through it. "I want you."

He reaches me in two long strides. The heat in his eyes, dark and glowering, crackles the night air. My heart pounds with excitement as he hauls me into a deep, urgent kiss. This one wilder than the public version. That I have the power to do this—turn him in mere seconds from casually offering me a drink to wanting to fuck my brains out—is a heady trip.

I feel Mick grasp the folds of my dress, dragging them upward. The warm breeze gusts against my bare thighs, then my bottom. His big hands squeeze the cheeks and trace the line of my thong. The rough sound he makes when finding my sex weeping with desire is almost enough to make me come. I ride his fingers, twisting my hips, sucking the tip of his tongue. Only the honk of a horn jerks me back to our not-so-private location.

"Can anyone see us?" I murmur, far less concerned than I should be.

"Maybe. But it's dark and too far away for them to make out who we are."

"Oh." I shiver.

"You like that, beauty?" His voice is deep and husky against my neck. "The idea of someone watching us?"

"Y-yes." Under the shroud of anonymity, the very thought feels sinfully risqué. "Is it a fantasy of yours?"

"Fucking you is my fantasy." His lips slide down my throat. "Anytime. Anyplace."

Then he drops to his knees and pushes my dress up to my waist. His mouth nudges away the thin veil of my panties and with his hands on my behind, firmly holding me in place, his tongue licks along my cleft, sliding me apart.

Gasping, I weave my fingers through his hair, clutching handfuls. The carnal play of his lips, his tongue, his entire mouth has my hips winding and my breaths stammering. It's decadent, thrilling. The way he spears his tongue into my sex, making me quake and quiver.

I hold his head, seeking an anchor, my self-control ripped away in tides of pleasure. I'm lost, completely helpless. Seized by the velvety strokes that now circle my clit. Round and round. Winding me up tight and tighter until I feel like I'm going to break apart.

And then I do. Only it's not a flash of an explosion. It's a hot, blissful unfurling. Beginning in my lower belly and billowing outward, downward. A release that is all of me, coming undone, shattering. I'm dizzy with it, spinning, my insides clenching, and Mick doesn't relent. He doesn't stop or slow. He holds me up and keeps licking, lapping at that tender spot until I come again, my hips driving up and up. My scarcity of breaths broken whimpers.

I fumble at him. Gripping his shoulders, sure I'm going to asphyxiate if he doesn't stop. Death by orgasm. Hell of a way to go, but he rises up and I live to see through my post orgasmic daze that his eyes are heavy-lidded, his chest rising and falling. My essence on his face. I should be done, out for the count. But all I want is more.

I yank at the snap of his waistband and carefully lower the zipper over his bulge.

"Poor baby." I gently squeeze him through the opening.

"*Dee*," he hisses in warning.

Turnabout is fair play. I pull his cock out. Thick and smooth. I run my fingers over the pulsing veins. Knowing his body well, what he likes, the way he likes it, I pump him from root to tip, tight and slow, drawing beads of pre-cum to the wide crest and rubbing it over the head.

He whips off his T-shirt and spears me with a dangerous stare. "Turn around."

Incited by the order and his impatience, I do as he says. The street is a main route to the French Quarter. I'm stimulated by the sights and sounds. By his hot breaths caressing my ear. By his shaft twitching anxiously against the bare cheek of my bottom.

"I'm going to fuck you now," he grits.

"Yes." I grip the metal rail. He snaps the string of my panties. A car engine roars, a brush of wind strokes over my pebbled skin. I bend at the waist and open my legs for him.

"Christ, that's sexy." He slides one hand down the crack of my behind and pushes it between my thighs, spreading me farther apart.

"Mick." My hips buck, chasing his touch.

"Tell me how much you want it."

Tension and need coil in my lower belly. "I want it badly."

"What do you want?"

"Your cock inside me. Fucking me, hard."

All teasing gone, Mick grabs the sides of my hips, his hands rough and chafing. As much as I anticipate it, crave it, I cry out from the full force of that first thrust, stretching me, filling me. My core melts and trembles around him.

He groans and slides in deeper before pulling out and plunging back in again, and again, shaking my body with slow, powerful drives. I grip the railing, my blood burns, sweat trickles between my bouncing breasts. With every thrust, his thighs relax then flex, his abs slap against my ass, the railing vibrates from the friction of our lower bodies crashing together.

"You love when I fuck you," he gnashes out. "When I claim you... take you..."

"Yes," I sob, so turned on by his unremitting possession and the erotic illusion of being on display. "Take me harder."

His tempo increases to a brute pounding. The wide crest of his crown unerringly hitting my g-spot. The onslaught, unbearable. My orgasm whirls through me like a tornado, with speed and inevitable might. My damp palms cling to the rail, my breaths tumble out in tattered moans.

"God, Dee. You are so fucking good." He keeps plunging through the clamp of my core, growing thicker. "I'm going to come for you now."

"No." I pant. "Not like this. I want to see you."

His pace slows. He withdraws, sliding out hard and wet. He turns me to him. His breaths are harsh and turbulent. I put a hand to his bearded jaw. "I want to see your face...your eyes when you go over the edge."

"You want to watch me lose it," he says hoarsely.

"I do." My open mouth presses to his, imbibing his breaths. The need to watch him is more exciting to me than the idea of us being watched.

Not wasting another second, he shifts us over to the bar. Then with my arms around his neck, he lifts me and sets me on top of the low marble surface. It's cool beneath my thighs but I'm heated by the steam pulsing off of him.

He pulls my hips to the edge and glides home. This angle is different, even better, in that I can see him. Our gazes fixed on each other, our bodies fused together—the magic is spun. Stroke to stroke. Eye to eye.

I rock my hips into his deep, steely thrusts, his eyes like flames in the dark. That feral look alone is an aphrodisiac. I've never wanted sex this much—the intimacy, the connection. It's as if each time with Mick only spurs my passion for more.

He grips my inner thighs, keeping me open. Fucking with unleashed urgency. A damp, wavy lock of hair falls like the letter C on his forehead. His teeth are gritted in sweet agony. The smell of hot, raw sex surrounds us.

"I want you like this forever," he rasps, pressing his thumb to circle my clit. "Spread open, tight and wet around my cock."

His words, his touch, flood me with ecstasy. My body screams, his name a litany on my lips.

He grunts through my orgasm, rubbing it out before his hips resume a fervid pumping, pushed to his limits, pushing me to mine. This is how I want him, how I wanted to see him, unbridled, his neck arched, lost to pleasure, eyes glazing over, consumed by a release that stuns me in its sweltering intensity. I hold him to me, my limbs caging him, my mouth absorbing his guttural groans, my core still pulsing as he keeps thrusting and coming, saturating me with his liquid heat.

"Christ," he whispers moments later, catching his breath. His heart pounds against mine. "You are my kryptonite." His hands cradle my face. "I love you, Dee."

WE WAKE SATURDAY MORNING, THE same way we'd fallen asleep— naked and wrapped around each other. At some point, we'd made it inside to wash up and crash on the bed.

"What time is it?" Mick asks, squinting his eyes open to the sun shooting across the bedroom.

"Just after 9:30." I stroke his chest where my cheek is resting.

"I haven't slept that late in I don't know how long."

"Guess you were worn out," I say teasingly, though I credit it more to the absence of his nightmares and the lack of him stressing over them.

"And you weren't, huh?"

"You do alright."

"Looks like I better step up my game." He tackles me onto my back and shows me once again just how spectacular his game already is.

I wish we could stay in bed like this for hours, making love, ordering up room service, then enjoying that Jacuzzi tub. But the world doesn't stop turning just because I wish it would.

THE WALDEN COUNTY CORRECTIONAL FACILITY for Women is a medium security prison with fenced penning around the perimeter. Paxton pulls up to the booth at the front gate where I lower my window to provide ID and Joyce's name. After the vetting process, the guard directs Paxton over to a place to park.

"Be careful, baby." Mick kisses me long and hugs me tight. I feel his reluctance about letting me go alone, but aside from him being a witness in the case, he's also famous. Micah Peters being seen at a women's prison in the Bayou State isn't the kind of headline we need.

I'm admitted into the building by a stern-looking guard. From there, I go through a metal detector and my tote bag is searched. At the desk, I sign in before I'm escorted to a visitation area with two long rows of picnic-style aluminum tables fixed to the ground and a low Plexiglas wall separating the inmate and the visitor.

Despite a decorating attempt, the series of landscapes cannot overcome the feel of the room. It's cold, hollow, and depressing. Three of the adjoined tables are occupied. I choose an empty one in the second row and take a seat.

Twenty minutes later, a female guard appears with Joyce. The heavy metal door loudly clicks into place behind them. I can't help but stare. The cute fifteen-year-old with the dimpled smile resembles none of the woman being ushered toward me. Her light brown complexion is now ashen; drained of color and life. Those big Franklin eyes are hardened and mean. Her dimples are lost to sunken cheeks. Her long dark hair is the texture of dried hay and she's rail thin beneath beige scrubs that dwarf her small frame.

"Stay behind the glass," the guard warns before she steps away, giving us a semblance of privacy.

Given Louisiana is a one-party consent state, I turn on the recording device inside my purse as Joyce kicks one leg, then the other over the backless bench. Although she sits, her body remains in jittery motion. Her knees bounce as if they have springs. Her bony hands—with nails bitten down to the quick—drum on the tabletop. Her cynical gaze darts all over me, seeming to take in my slicked-back bun and linen suit jacket. "They said you're a lawyer."

"Yes. I'm—"

"It's about time you got here," she accuses, abruptly cutting off my introduction. "That useless asshole told me to take a plea when the police jacked me up on some bogus robbery and assault charges. I always carry a knife for protection, just in case. But the cops didn't want to hear none of that." She scratches at the scabs on the inside of her arm. "Now look at where I'm at—in this hellhole 'cause I had some second-rate legal hack that didn't know his head from his dick.

"He railroaded me into taking a deal just to get it done and over. But I was reading about how you can appeal on what they call 'valid grounds,' like if I didn't fully appreciate the effect of the plea," she recites, the speed of her speech as jumpy as her body. "You can use that, right? Just tell the judge I didn't understand."

Considering her history of offenses, I doubt that what she declares is true. But her appeal isn't my concern. "Joyce, I'm not from the public defender's office," I say, clearing up the mistaken identity. "I'm not a defense attorney."

She blinks twice. "You're not here about my case?"

"No, I'm not."

Realization setting in, her eyes narrow to thin, leery slits. "Then who the fuck are you?"

"I'm Dwayde's lawyer."

CHAPTER TWENTY-SEVEN

Dee

"GUARD!" JOYCE SURGES TO HER feet.

"There a problem?" she asks, coming forward.

"No, Officer." I hope to stall. "Joyce." My eyes move back to her. "Just sit down for a moment and let me explain."

"Fuck you, lady. If you got no cause to get me out of here, you're useless to me."

"Please." I make another attempt. "It involves your parents."

That momentarily stills her movements. "You work for them?"

"No. Not at all."

She waves the guard away and plunks back down on the bench, her knees bouncing again. "Start talking."

"Dwayde is healthy and living with a loving family. He's smart, talented, doing well in school. He's happy."

"So?" She shrugs and chews a nail. "What's that got to do with me?"

I push past her cold response. "A couple of months ago, your parents found out where Dwayde was and began custody proceedings. He doesn't want to go live with them, he wants to stay where he is. It's my job to ensure that he does."

"And you came here looking for dirt on ole Charlie and Joan," she says shrewdly.

"Is there dirt?"

"Don't fuck with me, lady. The kid must have told you something, otherwise you wouldn't be here."

"He hasn't told me much," I admit. "But I gather there's something worth exploring. Something he might be afraid to tell me. That's why I'm here. To get the specifics from you."

"What's in it for me?"

"A chance to do right by Dwayde."

"*Pfft*." She spits out a piece of nail before attacking her finger again. "I don't give a shit about him."

My distaste for this woman curdles the contents of my breakfast. But I don't have to like her. I just have to get her talking. "What about your parents then?" I bait her, anticipating that's the hook.

"What about them?"

"They claim you gave them custody." I reach into my bag and pull out a file with the documents I'd printed off at work. I hold the custody agreement up against the see-through barrier. "Did you sign this?"

Her eyes scan the page and the blankness in her expression conveys she has never seen this document before. At least not in her sober mind. Yet that doesn't stop her from trying to play an angle.

"All depends."

"On what?"

"My daddy," she says with a trace of her Southern twang.

"What about him?"

"If he gets me a lawyer, a good one, I'll say I signed it. If not..." She lets the implication trail off.

"You think you can blackmail your father?"

"I wouldn't call it that." She taps at the page through the glass. "We'd just be helping each other out."

"Have you spoken to your parents in the last eight years since you left?" I ask, lowering the document back to the table.

"Never had reason to 'till now."

"I don't imagine your father is feeling too kindly toward you for taking off with his grandson."

"He'll get over it to get what he wants."

"Don't be naïve," I say bluntly. "Your father isn't going to be bribed into getting you a high-end defense attorney. Your signature on the custody agreement has already been verified by a handwriting expert, so either you signed it unknowingly or it's a good forgery. Whichever, your father doesn't need you."

Her colorless complexion reddens.

"That's the reality, Joyce. You don't have anything to bargain with."

"Fuck him. I have the truth."

"Then tell me what it is."

"And get dick-all? Naw." She flicks her hand at me. "I don't give something for nothing."

"Fair enough." I leverage an angle of my own. "Look at it this way, you took Dwayde from your parents for a reason. They claim you demanded $100,000 in exchange for custody and it's only when they refused to pay that you took off with him. But that's not true, is it?"

"Whatever you say, lady."

"I have a theory that you didn't leave with Dwayde because of the money. You took him as payback."

"Is your theory gonna get me out of this piss hole?" She sneers.

"No. But if you know something about your parents that would make them unfit guardians, then you'd prevent them from getting Dwayde back. I think you want that."

"I want out of here more. Think I'll take my chances with ole Charlie."

"A losing proposition, Joyce. Your father is too clever and arrogant to be outmaneuvered. If you have something on him that he wants to keep quiet, he'll feed you lies and promises to stop the truth from surfacing while he fights for custody. But in three weeks, after he's used you up and the case is over, he will have what he wants, Dwayde. And you'll still be right where you are, in here."

"Fuck you." She snaps out the two words like a whip. "You don't know shit."

"Oh, but I do. And more importantly, you've had enough experience with your father to know I'm right. But if you don't mind getting played..." Calling her bluff, I start packing up my papers.

She studies me, her eyes shifting in their sockets, the kinetic energy pouring off her in frenzied waves. "You trying to trick me."

"No tricks or gimmicks, Joyce. I've been completely honest. Our motives might be different, but our goal is the same. I don't want your parents to get custody of Dwayde and you don't want that either."

"You think you got me figured out?"

I stop packing. "Look at where you are, Joyce. Look at your life. I sense you lost your power to them. This is your chance to take it back."

"Like you care about me."

"I'm not pretending to care about you. I'm telling you how it is. The choice is yours. If you won't help me, I'll find another way to keep Dwayde from them."

"You really think you can beat ole Charlie?"

"I'm going to fight like hell to."

She eyes me hard. "You look all prim and proper but you got balls."

"Thank you." Then I wait, quietly, patiently.

"It makes no difference to me what happens to the kid," she says after less than a minute of contemplative silence and nail biting. "If you think I'm a bitch, I don't give a shit. But you're right about one thing, taking the kid wasn't about money. I didn't fucking want him, not ever. They would have paid me to leave him, that's for damn sure. Maybe I should have played it different, got my money and split. But I hated them too much for that."

"You must have had a good reason." I fold my hands together on the table.

"Yeah, I had good reason." Her tone drips with contempt. "If you didn't already know, ole Charlie inherited Franklin Farms from his daddy when he died. It had been in the family since his great granddaddy built it from the ground up. That business, that legacy meant everything to him.

"Finding the right woman to marry was part of it. My mother didn't exactly fit. She was what we called in the South, white trash. But she was pretty, smart, and had potential. She started working as a secretary at Franklin Farms. My father noticed her. Liked what he saw and classed her up to look and talk fancy. Then he moved her into a hostess position or some shit, greeting important clients and attending to his personal stuff.

"She was no fool. She recognized a good score and made herself indispensable. Within a year, Joan Ellis from the trailer park became Joan Franklin, Lady of the Manor. Only there was one big problem. The Lady wasn't so good at popping out babies. Just me. No boys to carry on the fine line of horsemen. I was Daddy's little princess. Finishing school. Cotillions. He dressed me up to look the part. But I still could never be what he really wanted."

A son. I got the picture. "Sounds like a difficult environment to have grown up in."

"I hated it. All the fake appearances of being a perfect family. It was so fucked up. But I had my horse. Starlight." For the first time since I arrived, her eyes soften with sadness, maybe longing. "I didn't care all that much about competing, that was my daddy's thing. I just loved to ride."

"You stopped after Starlight died."

"Killed," she corrects, her eyes going so hard again that if they were made of glass they'd break under the pressure of her anger.

"Who killed him?"

"Wyatt Alden," she spits out his name. "My fucking stepuncle."

My mind's eye goes back to the file I've read at least a dozen times. Alden, as I recall, was Joan's much younger stepbrother. Now deceased. An accident of some kind. He'd worked at Franklin Farms prior. Nothing particularly suspicious stands out. "Why would he kill your horse?"

She glares at me as if I'm clueless. "My mother didn't have much to do with her parents after she left. They didn't suit the Joan Franklin image. When her mama died, her daddy remarried. This woman had a son from a previous relationship. Wyatt. He came sniffing around Franklin Farms. My mother didn't want him there. She wanted no part of her old life. But he talked his way in. Fucking Charlie gave him a chance. Liked to think he was this do-gooder. *Pfft*. Put him to work as a ranch hand. Wyatt acted grateful but you could tell he resented being the hired help while my mother was sitting like a Queen Bee in the mansion."

"Why kill your horse?" I ask again, not drawing the connection.

"I'll get to that." She chews another nail. "He seemed nice enough, got along with the other staff; he was friendly, popular. Paid attention to me. I had a stupid girl's crush on him. I was too dumb to know that he was earning trust. He had access to the farm, to the horses, and to me." Her breathing accelerates and I know what's coming.

"One evening, I had just gotten back from riding Starlight. I was brushing him down when Wyatt came into the stall. He'd done that many times before. But this time, he didn't look friendly. He grabbed my arm and shoved me into the corner." She closes her eyes tight. "He covered my scream with his hard hand. I could taste the dirt from the day on it. He whispered in my ear that he was going to fuck the little princess and see how royal cunt felt."

I inhale a sharp breath. Expecting it, I realize, doesn't stop the shock of hearing the rancid words. "Did you tell anyone? Your mother? Your father?"

"No." She opens her eyes. They're vague and distant as if she's still back there on the farm. "I wanted to. But when he killed Starlight and said he'd do the same to me if I ever told, I just shut up and put up."

It explains why the light in her went dark. Why she changed so dramatically and quit riding. Wyatt Alden had stolen her childhood and murdered her beloved horse.

"I'm so sorry, Joyce." This hard-edged woman had made horrible choices, not the least of which was beating her son. But my sympathies are with the girl she had once been. "Your parents didn't suspect something was very wrong?"

"*Pfft*. Grief, sure. But when I whacked off my hair and started acting out, ditching school, smoking…putting a smear on the family name, they weren't so understanding."

"Did they try to get you counseling?"

"Lady, get real. My daddy wouldn't send me to some pencil-neck shrink to air out dirty laundry."

"How long did the abuse continue?"

"Five months of fucking hell."

I can't even imagine. "How did it stop?"

"I had burning when I peed and there were these yellow stains in my underwear. It got so bad, I finally had to tell my mother. She said it was probably a urinary or yeast infection. She took me to the doctor to get antibiotics. He ran some tests and found out that I had chlamydia. But an STD wasn't the worst of it, I was also pregnant."

"And you had no idea?"

"I should have. I'd missed my period. Guess I was in denial or something."

I nod, understanding the paralyzing fear of being young and suspecting you might be pregnant. But in my case, I had a boy who loved me. Joyce had been raped by her own stepuncle. "What happened then?"

"The shit hit the fan. I told them about Wyatt. About all the times he forced me into one of the horse stalls or wherever he could get me alone. I told them about him killing Starlight and him threatening to kill me. But none of it mattered."

"They didn't believe you?"

"No, they fucking did." She makes a snarling sound. "But they preferred the image of a teen pregnancy by an unnamed boy over the scandal of their daughter being raped by Joan Franklin's stepbrother. One made for gossip, the other would make news."

"Are you saying they covered it up?"

"That's exactly what they did—to protect their reputation."

But not their child. "What happened to Alden?"

"They sent him away and spun a lie about him getting a great job in Alaska on an oil rig. All very nice and tidy. The way my daddy likes things. He said we'd start with a clean slate and move forward as if none of that happened."

"Pretty hard to do when you're pregnant."

"*Pfft*. That was the best part for him. But for me it was like a death sentence. I couldn't have it. No way. I begged them to take me to get rid of it. I couldn't have an abortion in Kentucky at the time without parental consent. My father wouldn't hear of it. End of discussion. He spouted on about the miracle of life, like what happened to me was a blessing. He actually used that word when the doctor said I was carrying a boy.

"I tried to get rid of it myself. Took a hammer to my stomach. After that, they never let me out of their sight. So, I had their fucking demon seed. My father even named him after his granddaddy. Dwayde Davis. The apple of my father's eye. Made my skin crawl." She shudders.

There are women who choose to have babies born out of rape, and they love them. Joyce wasn't given any option or support. Instead, her parents added to the brutal assault by forcing their traumatized child to give Franklin a male heir.

"You waited until Dwayde was four to take him, why?"

"They wanted me gone."

"What do you mean?"

"I was using. Just weed and hash then. Pills sometimes. They threatened to send me away. Said they wouldn't tolerate drugs around their precious son. They called him that," she says curling her lip. "Their son. I knew they had a plan to get custody and raise him as theirs. I never signed that document. But I knew what they wanted. They'd already given up on me. The kid was all they cared about. So, I took him and ran.

"I would have paid to have seen their reactions when they woke up to find him gone with no idea where I'd taken him or what I'd done," she says with twisted pleasure. "I moved around to make sure they never found him. I did what I had to do to survive. Whatever it took. I wanted to make them pay. Make them suffer."

And in so doing, destroyed herself and hurt an innocent little boy in the name of revenge. "You told all this to Dwayde?" I surmise.

"Sho' did," she admits without a shred of remorse. "Every time I looked at him, it was like looking at the fucking devil. My father's eyes in Wyatt's face. You have no idea what that was like."

"No, I don't. What you went through, Joyce, is unconscionable. But it doesn't justify abusing Dwayde."

"*Pfft.* I could have sold him for a pretty penny to any pimp out there. I could have made money off him when the johns eyed him up. But I didn't. He got better than he deserved. You think he's going to grow up to be any different than the piece of shit his daddy was?"

"Yes, I actually do. Dwayde is an amazing child and he's going to grow up to be a good man."

"Yeah right. Tell yourself that if it makes you feel better about helping him. But good men don't exist. They're all fucking scum."

In her world, that's sadly true. I stand, feeling sickened by the tragedy of it all. I'd come here for answers and gotten the ugly truth in spades.

But it's not lost on me that the implications to Dwayde are far more reaching than just the case.

CHAPTER TWENTY-EIGHT

Micah

LATE THAT SATURDAY AFTERNOON, DEE and I board a private flight back to Chicago. She works for most of the time while I keep checking my watch, counting down the minutes until we land.

Right after leaving the prison, Dee had contacted Calista to confirm what she could of Joyce's chilling confession. The only reason information had been collected on Wyatt Alden was because he'd been a former employee at Franklin Farms and the stepbrother of Joan Franklin. There wasn't much in the PI report, no red flags at the time. Not so, when you know what you're looking for.

Alden had worked for Franklin Farms during the months Joyce claimed and they corresponded with the timeline of her horse's murder and her pregnancy. More than that, though—the smoking gun so to speak—were the two pictures of Alden that Calista emailed over. Placed side by side with Dwayde's, the shape of their noses and structure of their brow and jaw lines are too similar for it to be mere coincidence. Circumstantial from a legal perspective. But true just the same.

Only then did Dee share the recording and pictures with Victor and Isabelle. It sideswiped them, of course. We'd suspected Joyce might have been abused and that the Franklins were no saints. Yet none of us predicted they had intentionally covered up the rape of their own daughter and made her their unwilling surrogate.

The worst of it was that Joyce confirmed she'd told this to Dwayde. He'd known all along and kept it from us. Given the sensitivity of the situation, Victor and Isabelle contacted Dr. Sass for guidance and advice before speaking to Dwayde. But nothing was going to prepare them for how to tell him his long-held secret had just been blown wide open.

Christ. That poor kid. I check my watch again.

WHEN WE FINALLY LAND, WE drive straight to Victor's. Dwayde had taken refuge in the tree house out back and Victor and Isabelle show the ravages of stress.

"He got so angry," Victor recounts, rubbing his palm over his weary face. "We couldn't get through to him. No matter our reassurances, he thinks we don't want him anymore."

"He doesn't really think that." I put a hand on Victor's shoulder while Dee consoles Isabelle. "He's scared and ashamed."

"He has nothing to be ashamed of."

"We know that. But he doesn't. He's lived for years fearing he'd be just like his biological father. That messes with how you see yourself."

"Guess you know what that's like."

"Yeah."

"Jesus, Mick. I'm sorry, man."

"Dwayde is all that matters now. I'd like to try talking to him."

"If anyone can reach him, it's you."

I leave the kitchen and cut across the backyard. A cloud cover makes the evening as gloomy as the situation feels. I climb the wooden ladder to the platform of the elevated structure that's secured between two large trees. Victor and I built it the first summer Dwayde came to live here. A safe place for him to escape whenever he got the urge to run.

Rufus waddles through the opening, his paws greeting my shins in a flurry of excited barks. "Hey, boy." I give him an absent pat and glimpse Dwayde inside sitting on the futon, his thumbs working his game pad.

I duck to fit through the arched doorway. Rufus follows me in. I recognize the sullen demeanor and the pretense of ignoring me. But it's his eyes that have guilt coiling between my shoulder blades. They're shadowed and bruised with the mark of long, heavy tears.

"Hey." When he doesn't answer, I step closer. "Can we talk?"

"I don't want you here!" The fury in his voice doesn't mask the hurt. "You're nothing but a liar."

"I didn't lie to you, Dwayde. But I did go behind your back and for that I'm sorry. I thought finding out the truth would help. I never wanted to hurt you."

"You didn't help," he accuses, his eyes bright with the threat of tears. "You made it worse. She didn't want me and no one here's gonna want me either."

"That's not true, Dwayde. Joyce was screwed up because of what happened to her. She was wrong to blame you. But we don't. We know none of this is on you."

"You're just saying that. Everybody's gonna think I'm just like *him*. Aunt Maria's not gonna want me around Dani."

"Listen to me, Dwayde," I crouch beside the futon. "None of us could ever think you'd be capable of hurting Dani or anybody else. What Joyce told Dee doesn't change how we see you or how we feel about you, not even a little bit."

"You're lying!" he shouts, scrambling off the end of the futon and jumping to his feet. "You're all lying."

I reach out a hand with the intent to stay him, but he rears back.

"You gonna hit me? Like your father."

His accusation lands as intended, like a lead punch to the gut. "You're mad, I get it. But taking verbal swings at me isn't going to make you feel any better."

"I hate you!" He pitches himself onto the futon, and giving me his back, curls up into a ball.

Rufus, sensing his distress, climbs up and snuggles in against him. I sigh at the picture they make. A runaway and a stray, both of whom Victor had found on the streets and brought together. I slide the lawn chair from the corner to place it beside him and take a seat.

"Dwayde?" I lean forward, my gaze at his back. My heart in my throat. "I won't insult you by suggesting I know what this is like for you. What I can share, though, is what it was like for me. I felt the shame of Malcolm's abuse. I felt responsible for him hurting my mother and not being able to stop it. I felt I couldn't be any good if I came from him."

Dwayde shifts, tucking in his knees tighter.

"I spent my childhood and most of my adult life believing in the DNA curse. I made bad decisions because of it. I let Malcolm blackmail me. I kept it a secret from my family. Not only because I was protecting them from him. But because I was protecting myself too. I didn't want them to know. I didn't want them to think I wasn't worthy of their love.

"It took a long time…too long for me to finally realize I'm not him. I'm my own person."

"That's you," he says defensively. "Doesn't mean it's the same for me. What if I become him?"

"You won't. That's not who you are."

"You're just saying that."

"I'm not. I know it's true because I know you, Dwayde. I see the person you are. Kind and good. You're the kid that got Dani's doll down out of the tree when Justin threw it there and made him apologize. You're the kid that defended Joel when he was getting bullied at school."

He turns over and sits up, pulling Rufus onto his lap, keeping his gaze lowered from me. "I got a black eye," he grouches. "That sucked."

"Sometimes heroes get banged up," I say with pride. "Didn't take away from what you did for Joel."

"I just wanna be like you and Victor and Papa T."

Aw, Christ. "You are."

His bottom lip trembles. "I didn't mean what I said about you hitting me and being like your father."

"I know you didn't."

"I shouldn't have said that or that I hate you. I don't."

"I know that too." I get up to take a seat next to him on the futon. "I understand why you were afraid to tell us the truth. You didn't think we could know and still want you to stay. But we do. You're ours and we love you. Nothing could ever change that."

"Promise?" He looks up with big, searching eyes.

"Cross my heart." I draw an X over the left side of my chest.

Tears well up and slide down his face. I put an arm around him. He drops his head on my chest and cries big, aching sobs. I hold him while he unloads the burden of carrying that ten-ton secret, fighting back my own emotions and remembering the man who had guided me through so many difficult times in my life.

When Dwayde draws himself up, his wet cheeks are flushed with embarrassment. He wipes them away with the sleeve of his sweatshirt. "Are Victor and Isabelle mad at me?"

"No."

"I said shitty stuff to them too."

"Sometimes we say things we don't mean in the heat of the moment. But it's nothing that a hug won't fix. A big one for Bells and she'll be over the moon."

"Yeah. Women like that stuff."

"Guys don't mind it either." I ruffle his curls. "Ready?"

"Yeah. Thanks, Uncle Mick."

"Us good guys gotta stick together."

That earns me a watery smile. I realize the days ahead won't be easy. Joyce's damage—that the Franklins set in motion—isn't going to be undone just like that. But when we get back to the house and Dwayde rushes forward into his parents' awaiting arms, I know it's a damn good start.

"MMM." DEE BREATHES IN WITH appreciation. "Smells delicious."

She's standing in the kitchen entryway, her curls tousled from sleep, wearing a short white robe. I imagine from the soft sway of her breasts that she's naked beneath it. I imagine peeling it off her.

"Just coffee and eggs. I used basil."

"Fancy." She gives me a quick kiss on my lips. "Can I do anything?"

"I'll take another one of those."

She obliges, giving me a longer taste of her sweet mouth. "You were up extra early."

"I didn't want to wake you. So, I went out for a run."

"Couldn't sleep?" She puts her arms around me from behind while I stir the eggs in the pan.

"I slept alright." But Dwayde and the case are never far from my mind. "You think Jackson knows about what Alden did?"

"Doubt it. I don't think the Franklins would tell that to anyone, not even their attorney."

"I wanted to out their skeletons. But it's a lot on Dwayde."

"It is. But he's strong and resilient, Mick. He has Dr. Sass and all of us. He got so much love at brunch yesterday. He knows we're all there for him."

"Yeah, he does. It's just the thought of him having to spill all those details to a judge."

"I'm confident if it comes to that, he'll be okay." Dee slips away to drop two bread slices into the toaster. "Dwayde has started talking. That's the best thing to come out of all of this. You made it possible."

"I just said to him what Cayo said to me many times. You did all the work with Joyce."

"You're being modest," she remarks over her shoulder. "But we'll call it a team effort. As for the case, one step at a time. I'll start by meeting with Jackson."

"My bet is on you, Counselor." I turn off the stove when the toast pops. "You're going to kick ass."

"I plan on it." She twines her arms around my neck. "Thanks for the vote of confidence, though."

"After the case is over, we'll go somewhere and celebrate."

"What do you have in mind?"

"A private island where you can lie naked on the beach."

"Hm...why am I not surprised that your vacay choice includes nudity?"

"Because you know how much I love having instant access to your body."

"I love that too."

"Then you won't mind..." I tug at the knot of her belt and open the robe, revealing creamy olive skin and tightened nipples. "Very nice."

She nibbles on my lower lip.

If Dee is fighting the tapes in her head about being bared to the morning light, it doesn't show. Her blossoming confidence takes my arousal up another notch, spiking it through the roof. I grip her ass and lift her onto the counter.

"You have a thing for countertops," she murmurs, referencing the bar of our hotel.

"I have a thing for you."

She trembles on a gauzy sigh. I catch the sound, finding her mouth soft and wet. I've experienced many kisses over the years. They were like summer rain showers—brief and inconsequential. With Dee, kisses are like a storm—thunderous and breathlessly exhilarating.

My palms cup her breasts. I squeeze their generous weight and lower my head, alternating between nipping the peaks with my teeth and rolling them with my tongue.

Moaning, Dee arches her back seeking more, giving more. I move one hand between her legs and groan roughly. My dick hardens to the point of pain at finding her soaked and ready for me.

"I need you." She grinds into my touch.

"I need you too." Not just because sex is always amazing with her but because it irrevocably joins us and binds us to each other.

I shove down the front of my joggers and underwear. Gifted by Dee's openness, by her surrender, I sink my cock into the juiciest cavern a man could ever know.

"Mick." Her body shakes and her inner muscles contract, sucking me in deeper.

I slide my hands beneath her thighs, pulling her to me and canting her in place. She digs her fingers into my biceps, gasping when I put the force of my desire behind my thrust, surging over and over through the tight clasp of her pussy. I rumble a low roar when she climaxes, milking the entire length of me.

That's all it takes.

I come with the velocity of a fired missile, shooting off in a blaze of curses and heated spasms. Her cries overlapping mine, her body trembles. I crush our lips together, my tongue pushing into her mouth as I pump out the rest of my orgasm.

When the sensations finally ease, I wrap my arms around her.

"Now breakfast is cold," she says in a breathless voice against my ear.

I ease back to look at her with a satisfied smile. "Cold breakfast, hot woman, I'll take that trade."

We decide to shower first since we're going to have to warm up the food anyway. Washing each other turns into more foreplay. I slip my hands between her legs, staking my claim, and she fists me, staking hers. It's another thirty minutes before we emerge from the steamy bathroom wrapped in towels.

"Awesome start to the day." Dee smiles and disappears into the closet.

I feel loose and energized. Making love with Dee has that effect. I pull on boxer briefs. My phone buzzes. I walk over to the dresser and recognize the number across the top of the screen. Dread tangles in my chest like choking vines.

"What's wrong?" Dee asks, reappearing with her suit in hand to catch me glowering at my phone.

"It's Malcolm."

"Aren't you going to answer?"

Between the trip to Louisiana and the case, I'd pushed the looming deadline into that dark corner of my mind. "We have enough to deal with right now. This can wait."

"You're capable of handling more than one thing at a time," she says with gentle encouragement. "Whatever he wants or has decided, won't go away by avoiding him."

"I'm not avoiding him."

She gives my buzzing phone a pointed look.

Dammit. I swipe to answer and lift the phone to my ear. "What?"

"Hello, *son*."

Already primed and agitated from him encroaching into my space with Dee, his congenial tone—that I don't trust for a second—tests my patience. "I'm not interested in playing games. Get to the point."

"You sound stressed."

"The point, Malcolm."

"I've been mulling things over."

"And?"

"Once I got past that little stunt you pulled last week, I got to thinking it might be a good time for me to move on."

I tense up, skeptical by his too-easy assent. Dee watches me in question. "You're going to sell me the house and leave?"

"Not much happening in this sleepy town. There's a whole world out there. I can spread my wings like an eagle."

Only he's more like a vulture.

"Might head down to Destin for my retirement, do some deep-sea fishing, find me a Floridian honey. I'll send you a postcard."

"Don't bother. But if you break our deal, not only will I hunt you down, they will hear all about your fatherly ways in Destin or wherever the fuck you go."

"Yeah…yeah… you got me on tape. Relax, Cujo. I know the terms. Just get me my money. All of it upfront and I'll be on my way."

"You'll get it as soon as your resignation is announced and the deed to the house is mine."

"How do I know that you'll pay up?"

"I want you gone, that's how you know."

"Still…gotta protect myself."

"I'll put the money in escrow and have the papers drawn up. But if you don't sign them and tender your resignation by Friday, the deal's off."

"You finally got balls, son. Kinda admire that."

Like hell he does. "Friday, Malcolm."

"Friday it is."

I disconnect and spear a hand through my damp hair. "He's taking the deal."

"That's good news, Mick."

"It doesn't feel right. I threaten to expose him, to take away his power hold as sheriff, and just like that he agrees without a fight."

"You took away the power he has over you. That's what he thrived on. Without it, why not leave? $5 million is a lot of money for a new start."

"It just seems too good to be true."

She lays her suit on the bed and crosses to me. Her hands brace my jaw, bringing my face down to hers. There's love and pride in her eyes. The things I treasure like air. "You're free of him, Mick. You did that, whether he leaves or not. You've slayed your dragon. It's over."

Then why doesn't it feel over? I circle her waist and draw Dee close, fighting off the ominous dread that I could still lose all this.

CHAPTER TWENTY-NINE

Dee

THE LAW OFFICE OF BRYANT, Jackson & McGuire is located in the heart of downtown in a nineteenth-century brick-and-terracotta building that had been restored back in 2002. I'd agreed to meet Thomas Jackson on his turf, allowing him the illusion of the home-court advantage.

Calista won't be joining me. We'd debated it before coming to the conclusion that a one-on-one with Jackson would be more effective.

Armed and ready, I'm seated in an ornate lobby. Flaunting affluence and old-world tradition, it's decorated with dark wood, marble statues, and tufted couches. Given my impression of the pompous attorney, the cliché environment fits to a tee, right down to the young, bombshell receptionist.

For the meeting, I'd chosen a gray tweed suit, white blouse, and low-heel pumps. My hair is pulled back in a bun and pearl studs adorn my ears. Mick had teased me this morning about hiding my kick-ass under a bushel.

It was good to see him smiling and playful again. He'd been unusually quiet and distracted these last few days. Aside from the case, I know his distrust of Malcolm's intentions is weighing heavy on his mind.

At ten o'clock, an assistant in classic Chanel approaches with polite efficiency. "Mr. Jackson will see you now."

She leads me down a mahogany-paneled hallway, passing offices and framed art renditions of the three male partners. When she opens the last door at the end, I hear voices. Sitting at a long, polished boardroom table are Jackson at the helm and Mr. and Mrs. Franklin to his left.

I hadn't expected them. Their obvious intention. But if they thought intimidation came in numbers, then they are the ones in for a surprise.

"Ms. Chase." Jackson stands, expertly coiffed, not a single strand of silver hair out of place. He offers a manicured hand. "Good to see you."

"You as well, Mr. Jackson." I give his hand a firm pump. "Appreciate you making the time."

"My pleasure," he continues the phony charade. "You remember my clients."

"Yes, of course."

Charles Franklin, with his neatly groomed afro, is more formidable in a suit than the jeans and Franklin Farms monogrammed shirt I'd seen him in last time. He rises and moves behind Jackson to grasp my hand in a double-palm shake. "Ms. Chase. As lovely as I remember." He lays on the Southern charm.

"Mr. Franklin. Mrs. Franklin." I look over to where she's seated.

"Hello, Ms. Chase." Her voice sounds automated and her greenish-blue eyes stare back through the same hazy, far-away expression that I recall.

"Please sit," Jackson invites. "Would you like coffee?"

"I'm fine, thank you." I set down my tote bag and take the chair adjacent to him and across from the Franklins. "I'll get right to the point."

"Please." Jackson flashes capped ivories. "You said you have a mutually beneficial solution to discuss."

"I do." My eyes meet him with authority. "I'm giving your clients an opportunity to withdraw their petition for custody before scandalous facts about them become a matter of public record."

Joan Franklin's thin fingers clutch the cameo pendant hanging around the neck of her navy dress and Franklin snaps open his mouth to speak. Jackson intercedes him.

"I'll handle this, Charles. I assure you, Ms. Chase, that we are at a loss for what you are talking about."

"You may be. But your clients are not. Let's start with Wyatt Alden."

"*Oh God*," Mrs. Franklin gasps while her husband blusters. "What the hell is going on?"

Jackson puts up a silencing hand, his brow pleated in what appears to be genuine confusion. "Where are you going with this, Ms. Chase? Mr. Alden is deceased."

"Yes, and it's most unfortunate that he can't be held to account. But your clients can be."

"Watch it, Ms. Chase," Franklin warns in a menacing tone.

"Charles!" Jackson turns to him. "Not another word." Then to me: "Whatever you think Mr. Alden may have done is irrelevant to my clients and the case."

"I would say it's highly relevant that your clients covered up Alden sexually assaulting their daughter when she was just fifteen years old and impregnating her."

Joan Franklin takes in whimpering breaths and her husband pins me with a spearing look. "How dare you come in here with these lies!"

"It's the truth. Look at your wife's reaction."

"My wife is emotional and highly susceptible."

"I think it's called guilt."

"Ms. Chase!" Jackson chastises. "I'm sure you can see the distress you're causing my clients."

"My sympathies lie elsewhere. With Dwayde, who has a detailed account of what your clients did to Joyce Franklin. He bore the weight of that. Joyce's abuse of him stemmed from your clients' neglect to get her help or justice. Instead they forced her to have a baby to raise as their own. Mr. Franklin wanted a male heir so badly that he put his own selfish needs ahead of his daughter's, and Mrs. Franklin went along with it."

"I'm going to be sick." She clutches her stomach, her face contorted and sheet-white, the rouge on her gaunt cheeks standing out in ghoulish contrast.

"Have you no sense of decency?" Franklin charges, which is the epitome of those living in glass houses.

"Charles, you need to let me handle this." Jackson assesses his clients and the situation. "I think it's best that I speak with Ms. Chase, alone."

"That's not an option. I will defend myself against these malicious allegations."

"That's my job, Charles. Let me do it."

"It's my reputation. I'm not leaving."

"Your wife..." Jackson indicates, shifting his gaze to Mrs. Franklin whose eyes are too bright and breaths too rapid.

"Get someone to tend to her," Franklin orders, then softens his tone when he takes his wife's trembling hand in his. "It's going to be alright, darling."

Jackson's face pinches with disapproval. Nevertheless, he picks up the phone on the credenza behind him. "Gretchen, Mrs. Franklin isn't feeling well. Please see that she gets some tea and put her to rest in my office."

Within moments, the assistant I'd met earlier arrives. Franklin whispers something to his wife. She nods obediently and allows Gretchen to take her arm and escort her out of the boardroom.

Both men turn to me. Their expressions are contemptuous. Undaunted, I pull out the photos from my file and place them on the table. Alden and Dwayde, side by side. Not an obvious match at first glance. But if you take a closer look, it's undeniable.

"What does this prove?" Jackson dismisses the pictures with a shoo of his hand. "Alden is dead and buried. You've got no DNA. No evidence. And even if you did, it doesn't implicate my clients. All you have is hearsay from a twelve-year-old boy who was told drug-induced fabrications by an unstable young woman. A judge would laugh you out of court."

"Is that what your clients want—for this to go to court? To have their secrets exposed? For their grandson to lay out all the sordid details on record?"

"Our grandson has been fed lies. Joyce was a very sick girl."

"That's enough, Charles," Jackson cautions again. "Let me do the talking."

"I can speak for myself." Franklin whirls on him in remonstrance. "I warned you of the risk of not being able to see our grandson. I told you that in Joyce's state she may have lied to him about us and the Torreses could exploit that. We needed time with Dwayde to correct any misperceptions yet you advised against a court order, claiming that would make us look insensitive. Now look at where we are."

"*Charles*," he hisses in a stage whisper, "this is not the time or place to critique our legal strategy."

"Don't tell me about time or place. Just fix this."

Jackson turns to me, his face flushed with embarrassment and annoyance. "Ms. Chase, might you give me a moment alone with my client?"

"Of course." I have them rattled. "But for the record, Detective and Ms. Torres haven't exploited anything. They only learned of Alden when I found Joyce and spoke with her. She enlightened me on the details of your clients' horrific actions."

The shock on their faces is priceless.

"You can't really believe a thing she said!" Franklin recovers in outrage.

"Yes, I really can. Have a listen." I pull out a copy of the recording. Then I walk out with my tote bag, leaving the USB on the table, along with the pictures of Alden and Dwayde.

Gretchen, who Jackson must have alerted, arrives to show me back to the lobby. On the way, I note the restroom across from the boardroom and the name plates. I wait until Gretchen disappears down the other corridor to ask the receptionist for the ladies' room.

"Last door on your right." Oblivious to my intention, she smiles and points a pink polished nail toward the hallway I'd just come from.

"Thank you." With time being of the essence, I move quickly to the office with Jackson's gold-plated name plaque.

Pouncing on a vulnerable, unsuspecting woman isn't my typical style. But this woman, no matter her delicate condition, is as culpable as her husband. I turn the knob and peer inside. There's a stately desk with two guest chairs, a built-in library filled with law books, and across from that a maroon leather couch.

Joan Franklin is lying there with her head propped up on the armrest, her stocking feet crossed at the ankles, one arm draped over her eyes and the other arm clutched across her waist as if she's trying to hold herself together. This woman had once been a force. The Lady of the Manor, as Joyce had described her. Now a frail, shadowed version of herself.

"Mrs. Franklin?"

Her arm lifts, her eyes blink open. It takes a moment for awareness to dawn. Her gaze then jumps and her unpainted mouth starts pushing out quick, audible breaths. "Wh-where's Charles?"

"He's with Mr. Jackson. We need to talk."

"N-no." With effort, she swings her thin legs to the floor and sits up, pressing her fingers to her temples. "I-I'm not supposed to talk to you."

"Is that what your husband said?"

"Charles knows wh-what's best."

"Do you really think that what happened to your daughter was for the best?" I ask, closing the door behind me and pulling a guest chair up to the couch.

Her glassy eyes flicker.

"I saw Joyce on Saturday."

"Th-that's not possible."

"It is. I saw her and she's nothing like the girl she once was."

"Please." Her hands move to cover her ears.

"Don't you want to hear how your daughter has fared after running away from you?"

She shakes her head swiftly from side to side.

"Joyce had heroin tracks on the inside of her arms. She's been hooking, selling her body for drugs. And now she's locked up in a Louisiana jail for the next four years because she lured men to a motel room for sex and robbed them at knifepoint. That's how your daughter has been living."

"Nooo." Joan Franklin gulps as fat tears pool in her eyes and spill over. "How do you think it was for Dwayde?"

"Pl-please."

"For five years, she beat him. He has scars and broken bones that never healed properly. He was exposed to her bringing strange men back to whatever rundown dump they were living in and screwing them right in front of him. Some of the men wanted him too."

"Stop. Pl-please."

"Your daughter had a scrap of decency left not to sell him. But what do you think witnessing that would do to a child?"

"We-we tried to find them."

"Joyce would not have run in the first place if you had protected her. Instead she took Dwayde away from you as payback. And she abused him out of all that pain and loathing."

"It-it was the drugs."

"That's what you want to tell yourself to cope, even though you know it's not true. Drugs weren't the cause, you and your husband were."

"I-I didn't...do you think I would have let him hurt Joyce if I had known?" she inadvertently confesses.

"I don't blame you for the rape. But..." I lean in closer, right in her ghostly face. "You are responsible for what happened after Joyce told you. Not getting her help, sending Alden away without consequence, forcing your teenage daughter to have a baby to give your husband a son. You allowed that."

"You-you can't understand," she says, weeping.

"You're right, I don't understand. Joyce told me you blamed yourself for not giving your husband a male child. But that doesn't justify your actions."

"Pl-please."

There's a soft knock on the door prior to it clicking open. "Ms. Chase?" Gretchen startles, holding a tea cup on a saucer. It rattles in her hand. She observes what she can only perceive as a defenseless deer being attacked by a ferocious lion. "I'm getting Mr. Jackson." She purses her lips and exits the office.

I have mere seconds until the cavalry arrives. I direct my attention back to Joan Franklin, who is sobbing on shallow breaths, her narrow shoulders quaking, her face buried in her palms. I'm not impervious to her anguish. She may not be a bad person but she did a terrible thing.

"Mrs. Franklin, you can't undo the damage that's been done to Joyce. But you can do the right thing for Dwayde. Don't let your husband's ego and selfishness ruin another child."

She lifts her face. Mascara-streaked tears run down her blotchy cheeks, over her mouth and chin.

I hand her a wad of tissues from a box on the desk. She wipes her nose and dabs at her face, snuffling. "I-I just w-wanted us to be a-a family."

"Not another word, Joan." Jackson comes marching into the room like an army sergeant with Franklin fast on his heels. "Ms. Chase!" His tone is scalding. "Your tactics today are reprehensible. Mrs. Franklin is in no position to be interrogated. Whatever you may have coerced her into saying will not stand."

I rise to challenge his glare. "If I were you, Mr. Jackson, I'd worry more about your clients' tactics."

Franklin shoulders past Jackson and me to get to his wife. "Ssh, darling."

"She-she saw Joyce."

"Ssh, now." He sits beside her and strokes her hair.

"She-she's in jail, Charles. Our little girl. What have we done, what have we done?" Mrs. Franklin cries, rocking in her husband's arms.

"How dare you do this?" he spits out, all but frothing at the mouth. "You have no idea what we've suffered over losing Dwayde."

"What you've suffered?" Is he really that blind to their wrongdoings or does he just not give a damn? "You should see the shape your daughter's in. She's hard and brittle, street-worn, and utterly destroyed."

"I'm ordering you to leave this instant, Ms. Chase." Jackson stretches his arm toward the door.

"And let your clients off the hook? I don't think so." I pivot back to them huddled on the couch. "Dwayde still bears the brunt of your heinous actions. Until days ago, he hid the fact that he knew anything about his biological father. He did so out of shame. He thought Joyce's abuse was his fault because of what Alden did to her. He's been living in fear that he'll become just like him. That's been your grandson's burden."

"Because of Joyce's lies." Franklin continues his indignant denial.

"No, because of yours," I persist. "You owe Dwayde the truth. If you care anything about your grandson, as you claim to, you will tell him that the reason Joyce didn't love or want him is because of your mistakes, not because of him. He's a remarkable kid, in spite of you. He doesn't deserve to be saddled with your sins."

"If you have the audacity to repeat any of these false claims, I will sue you for defamation." Franklin punctuates his threat with a wagging finger.

"Stop!"

The room falls silent on Joan Franklin's pitched sob.

"No more," she pleads. "No more."

"Joan, as your lawyer, I'm strongly advising you not to say anything."

"I'm so tired." Her posture sags. "So tired of pretending."

"Joan, for Christ sake's," Franklin beseeches. "I will take care of this."

"That's what you said before." She stares back at him as if seeing someone she doesn't recognize. "You promised it would all work out. That we'd be a family. But Joyce was never the same. I was never the same. Our grandson hates us. He couldn't even stand to be in the same room."

"Darling..." Franklin tries to soothe. "You don't know what you're saying. Ms. Chase has confused you."

"I'm not confused. We ruined her, Charles. We ruined our daughter."

"Stop talking, Joan." Jackson threads his words.

"She's already said all I need to hear." My eyes encompass them. "I have more than enough."

"Joyce is a lying junkie and my wife is unwell."

"Let this go, Mr. Franklin." I give him one last opportunity. "Do what's best for Dwayde or it will all come out in court."

"You wouldn't dare." He postures. "You wouldn't have Dwayde testify to any of this disgraceful nonsense."

"Why shouldn't he testify to the truth?" I challenge. "Dwayde has nothing to be ashamed of. But you do."

"Put an end to this, Thomas!" Franklin barks. "Now!"

Jackson spares a withering glance at his client, then turns to me. "A word outside, Ms. Chase?"

"Sure." I hitch my bag onto my shoulder and follow him out into the hall.

"What is it that you want?" he asks.

"That's obvious. For your clients to drop the case and confess their behavior to Dwayde. Did you listen to the recording?"

"Some of it. But you and I both know that convicted felons and drug addicts aren't very credible witnesses."

"Generally, that's true. And if that's all I had I might be worried. But your plan to intimidate me by having your clients here, backfired. Not only do I have a recorded version of Joyce's account, I have a confirmed confession from Mrs. Franklin. What they did to their daughter is unthinkable. They are not fit to have custody. You heard that for yourself. The question is what are you going to do? Continue this charade and let Franklin lie in court under sworn testimony? Put your career on the line for him?"

Beads of sweat break out across his unnaturally smooth forehead. "I don't believe what I heard today was credible. Mrs. Franklin is under enormous stress."

"Hm. Seems to me a woman whom you and Franklin say is *confused*, *not well*, *highly susceptible*, and *under enormous stress*, wouldn't be an ideal candidate for gaining custody of a twelve-year-old boy in need of support and stability."

"You're twisting our words."

"I repeated them verbatim."

Backed into a corner, he can keep fighting or negotiate. He chooses the latter. "Hypothetically speaking, if my clients were to drop the case, what are you offering?"

"Not to expose their sham of a reputation."

"That isn't what I meant." He sighs. "Hypothetically, I might be able to convince them, if the Torreses decline pursuing adoption so that their grandson retains his identity as a Franklin. And if you were to offer visitation with the boy…we could start with monthly weekend visits in Kentucky."

"Hypothetically or otherwise, Dwayde and his guardians won't agree to any of that. However, if your clients come clean and admit the truth, perhaps in time, there might be an opportunity to have some form of contact."

"Ms. Chase…" he drawls, "you're asking for the universe without giving anything in return. Let's be reasonable, Charles Franklin hasn't even admitted to these allegations."

"That's the problem. He continues to put his self-interests first. Dwayde is not some trophy of male pride for Franklin to own and flaunt. If he truly cares about his grandson's well-being, he will own his mistakes with remorse and compassion. If he can't do that, there's no basis from which to start."

"That sounds all very well and good from your side. However, on the presumption that it's true, which again is hypothetical, that kind of admission would be costly to Mr. Franklin. He runs a well-known and highly respectable business. He has put his life's work into building a legacy, one that will benefit his grandson as heir to Franklin Farms. His reputation and status in the community are paramount to him."

"Then he should appreciate that a scandal could destroy it. That's why your clients sent Alden away, to avoid a massive stain on their reputation. What do you think will happen if they pursue custody and their filthy secrets become a matter of public record? Even with Franklin's denial, there will be speculation, doubt, people will put it together and see your clients aren't so squeaky clean after all. I'm giving him the chance to do right by Dwayde and still keep his reputation."

"You're offering a one-sided deal."

"I'm offering way more than the Franklins deserve."

Tension strains the vein between his impeccably trimmed eyebrows.

"Seems you and your clients have some talking to do, Mr. Jackson."

CHAPTER THIRTY

Dee

THE HOUSE IS DECORATED WITH balloons. Pulled pork tacos and pepperoni pizza are being served. Dwayde's picks. Mason is strapped into a booster seat, squishing up baby crackers in his chubby fists and sticking them in his mouth. Laughter and animated chatter fill Mama T's kitchen.

This isn't just any Sunday brunch.

It's a celebration.

The Franklins had withdrawn their custody petition soon after that fateful meeting, two months ago. The right decision for the wrong reason. When it came down to it, Franklin chose to maintain his innocence and honor the fraud of his reputation. As for Joan Franklin, she'd stood by her man. Neither of them had taken responsibility. They hadn't owned up to their mistakes or tried to unburden Dwayde. But they had forever lost the child on whom their moral crimes are based. I suppose, in that, there's poetic justice.

Dwayde has been through so much, but with counseling and the love of family, he's doing okay. Better than okay now that the adoption has been finalized.

Before we eat, Victor calls for everyone's attention. "I've never been a particularly religious man," he says, choking up. "But I believe fate or some higher power put Dwayde in our path. He was meant for us, meant to come into our lives and be part of this family. And for that, we are truly blessed. To Dwayde Torres!" Victor raises his bottle of Coke, his smile spreading white and wide across his handsome face. "Our son. And to my incredible sister, Dee, who was also fated to us. Thank you for fighting like hell to make it all official. We are beyond grateful. We love you both."

Enthusiastic shouts and applause ring out around the table. Mick squeezes my knee. Dwayde grins from ear-to-ear. Isabelle's eyes are joyfully misty and Mama T's wholesome face flushes with happiness. I knuckle away my own tears and turn to hug Dwayde. This is my world, my family. A lost treasure, found.

"You did it, Counselor!" Mick says, pulling me into his arms when we find a moment alone after brunch.

"We did it." I kiss him and feel a delightful shifting. As if everything is aligned and as it's supposed to be. With us, with Dwayde, with Malcolm taking the deal and leaving town.

"Isabelle said we'd get our happy endings." I nuzzle into him. "Looks like she was right."

"Ending?" Mick eases back with a twinkle in his eyes. "This is only the beginning, beauty. The best parts are still to come."

Micah

WEEKS AFTER THE CELEBRATORY BRUNCH, Dee and I are having a casual Friday night dinner in front of the fireplace. She lifts the last cracker and piece of brie off the charcuterie board and feeds them to me.

"Yum." I nip her fingers, making her laugh.

It had taken me a while to believe that Malcolm was really gone, that I was truly free of him. But with confirmation that he's still down in Destin, and with the case over, all hope for the future springs to life. "I think I owe you a trip."

"So, you do." She grins. "The one with me naked and sunburned on the beach."

"Not on my watch." I catch her hand and bring her in for a kiss. "I'll make sure you're well-oiled and lubricated."

"I'm sure you will." Her pretty eyes roll. "But your one-track mind aside, I'm up for a trip. I can probably find space in my calendar next month."

Next month is not what I have in mind. Dee gets up with the tray and disappears into the kitchen. My pulse goes a little haywire.

"I've never been on a beach vacation," she says, returning to the living room.

Free of makeup and wearing one of my T-shirts, Dee packs as much of a turn on in cotton as she does in lingerie. It's her natural sensuality and luscious body that make her a dream to fuck. But it's her big, generous heart that makes her a dream to love.

"I found this private resort on Mystique Island," I say. "The beach-front property is located on a lagoon. All the rooms have views of the water and white sand for miles."

"That sounds wonderfully decadent." She walks closer.

"I thought it would be an ideal spot for our wedding."

Her silky bare legs come to a stumbling halt. Her expression goes slack-jaw. Good. That's how I want her, caught off guard. I stand and meet her in the middle of the room. It's not pomp and circumstance. No grand, elaborate gesture. Neither of us is about that. I pictured it like this, proposing in our cozy house where we have shared some of our best times.

I look into her eyes, more golden in the candlelight. "There's no other woman more perfect for me than you are. You have made me a better man. A stronger man. A happy man. I loved you madly at eighteen and yet it's nothing compared to how much I love you now.

"You light up my entire world, Deeana Rae. Through all the darkness, you've filled it with stars and sunbeams." I go down on bended knee in front of her. "Will you have me as your husband and the father of your children? I vow to spend my life being the best I can be at both."

"I think I'm going to faint."

"I'll catch you, beauty. I'll always catch you."

"I know." She kneels down with me and wraps her arms around my neck, her tears wetting my cheek. There's no question or hesitation this time around. "Yes, Mick," she breathes. "Yes-yes-yes, a million times over, yes. To marriage, to children, to forever."

Filled with joy, I shift back to retrieve the ring that I'd concealed in the front pocket of my lounging pants and take her hand. The emerald-cut ruby, set in a delicate platinum band, is haloed by diamonds.

"Wow!" Her eyes round through damp lashes.

Smiling with pleasure, I read Dee the tiny engraving. "My first. My last. My only."

"Oh, Mick."

I slide the bespoke engagement ring onto her finger. It has the exact effect I was looking for. The deep, vibrant red against her tawny-beige skin. The sparkle of diamonds glittering in a rainbow of brilliance, complementing her elegant hand.

"It's beautiful," she says, holding the ring out in front of her, then looking back up at me. "I can't wait to be your wife."

My kiss against her lips is fierce and earnest. "Marry me next weekend."

"What?" She blinks rapidly. "You want to elope?"

"No. I want our family and your friends there. I just want to marry you in a private, intimate ceremony on a beach where there's only us and the people that matter."

"How would we arrange that so quickly?"

The fact that Dee's asking indicates she's not immune to the idea. "We'll all fly down on a chartered flight next Friday for the weekend. There aren't any residency requirements. It's a fast and simple process. No wait times."

"Okay, but still, not everyone will be able to get away with such short notice."

"I've got that covered, beauty. I asked for Mama T's blessing and spoke to everyone prior. The resort is booked."

"You planned it all without me knowing. How?"

"When I want something, I make it happen."

"Was my answer that much of a foregone conclusion?" Her lips quirk up on one side.

"I take nothing about you for granted. But you do seem pretty sweet on me, so I figured my chances weren't half bad."

"Uh-huh." She smiles drolly and slides her arms back around my neck. "Do I at least get to plan any of the wedding?"

"The details are all yours. I'll put you in touch with the resort manager," I say, confident in his discretion.

"So, you seriously want to get married next weekend?"

"Yes." I lower my head to kiss her. "I've waited over fifteen years for you to be my wife. I don't want to wait any longer."

Dee

I MARRY MICAH ANTHONY PETERS the following Saturday on a private beach, surrounded by the people we love. Lexie and Jordyn are beside me as my co-maids of honor and Victor and Dwayde are next to Mick.

I couldn't be happier. The sun shines high in a crystal blue sky, the flour-soft sand is warm beneath my feet. I'd been lucky to find a dress on such short notice that I feel amazing in. It has an ivory embroidered sheer lace bodice with capped sleeves, fitted from breast to waist. The tulle skirt floats down to my bare feet like ocean waves. My makeup is minimal and my hair is styled in a wind-swept low bun, accented with a floral vine of red roses and baby's breath. The look is boho-chic and seaside romantic.

Our officiant has kind eyes and a comforting manner. He reminds me of Papa T. I wish my foster dad could be here to share the momentous occasion. But I carry him close in my heart.

Mick and I face each other as the ceremony gets underway. My handsome groom is wearing relaxed linen pants the color of wheat, rolled up at the ankles, and an untucked pale blue shirt opened to mid-chest. He's barefoot too. His smile is bright like the Caribbean sun. I offload my bouquet to Jordyn and he takes my hands in his.

Tears well up in my eyes as Mick repeats his vows; his voice solid and sure. There's no doubt as to how much he loves me.

I can scarcely keep it together when it's my turn. We exchange rings. Mick slips a slim diamond band on my finger that matches my ruby and diamond engagement ring. I'd gotten him a wide platinum band. The strong simplicity suits him and complements the black diamond ring he still wears on his right hand.

"I now pronounce you husband and wife." At the utterance of the official confirmation, Mick hauls me into his arms and kisses me senseless.

Cheers and applause fill the afternoon air. Our family and friends approach with hugs and congratulations. Justin and Dani, our ring bearer and flower girl, bounce excitedly and ask if it's time to go swimming yet. Mason babbles and slobbers on my neck. I'm so glad we married here. The ceremony was everything I could have hoped for. Deeply intimate and personal.

"Mi hijo, mi hija." Mama T holds out her hands to us. We take each one. She's glowing in a soft pink tunic and capris set; her hair is one long braid, her cheeks rosy. "Felicidades! The wedding was beautiful. It does my heart good to see you married and so in love. Cayo would have been pleased and proud."

Mick's eyes water and he kisses her cheek. I give her a hug, forever grateful to Rita and Cayo Torres. They took in a lost and grieving fourteen-year-old and made me theirs. They nurtured the abused and broken-hearted little boy next door, giving Mick the support and affection he desperately needed. They contributed to him growing into the fine man he's become. My husband.

I hold on to Mama T, and Mick circles his arms around us both. We stay that way, crying under the sun until the officiant calls us away to sign the register.

"You're officially mine," Mick says after scrawling his name.

"And you're mine."

Once the documents are secured in a safe located upstairs in our beach house, we all enjoy a buffet spread on the veranda below. The kids swim. We dance in the sand until late in the evening. We cut a red velvet wedding cake, feed it to each other, and toast our future with chilled, non-alcoholic bubbly.

It's after ten when everyone finally settles into their respective bungalows. Our master suite is as impressive as the rest of the house. A king bed is framed by mosquito netting, and above it, blades of a fan swirl leisurely. The terrace doors open onto a hot tub and an infinity pool that overlooks the moonlit ocean.

Mick comes up behind me. We're quiet, standing at the window, taking it all in. The view. The moment. Just us and the stars. When his hands touch my shoulders, a shiver of anticipation courses through me. I'd imposed the no-sex-until-we're-married rule after our engagement. Mick had grumbled like a bear. Given our avid appetite for each other, we'd spent a week of longing, fraught with sexual tension. Heated looks and hot kisses cut short nearly drove us crazy.

I turn to him. His dark eyes move over me in a forever that seems to fit into the space of a single breath. Then his fingers slide up my neck. His touch, a whisper.

"Today was perfect." His hand curves around my neck and his head lowers to kiss me. Infinitely slow and soft. "I don't want to rush tonight. I want to savor every minute of it."

I slide my arms around his waist and nestle closer, feeling the heat of him through the thin linen of his shirt and the material of my dress. We stay like that, swaying without music. For all the pent-up yearning and fevered anticipation, I'd expected for us to let loose our lust in frenzied impatience. Instead, a delicious restraint winds through us like a gentle current. Sensuous and warm. We don't have to rush. We have a lifetime.

"More champagne?" he asks.

"Not right now, thanks. I'm going to get out of this dress."

I kiss him and disappear into the bathroom. I'm nervous. We've made love dozens of times, but this is our wedding night. I take out the hair vines and shake out my curls. They fall in a messy mass around my shoulders. Next, I take off my dress and hang it behind the door. The ivory strapless bra pushes my breasts up and together, the matching thong cuts up high on my thighs. I slip on the long, sheer, belted peignoir. It's delicate and sexy.

Mick is sipping from a crystal flute when I return to the bedroom. He pauses. His eyes coast over me. I see his breaths quicken in the movement of his chest. I don't feel the flutter of self-consciousness. It isn't just because of the safety I experience with Mick. It's me. It's the work I've done to weed out the negative thoughts and messages. I still have moments of insecurities, but not as often. And definitely not now.

"My beautiful bride," he whispers before setting his glass down and coming forward. He lifts me up in a cradle.

I slip my arms around his neck as he brings us to the bed. Inside the netting, he lowers me onto the downy-soft duvet. He separates from me just long enough to remove his shirt. I feel tingly all over. But it's not the giddy heat of desire that I got in the beginning with Mick. As potent, but not the same. This is a cultivated burn that comes from down deep, it flames like a torch and spreads from my feet into my limbs and up into my chest and throat, filling me everywhere.

He settles on top of me and we meet in a reverent kiss. He tastes like the fruit from the champagne and Mick. His hands glide unhurried down the sides of my body. Emotion overwhelms me.

Mick and I have opened up all the hidden parts in each other. He sees who I am. Beyond my childhood hurt and insecurities, he saw me right from the start. Not as flawed or broken but as perfectly lovable and whole. And I saw him too. Not as the bad seed he thought he was. Or the popular jock that his father and the town wanted him to be. I saw all the beautiful layers in him. The talented writer, the boy who adored his surrogate family, who survived his father's abuse, who grieved his mother. The boy who loved me to distraction and loves me still.

We'd unintentionally hurt each other and lost fifteen years. We'd lost a baby. But we're healing together. And growing.

"You're trembling." Mick lifts his head, his eyes concerned.

"Yes." I gaze up at him. "I'm feeling so much, I don't know what to do with it."

"I'm feeling it too, beauty. This has been a long time coming. But maybe we had to go through all that we did to get here."

We slowly undress each other. Kissing and touching in between. My full breasts caressed by his hands, his lips surrounding my nipples, gently tugging and sucking, one then the other.

I stroke my fingers over his chest. Muscled and defined beneath my palms.

"You're so beautiful," he murmurs, trailing a hot path down my torso and turning me over to place moist kisses down my back, over the cheeks of my bottom, and down the backs of my thighs.

I moan and close my eyes, enraptured by his intoxicating touch. By the time he eases me onto my back again, I'm limp with pleasure and aching with arousal.

"I want you," I gasp.

"You have me. All of me." When Mick says it now, I know that I do.

Braced above me, there's a soft look on his face but there's fire in his eyes. He lowers, giving me his weight, his heat, and all his love.

My throat closes, smothered by tears.

He sips at my damp cheeks and I clutch his shoulders as his thick erection enters me for the first time as my husband. I pull him to me, pressing my mouth to his. Our breaths mingle, hot and gasping. His hips roll against mine, filling and stretching me so good.

My heart flies as if it has wings; passion soars. We move, falling into a glorious rhythm. The rhythm of us. Our bodies gliding, muscles tensing and releasing, our wedding bed a chorus of moans and whispers.

Slicked together, chest-to-chest, heart-to-heart, my inner flesh tugs and tightens around his slow and measured surges. The tender fucking is exquisite. A tempered greediness that is all the more intense for its unyielding restraint.

"Mick!" I sob somewhere between euphoria and bliss. The quiet roll of my orgasm is no less devastating than an earthquake pounding through my veins, my blood, and centering in the rippling beats of my heart.

And Mick is right there with me. His fingers gripping mine as we come together as husband and wife. As one.

Much later, we eat chocolate covered strawberries and sip non-alcoholic champagne into the wee hours. We skinny dip in the heated pool. The warm salt water feels delectable on my skin. We crawl back under the covers after making love in the sprawling glass shower with jets that hit all the right spots. I tuck myself against Mick and fall asleep as secure and happy as I've ever been.

"*YESSS*," I SHRIEK, MY FACE buried in the pillow, my butt in the air.

Mick had awakened this morning rough and ready. Commanding me onto all fours. Now, he stands at the side of the bed, lunging again and again, pounding hard and deep.

"You're so tight and creamy." His fingers dig forcefully into my hips, his thrusts beating a ravenous tempo.

I squeeze my eyes shut, seeing stars. It's simultaneously all too much and not enough. This raunchier side of Mick never fails to unleash my sexy beast.

"More," I beg, and he gives it to me.

The not-so-gentle push of his wet thumb into my puckered rear is a dark and erotic pleasure. Consumed by a barrage of sensation, my nails claw at the sheets, my body writhing like a woman possessed. On occasion, we've experimented with sex toys but there's nothing as good as feeling Mick's touch all over and inside me.

"That's it, baby," he urges. "Go wild for it. You feel so fucking good."

His words and voice hasten my need to climax. I shove one hand between my legs and circle the nub of flesh with my fingertips. The pounding from behind rakes my breasts over the sheets, abrading my nipples. I silently scream into the pillow when the first hard tremor hits like a freight train. Its roaring power smashes through me. I can hardly breathe. My core and ass tighten, clenching down on his cock and thumb.

When I've ridden out one of the longest orgasms I've ever had, Mick flips me onto my back and pulls my legs forward to finish himself off. "Christ, you're sexy."

I imagine what he must see, a flushed and well-fucked woman. I've thought about what we might look like together. Mick is a visual man. He rarely closes his eyes during sex. And anything that gives him pleasure is a turn on for me. Eying his cock all hard and glistening—the roped veins pulsing, pleading for release...

I scramble onto all fours, this time facing him. My breasts bob as I crawl forward and wrap my mouth around his raging hard-on.

"Jesus, Dee," he hisses and works to regain his footing.

I suck avidly on the head and fist one hand around the base, pumping with a tight, fast friction. His hips work without volition. The urge to come driving him. I give Mick a good view of my breasts bouncing and he holds back my hair to watch my mouth working his shaft. The picture I have of me on my knees, greedy for his climax, makes me hotter.

I pick up the combined juices from my orgasm and his pre-cum to lube my finger. Then mimicking what he'd done to me, I clutch his thigh with one hand, and with the other, reach beneath him and rub against the entrance of his rear.

"*Dee.*" His girth expands in my mouth.

I slide my finger deeper, massaging that tender spot, while sucking him off. He curses and pulls at my hair. I have never done this, but watching Mick in the throes of breaking apart—being the source of that pleasure, sharing it with him—is an erotic trip.

I thrust and suck harder. Mick lets loose, powering into my mouth. "Oh fuck." He holds my head, his hips pumping. "Christ...ah, Dee..."

He comes in a copious rush. I can feel the flexing spasms against my finger, the wrenching contractions at the back of my throat that drain him empty. I don't stop until he does.

Clinging, gasping, we fall onto the bed in a shaky, sweaty heap. I love that we can be this way together—free and without inhibition.

BRUNCH IS SET UP UNDER a large tent on the beach. After we're showered and dressed, we join our wedding guests. Mick makes a heartfelt toast. The kids play in the sand and get in a last swim before their flights. I give Lexie and Jordyn each an Infinity bracelet. I cherish these two women. They welcomed me into their close-knit relationship when I was so alone, and now I get to include them in the family I've always wanted.

When Mick and I have the resort to ourselves for a mini honeymoon, we decide to explore the island by boat. Mick is adept at navigating the catamaran and looks like a sun god, shirtless and in nautical blue boardshorts.

The turquoise ocean is tranquil and so clear it's transparent. We dock at a waterfall, sheltered within a tropical forest. I slide off my sunglasses. A niggling of self-consciousness runs through me as I reach for the short hem of my cover-up. Mick has seen me naked, in the dark, in the light, he's seen me in bra and panties, but he's never seen me in a swimsuit. I haven't worn one since I was a kid. Though my nerves seem silly, I recognize they are part of my journey. I push past the lingering insecurities to lift the dress up and over my head.

"Damn!" Mick's gaze sweeps over me in the cherry red one-piece suit with a plunging neckline.

"You like?"

"You look good enough to eat."

"Help yourself."

He growls into my neck and devours me under the springs. The perks of having a slice of paradise all to ourselves.

THAT NIGHT WE DINE ON buttery lobster, take a walk along the beach, and soak in the hot tub. I don't want the time to end. But early Monday morning, our bags are packed and in the limo.

"I hope you enjoyed your stay," the resort manager says in a creole-influenced accent. "It was a privilege to have you, Mr. and Mrs. Peters."

"Everything was superb, thank you." I slide across the backseat.

Mick joins me and takes my hand, lifting it to his mouth for a kiss. "Mrs. Peters has a very nice ring."

"I like it too." Except I won't be Deeana Peters back in Chicago. I'll still be Deeana Chase. From secret girlfriend to secret wife.

Mick smiles at me, making my chest hurt. I struggle not to let my thoughts deflate the amazing high. We both value our privacy. Hiding is a practical solution. It doesn't make our marriage any less real. Or our love, any less valid. We exchanged vows in front of the people we care about the most. That's all that counts.

But I turn to stare out the window before Mick can read anything other than joy on my face.

CHAPTER THIRTY-ONE

Micah

"WE'RE BACK ON SCHEDULE," NADIA confirms after a snow storm had shut down construction for a week. "We added a buffer for the winter build."

I look over the plans. Through Jordyn's design, in a matter of months, my vision will be brought to life. A campus-style community that is integrated with educators, counselors, and protective services to provide transitional and long-term support to homeless youth.

"I'm pleased with the work you're doing," I tell her.

"Thank you. The framing is underway and should be completed in six weeks. We can go out to the site then and see the progress."

"I'd like that." Standing, I shake the project director's hand. "Text me some dates."

"Will do." She walks me to the door. "By the way, thanks for the referral. We just got the RFP."

"I give recognition where it's due."

"Well, I appreciate that. I read about you donating the property to your hometown."

"I'm glad I could do it. The place was once a farm and outdoor play area with massive snow hills." I remember fondly.

"Worked out that your father decided to retire and sell it."

My spine stiffens. The sudden retirement of Sheriff Peters from his long-held post had shocked the residents of Springvale, except for Mama T, who knew why Malcolm had taken the deal and split. An arrangement that had cost me five million dollars and my silence. This time, my choice, my terms. An imperfect justice. But I can live with it to have him far gone and out of our lives.

Keeping a smile plastered on my face, I respond to Nadia with a whitewashed truth. "The timing was opportune for it to all come full circle and be a place that kids can once again enjoy."

"It's a great project. I'd be thrilled to work on another of your endeavors."

"I'm hands off on this one," I tell her. "It's strictly a donation. But I do hope the city council's decision goes in your favor."

Smiling, she raises crossed fingers.

I leave for my next appointment, a start-up gaming firm in the virtual reality space. I spend two hours with a group of young guys looking for venture capital money. I like their energy and drive. I'm not a gaming aficionado. But their prospectus was impressive and Dwayde was psyched about the new technology they're using.

I hadn't known where life would take me after basketball. Starting up Papa's Kids was to honor Cayo. I hadn't expected it to become such an important part of me. Now I'm a philanthropist, aspiring writer, and businessman. A husband.

The wallpaper behind my lock screen is a picture of Dee. It was hours before we left the island. She's sitting in bed, surrounded by netting. Her skin is sun-kissed. Her white nightie, vapor-thin like smoke. The silk is held up by two teeny straps. Her breasts are a lush valley of cleavage, her hair is wild and messy. She's looking at me with that unguarded smile I adore. It was all I could do to not dive back in bed with her. Instead, I'd grabbed my phone, compelled to capture her at that moment.

No one would know that we'd just made love. No one, other than a handful of those close to us, would know that she's mine. That she's my wife.

The rush of guilt feels like a punch to the gut every time.

With my meetings over for the day, I take my wedding band out of my jacket pocket and put it back on my finger.

THE FOLLOWING FRIDAY, I PULL into the carport and exit my Porsche. Remnants of the March snowstorm still cling stubbornly to lawns and bare trees. After an unseasonably warm fall, winter seems to be lingering until the bitter end. Hunching my shoulders against the nip of cold air, I make the short jaunt to the house. Dusk has fallen and lights shine through the windows, welcoming me home.

"Hi, beauty," I call out, sliding off my cap and hanging it on the rack with my coat.

"Hey." Dee greets me with a warm smile and warmer kiss.

She'd gone to an exercise class after work. Curls spill from her ponytail and she's wearing a yoga jacket and leggings that mold to her curves. Gone are the baggy T-shirts she used to wear to the gym.

"Dinner's almost ready. Hope Thai bowls are okay. I went for something quick and easy."

"Sounds great." I pull off my boots and follow her into the kitchen. Rice simmers on the stove and a chopping board loaded with veggies sits on the counter. I wash my hands and snag a carrot.

"Know what tomorrow is?" she asks, pulling out a sauté pan.

"Yep. It's Saturday."

Dee glances over her shoulder at me, her eyes narrowed. "You better be joking."

"Maybe." I wink, messing with her.

"*Mick.*"

"Come on, beauty. How could I forget that it's been one month since I married the girl of my dreams?"

"Aw." That pleases her. "We should do something to celebrate, or is that too cheesy?"

"No. It's an excellent idea." I rub my chest and smile. How could I feel anything but happy that she wants to celebrate our marriage? There were a few days after we returned from the island that she'd seemed a little withdrawn. Postwedding blues she'd called it. I was concerned, but then it quickly passed and I didn't question her further. Maybe I'd been afraid to.

"Oh!" Her sudden outburst startles my thoughts. "I want to show you something."

"Jesus, woman, are you trying to give me a heart attack?"

"Sorry." She laughs and tugs on my hand, leading me into the living room. Her iPad is set up on top of the fireplace. She pulls it to her and awakens the screen. "I can't decide which color frame I like better for our wedding photos. I'm thinking of doing a collage above the mantel. What do you prefer?" She turns the image to me. "Pearl or..." she slides to the next option, "vanilla cream?"

Both frames look white to me. But a smart man knows better than to say that. "Um...the pearl."

"Really?" She makes a face. "I'm worried about the shine. The vanilla cream matte might be better against the wall." She holds it up. "It will also bring out the..."

I lose track of the words, watching her full lips moving. Pink and unpainted. My thoughts stray far from frame choices to taking Dee's mouth. Then taking her.

"Mick?"

"Huh?"

"Are you even paying attention?"

"I always pay attention to you."

Her eyebrow arches and she sets down the iPad on the coffee table. "Then what did I just say?"

"Something about shiny things."

Laughing, she smacks me with a throw pillow. "Remind me again why I married you."

I wrestle away the cushion she has poised to strike again and pull her against me. "Because I make you hot."

"*Humph.*"

"Speaking of hot, I like what you're wearing." I nip her earlobe.

"You're trying to distract me."

"That too. But I mean it." Dee is all the more radiant when she feels good about herself. It brightens everything around her, including me. "I love seeing you confident and showing off that sexy body."

"I'm getting there."

"It's hard to top perfection." My hands push into her falling hair. "But you're constantly progressing."

"That's the best compliment." She presses her lips to mine and I seize the opportunity to deepen the kiss.

It's just heating up when Dee eases back and slides her hands up my chest and over my shoulders. "Dinner first, then dessert."

"Dessert now sounds better."

"I'll make it worth the wait."

My wife can be such a tease. One of the many things I love about her.

"Why don't you look over some of the collage ideas I found on Pinterest while I finish up the bowls?"

My phone buzzes then. "Saved by the bell."

Her lips twitch with humor that she tries to hide behind a scowl.

Love you, I mouth, and fish my phone out of my pants pocket, watching Dee's sexy retreat. She's always the best and most invigorating part of my day. I look down at the screen. It's Asher Dumont, my Publicist & PR Manager.

In his midthirties, out of all my business relationships, I'd say ours is the closest to a friendship. While we haven't hung out as much lately, I like Ash on both a personal and professional level. He's been in charge of my media relations and branding since I left the NBA and started Papa's Kids. Asher doesn't have a rolodex of celebrities. I didn't want that. He's skilled at messaging and navigating the nuances of the press. And most of all, he understands that my priority is to do the cause justice, while keeping my private life out of the media.

"Hey, Ash," I answer, putting the phone to my ear.

"Hey, Mick. Got a minute?"

"Just about to have dinner. What's up?"

"I won't keep you long then. Are you familiar with the Chicago Children's We Care Foundation?"

"Sure, I've heard of them. They promote and fundraise for children's charities. Why?"

"Here's the why," he says with an upbeat lift to his voice. "Their board selected you to receive the Generosity of Spirit Award for civic and philanthropic leadership. Major kudos, my friend—congratulations!"

An appropriate response would be that's amazing news or I'm honored, but I say neither. In fact, I say nothing.

"Mick?"

"Yeah, still here."

"Shocked you, did I?"

"You could say that."

"Don't know why. You're doing great things for the city. Getting kids off the street. The new facility is gaining lots of attention. The board's chairwoman is anxious to issue a press release on Monday. The awards dinner and gala will be held later next month and she wants to announce the guest of honor."

"Does acceptance require me to attend?" I ask, processing my options.

"I don't know if it's required but it's customary. What kind of question is that?"

"I was thinking my managing director could accept on my behalf. Eden runs the show and deserves the credit."

"Bring her, but with all due respect to Eden, people will come expecting to see you and hear you speak. This is not a quaint little fundraising luncheon, Mick. This is a major event."

"I'm aware of that."

"Then it won't come as a surprise that recipients are featured on *Sunday Nights with Bianca Keller*. It'll be a friendly interview, aired a week or two before the gala, shot in your home. I know you value your privacy. But frankly, I think it's a good idea. Connect more of the man to the cause. You're beloved by the city, dude, and that intimate touch will draw people in."

I glance across the room, past the wall divider into the kitchen. Dee is setting the table. "There's a lot to consider. I'll have to get back to you."

"On the interview?"

"The whole thing."

"You can't be serious. An event like this with you headlining means attendees with fat wallets. Bianca's show will mean national and even global awareness for Papa's Kids. What's there to think about?"

"Just leave it with me," I hedge. "I'll call you tomorrow. Gotta go."

"Alright," he says in confused resignation, unaware of Dee and my new marital status. "Tomorrow then."

I disconnect and toss the phone down onto the sofa. Shit!

It takes me longer than it should to enter the kitchen. Dee is adding the chicken and vegetable to the bowls, her ponytail swinging with the movement. I swallow hard and clear my throat.

"What can I do?"

"It's all done." She looks aside at me. "Everything okay?"

"Mm-hmm."

"You seem bothered."

It amazes me how well she reads me, but I keep up the pretense. "I'm fine."

Her radar goes off. She faces me. "I know that *I'm fine*. I've said it often enough when it wasn't true for me, either. Who was on the phone, Mick?"

"Let's talk about it later." I grab the bowls and bring them to the table, attempting to stall. To think. To figure out what to do.

Dee doesn't move from her spot. "If you're upset about something, we should talk about it now."

"I'm not upset."

"Don't do that." Her tone sharpens with irritation.

"Do what?"

"Shield me. That's what you're doing."

My mouth opens in denial. But we're past the lies and omissions. "It was Asher."

"Your publicist?"

I nod and release a breath. "The Chicago Children's We Care Foundation is having a fundraising gala next month."

"They want you to attend?"

"Not just attend. They're giving me an award."

"The Generosity of Spirit Award?"

"You know it?"

"Of course. Wow!" She surges forward and throws her arms around me, her voice hitching with excitement. "That's amazing! You so deserve this. You don't just front the money, you give your time. Your heart. I'm so happy for you." Then as if remembering how my admission had come about, she pulls back, her brows pinched. "Why didn't you want to tell me?"

I look at her beautiful face. There's no longer any pleasure in it.

"The award includes attending the gala dinner and doing an interview with Bianca Keller. At home. Broadcast across the country."

"And you don't want that." Her hands fall off my shoulders and she takes a step back. "Because of me."

"It's not you, Dee. It's the situation. How could I possibly give a speech and not acknowledge you or do an interview at home and pretend I'm single. That's not even a consideration. But saying yes would mean exposing you and our relationship to the media and to the public."

"I'm aware of the exposure." She bristles. "Do you intend to hide me forever?"

"I haven't been hiding you, dammit. I've been protecting you." I pace away along the narrow galley, my jaw set. Because treating the woman that I love as a secret—no matter the reason—isn't something I'm proud of.

"Once you're out there, Dee...there's no turning back. Your life will forever be changed. Your anonymity gone."

"I know it won't be easy," she says. "A celebrity dating a non-famous person increases the hype. That's going to bring all kinds of attention and speculation. Some of it will be unkind. Unflattering. Even mean. I get that, Mick. But I can handle it."

"I don't want you to handle it."

"Because you don't think I can."

"We've been over this before, Dee." I grit my teeth in frustration. "You're the strongest woman I know."

"I know you believe that but you don't act on it."

"What the hell does that mean?"

"It means you won't let me prove it."

"You don't have to prove anything to anyone."

"I do, Mick. I need to prove it to myself. I've been talking about it with Dr. Roland."

I zero in on that nugget to justify my defense. "You talked it over with your therapist, but not me?"

"You don't exactly invite any discussion on this topic but that's no excuse. I should have told you before we left the island that I didn't feel good about starting our marriage this way."

Her admission blisters. "So, it wasn't postwedding blues after all?"

"No."

"What was it then?" I scoff with a head on my anger. "Disappointment...regret?"

"That's not fair. I don't have regrets about marrying you."

"*I didn't feel good about starting our marriage this way,* doesn't sound like a ringing endorsement."

"I take responsibility for not being honest about my feelings. But you haven't been honest either."

"How exactly haven't I been honest?"

"You said we wouldn't hide forever and yet here we are, still hiding."

"Stop using that word as if I'm ashamed of you or of us. That's not what this is about."

"I know. But sometimes, my insecurities get the better of me and I feel that way."

Jesus. Her words kill me. "There's no shame here, Dee. I love you and what we have, that's what I'm protecting."

"I love you too." She holds up her left hand, the ruby and diamonds catching the light. "I took vows, Mick. I'm all in. Not just for better or for worse. For good. I want to stop sneaking around. I want to wear my rings in public. I want to be able to take your name."

"I want that too. But going public comes at a cost."

"So does hiding."

What can I possibly say to that? I go with the inadequate. "I'm sorry."

"I don't want you to be sorry. This isn't about blame. It's about how far we've come. And where we go from here. You've just been presented with a tremendous opportunity. It feels like the right time to go public. And for the right reason. I want to share it with you, Mick, as your wife."

318

Hit at the very core, my heart pounds. Drumming out of my chest. These battles of inner reflection are pure hell. Like staring down the barrel of your own bullshit. I justified to myself that my reasons and actions were to safeguard her from O'Malley, from Malcolm, from the press...the public. But to what end? At the expense of Dee's burgeoning self-esteem? At the expense of our marriage? I'd nearly lost her before by trying to protect her.

I look into Dee's gold-flecked eyes and face the moment of truth. Do I hold on to my deep-seated urge to shield her from the things I can't control, or let go and trust in us to handle whatever going public throws our way?

I frame her hopeful face with my hands and take that picture into my heart. "You don't deserve to be hidden away, Dee. You never did. I've been holding you back. Dimming the light of your courage and confidence because of my own fears and needs to keep you in this safe bubble of my making. I was wrong."

"I want you to take my name. No more sneaking around or pretending that we're single. I want to build our life in the brightest of lights, not drape it in shadows. I want to shout my love from the rooftops, or in this case from the television screen."

Tears swim in her eyes. "Do you really want that, Mick?"

Do I want to put her out there in the public, with the press and social media? Hell no. There isn't any part of me that wants that. But do I want Dee to feel that I cherish her and our marriage, above all else? Then that's an unequivocal yes.

"Let's try this again, beauty." I fix my gaze on her and take that leap. "Deeana Peters, will you grant me the honor of doing the interview and going to the gala with me?"

"Yes!" Her elated smile is like a sunrise. "I want to be by your side for both, Mick. For everything."

I hold her close. My incredible, brave wife who loves me more than I ever knew it was possible to be loved. Who believes with unwavering conviction that our marriage is worth any risk, any battle, any sacrifice.

I kiss her neck, feel the flutter of her pulse. The soft underside of her jaw, the sweet moistness of her lips. I kiss her with tenderness and feel a sense of calm. Like the waters have settled. I cling to that, knowing that nothing in life is ever constant.

There will be rough and choppy waters ahead. Dee and I may face things I can't even imagine now. But somehow, I know we'll face them together, with the strength of love as our anchor.

CHAPTER THIRTY-TWO

Dee

ASHER DUMONT IS ALMOST AS tall as Mick. He's lankier and urban hip with a Vandyke beard and man bun. We'd recently met on a video call and I found him to be outgoing, energetic, and full of humor. I liked him right away.

"It's nice to finally meet you in person," I say upon his arrival.

"You are even prettier than I thought." He gives me a long, effusive hug and kiss on the cheek. "Mick is a lucky man."

"Stop pawing my wife." Mick shoves him away.

"He's jealous because I'm better looking," Asher quips with amusement.

I smile at the banter, feeling some of my anxiety fade. "Come on in." I lead him into the living room where we're going to do the interview in an hour. "This is my friend, Lexie."

She walks forward in ripped jeans that look chic on her and a sleek indigo jacket that matches her eyes.

"Mick mentioned you're in public relations too," he says, shaking her hand.

"Yes. At Chatman's."

"Good firm," he acknowledges, impressed.

"Lexie's been of tremendous help to me."

"Dee didn't need much." She demurs. "I've just been giving her a few tips."

"Right." I bump my friend's shoulder. "I didn't even know the basics of what to do or expect."

"You're going to be great," Asher assures. "Smart, gorgeous, and sophisticated. A child advocate to boot. You're just right for Mick's image of businessman and philanthropist."

"She's not an ornament," Mick snaps.

"See?" Asher shrugs. "That's why I don't usually take on celebrity clientele. Too temperamental. But he begged me."

Mick gives him the finger. It's plain to see they get along well, ribbing each other in the way that men often do. I hadn't seen Mick engage with another male his age, outside of Victor and James. I hadn't shared that part of my husband's life until now.

"Nice place." Asher strokes the length of his beard and surveys the cream-colored living room with splashes of marigold and gray sage echoed in the pillows and area rug. His eyes track to the leafy floor plants, brick fireplace, and up to the family pictures on the mantle and our wedding collage above it. "Bright and homey. It'll show well on camera."

"Thanks. We like it too." Which is why Mick would have preferred to do the interview at his condo. That's where he works during the week when he's in the city. The condo doesn't hold any special meaning to him. Unlike our house. Our sanctuary. But that's the very reason I needed to be here. In the comfort of my happy place.

I loop my arm through Mick's and smile up at him in a show of thanks. He's been so good about easing my nerves when I know he's feeling his own stress about putting me and our relationship out there. Especially when questions about how we met are on the list and will mean exposing our past.

The crew arrives on time; lugging in cameras, tripods, lighting boxes...

I try hard not to freak out. But really, it's Bianca Keller. She sweeps in with a flipped blonde bob, laughing green eyes, and ageless skin. Although her show is filmed locally, it's nationally syndicated and airs opposite *Sixty Minutes*.

"Micah Peters, it is indeed a pleasure to see you again," she gushes and extends her hand.

"Likewise, Bianca."

While my knees are knocking, I watch Mick casually shake her hand as if having a television personality in our house is no big whoop. Though I guess for him, it isn't. Aside from his own celebrity, Mick is a powerful presence. Even his laid-back appearance doesn't diminish it any.

Jeans and a sweater fit his tall, muscular body like a hug. Dark facial hair frames his sensual mouth and dazzling smile. Shifting his gaze to me, he slides an arm around my waist. At a time when I'm feeling a little unsteady, he's there to hold me up.

"I'd like to introduce you to my wife, Deeana Peters."

"It's nice to meet you, Deeana." Her response is friendly and disarming. Trained to be that way, but I recognize I'm being assessed.

"Dee is fine," I say. "And it's nice to meet you too."

"Your first television interview?"

"Does it show?"

"Nerves are normal," she consoles. "Look at me, not the cameras. Make it conversational and you'll do just fine."

"Thank you. I'll try that."

While the crew sets up, Lexie and Asher are kind enough to take on the task of getting them drinks and coffee. I excuse myself and go to the bathroom. Washing my hands, I peer at myself in the mirror above the sink. This all just got very real. I'm going to be on TV. The girl who used to be too self-conscious to even pose for a photo is going to be broadcast across the country with Micah Peters. Crazy! But I asked for this. To leap from my safety net, and acknowledge my husband's accomplishments and our marriage.

Thankfully my hair cooperated today. The new cut has thinned some of the volume and the shorter curls graze the tops of my shoulders in a glossy bounce. I'm wearing medium gold hoops, mascara with a dusting of taupe eyeshadow, and nude matte on my lips to give them a natural hint of color.

Selecting an outfit had been a stressful event. I knew I had to keep it casual for a relaxed-at-home vibe. But I'd agonized over what would be most slimming on camera. In the end, I'd stopped obsessing over how to minimize the pounds and picked a cinnamon, off-the-shoulder sweater with ankle-length jeans.

Once upon a time, I would have covered up in the armor of dark, baggy clothing. I would not have even considered going on camera or sharing any part of myself. I've since stripped away those layers. Bit by bit. I won't profess to have all my insecurities under control. I don't. But I'm starting to focus less on my flaws to see more of what's pretty good.

When Lexie knocks on the door to tell me they're ready, I take a slow, deep breath and exit the bathroom. Mick's gaze flies away from Asher as I re-enter the living room. Whatever he'd been saying dies on his lips. He approaches and takes my hand. "You okay?"

"Yes, actually. You?"

"If you're good, I'm good. Ready to do this?"

I nod, feeling my pulse skip.

Mick gives my hand an encouraging squeeze and leads us over to the sofa to sit in our designated spots. His arm goes around my shoulders and I lean into him. He smells divine—clean skin with whispers of sandalwood from his body wash and cologne.

Our faces are dabbed with powder and we're run through a sound check. One of the crew adjusts the throw pillow beside me and another smooths down a piece of my hair. When satisfied that we're good to go, Bianca takes the chair opposite us and crosses her legs. The room goes quiet. The camera lights shine in my eyes. I remember not to stare at them.

On cue, Bianca flashes an engaging smile, introduces her show, then segues to the interview. "Today, I have the privilege of being in the home of one of Chicago's own— former Bulls guard, Micah Peters and his lovely wife, Dee. Yes, folks, you heard it first on *Sunday Nights with Bianca Keller*." She beams then directs her attention to us. "Congratulations to you both on your recent marriage. And, of course, Micah, on your Generosity of Spirit award. I want to hear more about that and Papa's Kids in a moment. But I'd be remiss if I didn't ask how you two met. It all seems to have happened very quickly."

Mick is such a private man when it comes to his personal life. He's done a few interviews since his retirement, all of which have been focused exclusively on Papa's Kids. But he's made this exception for me. A declaration of his commitment as solid as the wedding rings on my finger.

"There was nothing quick about it," Mick answers in a voice that could melt butter. "Dee and I first met as teenagers. I fell hard for her heart, her intelligence, her beauty. We were young and it wasn't meant to be then. But our story wasn't over. When I saw Dee again several months ago, I knew she was still the one. The only woman I've ever loved." He lifts my left hand off his thigh and brings it to his mouth for a kiss.

Under Bianca's professional demeanor, I notice her swoon. I mean, really, what red-blooded woman wouldn't?

"The public hasn't seen this side of you," she enthuses. "Dee, give us the inside scoop on what Micah Peters is like as a husband."

"Well, for starters, he's Mick at home." I smile up at him and back at Bianca, managing to stay my nerves, speaking about my husband with ease. "He's considerate and loving. He respects my independence and gives me room and support to grow. Life with him is amazing." I smile again. "Mick has a romantic streak—surprise dinners, thoughtful gestures. He's fun and spontaneous, which keeps things interesting. I'm proud of all he's accomplished with Papa's Kids and the good man that he is. I'm proud to be his wife."

Mick's eyes wash over me with heated intensity. "I'm just as proud to be your husband."

"Oh my." Bianca touches a hand to her chest. "You both light up when you look at each other. It's very refreshing. I wish you all the best."

"Thank you." I exchange another grin with Mick.

"Let's talk about something you two have in common. Your affinity for kids in need," she says. "Dee, I understand you're a lawyer for foster children."

"That's right."

"It's a unique focus. Where does that come from?"

"I was a foster child."

"That must have been difficult." Her head tilts with compassion and she leans forward.

"It was," I admit. "But don't get me wrong, foster care is a wonderful thing. It can provide a necessary home until a child can be safely reunited with his or her family. It can also provide a longer-term solution that even leads to adoption. However, it doesn't always work out that way. I know what it's like to be bounced around and not have any sense of stability and permanence. Those are the kind of cases I tend to take."

"Sounds like you channeled your experiences into helping others."

"It has been a catharsis of sorts."

"In what ways would you say your life as a foster child has shaped you?"

I pause. We'd expected questions of this nature and gone over surface responses. But that suddenly doesn't feel right. Malcolm had wanted to use my past against me. Some reporters would too. I don't want rumors out there. If anyone's going to tell my story, it's going to be me. And I'm going to do it with honesty and without shame.

"I struggled with insecurities and a lack of self-worth."

"Tell me about that."

I hear the subtle intake of Mick's breath. The sound of his protective instincts kicking in. But I also sense his restraint as if he's holding himself back to let me handle it.

"My father left when I was four. My mother suffered from severe depression and couldn't care for me when she was off her medication. I didn't understand the challenges of mental illness back then, I only knew that she sent me away when she couldn't cope. I was in and out of foster homes for ten years until my mother died of an overdose."

"I'm so sorry. How did you deal with all that?"

"Not well for a long while. Because life felt so unpredictable, I sought control in emotionally destructive ways. I closed myself off to others and used food as both comfort and punishment. At an early age, I fell into an unhealthy pattern of overeating then starving myself. I dieted obsessively and battled a negative body image. I thought if I were thinner, prettier...I'd be more lovable. I thought that's why my parents hadn't wanted me. Because I wasn't good enough."

Mick's hand stays on mine and his eyes never leave me. I imagine it's hard for him to hear me revealing so much about myself in such a public way, but I'm compelled to see it through.

"I blamed every rejection or upset in my life on my perceived flaws and inadequacies. Feeling like I wasn't enough made me miserable. I hit rock bottom a couple of years ago. My system rebelled against the way I was abusing it and I ended up in the hospital. I realized then that I needed help. The problem wasn't so much what I saw in the mirror, the problem was on the inside. The way I felt about myself.

"I started seeing a therapist and soon after, I started up my child advocacy practice for foster children. That's how I channeled my issues into something more constructive. It's taken me a long time to flip the negative script and realize that I'm not lesser-than or unlovable. That neither my childhood or the size of my body define me.

"Unfortunately, I wasn't in a good place when I first met Mick, to let him or the amazing foster family I had love me then. But I'm in a good place now. I've come to like myself. The woman I am and still becoming."

Lexie and Asher, standing with the camera crew, raise two enthusiastic thumbs-up.

"Thank you," Bianca says, giving me a kind smile. "Sharing that could not have been easy."

"It wasn't. But I've found through having Mick back in my life, that talking has helped me heal. Anyway," I smile and redirect the conversation, "that's enough about me. We're here to discuss my husband's award and Papa's Kids."

"We certainly are." Bianca shifts her attention to Mick.

It takes him a moment to unlock his gaze from me and respond. The interview had gotten more personal than either of us expected. He'd obviously been thrown but he gets back on his footing.

"Across the US, over 700,000 youth between the ages of thirteen and eighteen are homeless, and unaccompanied by a parent. Most are living alone on the streets because of addiction, mental illness, or abuse. That's the unacceptable reality."

I can feel everyone in the room riveted now to Mick. To the deep baritone of his voice and his passion for the topic. He speaks at length about Cayo, the man he reveres; about the positive influence he had in his life. About being taught the importance of gratitude and paying it forward. Although Mick doesn't share the more intimate reasons for why he picked a cause that supports many abused children, it's because he believes that but for the grace of Mama and Papa T, he might have been a statistic.

I couldn't be prouder of the way he carries himself and honors the man that was a father to us both.

"Do you see yourself returning to the public eye?" Bianca asks in closing. "I know there's plenty of interest."

"That's all behind me." Mick's hand flexes in mine. "I'm happy with where I'm at. Expanding Papa's Kids and focusing on my future with Dee."

After Bianca winds down the interview, we're met with a round of applause and praise. Bianca thanks us for letting her have the exclusive on our marriage. We pose for a few photos. Lexie tells me I was stellar and Asher is ecstatic.

"You both killed it!"

"Don't get any ideas about making this a regular thing," Mick comments wryly.

"Am I that transparent?" Asher laughs.

"Like tracing paper."

Although said with a tinge of good humor, I wonder how Mick is feeling. I'm all too aware that I've pushed him beyond his comfort zone. I'd been the one to urge him to confess his painful story of abuse and blackmail to his family, to confront Malcolm, to go public. I'd done it all out of love but had I pushed him too far, too fast?

That's still weighing on my mind when the crew has packed up and everyone is gone, except Asher. I say good-bye to him, and leave Mick and his PR manager to talk press and social media strategy.

I change into one of Mick's T-shirts. It's barely noon. But getting up at the crack of dawn to prepare for filming, had made for a long, exhausting morning. I pull my hair up into a top knot to wash the makeup off my face.

I'm in the bathroom when Mick joins me. He pauses on the doorjamb. His eyes study my sudsy reflection but his gaze gives little clue as to his thoughts.

"Everything good with Asher?" I ask.

"He couldn't be happier that our marriage will soon go viral."

"I'm sorry."

"For what?" Mick frowns.

"The purpose of the interview was your award and Papa's Kids. I didn't want that to be overshadowed."

"I don't see it that way." His gaze sharpens, narrowing to laser focus. "Are you having second thoughts?"

"No." I look over to him. "Some nerves, yes. But no doubts. It's odd for me to feel this okay when I have no idea what the reaction will be."

"Fuck what anyone else thinks. I'm really proud of you. That took guts."

I shoot him a look of surprise. "I wasn't sure how you felt about it."

"What you feel is more important."

"It felt right for me," I say, returning to the mirror to rinse my face with a soft, damp cloth. "But I realize we didn't discuss me sharing all that."

He leans against the door. "I admit that I initially wanted to jump in and save you from answering."

"You didn't."

"No. But it took me a minute to realize this wasn't Malcolm, O'Malley, or anyone else trying to exploit you for their gain or as some vendetta against me. In this context, I recognized you were in charge. It was your story to tell and I needed to let you tell it."

My lips curve in appreciation. "That's a big step."

"I've been slow on the uptake."

"Have I pushed you too fast?"

"I don't think so. I pushed you hard in the beginning to open up but I didn't challenge myself to keep pace. You gained your grounding before I did and pulled me along. I needed that."

"So, no regrets about outing our marriage?"

"None." His gaze turns all primal and possessive. "You're mine, and tonight after the show airs everyone will know it."

I wrinkle my nose at him. "Remember this when the press is outside our door come morning."

That earns me a rueful grimace. "I'm not looking forward to that. I've increased security but I still don't like the idea of you going off to work and carrying on as usual."

"We've gone over it, Mick. I'm done with hiding." I rub moisturizer on my face. "Even Asher and Lex said if I avoid the press after the interview airs it will only prolong the curiosity. I want to get that part over with and live our lives."

"I won't argue with that."

I know Mick's acceptance is more indulgence than surrender. But I use the opportunity to tease when I brush past him. "I like this agreeable side of you."

"Oh yeah?" He gives my ass a playful swat that stings my flesh. But it's the sudden desire burning in his eyes that sends goosebumps racing across my skin.

Following me into the bedroom, Mick strips out of his clothes and I eagerly climb onto the bed. With the daylight surrounding us, I pull the scrunchie from my hair, toss out my curls, and beckon him with the crook of my finger.

Mick approaches, all deliciously hard. He crawls over me, braced on his arms. We're barely touching and yet I can feel that electric heat pumping off his body. He's so powerfully male, I only have to think of him to want him.

I push Mick onto his back and straddle his thighs, feeling him thick and pulsing against the silk of my panties.

"Taking advantage of my agreeability?" he asks, placing his big hands on my hips and directing me over his cock.

"Ha." I look down at him. "As if I don't know you're still controlling things. Topping from the bottom."

He removes his hands and clasps them beneath his head in a gesture of submission, but the smile on his face is pure unapologetic dominance. "I'm all yours, Mrs. Peters. Feel free to have your way with me."

"Oh, I will." I rotate my hips and comb my fingers down his chest. "I'm about to rock your world."

"Beauty..." His eyes glimmer with a depth of emotion. "You did that from the moment I met you."

CHAPTER THIRTY-THREE

Dee

MONDAY MORNING BRINGS APRIL SHOWERS and the press. Several news vans are parked at the curb and more than a dozen reporters are huddled on the sidewalk under umbrellas. Mick's tension manifests itself in the form of a drill sergeant.

"Stiles will drive you today," he says, standing at the dresser, barking out orders. "Keep your head down. Don't react, don't answer."

"Yes, sir." I salute.

"This isn't a joke, Dee. I should go with you."

I finish tucking my blouse into my skirt, and send him an adamant glance. "You are not going to take me to work. I can do this."

"I know you can. But you haven't faced this before. So, humor me."

"Why do you think I married you?"

He huffs out a laugh. "You're a riot."

I smile and give him a hug. "I promise I'm not taking any of this lightly. I just need to do it without getting all freaked out in my head."

He inches back. The stubborn lines of his jaw yield as he regroups. "I don't want you freaking out. Just aware."

"I will be. So just shut up and kiss me."

"I think I can handle that."

One hand goes to my ass urging me against him, the other to the nape of my neck, holding me still as he lowers his head. No one kisses like Mick. His lips are soft and yet they exert a perfect, firm pressure; his tongue dips inside my mouth in gentle, demanding thrusts that are on the right side of aggression. If his goal was to distract me, then mission accomplished. By the time he lets me up for air, my skin is flushed and my chest is rippling on unsteady breaths.

"I like this," he murmurs, his hand tracing the curve of my behind.

"My butt?"

"That goes without saying. I meant I like the skirt on you."

"Thanks. It's new." The pencil design, I used to envy on Lexie, skims my lower body from waist to calf. It's black and paired with a tapered pinstripe blouse. My hair is pulled back into a low ponytail and the diamond drops Mick bought me for Christmas dangle from my ears. "If you keep touching me like that I'm never going to leave."

"That's the idea."

I smile against his lips. "I have to go."

He holds me a moment longer before he reluctantly releases me.

In the foyer, I slip my stocking feet into a pair of high heels while Mick gets my coffee ready. Joining me again, he sets the travel cup down and helps me into my trench coat.

"I'll see you later." I rub my thumb over his lips, rubbing off the shiny residue of my gloss. "Go write. Finish your book and add author to your list of accomplishments."

"I'll be thinking about you the entire time. I love you, beauty."

"Love you, too." I reach down for my gym bag.

"I thought you might reconsider going to the gym this evening."

"I made plans with Lex and Jord. If the press show, they show. I'm not going to let them dictate my activities." But aware of his disapproval, I touch his arm, not wanting to leave on a sour note. "Think of the benefits." I make my voice low and sultry. "After an hour of cardio and Pilates, I'll be coming home to you all sweaty and limber."

That coaxes a gleam in his eyes. "You play dirty but drive a hard bargain."

"Hard being the operative word."

"Keep that up and you won't be going anywhere."

I pucker my lips in an air-kiss and take the travel cup of coffee from him. "I'm going to be fine, Mick."

He answers with a brusque nod and opens the front door. Stiles is waiting on the porch, under the awning. His posture is rigid and at attention. I look out at the flock of reporters and paparazzi.

Holy crap. Camera flashes light up the dreary morning; shooting off in rapid speed like a firing squad. Maybe I'm not as ready for this as I thought.

"Ignore them," Mick says gruffly, then to Stiles: "Take care of her."

Stiles flips open an umbrella and holds it over my head with one hand, his other takes my gym bag. Sheltering me with his large frame, we walk briskly through the buzz of questions and prods of microphones. I keep my head lowered and slide into the back of the SUV. Only when the door closes behind me do I breathe normally again.

"Whew." I slack against the leather, glad to be insulated for a while and just blend in with the morning commuters. "Thanks for getting me through that, Stiles."

His eyes, black as night, glance at mine in the rearview mirror. He's not one for conversation. His demeanor is reserved and emotionless, perhaps by nature or by military training, I can't say for sure. But in this moment, his hard, rugged features smooth out, briefly.

"You're welcome, Ms. Peters."

Jordyn's assumption that Stiles runs deep might be so. He's a complete mystery. I still don't even know his first name. But there's something about him, beyond his physical size, that's solid and dependable.

During the quiet forty-minute drive, I sip sweet coffee and turn on my phone. There are several texts from previous colleagues who had either watched the interview or clips on the news. People I haven't seen or spoken to in years, coming out of the woodwork. The only work acquaintance I had given a heads-up to before the show aired was Calista. I owed her that after keeping my relationship with Mick a secret during Dwayde's case. To say she was shocked would be putting it mildly. I didn't take offense. I would have been too, had the roles been reversed. If you don't know Mick, just his celebrity image, you couldn't imagine that he would be content living in a modest home in the suburbs with a woman who isn't a supermodel.

There's a message from Dr. Roland. I hadn't expected to hear from her prior to our next appointment. *I watched your interview. I thoroughly enjoyed seeing you in your element; owning your story with honesty and strength. I look forward to discussing how that was for you when we meet in a couple of weeks. Be well.*

I email back my thanks for all her support. Once I opened up and truly embraced therapy, that, along with my will to progress and Mick's love, saw me over the hurdles. I feel as if I can face anything.

Maybe that's what has me setting aside caution and pulling up Google. I enter *Micah Peters, marriage*. In an instant, numerous Top Stories pop up and it hasn't even been twenty-four hours. I scroll through the headlines from various sources including *People, USA Today, Enter-*

tainment Tonight, and *CNN*. My breaths quicken. Mick and I had deliberately not watched the news or checked social media. Now, I'm wishing I had stuck to that plan. It was one thing to be featured in a contained interview shot in our house. Quite another to see Mick and me splashed everywhere for the world to see.

Micah Peters ties the knot with children's attorney Deeana Chase on a private island

Sunday Nights with Bianca Keller breaks the news that Micah Peters married his high school crush

Wife of Micah Peters bears it all on her weight struggles and being married to the former NBA star

One Twitter post called us the new *It couple* with a hashtag, #McDee. There's scant mention of Mick's award and Papa's Kids, the purpose eclipsed by the hype of our marriage and my tell-all. Overwhelmed, I close Google and lean back, shutting my eyes for the balance of the trip.

ALL TOO SOON THE CAR reprieve is over. Stiles escorts me through another crowd of reporters. It's for this reason that I hadn't scheduled any in-person meetings for the next week. I'd told Lena she could work from home. But I arrive to find her at her desk and no worse for wear. In fact, her heavily lined eyes greet me with excitement.

"I felt like a rock star."

I suppose at twenty-four and fame-hopeful, Lena would have that perspective.

"How are you dealing with it?" she asks.

"Not with the same enthusiasm." I remove my coat. "I assume they'll tire of this soon enough and move on after the gala next Saturday."

"I don't know." Her tone sounds dubious. "That interview was fire, Dee. You put it all out there. I didn't even know some of those things about you. Now I understand the changes I've seen in you over the last few months."

"I didn't intentionally keep any of it from you. They just weren't issues I talked about. I wasn't expecting to reveal that much on TV."

"Well, I think it's dope that you did. You and Mick are trending on Twitter."

"I saw the #McDee." I make a face.

She laughs. "It's cute."

Even so, I'm not going to let that matter. Because if I soak up the flattery, I can just as easily drown in the insults. "Any calls?" I ask, switching gears.

"Mostly from reporters. I said *no comment* like you told me to."

"Thanks. Mick's publicity manager will handle those."

"There are a couple of new cases that just came in. I made up files and put them on your desk. Oh, and this person called." She hands me a pink message slip. "She said she knew you from Springvale."

Curious, I look down at the note. Molly Whitaker. She was my back-stairwell lunch partner in high school and we worked together at the library. We weren't what you'd call friends. I didn't have friends back then. I put her number aside for later and remove the framed wedding picture from my tote bag. We're barefoot in the sand and smiling under the sun. The resort's photographer had caught some fabulous candid shots. In this one, there's a playful familiarity between us that captures the way we are together.

I place the picture on my desk. That I can now do that, is a welcome touch of normalcy. I angle it for my line of sight and get to work.

The morning flies by in a blink. My caseload stretching capacity. Lena, bless her, has taken on as much as she can. It's inevitable that I will need to add another lawyer or find a partner. I've resisted that, reluctant to give up control. But I recognize that another attorney would enable me to serve more clients and would offer a myriad of personal perks, not the least of which is more time with Mick.

Mama T checks in on me while I'm eating lunch at my desk and Mick calls for a second time.

"Stop fussing."

"Grandmas fuss, I'm an adoring husband concerned about his wife."

"Your wife is doing fine," I assure him with a smile in my voice. "Are you writing?"

"Yep."

"I can't wait to read it."

"You'll be the first."

"It's going to be a bestseller, I know it."

"Love your faith in me, beauty."

"Always." My eyes catch the edge of the pink message slip under the files. I pull it out. "Hey, guess who called me?"

"Who?"

"Molly Whitaker."

"The girl we went to school with?"

"You remember her?"

"Sure. She made it possible for us to sneak away to the lake. I owe her big time."

"You do, at that." I laugh. "I'm going to call her back. It'll be nice to reconnect. See you tonight around 8:00."

"Want something cooked or ordered?"

"Surprise me."

TOWARD THE END OF THE day, I get around to calling Molly. She answers on the second ring. "Molly Whitaker."

"Hi. It's Deeana Ch—Peters," I amend. "Dee."

"Dee! It's great to hear from you. Congratulations!"

"Thank you. I'm sure the news came as a surprise."

"Not so much."

"Oh?"

"I suspected you had a secret boyfriend back in senior year. All those evening shifts you asked me to cover. You were too excited for me to believe you were babysitting. And the way Mick took down JT...I had an inkling."

"It was complicated."

"Most relationships are."

True enough. "So, how are you?"

"No current complicated relationships to speak of. We should meet and catch up. I always wondered what happened to you."

"Sorry that I took off without ever saying good-bye."

"No apology needed. I wish I had been a better friend."

"It wasn't you. I wish I could have been a friend to you, too."

"We both could have used it. But from what I saw last night, you have come into your own. A children's lawyer just like you planned. You looked so confident and together."

"Still a work in progress. What about you?" I picture the tiny awkward girl with a mouth full of braces. Head bowed and shoulders scrunched like a turtle trying to hide in her shell. I recognized that posture. I had it too. "You don't sound like the timid girl I remember."

"Not as much, but I still prefer to stay behind the scenes."

"Mama T mentioned that you work for the Women's Network in Chicago."

"I produce *Women Like Us*. Do you know it?"

"Yes. I've seen a few shows. Very well done. You touch on important issues."

"Thank you. We try to make it relevant and meaningful. Which brings me to one of the reasons for my call."

"What's that?" I ask.

"I'd like to invite you to speak at our Women's Symposium in June. We usually have a couple hundred attendees and broadcast it live."

I'm rendered speechless, which is pretty ironic. "You want me to give a speech?"

"Yes. You present well...you're relatable. Your message about body positivity and self-love really struck a chord. You're trending online. Women are responding."

"I'm flattered. Thank you. Really. I'm glad the things I said resonated, but I'm not looking for a platform or to do anything so public again."

"I hear that. But the platform may have found you. Just think about it. No pressure. Let's meet for lunch. We can either explore it further or just catch up."

"Catching up sounds good."

We set a date for a few weeks out.

"WHAT'S THE J STAND FOR?" Jordyn sits between Lexie and me in the back of the SUV, leaning forward through the space separating the front seats. Stiles had picked my friends up on the way to the Brockville Women's Fitness Center. Jordyn's been poking at him since.

"John? No, it's a solid name but not unique enough."

Lexie and I exchange eye rolls.

When Stiles doesn't respond, she continues. "Joshua? Definitely not. I once dated a Josh and he was a complete dweeb. Jerimiah?" She puts her hand beside his head rest, pulling herself even closer. "Nah, too biblical for a man that looks like he's made for sin."

"Ms. Sinclair." His voice is level, unaffected. "For your safety, you are required to sit back and put on your seat belt."

"So, no hints, huh?"

"*Jordyn*," Lexie hisses under her breath and pulls our outrageous friend back by the shoulder. "Have you no shame whatsoever?"

"Nope." She laughs and settles between us. "He likes me," she says loud enough for Stiles to hear. "You're just playing hard to get, aren't you, J.D.? That's okay. I like a challenge."

Poor Stiles, though he seems more than capable of handling himself.

When we arrive at the gym a short time later, it's paparazzi-free. Thank God. I just want to have a good workout with my friends. Only once inside the fitness center, I'm reminded of what Mick had warned about my anonymity being gone and my life not being the same.

Women gawk and whisper. Heads turn in my direction. Some of the regulars come up to me with congratulations and ask to take selfies. It's awkward and weird. But I politely pose and try to make it seem natural. My friends are no help. They think the positive attention is great, which is why I should not have told them about the Women's Symposium.

"You should absolutely do it," Jordyn says, setting down her water bottle at the back of the studio next to mine.

"I agree," Lexie puts in. "Body positivity is such a hot topic and affects so many women."

"I know that but I don't have the time or experience."

"Bull," Jordyn scoffs. She's wearing black bootie shorts with a neon lime sports bra, the color as bold as her personality. "You can find the time and your life is your experience."

"Let's be real, Jord." I shrug out of my yoga jacket. "Molly only asked me in the hope that I'll draw a large audience as the wife of Micah Peters." When they both frown at my assumption, I add: "That's not a put-down of my worth. It's true."

Lexie shakes her head. "I think Molly recognizes, like we do, that women will be drawn to *you*. You're engaging and so is your journey. You're right that being Mick's wife gives you a bigger spotlight, but what's wrong with that?"

"Nothing, except Mick and I don't want the spotlight. We just want to get past all this post interview hoopla and lead a normal life."

THE EIGHTY-MINUTE CLASS LEAVES me jonesing for a hot soak. I take a long swig from my water bottle and dab a towel over my face as we exit the room into the common area. I can only hope no one wants to take a selfie with me looking a sweaty mess.

I sense it immediately. The atmosphere is different. The way the women are looking at me isn't the same as when I arrived. Their expressions are of pity...embarrassment. My friends notice it too.

Jordyn puts a hand on my elbow and steers me into the change room. There, Lexie enters the combination on her locker and retrieves her phone, which isn't permitted in the studios. Moments later her face pales.

Oh God... "What is it?"

"Let's talk over here."

Suddenly cold, I pull my yoga jacket over my tank top as Lexie leads us away from the lockers. She glances around to ensure we're alone in the nook where the week's class schedule and notices are posted.

"A video has gone viral."

"What kind of video?"

"It insinuates that Mick is having an...an affair."

My stomach roils. I think I'm going to be sick. But I need to face whatever scandal is brewing. "Show me."

She hesitates out of sympathy, then hands me her phone.

Feeling shaky, I take it and lower onto the bench. Jordyn sits beside me, silently offering her support.

Staring at the screen, my chest tightens like a vise, pushing my breaths out in short, quick bursts. *Newlywed, Micah Peters proves old habits die hard.* Below the taunting caption plays a clip that is a lash to the heart. It's date stamped, four days ago. I want to take the image away, escape it, if only I could. But my stare latches on to Mick. He's in the hallway outside his penthouse. Leaning against the door. His eyes are closed. His neck arched. His mouth partially opened. A woman with slender curves is pictured from behind. She's pressed against him, wearing a short robe that shows off toned legs that stretch for miles. Her arms are lowered and in motion. Her hands aren't visible, but the look on my husband's face offers more than a hint as to where they are.

"Is that woman who I think it is?" Jordyn seethes. "The condo neighbor?"

I nod, swallowing the sob that claws up my throat. Witnessing Mick with Lisa is like a sharp, jagged twist of déjà vu.

The old tapes that I've worked hard to silence, start up on replay. It's as if someone had tapped into my psyche and used just the right image to set off all my triggers. In that inescapable moment, I'm the fat girl that catches her boyfriend on the deck with his hands on the slim hips of Tamara Scott. I'm the fat girl that gets discarded. The fat girl that nobody wants.

Hot tears spring to my eyes. They blur the video on the screen. Yet I still feel its searing effects. Burning in my chest, my stomach, everywhere.

Jordyn wraps me in a tight embrace. Lexie takes the phone and stands guard, stroking her hand over my hair.

Commotion from outside the locker room jolts me. I straighten away from Jordyn hearing two loud voices: one shrill, the other deep and unrelenting.

Mick.

My friends exchange startled glances. Already on my feet, I swat at my wet cheeks and rush forward past several wide-eyed women in various stages of undress, getting to the change room door.

"You can't go in there!" a woman yells.

"Try to stop me."

I yank the door open and run smack into Mick. He grabs my shoulders, instinctively to steady me. But he doesn't let go. Instead his grip intensifies.

Just seeing him splinters a sob free. Guilt and fury slice across his face. He knows I know.

"Dee—"

"Don't..." I say, my heart hurting for us. This isn't the time or place. But pushed past reason, my caution is no barrier.

"I realize how it looks..." his words race, heedless of our audience. "But I swear to you that video wasn't from days ago or how it seems. I haven't been with any other woman or wanted to be, since you. I would never—"

"Ssh..." I try to calm him. "I trust you, Mick."

"—do that to us—what?"

"I said, I trust you. Of course, I do."

He exhales a hard, audible breath. To Mick, my faith in him is as precious as my love. He doesn't have to explain the video to me. Trusting him, the way I do, there is no doubt in my mind about my husband's fidelity. "I know you, Mick. That's all I need to know."

Making a savage sound, he cups my face and seals his mouth over mine. I'm dimly aware of the gasps and whispers as he kisses me with soul-wrenching passion. My hands spear into his hair and his body presses against me, straining to be as close as one. I couldn't care less about the spectacle we're making or what anyone else thinks. Mick is conveying in more than words that he belongs to me, only.

Jordyn's boisterous hoot from behind has us slowly coming back to our surroundings. Mick eases his mouth away. His lips are damp and reddened from the fervor of our kiss. His gaze on me is tender, his anger and panic tempered by my reassurance. "I love you," he says.

"I love you too."

Mick smiles and puts on his game face. With his hand at the small of my back, he turns to address the manager, who'd tried to stop him, and the handful of women that have gathered. "Ladies, I apologize for barging into your gym like this. It wasn't my finest hour. But the claim of an affair is an outright lie and making sure my wife heard that from me was my priority."

They could think whatever they wanted about my husband's faithfulness but judging by the number of fan-girl grins, they are not immune to his charms.

"Ready to go home, beauty?" Mick asks.

"I just need to get my bag."

"Holy shit! That was hot." Jordyn fans her face when we're back in the change room. "Anyone can see the man is totally into you. Mick wouldn't screw around. But making it look like he did right after he announces his marriage is taking the Internet by storm."

"Exactly," Lexie says, tapping on her smartphone. "So, let this go viral."

"What did you just post?" I gape at her.

"Nothing yet. I sent a pic to Asher. He'll make sure it's strategically released to the press and on social media. Don't worry, it's good." She turns her phone to me, smiling wide.

Oh wow. That is good. I won't lie. I'm relieved it's not a full-body shot of me in leggings. Rather, it's zoomed on our faces. Lexie had captured us in a steamy, all-consuming kiss. It says, let the world talk, we don't give a damn. We know what we have.

I return to the common area to find Mick being chatted up by several of the women. He seems cool and collected. But my man is far from. His brain must be going a million miles an hour. His character had been slandered, his fidelity publicly challenged. His wife, humiliated. Mick will never stand for that.

He excuses himself and takes my bag in one hand, my palm in the other. He tells Jordyn and Lexie that Stiles is waiting to drive them when they're ready. My friends give him hugs as a show of their support. I love them for that.

The short trip from the gym to our house is usually less than ten minutes. This evening, with reporters shoving microphones at us and shouting out salacious questions that insinuate Mick's guilt, doubles the time. The idol-worship and popularity of Micah Peters in Chicago rivals that of Michael Jordan. Yet it had all been cast aside because the rumors make for better news. I can see that it takes Herculean effort for my husband to keep forging ahead without stopping to defend himself and our marriage. Mick knows the damage an impulsive response can cause.

His phone rings after we enter the house. From his end of the conversation I gather it's not Asher this time. During the drive home, they'd spoken for most of it about a press release while I assured Mama T and Victor that we're managing...all things considered. Like me, they had dismissed the rumors out of hand. Still, it hurts to have them out there.

Inside the kitchen, I find uncooked food and pots left on the counter. Mick must have been preparing dinner when he'd gotten the news from Asher and rushed out. His reaction would have been—murderous. The same way he sounds in the foyer.

"Goddammit, don't give me the worst-case scenario. A subpoena will take too long. Do your fucking job and get me a copy of the security surveillance ASAP or I'll find another lawyer who can."

Mick disconnects with a curse and slaps his phone down on the hall table. He comes to me, standing close in the narrow space. I can see the burn of anger rimming around the edges of his coffee-brown irises. He wants so badly to prove the video isn't recent or as it appears. I want that too. Not because I need proof of his innocence but because he does.

"I'm going to fix this, Dee."

"Do what you need to do to clear your name, but not because you think I have doubts. I don't. There's nothing to fix with us."

"When I got to the gym, you'd been crying," he says, his voice worn.

"I hated seeing you in a suggestive position with another woman." And not just any woman. But Lisa. Toned and lean without dimples on her butt or lines on her stomach. "It took me back to a bad place. To feeling rejected and unwanted. To seeing you with Tamara on your deck."

"Christ." He makes a pained sound of remorse. "I'm so sorry for what you saw and for what it did to you."

"You have nothing to apologize for." I touch his forearm where the muscles are corded and stretched tight. "I don't blame you for something that happened before us."

His head drops. His breaths roughen. Then he looks back up. His features are overcome by a volatile emotion that scares me.

"What is it, Mick?"

"I said that what you saw in the video was before you."

I still, my heart thudding like a fist against my ribs. "When...when was it?"

"The same day that I came to your office." He swallows. "Later that night."

I process the timing. Our first encounter after fifteen years. We had lashed out at each other. Emotionally, physically.

"I was fucked up over seeing you...touching you." He scrubs a hand through his hair. "I went for a jog to try to burn it off, and when I got back Lisa was there. Instead of brushing off her advances like I usually did, I let her put her hands on me. It was fucking careless. I didn't consider the security cameras or the consequences. I just wanted to block out everything."

It's an explanation I understand, knowing what it's like to just want to escape the pain.

"It was a difficult time for both of us." My arms go around him. "You don't have to explain."

"I need to." His hands gently push me back. "It didn't go any further with Lisa. I never slept with her. I didn't lie to you about that. But I was wrong to let her touch me that way after seeing you. I was wrong to use her as some poor substitute when I only wanted you. When I was only picturing you. Imagining you. I know it sounds like the same bullshit again with Tamara. I'm not proud of it, Dee. I have no excuse. But I don't want you to think that I would go to—"

"*Mick.*" I bracket his face, forcing him to stop. "That's all in the past. We've both changed. For ourselves and for each other. I'm not worried about you going to another woman in a fit of anger or for any reason. Seeing the video shook me at first. It brought up old memories and insecurities. But it didn't break me. It didn't break us. Nothing can."

CHAPTER THIRTY-FOUR

Micah

WHOEVER COINED *PATIENCE IS A virtue* should have their ass kicked. Twenty-four hours in and I'm no closer to clearing my name.

"I appreciate this isn't what you wanted to hear," Nolan continues apologetically, "but our only course of action is a subpoena. I will file the documents first thing in the morning and have it expedited. Barring no unforeseen issues—which I don't expect—the video should be in our hands, end of week."

Not long by normal standards. But the longer the rumor circulates, the less the truth will matter. My marriage—sacred to me—is being tainted by the hour because of a malignant lie. I'd vowed to protect Dee from my fame. I failed.

I want to put my fist through the office wall, rip something apart. Fire Nolan. But what good would that do? He's a trusted legal advisor that's been working around the clock for me. Everyone on my team has. Asher putting out media fires, Stiles tracking down information.

None of this resembles the normal life I wanted to give Dee. I scrape my fingers through my hair, hating that horrible feeling of helplessness and lack of control.

"I'm sorry, Mick. It's the best I can offer." Nolan pauses and clears his throat as if waiting for the ax to drop.

"Do what you need to do." I disconnect and wait several beats before facing Dee.

A single lamp glows in the bedroom. She's changed into pajama bottoms and a peach camisole with spaghetti straps; the outline of her plump breasts is visible beneath the soft stretch of cotton. She's sitting up in bed against the headboard; her legs bent at the knees, her feet nestled in socks, writing in her notebook. The light shines on her sable curls and freshly scrubbed face. She looks up. Her wary eyes watch me in a way that makes my heart pound.

I take a breath. "Management won't release the video without a subpoena."

"I'm so sorry, Mick."

"I'm the one that's sorry." I lower to her side of the bed and brush my fingertips down her cheek. "I wanted this to be over and done with. Quickly. For you. For us."

"I know." She sets the book aside and catches my hand to hold in her lap. "What reason did they give?"

"Lisa got to them with threats of suing over privacy issues."

"That's crap!" she snaps. "The video is already out there, what claim of privacy could she possibly have?"

"None. But it spooked them just the same. Their lawyers responded that they wouldn't get in the middle of a personal dispute between two condo owners."

"Lisa knows the video will clear you and is obviously trying to stall the truth from coming out for as long as possible."

"I'm going to talk to her."

"*No, Mick.* You can't reason with her."

"I'm not planning to reason with her. Right now, Lisa thinks you and my marriage are my weak spots. She's exploiting that. She needs to know having a weak spot doesn't make me weak. It makes me fucking ruthless."

"You go to her all guns-a-blazing will play right into her hands. She wants you riled up and angry. But more than that, she's craving your attention. Trust me, if you give it to her, there will be no end to her vindictive ploys and tactics. You don't want that."

"No," I concede, my blood boiling. "But I can't just wait it out while Nolan works on getting a subpoena."

"You have to." She puts her arms around me, and strokes my back to soothe. "It's not weak or passive to wait. It's smart and strategic."

"The shit that's out there—"

"Can't touch us." She pulls back to look at me. "I know what people are saying, Mick. I know the comparisons they're making. You going after a woman like Lisa is expected. Me, not so much."

"Dee..."

"It's okay. I've stopped going on social media. But I know what's out there. It's hard not to let it matter, to just let it roll off. That's what I was writing in my journal."

"What?" I ask, my throat tight.

"To hang tough in the face of all this. To not give up my personal power or sense of worth. To believe in who I am and what we have. Those people don't know me. They don't know us. But I do. We're a team and we're going to get through this."

I stare at her for a moment. "You're a wonder, you know that?"

"Thanks to counseling and your love."

"It's all you, beauty."

"I'm pretty sure you have something to do with it." She smiles and pulls me down for a kiss.

Anyone who thinks Dee is less-than and can't see the beauty that's so obvious, is a fucking fool. I love that she's round and soft. That arouses me immensely. But she's also solid and strong. That arouses me too.

I settle in the space she makes for me between her luscious legs and hear her moan into our kiss. To hell with everything else tonight. Being with my wife is as close to heaven as I can get.

THE NEXT MORNING, WHILE NOLAN is at the courthouse filing for a subpoena and Dee is at work, Stiles arrives.

"Come in." I step back to let him inside and close the door on the shouts from reporters. They've been staked outside the house for hours, anxious to get a comment from me.

Many in the mainstream media had run with the unsubstantiated online claim. Afraid they might get left in the dust of a possible scandal, they were using language, such as *allegedly* and *purportedly* to cover their asses as they still benefited from the coverage.

Social media is worse. People hiding behind their screens while they lob attacks and insults about my wife without any care for who they hurt, or interest in the truth. Our passionate kiss at the gym had been a distraction for all of five minutes.

I'd met the smears with an unequivocal denouncement in a press statement and posts on all my accounts. Former teammates and celebrity friends came to my defense. Many fans had too. But with the award gala being next Saturday and my reputation in question, the conservative board members were antsy.

Asher had assured the Chairwoman that I was close to obtaining proof that the affair was falsified. She had agreed to go to bat for me and buy more time. I don't care about the award. But I do care about what taking it away would mean for Papa's Kids and Cayo's memory.

The fake story had attempted to discredit me and embarrass my wife. Anger burns through me with a thousand flames. I blow out a fuming breath and drop into the chair behind the desk.

Stiles pulls up a seat on the opposite side. "How you holding up" he asks, crossing one boot over the jean-clad knee of his other leg.

"I hate this shit for Dee. But she's handling it better than I am. Keeping her head high. Never once doubted me."

A trace of admiration causes the austere lines of his face to briefly relax. "Your wife is stand-up. She's tough and has your back."

Stiles knows of what he speaks, having seen Dee go toe-to-toe with Malcolm. That was my wife. Whether facing down my demons or ugly rumors, she did it with that warrior determination of hers.

Early in our relationship, I'd feared that I might not be able to hold on to Dee. I wasn't sure she would stick when the going got rough. But she's been the glue through it all. My biggest supporter and defender.

"Tell me you have something," I ask with bated anticipation, because not knowing is driving me out of my mind.

"A little more than I did earlier. We used a device fingerprint to dig deeper into the concealed IP address of the anonymous post. It's registered to Gavin Baxter."

Not the name I'm expecting. "Who's that?"

"No one as far as I can tell. He doesn't exist. Looks like someone went to a lot of trouble to cover their identity."

O'Malley? Malcolm? Both have motives. But posting a video where the timing could be disproved isn't Malcolm's style. He wouldn't strike to merely disrupt, he'd strike to destroy. "The video sounds like O'Malley. Falsifying a story is his MO."

"Thought of that. Got a tail on him and checked his phone records. He hasn't made any physical contact with Ms. Manning and there aren't any calls between them. Not ruling it out, though. We're looking at all possibilities, including how anyone could have gotten a copy of the video. Security protocols are strict. Only the director and his two guys that monitor the CCTV room have access to any of the footage."

"People can be bought. Lisa knew the video existed. She could have paid off someone in security to get her a copy."

"True enough. But doesn't tell us why and how O'Malley comes into play."

"Anyone following me on social media would be aware of O'Malley's disdain; that he thought my image was a fraud and wanted to expose it. Lisa could have reached out to him after the interview aired. Through DM, which wouldn't show up in their phone records. With a mutual interest in taking me down, they could have easily planned it and covered their tracks. O'Malley would know how to do that. He's done it before."

"We'll keep following that angle. But what strikes me as off is that O'Malley stopped blogging about you months ago. He didn't even retweet the video or comment. Seems out of character for someone who used to be all over you to just ignore potential dirt."

"He's not ignoring it," I say in frustration, wanting action over discussion. "He's found a different way to come at me and stay beneath the radar."

"Could be. But we should also consider that Ms. Manning acted alone."

I reject that notion, shaking my head. "Don't see it. Lisa isn't savvy enough to pull off something like this on her own."

"With respect, sir, I wouldn't underestimate a woman scorned."

"Fuck!" I exhale harshly and push to my feet. Pissed at the lack of info. Pissed at myself for contributing to this mess. After I got sober and joined the NBA, I'd been discreet and careful. No random hook-ups or groupies. I chose women that were high profile and had their own reputations to safeguard. I never wanted to embarrass my family or myself. The fact that I'd brought this scandal on Dee fucking kills me. I will take that blame, own it. But I will not let anyone else responsible get away with hurting my wife.

"I want answers, Stiles." And I'm past the point of sitting back and waiting for them.

LESS THAN FIFTEEN MINUTES LATER, I wade through the flash of cameras and shouts of debasing questions. "Do you miss your old lifestyle, is that why you cheated?" "Are you still involved with the woman in the video?" "Are there others?" "Is your wife standing by you for the money or because she lacks the confidence to leave?"

Profane retorts scald my tongue. I hold them back and climb into the passenger's seat with a slam of the door. "Let's get the hell out of here."

Stiles puts his foot on the gas and speeds off before we're followed, taking several detours to make sure of it. He'd suggested his SUV to avoid my car being seen at O'Malley's.

When we reach the south end of the city, I'm operating at a low simmer. Rows of linked townhomes line both sides of the street. Stiles rolls into an empty space and cuts the engine.

"That's his place on the right, 907." He directs my attention to a narrow, two-story brick house. "Max reported that O'Malley hasn't left yet. His routine has been to pop out to get lunch around 11:45. If that holds, he should surface in fifteen minutes."

"Got it." I pull out my phone and call Dee's mobile. She knows I only ever use that number while she's at work when it's important.

"Hi." Her apprehension ripples over the line. "You okay?"

"Yeah. Got a few minutes?"

"For you, of course."

I take a moment to let the warmth of her voice calm me. Then I catch her up on my suspicions and add: "I'm with Stiles, sitting outside of O'Malley's house."

"That doesn't sound like a good idea."

"Planning just a casual bump-in on the sidewalk."

"In other words, an ambush."

"I want to catch him unexpectedly. See his reaction."

"O'Malley is a sleaze," Dee says, "but it doesn't add up for me that he colluded with Lisa, and covered his tracks. It wouldn't be worth it to him without taking the credit."

"He wouldn't want credit for another fake story. He could just want to fuck with me. That's why I need to see his response. I'll know then what I'm dealing with and so will he."

"*Mick.*" Her tone conveys a wealth of warning.

"I know you don't like it, Dee. I didn't think you would. But I listened to you about staying away from Lisa. You were right about that. I'm right about this. I can feel it in my gut. It's something I have to do. And rather than tell you about it afterward, I'm telling you now."

"Playing that card, are you?"

"What card?" I feign innocence.

"The I'm-telling-you-upfront-so-you-can't-be-mad-even-if-you-don't-agree-with-what-I'm-doing card."

"See how I'm learning?"

"I see that you're topping from the bottom again."

"You love that."

"In bed, yes, out of bed, we compromise."

"Here's the compromise, baby: I have to do this but I'll alleviate your worries with a promise that I'm going to keep my cool. I have too much to lose by going off on him in a public place. Trust me."

"I do."

"That's all I need. I'll call you soon."

"K. Be careful. Oh, and Mick?"

"Yeah?"

"Thanks for telling me." I can feel her soft smile.

"Love you, beauty."

I end the call to Stiles dividing his gaze between O'Malley's front door and me. "Got it squared away with your wife?" he asks with a rare hint of amusement.

"Calling me whipped?" I blow out a short chuckle, secure in my manhood.

"Nope. Marriage suits you."

I'm surprised by his comment. "Thanks. It's changed me in all the best ways."

"I can see that."

"You married, Stiles?"

"No." His mood changes. Like a dark cloud has suddenly swept in. He looks back out the window. I don't have the opportunity to probe the shift. "There he is," Stiles says, diverting my attention. "Right on schedule."

My gaze slides over to where O'Malley has stepped through his front door. As disheveled as ever, he's dressed in khaki pants, a sloppy T-shirt hanging out of his windbreaker, and bad comb-over flapping in the breeze.

I slip on dark shades beneath my cap and cross the street. As O'Malley jogs down the steps, I intercept him at the bottom. Even with a one-stair advantage, he has to look up to reach my face. His open-mouthed shock is worth the price of being here.

"Fancy running into you, O'Malley."

He recovers in a snap. "Well, if it isn't the newly married Micah Peters. Congrats on your nuptials. To what do I owe the pleasure?"

"Thought we should talk."

"About what?" He shoves his hands into his front pockets in a casual stance. Anyone walking by would just think we're two guys shooting the shit. They'd be wrong.

"About your involvement in posting a fake video."

That slaps the smug out of him, and replaces it with a flicker of fear in his eyes.

"I don't know what you're talking about." His gaze darts around. "I had nothing to do with that video being posted."

"You seem awfully nervous for an innocent man."

"Give me a break, Peters. How would I have even gotten it?"

"You tell me."

"I can't because it didn't happen. Seems to me you should be going after the woman in the video."

"What do you know about her?"

"Nothing. Jesus." He withdraws his hands in an effort to stay down his meager strands. "You got caught with some broad giving you hand action and you come here trying to pin this shit on me."

"You're the one with a reputation for falsifying stories."

"It was one time. A stupid, costly error in judgment."

"You don't strike me as a changed man. I have people tracking down the anonymous source. I will find out."

"It. Was. Not. Me. For fuck's sake, I'm trying to get my career back. I'm trying to live my life. I stopped blogging about you. I stopped looking for a story. What more do you want?"

"The truth."

"I've given it to you. You think I'd chance posting that video—even anonymously—and risk another beat down or worse?"

"I'd hardly call busting your lip a beat down."

"Playing dumb, Peters?"

"Playing dumb about what?" My patience is waning. "Stop talking in fucking riddles."

"Look..." he puts his palms up. "I didn't post anything. I got the message loud and clear."

"You're pissing me off, O'Malley. Spit it out."

"You really don't know. Jesus." His hands shaking, he pulls a cigarette out of his jacket pocket and lights the end. "I was good at my job. Too ambitious maybe. But I was good. Smart. An astute reader of people and situations. I fucked up on one big story. I reported what I knew was true, but without proof, I made up the sources. I lost everything. I would not fuck up like that again.

"I was chasing real stuff. I knew basketball had to be the source of the dynamic between you and your father. It's a common tale. Controlling dad, living vicariously, forcing his will. Obliging son, dispassionate about the sport but desperately wanting his father's approval. Only that wasn't quite you, was it? You didn't care one bit about your father's approval. No, it's Cayo Torres who mattered to you. He was the man you looked up to. So, I asked myself, why would you play basketball all those years for someone you didn't seem to give a shit about?" Squinting, he drags the nicotine through his lungs, and blows a plume of smoke.

"You wouldn't, unless there was some compelling reason. That was the story I knew could get me my career back. Real investigative journalism. While nobody else wanted to look beneath that golden boy image of yours, I was going to be the one to unearth those buried secrets.

"Your denials, your refusals to sit with me for an interview, never revealing anything personal about yourself, all made me more suspicious and more certain. Ah, then you clocked me in the face and that really turned me into a dog with a bone. I couldn't let it go. When I learned from a source about your night at the Lemon Lounge, I followed you to the deli the next day.

"I didn't know then that the woman in question was Deeana Chase or that she was part of your past, but I knew from your reaction that I'd stumbled onto another hidden gem. I left the deli and called your father. For months he wouldn't budge, wouldn't speak to me. But this time when I mentioned a woman that went against your type and revved up your protective defenses, that got his attention. He agreed to meet me. Suggested it. I was too excited to be skeptical. I went all the way out to this dive."

O'Malley's face turns red. He finishes his cigarette, drops it to the stair, and stubs it out with his shoe. "That's when I got jumped—soon as I exited the car. This scrappy dude with a scar down his face, punched and kicked the hell out of my stomach and ribs. When he was done, and I was lying in a heap on the ground, hardly able to move, he gave me your father's warning: *keep digging and you're dead.*"

My blood runs cold. But I retain my neutral expression and give nothing away. "You want me to believe that this one alleged beating kept you quiet about me?"

"It didn't stop there. That thug, the kind of ex-con that dirty cops keep around to do their bidding, paid me more surprise visits—same warning. Then small bags of cocaine were planted in my car, in my house, in plain sight. I could have been arrested. Your father was letting me know he had the power to take me down any time I stepped out of line."

"If you were so sure it was my father, why didn't you go to the police?"

"Are you crazy?" he scoffs. "I had no proof. You think I could crack the blue wall on my word? Your father, the big, popular sheriff, and me, the ousted journalist who falsified a story. Come on, Peters. You know I couldn't."

Yeah, I did know that all too well. "Have these threats stopped?" I ask, needing to know.

"If you mean the beatings and planting evidence, there's been nothing in the last few months. I read that your old man retired and left town. But I'm not stupid enough to think he can't reach me from wherever the hell he is."

"And this sob story is supposed to make me believe you didn't post that video?"

"It's not a sob story." Spittle forms in the corners of his mouth. "I'm done with anything having to do with you. That means I've sat on a story that's worth millions, worth my career. You at least owe me for that."

"Think you can shake me down, O'Malley? Think again."

"You're a real piece of work." He shakes his head in disgust. "You can play the innocent here, but you knew your father had silenced me somehow and that makes you no better than him."

His arrow hits on target and pierces deep. My phone pings in my back pocket. I turn away from O'Malley but not his accusation; my head pounding, my thoughts reeling. I retrieve my phone and look down at the text from Stiles.

Meet me back at the car. It's not O'Malley.

CHAPTER THIRTY-FIVE

Dee

ASHER'S CHEERFUL FACE APPEARS ON the iPad for our video call. I settle in beside Mick on the sofa and press my hand to his back. Through the ribbed Henley, his skin is feverishly warm, his muscles rigid and tight.

A lot has gone down in the last several hours and my husband was bearing it all.

"This is great news!" Asher beams. "Your man, Stiles, came through."

Apparently, his tech whiz had unraveled the elaborate process used to conceal the originator's identity. That unmasking led to Kyle Duncan, avid technology buff, who also happened to work in the CCTV room at Mick's condo. It didn't take much for him to point the finger straight at Lisa.

According to Duncan, the former Knaughty Kitten model approached him during his Sunday night shift after the interview aired, and used her ample wiles and bank account to entice him into posting the video and covering their tracks. The twenty-three-year-old said when faced with a cool challenge, hot woman, and cash, he couldn't say no, as if that somehow let him off the hook. They were both guilty as sin. It had cost Lisa $5,000 to exact her revenge. While my husband's reputation, worth more than money, was put through the wringer.

Duncan has since been fired and management is in the process of releasing the video with groveling apologies to Mick. They have also opened an investigation into Lisa's conduct and the condo board will decide the fate of her continued residence. Not nearly enough. But she's not worth the energy.

"We need to get out there," Asher continues. "Fast. The press is at your condo where Lisa Manning is denying all of Duncan's allegations. We can't let her narrative hog the limelight."

"I don't give a shit about what Lisa says," Mick rebuts, heatedly. "Once we have the video as proof, I'll make a statement. I'm not going to entertain her denials."

"That's the way this works, Mick. You make another statement to pre-empt the video."

"To say what I've already said? Waste of time."

"Sure. Of course," Asher mocks. "Let's do it your way. I'm only the media expert."

"Now what, you're going to sulk like a baby?"

"I'm not the one sulking, Mick. You are and I don't get it. Why aren't you happy about this development?"

"What the fuck is there to be happy about? Proving something I already knew was a lie."

I send Asher a look of apology. "Thank you for your advice and all you've been doing. We both appreciate it. Let's just take a breather and circle back."

"Alright," he relents, somewhat mollified. "We'll touch base in another hour."

"Sounds good. Bye, Ash."

"You don't have to coddle him." Mick turns to me when I kill the call. "It's his job to give advice and my prerogative not to take it."

"True." I study the deepening shadows in his eyes and the ticking of his jaw muscle. "But we both know that's not what this is about."

"I'm fine, Dee."

"You're not fine, Mick. You're churned up about what O'Malley said."

"Really?" His tone drips with sarcasm. "Don't most fathers plant evidence and send death threats?"

"No, they don't. But Malcolm did and that has nothing to do with you."

"Whatever." He pushes to his feet and stalks out of the room.

He's halfway to the office when I catch up with him. I grab his arm. He comes to a halt, his whole body radiating an angry guilt.

"Talk to me. Please."

"What do you want me to say, Dee?"

"Whatever you're feeling. Just don't shut me out."

"I should have listened to you and Stiles about O'Malley. I should never have gone there."

"Knowing now what Malcolm did doesn't make you responsible for his actions."

"Right." He stares away as a turbulent silence descends, taut with echoes of a painful past.

"It doesn't, Mick." I cup his hardened face and look into his eyes. "How could you possibly bear any of the blame?"

"Because I know Malcolm." He pulls my hands away. "Goddammit, Dee. I knew he hadn't bought O'Malley's silence without strong-arming him in some way. But the truth is I didn't care because it served my purpose."

"You think if you'd known, you could have stopped Malcolm?"

"I wouldn't have wanted to stop him."

"I don't believe that."

"They say love is blind. Guess it is."

He wants to pick a fight but I won't give him one. "I'm not blind, Mick. I just know you. At the time, you didn't want O'Malley pursuing a story any more than your father did. And yet, you never threatened him or sent anyone to kick him around. Instead you hired bodyguards to keep me safe. Because hurting people is who Malcolm is, and protecting them is who you are."

"Don't go pinning a medal on me, Dee. I'm not going to lose sleep over O'Malley. He tried to use the situation to get money out of me today. He was dogged in his pursuit of a story and he wouldn't have cared who he hurt, including you. O'Malley is a prick."

"He is, but how you're feeling isn't about O'Malley's character, it's about what you think this situation says about yours. When he said you are no better than Malcolm, that cut deep. It opened up old wounds."

"Just let it go, Dee."

"I can't do that." I put a gentle palm to the center of his chest. "Hearing what your father did has made you doubt yourself. But I'm here to tell you, Mick—the love of my life—that you are a good man, through and through."

"Dee." His voice is gruff with emotion.

"It's okay for you to feel bad, angry, conflicted, and any number of things you might feel. But it's not okay to blame yourself. I won't let you."

"No," he breathes out a humorless laugh. "You never do."

"Remember what you told Dwayde about his father's bad deeds not being his responsibility? You said that because you know it's true. So, remind yourself about that now. Don't take on Malcolm's sins."

He slides his hand beneath my curls, his look filled with gratitude and a love so deep, I can feel it seep into my chest and glow warmly around my heart. "Thank you, beauty."

"You don't have to thank me."

"Yeah, I do."

His smartphone buzzes, interrupting the moment. Mick presses a soft kiss to my forehead and returns to the living room where it's vibrating on the coffee table. He answers, listens, then looks over at me with a spark of renewed vigor.

"We have the video."

ON THURSDAY, THE PRESS CONVENES at the downtown convention center. It's a clear spring day. Natural light pours through the solarium windows of the Garden Room that faces Michigan Avenue and Grant Park. I'd chosen a mid-calf wraparound dress in blush taupe with nude high heels.

Early comers have filled the rows of seats, while the rest of the room—rustling with activity—is standing only. There's a table set up at the front with a microphone.

Mick and I wait off to the side, concealed by a curtain. He slips his palm in mine and squeezes. There was a time when he wouldn't have wanted me here. He would have wanted to shield me. Now, he holds me firmly by his side.

I gaze over at him. He's dashingly handsome in an olive gray suit. The growth of his wavy hair curves against the back collar, his strong jawline is relaxed and lightly bearded.

He catches my stare and winks. "We've got this, beauty."

Asher goes first to call the press conference to order. Then keeping our hands joined, we walk out to a blaze of camera fire, and move to stand at the microphone.

"Good morning," Mick begins, his voice clear and steady. The crowd of reporters settles. "These past few days have been hell, as rumors and lies have swirled about us. I want to thank my incredible wife for her depth of loyalty and unwavering faith in me. I also want to thank our family, friends, fans, and everyone who took to social media to defend me against the baseless claims. Thank you to the Chicago Children's We Care Foundation for their continued patience while I sorted this out. And finally, appreciation goes to those of you in the media that reported the events with professional integrity, allowing the facts to bare out.

"Unfortunately, not everyone was as concerned with the truth and many were downright cruel. I kept our relationship out of the public for that very reason. I didn't want Dee to have to deal with vicious attacks. But she has, proving herself to be stronger and more resilient than ever.

"I love and respect my wife. I value our life together. I did not and would not have an affair. Many of you were duped by a fake story. It dismays me how quickly there was a rush to judgment. But here are the facts as you will see for yourselves."

Asher cues up the system. I know it guts Mick to have me watch the video again. That because of Lisa's vindictiveness, it will forever live on the Internet. Unfortunately, we can't change that, but I can let Mick know that it can't hurt me or change anything between us.

I give him a tender smile, then mouth "it's okay" before I turn my head and stoically face the screen. Mick pulls me close and together we watch the videos play side by side. Two almost identical clips. The one that went viral had been digitally altered to show a recent date stamp and the ending cut short. While the unedited, longer version, shows the real date from back in October and Mick ultimately rejecting Lisa's sexual advance.

Murmurs follow as we pivot back to the front. A few reporters even have the grace to bow their heads knowing they were part of perpetuating the lie.

"As is obvious from the footage," Mick resumes, "the video was taken before my relationship with Dee and did not accurately represent the full story. Nevertheless, I regret my poor judgment and apologize to my wife for being dragged into an attempted scandal."

He ends the statement to a flurry of questions.

Lisa Manning denies posting the video. Do you believe her?

"No comment."

Is she obsessed with you?

"No comment."

Are you going to seek legal action against Mr. Duncan and Ms. Manning?

"I'll leave that with my legal team to comment on. As for Dee and I, we are anxious to put this nightmare behind us and move forward."

"That's all." Asher steps in and holds his hand up. "Thank you for coming."

Mick ushers me away through the blaze of camera explosions to the limo where Bernard is waiting out front.

Micah

I DON'T HAVE TO GUESS how pleased Dee was about the press conference. Her affectionate demeanor and excited praise during the drive home leave no room for doubt. Nor does the way she attacks me the instant we're at home and behind closed doors—like a sexy tigress. Her tongue licks into my mouth. Her hands shove off my suit jacket, pulling my shirt out of the waistband of my pants, pushing beneath the material to claw her fingers over my muscles.

"If I had known press conferences were such a turn on—"

"They're not." She pants with impatience. "But you are. Commanding the audience, pledging your love...I want you. *Now.*"

On an aroused laugh, I toe-off my shoes. Seconds later Dee pulls away and my amusement dies. Her curls are piled up on top of her head in an alluring style, with a few loose wisps falling along her graceful neck and framing her beautiful face. Watching me, she unties the belted bow at her waist, and without hesitation, slithers out of the wrap dress. It drops quietly to the floor, pooling at her feet.

I stand frozen in place. Only I don't feel anything close to cold. I feel in-the-desert-at-high-noon hot. She's wearing a translucent bra and panty set, sheer thigh stockings, and high nude heels. She's naked but not. I can't tear my eyes away from the decadence of Dee. Her milk-chocolate nipples are pebbled through the gauzy material, her full breasts swell above the demi-cups. Her landing strip peeks through the sheer V between her voluptuous thighs.

Looking at her makes me primal. Like a caveman on steroids. I put my hands on her waist. Slide them up her ribcage. She breathes out a tiny giggle. I'd first discovered her ticklish spots when we were fifteen and I was trying to wrestle out of her the answers from a test. I would use any excuse back then to touch her. How lucky am I that I no longer need one?

I trail my palms higher to the under curves of her breasts. I cup them through the thin layer, hefting their weight, gently squeezing.

"Mick," she moans when I rub my thumbs across her hardened nipples. "I'm supposed to be seducing you."

"You are...just by being you."

"Let's go to the bedroom." She unbuckles my belt and undoes the button.

"Too far." Deepening the kiss, I walk her several steps in a slow dance to the living room. "Leave the heels on," I murmur, lowering her to the area rug.

My mouth finds hers again, hot and sultry. Her arms circle my neck, holding me to her. My fingers encounter her belly above the bikini line of her panties, softly rounded, quivering when my knuckles sweep across the skin.

"Ohh. You make me so wet."

"Show me." I extricate myself from her grip to look.

Dee slides her legs apart. With the thong pushed askew from the movement, and her pink and glistening, she has that wanton, fuck-me look that makes my dick ache to be inside her wet snug heat. But I long for a taste first.

Sliding down into a prone position, I nudge the thin line of her panties away and lick in long drags along her creamy channel.

"Soo good." She arches, her heels digging into the rug, her juicy pussy lifting into my mouth.

I seize Dee's gaze, forcing her opaque eyes to stay on me as my tongue swirls around her clit and my fingers twist and rub her taut nipples. She gasps and writhes. The multiple stimulus working her into a frenzy. And me too. I tease those sweet, tender spots until she cries out. Her neck and back arch, her hips bow up and down. Watching Dee come takes me straight to the edge.

I rise to my knees and shove my pants and underwear down my legs. With her panties still pushed aside, I plant my palms on the rug, lever over her, and drive my cock through the slick clasp with an ecstatic groan.

"*Mick.*" Her short nails beneath my shirt scratch at my back, marking me. "You feel so hard."

"That's all you...what you do to me." I lower my head to kiss her, then up the pace. I fling her leg over my shoulder. Grabbing at flesh, my knees push into the carpet, gaining leverage to drive harder, to sink deeper.

"Yes," she sobs with every plunge. "Make me come again."

Her words drench my blood in feral heat. On the verge of exploding, I push my hand between her legs, rubbing her clit to another orgasm. When she comes on throaty moans, convulsing around my cock, clamping tightly, I lose my fucking mind.

Speed, heat, and power. My hips surge like well-oiled pistons. Sweat beads on my skin. I lower her leg from my shoulder and pin her down. Thrusting and kissing Dee roughly, I let go. The red-hot, knotted ball of tension releasing into a violent burst of flames.

Together, we clutch each other and move until the fire clears. Collapsing on the rug, we lie there winded and spent with the midday sun shining through the curtains, spreading dust crystals in the air.

I press my nose and mouth to her damp neck. Inhale sex-scented skin. When I can get my legs back under me, I rid myself of what remains of my clothes and carry my wife to the bedroom.

"You would have made a perfect lead in old movies," she says with her arms draped around my shoulders.

"Why?"

"Because carrying a woman harkens back to old, romantic films."

"Guess I'm a romantic at heart."

"You definitely are that." She smiles lazily. "I love the contrast of how raw and rough you can be one minute and tender the next."

"You have a little dirty side yourself, Mrs. Peters."

"I do with you. My inner sexy beast."

I laugh, thinking it suits her, and lay her down on the bed. She's still in those nothing-of-a-bra-and-panties. I remove her shoes and slide in beside her. She rests her cheek on my chest, right over my heart.

I can't imagine the chemistry and intimacy between us ever fading. It will change and shift over the years, mature but not dim. I can feel that throughout every day we spend together, getting closer, more entwined, our lives naturally and intricately threaded.

I gaze down at Dee. Her eyelids are still heavy, her body languid. "Tired?" I ask.

"Relaxed."

"What do you say, I make us lunch and we eat in bed?"

"I do have to work at some point."

"You're the boss." I stroke my hand over the curve of her hip. "Take the whole day off."

"Too much on my plate. But I'll work from home." Her fingers caress the pad of my pec. "I've been thinking more seriously about taking on a partner."

"You've mentioned it a few times."

"I was dabbling with the idea then."

"And now?"

"I'm ready. A partner would help with the workload and increase the capacity to take on more cases. But there's another reason."

"What's that?"

"Us. It would free me up to travel with you, to spend more quality time together, to…" She pauses. "Start a family."

I go still. A lump the size of a basketball forms in my throat. "I want that. Children with you."

Her expression suddenly fills with sadness. "I wish I could give you a baby that we make together."

"Dee," I say quietly. "Any child we have together, however that happens, will be ours."

"I know. Adoption is a great choice. So many children out there are in need of love and a family."

"We can do both. Adopt and try to have a baby."

"The chances of the latter are slim at best."

"You don't know that for certain."

"Pretty much. A doctor told me years ago that with the amount of scar tissue from my miscarriage, my chances were negligible."

"There are second opinions, specialists, new procedures..."

"I don't want you to get your hopes up." But I hear the wistfulness in her voice, see it in her eyes.

"When I say it doesn't matter to me how we make a family, I mean that." My lips graze her brow. "I just don't want you to give up on the potential of having a baby, if there's any possibility."

"What if we try and it doesn't happen or I miscarry again?"

"If for whatever reason it's not meant to be, beauty, we'll survive it."

"You seem so sure."

"I am." I take her left hand in mine, our wedding bands clicking as I interlock our fingers. "I've never been as sure of anything as I am of us."

CHAPTER THIRTY-SIX

Dee

"ZIP ME?"

"A husband's privilege." Mick slips the cherished pocket watch from Papa T into his jacket pocket, and crosses from the dresser to come up behind me.

I hold up the front of my strapless evening gown. A gift from Mick. Custom made by a haute couture designer, it's the most exquisite and expensive item of clothing I have ever worn.

His knuckles drift against my bare back as he reaches for the tab of the invisible zipper. There is something about Mick helping me dress that simultaneously melts my heart and turns me on. I suppose because, like making love, the intimacy of it belongs only to us.

I stand in front of my first full-length mirror—a recent purchase that marked a major milestone for me. I don't have to work so hard to see past my perceived flaws anymore. Instead I'm coming to accept my thick curves as just being a part of me.

As Mick raises the zipper, I watch the bodice tighten against my waist and breasts in an hourglass. The dress is stunning—pale gold and sequined with a split skirt that cascades to the floor like a champagne waterfall. Together with the sweeping train, dramatic eye makeup, and my hair styled in Jessica Rabbit waves, I feel glamorous.

Our reflections lock on to each other. Then Mick's gaze, in that slow burning motion of his, rakes me from head to toe and back up again. Pausing at my plump cleavage, red painted lips, and finally my gold and brown smokey eyes. "You look spectacular."

"Glad you like it."

"Like doesn't come close to describing my reaction." He keeps his eyes on me and lowers his mouth to the curve of my neck.

"Mm. I can't wait for you to show me later."

"I could show you right now. Christen the new mirror."

I shiver. The idea of watching Mick slide his big cock in and out of me is an erotic temptation. I gaze at his image, at that wicked grin and all his sophisticated hotness. In a black onyx tux that perfectly fits his lean, muscular frame, he's my very own 007. The pocket square is silk champagne to match my dress, and his shirt is crisp white with gold cuff links at his wrists. While my hair had taken the handiwork of a salon stylist, he'd passed his fingers through his with enviable ease. The result didn't suffer any from being effortless. Thick and tousled, his hair falls in the shape of moon crescents at his ears and against his collar.

I turn to him, highly conscious of how good he smells, of how good he looks. Of how much I want him. I straighten his bow tie and breathe through my arousal. "Getting sweaty with you right now would be a risky thing to do when it's nearly time to leave."

"We'll be fashionably late."

"Huh-uh." I spread my hands over his wide shoulders. "Tonight is too important. The award is to celebrate your generosity. But more than that, to me, tonight is a celebration of you. Your courage and mettle. You've conquered challenge after challenge with strength and class. I love you. Adore you. Admire you. I know how much you idolize Cayo and you are every bit of the man that he was."

His hands circle my waist, and he presses his forehead against mine, breathing hard. "I wouldn't be half this man without you. I never would have confronted Malcolm or told my family the truth. I would not have gotten through any of that mess last week without you beside me.

"You're not just my muse in writing," he says, making my eyes mist with the threat of tears. "I'm inspired by all I see in you. That pushes me to keep striving to be the best version of myself. The best man I can be."

I touch his bearded jaw, too choked up to speak.

"Reconsider Molly's offer."

"What?" I blink at the sudden curve ball. "Where did that come from?"

"I know we talked about lying low after tonight. Getting back to normal and staying out of the media. But Molly and others are interested in what you have to say. You have followers that are interested.

"I don't want you to hold yourself back from doing anything that you want to do. If body positivity, self-acceptance, or any other platform feels right for you, then go for it."

"Okay, wow. Not what I was expecting."

"You have a powerful journey to share, Dee, and I know you'd convey a powerful message. There's nothing you can't do if you set your mind on something, beauty. It's your decision. But I always want you to shine."

"Thank you."

He smiles and dabs at the tears beneath my eyes with the gentle brush of his fingertips.

Whether the symposium or the platform were the right opportunities for me or not, I still don't know. But it's his message that lights me up. My husband never wants me to feel hidden or invisible again.

OUR LIMO PULLS UP TO the front of the magnificent Grand Hotel. I lean forward to gaze through the black-out window, struck by it all. Guests are arriving, and fans, cordoned off by metal barricades, are huddled to get a glimpse of Micah Peters. On the other side, bordering the red carpet, media and paparazzi stand in wait behind velvet ropes. I can all but feel the current of expectation as necks crane to see who will emerge from the limo. When the valet opens the door and tonight's man-of-the-hour steps out, flashes erupt like a lightning storm.

The fans roar with enthusiasm and the press shout out his name, competing for his attention. One photographer, who tries to cross the rope, is immediately met by the stone wall that is Stiles. Mick waves to his fans, then extends his hand to me. Taking a steadying breath, I set my palm in his, and climb out of the back seat. I stand beside my husband. The flashes are blinding. Smartphones are raised to capture our every move. I smile and work to navigate the length of my dress while keeping my eyes from squinting against the bright explosions as Mick and I ascend the red carpet.

Our security team covers our entrance, their hard eyes trained on the surroundings while the police hired for the event keep back the melee of fans. Max ushers us into the sprawling lobby of columns and marble. There, security hangs back and we are met by the event handlers who guide us through the foundation's required photo ops. We pose for shot after shot.

My cheeks are hurting from smiling so much when we're finally led away and escorted up an escalator to the ballroom. Sparkly empire chandeliers provide atmospheric lighting. Round tables with seating for twelve are centered by elaborate floral and candle arrangements, and each place setting glitters with silver and crystal. It's a massive affair. Servers in black and white wear gloves and carry trays of tiny hors d'oeuvres and champagne.

Chicago's elite, a combination of old money and the nouveau riche, are blinged-out and dressed to the nines. The room hums with conversation and the full orchestra is playing Michael Bublé in the background.

Mick steers me through clusters of people, pausing often for greetings and congratulations. He keeps his hand on my lower back, proudly introducing me, slipping into his public persona with finesse. He's a natural at schmoozing, using every opportunity to fundraise and educate on behalf of Papa's Kids and youth homelessness.

I'm not nearly as confident in this situation as I am sitting across a mediation table or being inside a courtroom. But I want to represent Mick well and be an asset to his growing role of philanthropist.

He hands me a flute of champagne from a passing tray and we move several steps before we're hijacked by a finance mogul, whose much younger wife ogles my husband. I'm holding up my end of the conversation when a group in front of us disperses and I spot my friends.

Jordyn is dressed in a single-shoulder beaded jumpsuit and has styled the front of her short hair into a voluminous pompadour. She looks fabulous if not bored by Lexie's beau, Dr. Richard Schnauss. With his brown hair rigidly parted to the side and slicked back, he gives off an aristocratic air. Beside him, Lexie is a vision—long and graceful; her lavender column dress boasts a show-stopping feathered skirt. She's smiling politely at whatever Richard is saying, but appears no more entertained than Jordyn does.

Following the direction of my gaze, Mick makes our excuses. I set my glass down to exchange effusive hugs with Lexie and Jordyn. They extend the same warmth to Mick, while Richard offers him a perfunctory handshake and gives me a stiff kiss on the cheek.

"Yass, queen!" Jordyn snaps her fingers. "You and your boobs are killing that dress."

Richard's lips purse at her behavior and Jordyn scratches her nose using the middle finger.

"Behave," I warn beneath a whispered laugh.

When Mick is drawn into a conversation with Richard and Lexie, Jordyn leans over to me. "He is honestly the driest man I have ever met. I don't know how our girl does it or why."

"Lex may see a side of him that we don't."

"Not possible. There's only one side, BO-RING."

"Well, you seem to think there's more than one side to Robocop," I point out.

"Are you really comparing the sinfully delicious Stiles to Dr. Wake-Me-When-It's-Over?"

I feel Mick's hand slide up my back to the bare skin above my dress. "What are you two whispering about?"

"Your hot security man," Jordyn says.

Mick, aware of her crush, lust, whatever it is, shakes his head. "Good luck with that."

"I don't need luck. I've got this cat and mouse thing going with him. A slow chase to set my trap, and then..." she curves her hand and scratches it forward like a claw. "I'll pounce."

Mick and I laugh. Since Stiles is more grizzly bear than mouse, and Jordyn, more lioness than cat—should make it very interesting.

WHEN MICK'S MANAGING DIRECTOR OF Papa's Kids arrives, he introduces me to Eden and her partner, Trinity—a lovely couple that I plan to have over and get to know better. I'm also introduced to other members of the team that have an assigned table next to ours. Their rapport with Mick and each other is one of collegial friendship and mutual respect. The more I experience the various facets of Mick's life, the more connected to him I feel.

I'm thrilled that our family is here. They wouldn't miss Mick's big night for anything. Mama T shines like a diamond in a silver gown, her long, salt and pepper hair styled in a French chignon. "You look beautiful," I tell her.

James and Maria are jubilant, dressed up and sipping champagne, enjoying a rare evening without the kids. Victor and Dwayde make a handsome father and son pair in matching tuxes, with Isabelle wearing a blue princess dress—her pretty face rouged and powdered for the occasion.

Gabi, oh wow, catches my breath. She is a head-turner in a sparkling pearl trumpet gown that clings to her slim curves. The flirty updo shows off her gorgeous features and bare back. Mick and Victor step in the path of a young man who is doing nothing more than giving their little sister an appreciative once-over. Gabi will be graduating next month and off to Georgia Tech at the end of the summer to study bioengineering. We are all so proud of her but God help any guy who sets his sights on the smart and stunning Gabrielle Torres with Mick and Victor running interference.

BEFORE DINNER BEGINS, EVERYONE FINDS their assigned tables. We're located at the front. Mick pulls out two chairs for Mama T and me, giving us both a direct view to the stage. Our elegant meal consists of wild mushroom in puff pastry on a bed of warm greens followed by filet mignon topped with lobster. I don't eat much of mine—too nervous and excited for Mick.

I return from the restroom after freshening up my lipstick when Chairwoman Jasmine Clarke goes to the podium. She acknowledges the attendees and Mick. He sits beside me with an air of calm, his hand resting on my thigh under the table.

The chairwoman talks about the foundation's good works, then extolls praise on the importance of Mick's contributions—highlighting Papa's Kids, the land he donated for the new recreational complex in Springvale, and his charitable support of causes benefitting abused and homeless children.

"Without further ado, it is my esteemed privilege to welcome to the stage this year's recipient of the Generosity of Spirit Award. None other than, Micah Peters."

The room thunders with applause as Mick rises to his feet. He leans over to kiss my cheek then Mama T's. She dabs at her damp eyes and reaches for my hand as we both watch the man we love take the stage with long, lithe strides and confidence.

Chairwoman Clark presents him with the plaque. They shake hands and pose for a few pictures. Then she discreetly slips to the back and Mick has the floor. He smiles, seeming to take it all in humbly.

"Thank you, Chairwoman Clark and the Foundation, for this prestigious honor," he begins.

The deep baritone of his voice gives me goosebumps. Mick is a joy to look at and listen to. He is gracious and sincere. His speech sounds polished but unrehearsed. His voice catches when he talks about how

Cayo and Rita Torres were the role models that inspired him. He doesn't skimp on giving gratitude to all his family or sharing the credit for Papa's Kids with his team, having them stand for a round of applause. He speaks for ten minutes. Not long enough. I could listen to him for hours. When he brings it to a close, he looks right in my direction.

"I would like to share this award with the woman that lights up my life." He raises the plaque. "Dee, baby, this is for you."

I blush as the audience gets to their feet for a standing ovation. My friends and family cheer the loudest. When Mick beckons me to him, butterflies swarm my belly. I hug Mama T and meet Mick, where he's waiting for me at the bottom of the stairs. He offers his arm and escorts me up onto the stage. I greet the chairwoman with a friendly handshake, and Mick and I pose for more pictures.

Nerves be damned, there's no place else I'd rather be than right here, sharing this significant moment with my husband.

A SHORT TIME LATER, WE return to our table to enjoy a dessert platter with petite mousse cakes and Belgian chocolate truffles, that are almost as good as sex. Well, not sex with Mick, but still.

Our table is spirited. Whether a casual brunch at home or a fancy venue, that's us. The only one who seems put out is Richard. Censure is etched into the prudish pinch of his brow. Fortunately, that doesn't stop Lexie from delighting in my lively family, so different from the cold proper atmosphere that her mother and father created. It's the scarce occasion when I actually get to see her relax from the rules of etiquette and rigid expectation.

AFTER DESSERT, THE ORCHESTRA PLAYS for the mixed-age crowd, segueing from Sinatra to Ed Sheeran and even throwing in some Bruno Mars. I'm on the dance floor with my friends and sisters when Mick approaches and whispers in my ear, "Don't expend all your energy here."

Laughing at his meaning, I shove him away. We don't leave until well after eleven. Greeted by the paparazzi and an evening breeze, Mick drapes his jacket around my shoulders while Max and Hilton stand guard. The limos that Mick arranged for our family and my friends arrive before ours. We hug everyone goodnight, and soon after, Stiles pulls up. He doesn't usually act as limo driver but he put himself on our security detail, and assigned Bernard to Jordyn—much to her chagrin.

The first thing to go inside the luxury vehicle are my glittery heels. Made for fashion rather than two hours of dancing, I slide them off in sighing relief.

"Here." Mick lifts my legs onto his lap and massages my feet.

"Mm. That feels amazing."

"You had a good time?"

"Yes. I enjoyed it all, especially your speech."

"Given your orgasmic reaction, I thought you'd say the chocolates."

"Okay, those too."

"Hope I can measure up."

I dangle the gift bag that contains a box of the decadent truffles. "I have these just in case."

"You'll pay for that, Mrs. Peters." He teases the ticklish underside of my foot.

A reminder of our younger days, I try to wrestle away from his playful punishment in a fit of breathless giggles. Finally, with us both in hysterics, he shows mercy on me and relents.

I punch his shoulder in weak retaliation. He catches my hand and brings it to his lips. It's a tender after-moment. Sobering, I curl into him and rest my head on his shoulder. "Tonight was wonderful. Papa T would have been so proud. Thank you for including me in your honor, and his."

"I didn't want to embarrass you, but I wanted you up on stage with me."

"You didn't. It was really special."

"For me too."

I hug him, pressing my nose into the crook of his neck and breathing in his woodsy scent. "I love you," I whisper.

He lifts my chin and treats me to a heart-melting kiss.

I'm like putty when Stiles pulls into the driveway. Since Mick cleared his name, the paparazzi no longer plague our sidewalk, having moved on to the next shiny object. Yet still, Stiles scopes out the area before he comes around to open the back door.

Mick exits first and reaches for my hand. I join him in my stocking feet, carrying the shoes by the straps over my shoulder.

"Oh, the chocolates." I duck back inside to get them.

Mick looks at the bag drolly. "My competition."

"Never." I smile, then glance from Mick to our ever-alert bodyguard. Before I can thank him and say goodnight, his shout jolts me.

"Get down!" Quick as lightning, Stiles jumps in front of us just as Mick topples me to the ground.

We fall together hard, my head hitting the pavement with a dizzying thud. My vision blurs. Mick's body covers me. Pain. Radiating pain. Everything hurts. I can't move. There's a deafening pop, pop, pop beneath the incessant pounding in my head.

Mick! Mick! I scream over and over again but there's no sound, no light, nothing but darkness.

CHAPTER THIRTY-SEVEN

Micah

THE GUNFIRE FINALLY CEASES. HOW many shots there'd been, I couldn't say. More than three…maybe four, five. It had all happened so fast, yet felt like an eternity. In the chaos, I'd taken Dee down, using my body as a shield.

Sirens wail in the near distance. Breathing rough and frantic, I whisper words of encouragement in her ear: "Dee, baby, we're okay. It's over. The police are coming."

I'm met with an eerie stillness.

"Dee!" I panic and lever myself up enough to see her face. The side lights of the limo wash over her. Eyes closed, a stain of red on the pavement. So much blood.

"No! Christ no!" She is lying deathly still. Unresponsive. I press trembling fingers to her neck. A pulse! Slow, but steady.

I'm afraid to move her. Don't know where the blood is coming from. It's not on her skin or dress. The crimson spread is beneath her. Had she been shot before I got to her?

"Wake up, baby. Please wake up." I gently tap her face, the skin is cool, pale.

Flashing red lights appear. Voices, the pounding of footsteps. Quick. Urgent.

"Sir? Are you hurt?"

I lift away and look over my shoulder into the placid face of a medic. "My wife. Dee. She's unresponsive. Bleeding. She might have been shot."

"Alright, Mr. Peters," he says in recognition. "I need you to stay calm for me and move aside so we can take a look."

I nod and without going far, crouch against the limo.

"Dee." He calls her name. No answer. He carefully turns her onto her side.

I look and wish I hadn't. Can't stop from looking again. The back of her hair is violent red, wet, matted and sticky. I watch him shift through the strands while I hold my breath, shaking.

"The gash is wide," he says, "but I don't see any evidence of a gun wound."

My bent posture sags. But through the profound relief comes guilt. I had taken Dee down so hard, crushing her beneath me that I'd hurt her badly.

He checks her pulse and under her eyelids. Then with the help of another medic, they secure her head and neck, and load her onto a stretcher.

"We're taking your wife to Brockville General."

"I'm going with her."

"It would be better if you met us there."

"I'm going." I straighten, imposing my size and resolve. "I'm not leaving her."

He backs down. The gurney bumps along the ground with me following at Dee's feet. I long to hold her. To see those golden eyes open. To see her crooked smile. Fear overwhelms me.

I vaguely register the police cars and more medics at the end of the driveway. Where was Stiles? What the hell happened? All of it goes through my mind, but the center of my focus is Dee. My beautiful Dee. I hold her limp hand, talking to her, praying as the ambulance speeds through the night.

At the hospital, a medical team rushes Dee inside. No matter my protests and rants, the staff won't let me in while they examine her.

"Mr. Peters." A young doctor with short dreadlocks puts a hand on my shoulder in a kind but firm manner. "I'm Dr. Granger. How you can best help your wife is to answer a few questions. Does she have any allergies?"

"No."

"Previous head trauma?"

"No."

"Is she pregnant?"

"No. We don't...Dee doesn't think she can get pregnant. But we're going to try."

I don't know why I say all that. Those details don't matter to him. They matter to me. Would we ever get the chance?

"Alright," he says sympathetically. "I know this is hard. But let me do my job and take care of your wife. I will be out to you with news as soon as possible."

MY HAND SHAKES AS I fill out the medical forms. Then they put me in a private area to wait. I rip off my bow tie, undo the stifling top button of my shirt, and stalk the tiled floor like a caged panther. Terror chases my every step. I check my watch too often and badger the nurses for answers, who can't or won't tell me anything.

Nearing the sixty-minute mark, I'm losing my mind when Victor comes racing in. I stop. I hadn't called him. I hadn't called anyone. He puts his arms around me. I take the comfort I hadn't realized I needed.

"How's Dee?" he asks, visibly distraught but retaining his composure for my sake.

"I don't know." My voice cracks. "They're running tests. She's unconscious. Head wound. Jesus." I bend over at the waist, sucking in air. "I slammed her to the ground."

I feel his hand on my back. "She could have been shot, Mick. You prevented that. She's strong. She's going to pull through."

I nod because thinking otherwise is too much to bear. "I'm sorry I didn't call."

"That's okay, man."

It's not. I hadn't wanted to share my agonized worry. But more than that, I didn't think I could cope with anyone else's. "I'm glad you're here." I straighten, try to pull myself together. "Your buddies in blue told you."

"Yeah. Ivers. He was called to the scene."

"What happened?"

"Let's sit down."

"No." I shake my head, attuned to the gravity in his tone. "If you know something, just tell me. I heard gunshots."

"Stiles took down the shooter."

"Jesus. Is he alright?"

"Got hit but he was able to call it in. He's at St. Joseph's."

"What the fuck?"

"I know," he concurs bleakly. "Did you see anything? Anyone?"

"No. I had just helped Dee out of the limo when Stiles shouted for us to get down. We did. Then I immediately heard gunshots. Four or five of them."

"Did you see any of the shots being fired?"

"No. I was covering Dee the whole time. It sounded close at first, then got farther away. I didn't look up until I heard the sirens. Why are you asking me when I'm looking for answers?"

"I needed to know you weren't a material witness to the scene before I tell you anything. I wouldn't want to compromise the case."

"Jesus. Victor. Tell me."

"What I got from Ivers is that Stiles didn't see anything unusual until you and Dee got out of the limo. That's when he noticed movement. It seemed to be coming from your neighbor's property. Presumably he was lying in wait, outside of the range of your home cameras. He was dressed in all black as camouflage and looked to be armed. Thank goodness for Stiles' combat training and quick reflexes. The shooter had a rapid firing weapon. He could have gotten off a round before anyone knew what hit them. But Stiles intercepted his gunfire. An exchange, with Stiles ducking behind the limo and trying to get the shooter farther away from you and Dee, took them down to the end of the driveway. That's where Stiles took a bullet to the shoulder before he incapacitated the shooter. Looks like a clean shoot but the police have to investigate. They'll need to see your home camera footage."

Christ. Victor just described a scene out of an action film. Only it's not. My breathing hitches as the horrific reality sinks in. Someone had tried to kill me. Could have killed Dee. "Who? Who the fuck did this?"

Victor puts a hand on my shoulder as Granger had. But in the doctor, I saw cool efficiency. In Victor, I see compassion mixed with dread and anger. "Mick..."

And in that moment, I know. My whole body shakes with it. His name spits out of me in murderous particles. "Malcolm. He did this."

"I'm so sorry, Mick." Victor pulls me into another firm embrace. "I can't begin to understand what you must be feeling."

How could he? His father was Cayo, a man of honor and integrity. Mine was the fucking devil himself. That Malcolm had chosen the night of the gala for his vengeful return wasn't coincidence. He wanted to strike me down at my highest point. Married to the only woman I've ever loved. My name, cleared of scandal. An esteemed award that celebrates my work and is a tribute to Cayo. While, in his twisted, sick mind, I had taken everything from him. Basketball, his career, his power.

I pull away. The image of Dee—lifeless and bleeding—evokes a rage so vile, it boils inside me. Scorching my chest, my lungs, my heart.

"Is he dead?" I ask, I hope. Because if not, I am going to fucking kill him myself.

Victor's sharp gaze holds mine. My hard-edged expression gives him a window into my thoughts. "He's not worth it, Mick."

I ignore his warning. "So, he's alive?"

"Last I heard it looked bad. Two shots to the chest. He's at St. Joseph's in police custody. If he makes it, he's going away for a long time. His life is over."

And what about Dee's life? I need to see her. Touch her.

I pace away from the simmering worry in Victor's eyes. His presence is the only thing that keeps me from punching a hole in the waiting room wall.

"You need some rest," he says. "Mama and Isabelle are on their way. Lean on us so you have the capacity to be strong for Dee when she comes around."

That gives me a focal point. Being a rock for her.

"Have you called Lexie or Jordyn?" he asks.

"No." I shake my head. "No one."

"Let me do that so they don't first hear about this in the press. Media is already at the scene."

Absorbed in my own misery, I hadn't thought of the people who loved Dee finding out that way. *Father of Micah Peters attempted to shoot and kill his son and daughter-in-law.* Jesus!

I turn my phone on and hand it to Victor, giving him the code. "Call Asher too. They're all in my contacts."

"Okay. Take a seat, get off your feet for a few minutes at least. I'll go find you an energy drink or something to refuel."

The thought of putting anything in my stomach is enough to make me hurl. But I recognize that taking care of me shifts his worry off Dee. "Thanks."

He leaves the room with my phone under the auspice of locating a vending machine to avoid me hearing him relay the message about Dee and the shooting all over again.

I try to sit. Can't. Go back to pacing. Check my watch. Eighty-nine minutes and still nothing. What was taking so long? At minute

374

ninety-six, I look up and spot Dr. Granger coming toward me. His expression is unreadable. I charge forward and stop short of grabbing his arm.

"How is she? How is my wife?"

"She's in recovery."

"Dee's awake?"

"In and out, but yes."

"Thank God."

"She's woozy and disoriented. Tired. That's normal," he assures. "Your wife suffered a traumatic head injury where she lost consciousness. We stitched up the laceration. I'm sure the amount of blood gave you quite a scare, that happens with head wounds. Good news is there's no sign of a concussion or any internal swelling. Vitals are strong. We're giving her pain meds and letting her rest."

"I want to see her."

"Alright, just be aware, Mr. Peters, that memory loss surrounding the incident can happen. But she knew her name, the day, where she was. She asked for you. Those are all positive signs."

"Take me to her," I urge impatiently.

"I will. There's just one other thing."

"What?" My heart drops.

"You said your wife couldn't get pregnant."

"Yes, that's what a doctor told her years ago." I search his inscrutable face. "Why?"

"Test results show your wife is indeed pregnant."

Shock blows me back a step. "Dee's pregnant?"

"She is."

This is unreal. And changes everything.

"Your wife should see her family doctor or gynecologist after she's released."

"I want a specialist. The best."

"I can provide a couple of names. Congratulations, Mr. Peters." He extends his hand. "Let's go see your wife."

DEE IS LYING IN BED with a clear plastic drip feeding the tube in her hand. She's hooked up to a monitoring machine. A nurse helps her take sips of water from a straw. I stand in the doorway, staring at my wife. Awake. Unknowingly carrying our baby.

She looks up when I enter. Drowsy, her gaze stutters across the room. She blinks as if bringing me into focus. Then her eyes light up, golden-brown and all the more compelling for having missed them.

"Mick." Her voice is faint, a little croaky, but just hearing it is like sweet music.

My throat closes. I want to rush over and hug her, but conscious of her injury, I hang back and will my own voice not to break.

"Hey, beauty."

She tries to sit up and winces.

"Not too much yet," Dr. Granger warns and takes a light to each of her eyes. He nods his satisfaction at whatever he sees there. "We'll let you visit with your husband and I'll check in on you again in a bit. It's okay if she falls asleep," he says to me.

"Thank you, Doctor." I shake his hand again at the door. "Would you please have a nurse update Dee's brother, Victor Torres? Not about the, you know," I whisper. "Let me tell Dee first."

When we're alone, I go over to the bed, and anxiously scan her face. Some of her olive coloring has returned. Her amber eyes search mine beneath the fringe of her lashes. But the thick bandage around her head, protecting her wound, is jarring. I lean in and press a gentle kiss to her mouth. Breathing in her breath.

Dee's hand reaches up to lovingly stroke my cheek. I can feel her soft body through the hospital gown pumping with energy. With life.

That's what I needed at my very core. Her vitality. It settles and grounds me like nothing else. Easing back, I take her hand. "How are you feeling?"

"Hurts."

"I can get the doctor back."

"No." Her grip is reassuringly strong. "Stay."

"I'm not leaving." I pull up a chair close to the bed and sit at the edge, leaning forward. My thumb smooths over the skin and veins on the back of her hand.

She blinks, her lashes fluttering as if keeping her eyes open is a chore.

"Sleep, beauty. I'll be right here when you wake up."

"K." She tries to smile. "La yuh."

My heart clenches. "I love you too. Always."

She lets her eyes close and is asleep almost immediately. Only then do I allow myself the tears I'd been holding.

DEE DRIFTS IN AND OUT over the course of the day. The doctor explains that's typical for the first twenty-four hours. Because she tires easily and he wants to keep the stimuli low, he only permits two visitors at a time.

Bright, cheerful flowers decorate her room. My family is a rock. Dee's friends too. How could I have ever thought their emotions would be a burden? I'd been messed up and not thinking straight. Mama T sits with Dee and makes me eat something. Jordyn brings me a change of clothes and some of Dee's personal belongings. I leave the room only long enough to pee and get on a pair of jeans.

Asher handles the media. For now, I have no comment. Victor tells me that Stiles was soldiering through his injury and should be released in a couple of days. I owe him a debt of gratitude that can never be repaid.

Malcolm is still in critical condition, apparently touch and go. The speculation on social media must be spreading like wildfire. But the only thing that matters is Dee and our baby.

When night falls, a thoughtful nurse has a porter bring me a cushioned visitor chair. I doze off here and there, frequently checking on Dee. At some point, exhaustion must have won over for the sun is up when I jerk wake. Had it been a nightmare about Dee and the baby? Momentarily disoriented, my eyes dart around and land on my wife.

She's watching me. Not a dream. She's real. My heart somersaults in my chest.

"Morning, beauty."

"Your poor neck." She frowns.

"I'm okay." I take her hand and kiss the knuckles. "How are you feeling today?"

"Head still hurts. But so much better. My brain's not in a fog anymore. I need to use the restroom."

"Let me help you."

She eases up and swings her legs to the other side of the bed. I take her elbow as she gains the floor.

"Any dizziness?" I ask.

"No. I can make it."

"I don't mind."

"Mick," she chides, defending her independence. "I'm good."

It's such a Dee thing that it makes me smile. I let her go, but remain vigilant as she pushes the IV drip forward. Her steps are gradual but solid.

When she's done, I help her back into the bed and take my turn next.

"Flowers are pretty," she says, sitting up, looking alert. "That was nice of everyone. Sorry, I wasn't much company yesterday."

"No one expected that of you. We just want you to rest and feel better."

"I do. Like I got a second wind."

"That's a good sign."

Her beautiful eyes, clear and focused, bear into me. "What happened?"

The moment I've been dreading is finally here.

"How did I hit my head?" she asks in earnest.

My impulse is to stall. Shield her now and ask for forgiveness later. But considering the media fest, there is virtually no opportunity to sort through the aftermath slowly or in private. We are going to be all over the news for days, weeks, months.

I sit back down and take her hand. "Tell me what you remember from the night of the gala."

"Um...everything about being there and driving home. You gave me a foot massage and we joked about the chocolates. I remember getting out of the limo without my shoes. It all kind of goes blank after that, until I woke up in the hospital."

"The doctor said that's normal."

"It doesn't feel normal. It feels weird to have this huge black spot. I have no recollection of falling. I wasn't feeling tipsy, certainly not drunk. But maybe I can't handle champagne as well as I thought I could."

"You weren't drunk, Dee."

"Did I trip on my dress then? God, that's even more embarrassing."

"You have nothing to be embarrassed about. You didn't fall. I knocked you down."

"What?" Her face scrunches with confusion.

I take a deep breath. There is no delicate way to say this, so I just get it said. "Stiles saw a gunman and shouted for us to get down. In my urgency, I pushed you to the ground harder than I thought. With my body over yours, I didn't realize you'd been hurt until the gunfire ceased and I was able to check on you."

"What are you saying?" Dee stares at me, her eyes wide, her hand trembling in mine. "That someone shot at us?"

"Yes." I squeeze her cold palm. "It was Malcolm."

"No," she utters in disbelief.

"I'm sorry, baby. I know it's a lot to process."

"Oh my God." Her eyes well up. "You were right that he wasn't going to bow out just like that. I could have lost you."

"Ssh." I move to sit on the side of the bed and carefully pull her to me. "You didn't. I'm right here. Safe. You're safe. Malcolm is in police custody at St. Joseph's. Stiles shot him."

"Is Stiles okay?" Dee shivers against me, despite the sun warming the room.

"He got hit in the shoulder. But he's doing fine and should be home in a couple of days."

"He saved us."

"Yes."

"And you saved me." She looks up with tears clinging to her lashes.

"I knocked you out."

"A cut on the head is nothing. You saved my life, Mick."

"Your life wouldn't have been in danger if—" I stop abruptly.

"If what?"

If not for me. Only a week ago, I might have believed that. But it's not true. I didn't cause this. "If not for Malcolm."

"I'm so sorry." She hugs me as best she can. "What he did was beyond horrible. But you are not to blame."

"I know."

"You mean that?"

"Yeah." I set Dee back against the pillows but remain on the edge of the bed, facing her. I want to be the best husband and father I can be. Here and present, not battling my past. "Malcolm is fucked-up and evil. That's just who he is, but that's not on me."

"I'm so happy to hear you say that." Her golden eyes liquefy with love.

"I can say that because of you. Because of all you've given me."

"I didn't give you anything but the truth."

"I'm finally coming to accept that. Not just in here," I touch a finger to my temple. "But in here too." I tap my chest. "They aren't just words that I know I need to say to convince myself. I believe them." I link our fingers again and continue. "Malcolm's condition is critical. He may not make it."

"How do you feel about that?" she asks, softly searching my face.

"I thought about killing him myself."

"I would imagine you did. But that's a fantasy. It's okay to feel something, Mick. He's still your father."

"Not in any way that matters. I've wasted enough energy on him. If he dies, he dies. And if he doesn't, he'll go away for a long time. Either outcome is going to be a shit show in the press. I can't promise the next several weeks or months will be easy."

"We don't do easy." A heartening smile tugs at her lips.

I look at the woman I adore beyond measure and manage a short laugh. "No, I guess we don't. But what I can promise you, Dee, is that I'm not looking back anymore. I have too much in front of me." I place our joined hands on her stomach and kiss her mouth, letting go of the past in the shelter of Dee's love, and the overwhelming joy I feel for our baby.

"We're pregnant, beauty."

CHAPTER THIRTY-EIGHT

Dee

"IS ANY OF THIS PAINFUL?" Dr. Tia asks, sitting at the foot of the table between my open legs.

"No."

"Good." She smiles.

Tanned and fit, with frosted blonde highlights, the maternal-fetal specialist reminds me of Jennifer Aniston. I have the absurd thought of Rachel from *Friends* staring at my vagina. But that takes my mind off my nerves and from her gloved fingers probing inside me.

I still have to pinch myself. *We're pregnant.* My brain couldn't process it when Mick first told me. Even with confirmed test results, I spent several days in a state of shocked denial. Afraid to let myself believe it was true or possible, when all these years I'd been told it wasn't.

Since I was released from the hospital last Tuesday, Mick has been more attentive and affectionate than usual, which is saying a lot. He gets a kick out of rubbing and talking to my belly. It's really the sweetest thing. Our little miracle has brought a ray of happiness to a dark time.

Whenever I think about what Malcolm did, what he could have done to his own son, fills me with a potent mix of rage and pain for my husband. What kind of a monster would do such a thing? And yet, Mick is handling it better than anyone could rightfully expect. He's channeling all his focus and energy into taking care of me and our baby-to-be.

Mick is going to make an awesome dad. Fun and loving. Like Cayo. Nothing like his biological father, who continues to languish in the ICU with a potential charge of attempted first-degree murder awaiting him. For the last ten days, that story has been the headline. A media sensation. How could it be anything else?

Mick hasn't made an official press statement or said anything publicly about the case or Malcolm's motive. He will respond in his own time and in his own way.

Our people have been absolute gems. Isabelle and my friends helped me through a week of convalescence when I was on mandated rest. Lena has held down the fort in my absence. Gabi was my source of entertainment, regaling me with stories from school and TikTok clips. The kids and Dwayde drew us cheerful pictures. Mama T made us her Mexican Chicken Soup that she swears is the wonder remedy for whatever ails you. Maria and James prepared a host of organic meals that we can just pop into the oven or grab from the fridge. Victor, solid and reliable, is a constant source of comfort in just being there.

As much as we love and appreciate them, we haven't shared our pregnancy news. Mick, excitedly, wants to. But scared to jinx it, I'm adamant about waiting until after the first trimester.

When the internal exam is over, I sit up and Dr. Tia invites Mick back into the room. He looks at me seated on the table, a sheet draped over my lower half, and meets my gaze. A crackle of awareness fills the space between us.

"How did it go?" He comes to stand at my side and reaches for my hand as he often does. A simple gesture that conveys so much. Support, solidarity, love. It says, *we're in this together*.

"The pelvic exam went well," the doctor confirms, shifting her gaze from Mick to me. "Everything feels normal. I have reviewed your ultrasound scan and there is a fair amount of scarring on the uterus. But given its location, there appears to be adequate room for you to carry to term. We'll do another ultrasound after your first trimester."

"So, the baby's fine?" Mick asks.

"Yes." She's quick with a smile to relieve any worry. "Growing right on schedule. We'll get an image at Dee's next appointment that you both can see. Though it may still be too early then to determine the sex."

"I don't care," Mick says. "As long as Dee and the baby are healthy."

"That's the goal here." She wheels her stool over to her computer. "Let's check your due date. Dee, you said your last period was two months ago. Can you narrow that down?"

"Yes. I'm not regular so missing a month or two isn't unusual for me. But I'm fairly certain my last period was around February 17th, not long before our wedding." Touched that I could have conceived then, I glance up at Mick and we exchange a heated look of remembrance.

"Alright." Dr. Tia taps a few keys. "Ah, that puts you at ten weeks tomorrow and your due date at November 24th."

A Thanksgiving baby! How fitting.

"Have you had any morning sickness or nausea?" she asks.

"Neither."

"Any spotting?"

"No. My breasts have just started to feel fuller and tender."

"That's normal. Any issues from your head injury?"

"I got an all-clear from my doctor yesterday."

"Everything sounds great then." She finishes her entries and turns her stool toward us. "I'll give you some prenatal vitamins before you go. It's important to take them. Any questions?"

"Yes." I voice my worst fear. "What are the chances of me having another miscarriage?"

Mick's grip on my hand tightens.

"There is always some risk in any pregnancy. Your previous miscarriage and the scarring tissue can be factors. But you conceived against the odds. Let's not borrow concern when everything with your pregnancy looks good so far. Naturally, it's advisable to keep your stress low. I realize your situation in the media might make that hard. I can't even imagine," she adds. "But try your best."

Mick's shoulders stiffen. My poor husband, who likes to be in control, has none over the whims of the press.

"Any other questions?"

"I'd like to go back to the office next week," I tell her. "Would that be alright?"

"You can return whenever you're ready."

"And working out...is that okay too?" I pursue, afraid of doing anything wrong.

"Physical fitness is good for you," she says patiently. "You are a healthy woman, Dee. Keep up your normal activities and listen to your body. Balance is key. Don't overdo it but don't stop living, either."

"Does that mean sex is okay?" My cheeks warm and I don't dare look at Mick. "We haven't since I got out of the hospital. But we used to have it quite often and um...energetically."

"Excellent. When you feel up to it, you can have it quite often and with as much enthusiasm again. In fact, some women experience a heightened sexual drive during pregnancy and crave it with greater frequency."

"In that case," Mick says with an ardent smile, "You better give me some of those vitamins too."

WE LEAVE THE APPOINTMENT ON cloud nine. Dr. Tia had allayed a good deal of our worries. I'll be careful, cautious—of course—but we're not going to dwell on what could go wrong and miss out on embracing our second chance.

I'm soaking up the happy vibe when we pull up to our house and all the warmth and excited relief leaves my husband. The press is still camped out at the end of the driveway and on the sidewalk. Mick takes my elbow as we exit the backseat of the Range Rover.

By rote, we put our heads down and ignore the bark of questions and hail of camera flashes as the paparazzi try to get clear shots of us. Impossible to do through the security cover of three mountainous men—Max, Hilton, and the temporary addition of Grayson.

Stiles, in a cast, has been relegated to desk duty, which Mick said he's been grouching about. The bullet went through his shoulder, fracturing three bones. Thankfully, he's expected to make a full recovery and that the police concluded his role in the shooting was clean and in self-defense.

I'd sent him a card. Not that there are any words that could adequately express the depth of my gratitude for saving our lives. Mick had been more practical in his sentiment. He'd wanted to give a hefty bonus, but Stiles, being Stiles, refused. For him, that was the job. I can well imagine he finds the term *hero* embarrassing, but that's the label the media has bestowed on him. And the one that I think he rightfully deserves.

Mick closes the front door against the chaos, enveloping us in peace and quiet.

"Well, that was fun." I slip off my flats and attempt to lighten the mood.

384

He sends me an unamused look. "I don't like you having to deal with that."

"It won't be forever, Mick."

"It'll be long enough. I want to show you something." He guides me to the office, and taking a seat in front of his computer, pulls me onto his lap.

I push my hand into the fullness and length of his wavy hair. "Going to keep it this long?"

"You seem to like it," he says, waking his laptop.

"I loved it short too. But this gives me something more to hold on to."

"I noticed." He winks in sexual reference, his playful mood returning.

"Well, I may have horny hormones now so..."

"I'm at your service, ma'am."

I laugh and hug his neck. "What do you want to show me?"

"Give me a sec." He scrolls through several bookmarks, then opens one titled Sullivan Listings.

I peer at the screen and see that the link is to a real estate website.

"Check this out," he says eagerly.

A house...no that's not the right word for the aerial shot of a mansion on sprawling greenery that backs onto the lake. It reads: *At 8,500 square feet, this one-of-a-kind waterfront home offers a private oasis.*

The blurb goes on to describe the five-bedroom contemporary design in flowery detail, highlighting the in-home theater and gym, tennis court, and two pools. It uses words like secluded and remote, claiming to have everything one could need contained in a single place. The write-up then ends with: *This superb property has gated access and a state-of-the-art security system.*

I extricate my arm from around Mick and slide my gaze to his. "You've been house hunting?"

"Browsing. This one caught my attention."

"It sounds like a fortress."

"I'd hardly call it that." He frowns. "We'd be on the lake like we always talked about. And there's plenty of space for a baby and the family we want."

"There's no rush. A baby just needs a bassinet in our room."

"For a few months, maybe," he counters. "Then what?"

"We'll figure it out. I don't want to move yet. I love our house. I thought you did too."

"I do. But we need more."

"More security, you mean?"

"There's that," he allows. "We're far too exposed and accessible. The shooting proved that."

I would never want to diminish the trauma he went through. Because I have no recollection of the incident, that gives me a different perspective and gentles my approach. "A terrible thing happened, Mick. I understand that's fresh in your mind. Just as I understand your need to protect us. I don't discount any of that. Nor do I want us to live in fear or behind a gated wall."

"Taking precautions is not living in fear. It's keeping you and the baby safe from potential dangers."

"Taking precautions is fair," I concede. "But that house doesn't feel like us. It's too much, it's too um...rich."

"We are rich."

"But we don't live like that."

"Then we can find another house."

"Or..."

"Or what?" His gaze narrows.

"We could stay here and build a second floor with the bedrooms upstairs. Even add a split level with a great room or big play area," I add, growing increasingly keen on the idea. "Jord can draw up some plans and you can consult with Stiles on how to better secure our property without it feeling like we're behind a wall."

"Humph." He makes a scoffing noise. "I'm not hearing much of the 50/50 compromise you're always pushing for."

"This is a compromise," I say sweetly. "We try it this way first and if we can't find a solution that works for both of us, then we'll look for a house that we can agree on."

"You realize, we'd have to move while the house is under renovation."

"Right, so we hold off on selling the condo."

"You hate the condo," he balks.

"I don't hate the condo." I despised knowing Lisa lived there. However, that won't be an issue much longer as she's been ousted by the board and has sixty days to vacate.

"You said it's too bare and monochrome," he persists.

"I'll give it a homey touch. Besides, staying there would only be temporary."

"You have an answer for everything."

"Don't pout," I tease, without bothering to hold back my victorious smile.

"I'm not pouting."

"You are and it's cute."

"I'm on to you, Counselor," he says wryly.

"What?" I wrinkle my nose.

"Don't think I don't know how you *handled* me to get what you wanted."

"I did nothing of the sort. It's a reasonable proposal and you're a reasonable man." I wrap my arms around him again, and bring my lips to his in a smacking kiss.

THE NEXT MORNING, I'M UP early. Although I have no plans to go into the office until next week, I want to start putting out my feelers for a partner. It wasn't top priority before, but it is now.

Tucked against Mick's warm body, my feet sandwiched between his calves, I push my hair out of my face and watch my husband sleep. Waking before him isn't as rare as it used to be. He's been sleeping better, longer. No more nightmares, despite everything that's happened. No more blaming himself. It's as if being an expectant father is a fast-healing agent.

Filled with love, happiness, and gratitude, I snuggle with Mick a little longer, then slide away and slip quietly out of bed.

On route to the bathroom, I pass the full-length mirror. Pause. Then step back to my reflection. Ten weeks today. Another two, and I'll already be in my second trimester. I'm starting to feel pregnant. I think I'm starting to look pregnant too. I turn sideways and pull my thin camisole nightie tight against me, cupping my hand below my belly. It appears slightly more distended, and feels rounder and firmer. Soon all of me will expand. My butt too. But gaining weight doesn't worry me as much as I thought it might. Because I know that it's a healthy sign our baby is growing.

I face the mirror. My breasts are definitely getting bigger. Fuller. More tender. I gently cup their weight. My nipples tighten. I touch the sensitive tips through the soft cotton. It's been nearly two weeks since Mick and I have made love. Between the shooting, my injury, and fear of doing anything that could harm the baby, we've kissed and cuddled, but nothing more. I miss it. Sex has always been a key element of our relationship—an intensely passionate connection that we established early on. If pregnancy hormones spike my lust for my husband any more than how much I already desire him, then I'm liable to self-combust. Just thinking about it has me squeezing my thighs together.

I hear the mattress shift. Startled, I drop my hands and peer over my shoulder.

"Morning," Mick says with a knowing grin.

"Morning." I blush, a little embarrassed at getting caught. "I didn't know you were up."

"Oh, I'm up alright." I glance at his impressive erection tenting the sheet. "I thought I was having an erotic dream about my lusty wife touching herself in the mirror."

"I wasn't touching myself."

"Uh-huh." He lifts off the sheet and wraps his hand around his stiff cock, squeezing the wide head, and stroking the length in rhythmic slides—fully aware of how much that turns me on.

My core clenches in response. He's hard and thick. Divinely virile. Shameless in his arousal.

"Mick," I breathe, my eyes following the up and down motion, watching his hand quicken.

"See something you like, beauty?"

"Very much." I lick my lips.

Putting on a show, he treats me to a few more strokes before he withdraws his hand and climbs out of bed. Powerfully graceful, he prowls forward in all his hard, naked glory, his hot gaze zeroed in on me. A moment later, I'm whisked into his arms, and pulled against him.

My breasts, under the cotton, are crushed to his chest. The thickness of his erection presses into my belly. His hands at my lower back dip to cup my bottom as he ravishes my mouth. I respond with hyper urgency, squirming against him until I break away to catch my breath. "Do you want to?"

"Baby, you have no idea." He pants. "Are you sure you're ready?"

"Yes." Beyond ready.

"I'll be gentle."

"Don't be."

"Jesus, Dee." Lust darkens his eyes.

"The doctor said we can resume with enthusiasm," I remind him. "And you feel very enthusiastic." I slide my hand between our bodies, making him groan.

After several strokes, he removes my palm and presses a kiss to the center. "I don't want this to be over before it starts."

"I love making you come."

"Later," he promises against my lips. "Take this off."

I grab the short hem, lift the nightie over my head, and toss it aside.

"Now turn around."

The moment of self-consciousness is brief, lost beneath the hunger in his eyes and the brutal need in me. I turn. Our gazes meet in reflection. It's only with Mick that I have allowed myself to be this vulnerable. To lay myself bare and know I'm safe.

"Do you see what I do?" he asks.

I let my eyes travel over the image of my naked body in a way I haven't before. Without judgment, without criticism, without assessment. "Yes." I nod at him, thinking I finally do. What I see through his eyes, and what I'm beginning to see through mine, goes deeper than the physical. Deeper than the way I look. It's how I feel, it's what I am. My eyes move from my reflection to his. "I'm beautiful and strong and sexy."

He smiles a tender smile, liking what I've said. "You are, in every way, Dee. Watch."

His hands slowly trace the wide swell of my hips, the indentation of my waist, his long fingers fanning out to climb my ribs and skim the undersides of my heavy breasts.

"Tender?" he asks, gently molding them.

"Yes, but that feels good."

His caress is sublime, exploring their fullness, brushing his thumbs against the stiff peaks.

"I need you," I rasp, aching for more. "I need to feel you inside me."

"I need you too." He releases me and is gone, returning in a flash with the armless club chair from the corner of the room. He places it in front of the mirror.

My throat works on a swallow of nervous excitement. He sits back in the chair. Sleep-mussed hair, whiskered jaw, cock standing at proud attention. I step forward to straddle him.

He shakes his head. "The other way."

I've come this far. Executing what I hope is a provocative pivot, I give him my back, and a full rear view.

"You're killing me," he growls.

"It was your idea," I tease, feeling emboldened. "Should I stop?"

"Hell no. I want you to watch yourself riding me."

I bite my bottom lip and keep my gaze on the image of me lowering onto his muscular thighs. I slide my legs wide, giving us both a peek at my desire. Mick's breaths are rough and quick.

I want to make it good for him. Burn this image in his brain and hold nothing back. I arch my spine and lift my arms, joining my hands behind his neck. In this position, my torso is elongated and my breasts are high, round, and thrust out and upwards.

He makes a carnal sound of approval. Invoking my inner Sex Queen, I wind my hips over him and swivel my waist, mimicking a lap dance.

"*Dee*." I feel his temperature rise, exuding a sultry heat.

That's how I want him, on edge and on fire. When the teasing gets too much to bear, he clutches my hips and whispers with an authoritative bite, "ride me."

I lift up, seeking his stiff cock with my hand and position him against my core.

"Slow," he hisses.

I lower onto the bulbous crown, watching each thick inch disappear, slowly, deliciously, until I've taken him to the root. I breathe through the luscious stretch, loving the way he fills me, completes me. Puzzle-like pieces fitting perfectly together. All reflected in the mirror, from where we're intimately connected to the open-mouth, breathy expressions of pleasure on our faces.

I inch up and slide back down, watching the slick movements—watching his ferocious gaze consume the bobbing of my breasts and the bouncing action of my ass slapping against his thighs.

On a stream of curses and dirty talk, Mick brings one hand between my legs. His fingertips on my clit are like an electric current. Wild for him I cry out, my mind lost to the primal urge to fuck. I ride his fingers and shaft, my mouth parted on choppy moans. It's like watching an erotic movie with us as the stars. I bring my hands to my breasts. Squeezing them, stroking the tips as an orgasm bursts through me, the tremors radiating everywhere. We watch me explode, our gazes riveted to the insatiably hedonistic sight of me coming all over him.

And it only gets better when Mick lifts me off and turns the chair so I can grab on to the back and see us in profile. Him positioned behind me, hands grasping my hips as he slams into me.

"Fuck, fuck." Roars vibrate from his chest, the mirror capturing every carnal thrust.

"Mick...oh God, don't stop...so good." It's sensual heaven, the feel of him combined with the visual stimulation of watching him fuck me with ravenous greed.

His face, beaded with sweat, is strikingly intense. The firm muscles in his ass flex with the rhythm of his lunges, his arms ripple, his abs pull taut as he drives possessively toward his orgasm and brings me to another one that's even more mind-obliterating than the first.

Milking him, he pounds his hips at me with warped force and speed. "Dee!" He climaxes on a litany of gnashing groans and hisses of my name, his head thrown back, shuddering through each vicious spasm, coming hard and long.

Left boneless and breathless, wow is my only thought. Then I feel Mick's kisses on my back, down my spine, before he shifts to sit me in the chair. I have a few brain cells left to register that he's kneeling in front of me with a look that says, I'm not done yet. My chest quivers.

I can't. I'm too swollen and sensitive. I weakly fist Mick's hair intending to pull him away. But when his tongue flutters against my clit, need reignites in an instant. He slides his hands beneath my bottom, bringing me closer, almost off the seat. I wrap my legs around his shoulders and arch upward into his mouth. My fingers cling to the wavy strands of his hair, my moans quicken.

His mouth eats at me with avid intensity. I writhe, hovering on the verge of another orgasm I hadn't thought possible. His thumb enters my rear. The decadent fullness at the back and maddening laps of his tongue break me with pleasure. Watching us, I sob his name, coming apart in a million blissful pieces.

Slumped against the chair, Mick carries me to the bed. I'm too wrung out to do more just lie there limply at his side.

"You okay?" He strokes my hair, then down my arm.

"Mm-hmm."

I can feel his satisfied smile. "I've been fantasizing about christening that mirror for weeks."

"Did it measure up?" I murmur.

"Beauty, you are always more than anything I could ever dream of."

IT'S A WHILE BEFORE WE get up and shower. Mick washes me and pays homage to my belly. He kisses and whispers words of love to me and the baby. He can't see my tears through the spray of the water. I hold his head to me, looking forward to the little kicks and flutters that will start in a few months, and bask in the knowledge that our baby is going to come into this world wanted, valued, and adored.

We dry off and I slip into my robe. Mick pulls on boxer briefs and is toweling off his hair when his phone vibrates. He gripes at the intrusion but reaches to pick it up off the dresser.

He looks at the screen and his eyes squint in question. "Peters here." After a pause, he confirms: "Yes, it's Micah Peters."

Then a wave of tension pumps off of him. He paces, listening. When he stops, I move to his side and put a hand to his back. The skin is still dewy from his shower but the muscles are taut.

"I'll be there in an hour." He disconnects and tosses the phone onto the bed. His features, rigid.

"Mick?"

He rakes his fingers through his damp hair. "Malcolm's dead."

CHAPTER THIRTY-NINE

Micah

WHITE WALLS, ANTISEPTIC SMELLS. MY head fills with the still too-recent memory of being in a hospital waiting for Dee to wake up, the agony of not knowing if she would.

Because of Malcolm. Now the bastard's dead and his body is my responsibility.

Dee threads her fingers with mine and just that loosens my shoulders. I look over. Her face is somber but her arresting eyes on me are warm. I remind myself that she's okay. The baby's okay. We're okay.

Once upon a time, I would not have wanted Dee here. I would have wanted to shelter her from the ugliness of it all. Fix things on my own before they could touch her. Now, I can't imagine being here without her. She's strength and comfort. She's home.

The sound of the door clicking open has our heads turning in that direction. Dr. Randal Stevens, as he introduces himself, enters the stuffy room intended for families receiving bad news about a loved one. He is accompanied by Charlene something or other, a grief counselor.

I stifle the harsh laugh and politely shake her hand and the doctor's. They address Dee then join us at the round table.

"Thank you for coming." Stevens, an older man, graying at the temples, nervously clears his throat, seeming uncomfortable with this aspect of his job. "Your father passed away earlier this morning. We tried to revive him but the damage to his lungs was just too extensive. Given the...uh... criminal matter, we notified the police. They completed their process and so we are required to release the body into someone's care. Yours was the only name on file; however, if there is someone else, we can contact them."

"There's no one." Victor had offered but it felt unfair to pawn this off on him.

"We realize it's is a unique circumstance." Charlene steps in with a kindly manner. "I am here to support you however I can. If you'd like to see him," she couches her words, "if that's something you would like to do, I can make the arrangements. Some people find that it gives them closure."

"That's not necessary, thank you. I'm good."

The doctor clears his throat again and checks his watch. He can't wait to get the hell out of here. That makes two of us.

"If we could just get to the practical aspects of this meeting," I say, "I'd appreciate it."

"Of course." Charlene outlines the bureaucratic details and slides across the paperwork to be completed. "The hospital will send Mr. Peters over to the funeral parlor you choose."

I hadn't thought of a funeral. Arranging a service for him is out of the question. I won't pretend to celebrate his dishonorable life or mourn his disreputable death. I will do the bare minimum and be done with it... be done with him.

On a brisk handshake, Stevens books it out of there and Charlene gives us time alone with the documents. Dee puts a hand on my arm.

"How are you feeling?"

"I told you before that I'm fine." I return her gaze. "I'm still fine."

"I'm not sure anyone could be fine in this situation, Mick."

"Beauty, you're the one who encouraged me to get free of him. I'd say this is as free as I can get."

"Death doesn't necessarily equal freedom. I don't want you to gloss over whatever you're feeling. I don't want you going dark or quiet or numb."

"I'm not numb. That implies an emotionally-anesthetic state of coping. There's nothing for me to cope with, other than this fucking paperwork and making arrangements."

I grab the pen off the table and attack the first document, filling out my personal information before I turn back to her. "I'm angry, alright. I'm angry that he's dead. Not because I give a damn about him. But because he got off easy. Again. He didn't have to face the consequences or account for his actions. He didn't in life and now he won't in death. But there's also this relief that he's gone. He can never attempt to hurt my family. We won't get tied up in an investigation and possibly a trial. It's cleaner. We can move forward. Our lives and the world are better without Malcolm."

"That's true, he didn't amount to much and did so many awful things. But he did one thing right."

"What?"

"He gave the world and me, you."

"Dee." I shake my head.

"I'm not placating you, Mick. Your father was a vile human being and he never deserved you. But look at what you've become in spite of him. An amazing man. An amazing husband. And you're going to be an amazing dad."

"Beauty." I cup her face and lay my forehead against hers. A rush of love clogs my throat.

"Know what we should do?" she says with a sudden burst of energy.

"What?"

"Get out of here."

"We will. Soon as I get these papers signed."

"No, I mean get out of the city...out of the country. Away from the press. We could book a private flight out tomorrow and go back to Mystique Island, where we got married. Where we may have conceived. Spend a long weekend. Just you and me."

"Traveling's okay for the baby?"

"Yes, until the final trimester."

The idea is just what we both need. "Let's do it then."

THE OCEAN BREEZE COOLS MY sweat-covered skin after a long run on the beach. I'd left Dee sleeping under the mosquito netting with the balcony doors open, the sheer curtains blowing, the dapple of sunlight on her face and hair. She looked angelic. An innocent version of the hot siren who had worn me out last night, twice. The memory still vivid, my body responds. I start toward the house with the intention of waking her for another round before breakfast when my phone rings. As much as I wanted to shut out the world for our short getaway, too much was happening back in Chicago to be unreachable.

"What?"

"Hello to you too," Asher says, dryly.

"It's not even 8:00."

"It's 7:00 here."

"What is it?" I repeat, irritated by the interruption.

"Listen, I appreciate that you and Dee need some time away, but with your continued silence, the speculations are running amok."

"So, manage it."

"What do you think I'm doing? But it's like trying to hold a dam together with toothpicks and cheap glue. It's crazy here, Mick. And last night, Paul O'Malley posted that he's writing a book."

"Yeah, okay," I offer dismissively.

"It's not okay. He claims that he was getting close to a story when your father tried to shut him up. You can imagine the media play this is getting. What comment do you have?"

"None. I'm not dealing with this now."

"You have to, Mick. I can only say *he's taking time* and *please respect his privacy* for so long."

"I'll be back in two days."

"Two days in the media is two months. O'Malley's post is stirring the pot."

"Say what you need to buy more time and I'll decide how I want to respond on Monday."

"Dammit, Mick." His exasperation reaches me from thousands of miles away. "I'm trying to get you quickly out of the spotlight and you're making that a near impossible task."

"That's why you get paid the big bucks."

"Not nearly enough. I'm owed stress compensation."

"I'll send you a bottle of wine."

"Yeah, that should really cover it."

"Stop whining. I'll call you Monday."

I disconnect and look out over the ocean. Asher was right. I need to respond. I'd put off the looming decision for far too long. If Malcolm had survived, a police investigation would have required me to, willingly or not, reveal the closeted truth about the years of abuse and blackmail. But Malcolm's death has negated that. The case is closed.

Only Dee, her friends, and my family know the real history between Malcolm and me. What others are saying is purely gossip and guesswork. The most popular social media BS was that we were estranged because of my attachment to Cayo. Malcolm was said to have been jealous. Not mentioning him in my interview, coupled with receiving an award in Cayo's honor, had built Malcolm's jealousy and resentment to a violent boiling point. He'd snapped. Lost his mind. Only Malcolm wasn't crazy. Nor was he jealous. He was vengeful, he wanted me to pay. He hadn't snapped. He'd plotted and planned. He had delusions of being invincible and above the very law he'd taken an oath to uphold. He hadn't counted on Stiles.

Nonetheless, the prevalent narrative had enough red meat for the appetites of the press and public. I could latch on to those bits of truth and leave out the rest.

It does the job. Malcolm still goes out in a stain of his own making. His reputation had died before he had. What good was the whole truth now?

I linger on the beach, pondering that question.

"I FOUND YOU." SILKY ARMS encircle my waist. Dee's soft cheek rests against my back. She breathes out a contented sigh.

"I went for a jog. Didn't want to wake you up too early."

"You can wake me any time."

Smiling, I turn in her arms and kiss the tip of her nose. Her golden eyes, brighter than the sun, glitter up at me. She looks beautiful. Sable spirals that refuse to be tamed; naturally pretty face that doesn't require makeup; soft, feminine curves beneath a simple white cotton dress that skims the top of her bare feet and dips low at the neck. At ten weeks pregnant, her breasts are already fuller, her belly is rounder. Changes that make my heart swell.

I touch her stomach, feeling blessed by the miracle of it, awed by the responsibility. This little being will be mine, to take care of, to love, to nurture. I'll draw from all the things and the people that have shaped my life, and made me the man I am now, and the father I will be.

One day I'll tell our sons and daughters about Luiza, the grandmother our children will never have the joy of meeting. About how she taught me compassion and gave me the creative gift of writing. I won't paint her as a victim. She was strong. She loved and protected me as best she could. I would want our children to know that about her.

I'll tell them about the warmth and generosity of the Torreses. About how Cayo taught me to ride a bike and how Rita bandaged my knee when I fell off. I'll tell them of how they cared about a little boy next door and made me theirs. Of how they encouraged me to be my own person and find my own path. Of how they gave me a brother and sisters, and showed me that lasting bonds have nothing to do with bloodlines or DNA.

I'll tell our children about the day I met their mother—the girl of my dreams. I'll tell them about the way she would change my life with just one look. The way she would brighten my world and fill it with love and sunshine and hope.

There are so many things I will tell our sons and daughters. About being kind and good. About standing up for what's right. About honesty. About truth.

"You seem reflective," Dee says, breaking through my thoughts. She squints up at me against the sun. "Like you're weighing something heavy."

"Asher called. O'Malley posted that he's writing a book about Malcolm's threats to stop him from uncovering the dirt."

"That didn't take long."

"Nope."

"What are you going to do?"

"I don't know." I shrug. "Legal action will only spike up the curiosity and make him more relevant. As long as he doesn't say anything that hurts you or hurts us, I'm not sure I care."

"Wow, that's big."

"My priorities have changed."

"I can see that." She brings her palm to cover my hand that's still pressed against her belly.

"I've made a decision about addressing the shooting and Malcolm." I hadn't known what I was going to do right up until I saw her, carrying our baby. But looking into Dee's eyes, it feels right. "I don't want a PR event with a room full of reporters and the paparazzi. That's too impersonal. Bianca handled our interview with class. She wasn't out for blood. I like her and trust her."

"Me too. What have you decided to say?"

"The truth. All of it. I owe that to my mother. To the cause. And to myself. I want our children to be proud of me. To see that whatever bad things happen in your life don't have to define you. I learned that from you. I want them to know that I survived abuse and I'm not ashamed to openly admit it or talk about it."

She throws her arms around me, thrilled by my decision. "Our children are going to know that their father is a man of integrity, who is deeply good, intelligent, talented, loyal, and strong, and who taught me the true meaning of love."

Dee

LATER THAT NIGHT, WE WALK along the beach under the moonlight. Mick extends his hand. Our palms meet, our fingers interlock. Our steps sink into the soft grains of sand, falling in tandem. We've hit our stride. The bond between us grows stronger every day.

My husband smiles over at me. I feel it in the center of my chest. He doesn't say anything. I don't need him to. The depth of emotion echoes loudly through the quiet.

Our journey hasn't been easy. But we have persevered and come through it stronger, more confident, more resilient. We have emerged from thunderous storms, battled threats, and banished our ghosts to distant lands.

We have stripped away the layers to expose the raw. Bared ourselves. Our hearts. Our souls. Our very essence. There are no secrets between us, only honesty and acceptance. And in those, we found the infinite beauty of what it means to be loved naked.

BONUS SCENE

Boy or Girl? For an exclusive scene on the gender reveal, please visit me at leighcarron.com and subscribe.

I'm excited to share Dee and Mick's news with you. ;)

AFTER *A NAKED BEAUTY*

Dear Readers,

If you're anything like me, you may be finding it difficult to see the story of Dee and Mick come to an end. I haven't always agreed with their choices, but I have loved and rooted for them every step of the way. Their journey was challenging, filled with wonderful highs and painful lows. They fought for each other, and through the pain, they grew stronger, more resilient, separately and together. They found the beautiful forever love and self-acceptance that we all need and deserve. For that reason, I can now let them go.

The **Perfectly Imperfect** series continues with some of the characters from the first two books. That means you'll get a glimpse of how Dee and Mick's lives continue. But it will be in the background while you get to know Dee's friends as they experience their own passionate and emotional journeys.

Enjoy a sneak peek of Jordyn's story in the pages that follow....

*When an attraction of opposites doesn't go as perfectly as planned…
can something so wrong, turn out to be so right?*

AN IMPERFECT SEDUCTION

CHAPTER ONE

Jordyn

I HATE LOSING WITH A passion.

True statement, although the expression seems counterintuitive to me. I associate passion with good things, like sex, french fries, and Luciana Aymar—a field hockey legend. I admire the crap out of that woman! But I digress, which I often do. It's as if my mind is made up of a road map; some routes are direct and straightforward, others are a series of loops and winding detours.

The point is, as much as I hate losing, I don't whine or sulk. I take my loss on the chin, and congratulate the winners with a firm handshake and genuine respect. That's just good sportswomanship—technically, that isn't a word but it should be. Why do men get sportsmanship, manpower, mankind, and humanitarian? On the other hand, they're not batting a thousand with words like manipulative, maniacal, and man-baby.

Jeez, I sound anti-male, which I'm not. I like men. Some would say a little too much. But that's another one of those loops and detours.

At the game earlier, lazy passes, missed shots, and a goalie asleep at the net really pissed me off. At five-two, I'm the shortest player on the team, but what I lack in size I make up for in speed, agility, and aggression. I go balls-to-the-wall. Doesn't matter that it's recreational field hockey, my motto is, *give anything you do, everything you've got.* Half-assing is a travesty, a wounding blade to my competitive spirit.

But why add more injury to defeat by going home to nuke a frozen dinner when I can grieve the 2–0 blowout over a golden ale and double stack? With fries, of course.

At the stop sign, I turn the corner and pull into the customer parking lot, where Royal's Pub is sandwiched between a coin laundromat and a pawn shop. The neighborhood isn't the classiest. Royal's doesn't have the pedigree of being one of Chicago's famed historic pubs. It's not even Irish. Opened in 2017 by three brothers that look more like surfers than pub owners, they pooled their resources to buy an old, tired bar, and spruced it up with gallons of paint and shiny new décor. But the reason I come here whenever I get the chance is because the wooden sign out front is no word of a lie, "Our Burgers and Beers Rule."

On weekends, they entertain the twenty- and thirty-something crowd with karaoke, themed nights, and live music. But on a Tuesday evening, it's quiet—only a few cars and one motorcycle are in the lot. A behemoth. Black and sleek. Sexy. I look around to make sure I'm alone; wouldn't want to get caught by the driver—or is it rider? I slide my hand along the massive handlebars and over the wide leather seat. It's a beast of a machine. I imagine what it must feel like having all that power revving between your thighs. *Great*, I chide myself, *now I'm pissed, hungry, and horny.* Horngry. I should hashtag it.

Withdrawing my hand, I slip my credit card inside my phone case and tuck that into the waistband of my shorts, and stick my key fob into the top of my sock. Minutes later, I enter Royal's. Behind me, the door closes against the summer humidity, and I'm greeted by the welcome draft of air conditioning and pleasant smell of hops. Music and indistinguishable conversation leach out from the dimly lit bar.

"Oh, hey Jord." The youngest of the three brothers emerges from the office, looking happy to see me.

"Hey, Cam. How's it going?"

"Better now." He's shy of thirty, too pretty for his own good, with a teasing wink in his smile, and sun-streaked hair that he flips out of his face. "You coming from a game?"

"Yep. But..." I hold up my palm. "Don't go there."

"That bad, huh?"

"Worse."

"You should invite me to the next one," he says through a grin that oozes playboy charm and makes him ultrapopular with the female patrons. "I'll bring you luck."

I don't take him seriously. Men like Cam don't go for small-chested, athletic types. They go for gorgeous, buxom women, and usually more than one at a time.

"Too much competition for your affection," I tease back because he's harmless and I enjoy him.

"One day, you're going to stop doubting me, Jord."

"Yeah, yeah. So you always say. But if we hooked up and it didn't work out, I'd be forced to give up the burgers. And as cute as you are, I like the burgers better."

"Ugh." He feigns removing a knife from his chest.

"You'll get over it." I laugh and playfully jab his shoulder. He catches my hand and grins.

"Come on, let's get you a table and something to eat. Your usual?"

"Am I that predictable?" I ask, noticing Cam hasn't let go of my hand as we walk toward the bar.

"Jord..." he side-glances me, his smile gleaming. "There's nothing predictable about you, except for a double stack, fries, and golden ale."

"Good answer." I share his grin while taking back my hand. Just in case he has any ideas, I don't want to encourage him. I like Cam. He's flirty and fun, easy-going. I would chew him up and spit him out in a heartbeat, but as I said, I like the burgers too much to have sex where I eat.

Inside the bar, a few tables are occupied, one by a couple of women, their laughter reminding me of nights out with my best friends, Dee and Lexie. The older brother, Graham, is pulling beer, and two men are sitting at the long, polished, mahogany bar—a blond in a suit, who probably stopped in after work, and a darker figure at the far opposite end.

In that moment, my heart seems to stop right along with my feet. *Holy sh...* the expression, which is second nature, dies on my tongue. I squint hard. It can't be... But even before my eyes fully accommodate the twenty-foot distance; even before my gaze follows the line of his jaw, the outline of his lips, and the width of his broad shoulders; even before my brain computes that he isn't just a hopeful vision I'd conjured up, I know it's *him*. J.D. Stiles.

There's no mistaking his size... or effect—a visceral reaction, unparalleled to anything I've ever experienced. The kind that makes my pulse sing and my breaths dance. That brings to mind dark thrills, sweaty bodies, and tangled sheets. The kind of down-and-dirty that has consumed my waking thoughts, my dreams… my every fantasy. For months. Long by my standards. I usually go in for the kill. Wham, bam. But with Stiles, I've whet my appetite on a game of cat and mouse. Teasing and luring him like a piece of cheese in a trap.

So far, he hasn't taken the bait—not a sniff or a nibble.

I chalk it up to circumstance. Until now, the only time I'd ever seen Stiles was while he was on duty and on alert. He operates a security firm that specializes in the personal safety of CEOs, dignitaries, and celebrities. I'd met him when Dee reunited with former sports star Micah Peters. She affectionately refers to her sometimes-bodyguard as Robocop. An apt description for Stiles, on the surface. But beneath that rigid, unyielding mask of his, he's still a hot-blooded male.

It's then that I remember what I'm wearing when I normally wouldn't care. A royal blue sleeveless jersey, matching shorts, white knee socks over shin guards, and grass-stained cleats. On top of that I'm probably smelling a day old after running up and down the pitch in eighty-four-degree weather that hadn't cooled even with sundown. Okay, so I'm not exactly dressed for a perfect seduction. But I'm not about to let this prime opportunity go to waste.

Cam turns to see me stopped. "What's wrong?"

"Nothing. Nothing at all."

"Then why are you standing there like you're frozen in place?"

"I caught a glimpse of someone I know at the bar."

"Who?" Cam peers over. "The big guy?"

"That's the one."

Something in my face must give me away because his sea-green eyes regard me with warning. "Damn, Jord. That dude doesn't look like someone you ought to tangle with."

"I like living dangerously." The rush of challenge raises the fine hairs on the back of my neck. Stiles has yet to look over or even appear to notice me. He's facing forward, nursing a beer, his gaze lifted to the TV screen mounted above the mirror and bottles of liquor. His expression is inscrutable.

"You know I'm a safer bet," Cam points out.

"Safe is too easy," I say, planning my pursuit. "Hold my order. I'll just have a beer for now."

Frowning, he moves behind the bar and I join him on the other side, hugging the curve of the counter, my gaze remaining on Stiles. He seems so still, and yet there's this energy, as if he's emitting sonic waves. Soundless. Invisible. They vibrate across the room and seep inside, bouncing frenetically through my body. Unlike him, I can't remain still. The energy won't let me. I may never be still again.

"You're really into this dude." Cam scoops back his bangs, sounding a little put out.

If I didn't know better, I'd think he was jealous. More likely a bruised ego. Cam's a guy after all, he probably wouldn't mind sleeping with me, but he can tell by my body language that he's not the man I want. *That man* is busy sitting still, not even noticing me while he zings off silent killer vibes that make my palms itch and my pulse beat way too fast.

I lose track of whatever Cam is saying as he pulls the lever and fills a glass. "Jord." He grabs back my attention and slides the beer across with another warning. "Be careful. Seriously. That dude is not sending out boyfriend signals."

"Then it's a good thing I'm not looking for a boyfriend." I grin and slip away from his needless concern with a finger wave.

I can handle men, even Stiles. I taught myself how.

I'd grown up a tomboy and an athlete. I played soccer and field hockey, drawn to both because they're fast-paced and aggressive. I used to wonder if my unisex name had destined me. Had I been a Stefanie or a Lily, would I have preferred chasing butterflies over digging up worms, dolls over trucks, dancing in a tutu over getting a ball into a net? I'll never know. But as Jordyn—even with a "y" that my mom claimed gave it a female distinction—I'm what most would call a guy's gal. My knowledge of sports stats is extensive. I can cuss and make crude jokes with the best of them. Plop me down in front of any sporting event with a beer and a mustard-topped hot dog and I'm all set.

That affected the way guys saw me in high school and into college—as one of them. The girl you took to a game or hung out with. That you screwed in the basement or on the twin-size bed in a dorm room, but wouldn't actually date or bring home to mom.

I didn't have a boyfriend until I was twenty-three and met Theodore Price. Tall, dark, and bordering on dorky, in a cute and endearing way. He wasn't into sports. I wasn't his buddy. For the first time, I was someone's girlfriend, and I liked it. We met in the Master's program at Illinois Tech. We shared a deep respect for neoclassical architecture even though my designs leaned toward modern. We took a trip to Greece to immerse ourselves in the history. We worked on projects together. We challenged each other intellectually, but we also had fun.

Our relationship was easy, seamless. And for a dork, he loved sex. The wilder, the better. He liked that I was uninhibited, and I liked that he told me I was pretty and sexy. I thought he could be *the one*. I let him move some of his things into my apartment and introduced him to my family.

I thought... hoped he'd reciprocate. But every time he went home to Missouri, he never asked me to join him. I'd never even spoken to his mother on the phone. Finally, after six months, with a holiday coming up, I decided to broach the subject in a serious way. I told him how I felt—I didn't use the *L word*, but it was implied. He said I was the best thing that ever happened to him and then spread my legs apart. The sex had been great, but I wanted more. I wanted to know that he saw a future with me. I wanted to finally be that girl the guy brought home to mom.

The next morning, while Theodore was in the shower, his phone vibrated. He always had it with him. This time he'd forgotten. When I heard a message ping, I ignored my conscience. Some doubt or insecurity compelled me to roll over and retrieve it from under his pillow. The message that popped on the screen dizzied me.

Hi Teddy bear. Guess you're busy. Only a week to go. I can't wait until you're home. I miss you so much. For Easter, your mother is going to teach me how to make her potatoes au gratin. That way I'll have it down to a science by the time we're married.

I stopped reading there. I didn't know which disgusted me more, that a grown man allowed himself to be called *Teddy bear* or that he was a goddamn liar and a cheat. I didn't wait for him to finish his shower. I charged into the bathroom and ripped back the curtain, waving the phone in my hand.

"Fuck you, *Teddy bear!*"

Other than the shock of a crazed naked woman foaming at the mouth, he was rather blasé about getting caught. No denials or apology.

I felt stupid and gullible. I'd been so sure that he cared about me, even loved me. How did I miss it? Confused, I calmed down enough to ask why. And wish I hadn't.

"You're smart, Jord. Fun. We have a love of architecture in common. I really like you. The sex is off the hook, the best I've ever had. But to be honest, you're not wife material."

Furious. Insulted. I was reminded of that adage about a tiger in the bedroom and a lady in the parlor. I was the good-fuck tiger, while the *lady* was back in Missouri learning how to make potatoes au gratin.

I didn't cry. Theodore wasn't worth my tears. Instead, I tossed his clothes out the window and his ass out of my apartment. Looking back, my heart wasn't broken. Slightly dented, maybe. I was more peeved that he'd wasted my time, embarrassed that I'd been used. But I moved on.

Smarter, wiser. I wasn't going to ever be led on again. I control the reins. That doesn't make me jaded about relationships or love. I grew up with happily married parents that still act like newlyweds. My older brother proposed to his now wife, after knowing her a mere seven weeks, and they're still ga-ga and going strong three years later.

I can admit to momentary bouts of wishing the romance gene hadn't passed me by. But then I'm reminded that I like having the bed to myself, not sharing the remote, or having to account to anybody but me. At thirty-one, I'm a successful architect just named on the list of Chicago's Rising Stars Under 40. I own a brownstone that I've converted into rental apartments. I'm not rich but I'm financially solid. I have a great family and great friends. A great career.

I don't have the time or inclination for emotional attachments. I like sex and I like my independence. Period.

No promises. No expectations. No one gets hurt.

The kind of arrangement I think a practical man like Stiles would appreciate.

Locked and loaded, I finger-fluff the textured bangs of my auburn pixie cut that brings out the hazel-green eyes I'd inherited from my dad, and strut forward as if I'm wearing my most bolstering push-up bra rather than shin guards and cleats.

At six-one and supremely muscular, his broad chest and shoulders test the cotton threads of his army-green T-shirt. Whereas Eduardo—my friend-with-benefits—could be mistaken for a fashion model, you'd never make that mistake with Stiles. Never would you see a man like him walking down a runway in Calvin Klein or gracing the pages of GQ in a slim-cut Gucci suit. He's too rugged, too big. Too badass. The kind of man that should be featured on *Rider* magazine in leather and biker boots while straddling that huge piece of metal out back.

Stiles isn't handsome in the conventional sense. That word is too tame for him. He's more like a tall glass of mouth-watering maleness. His bone structure could be carved out of stone. His firmly etched mouth is full and wide, framed by a sleek goatee that resembles black felt, and matches his thick eyebrows. In contrast, his head is clean-shaven—the skin, smooth and polished like teakwood.

Not every man could pull off the look, but on Stiles, it just adds to that bad boy appeal. When I reach him, he turns his head toward me. His expression holds no surprise. Of course, he'd known I was there. A former military man, Stiles was trained to be observant. But whether it's training, his personality, or something else altogether, he registers zero emotion.

With an economy of movement, his gaze executes a quick once-over from my face to my blue uniform, and back again, not revealing a single clue as to his thoughts.

"Ms. Sinclair." He nods brusquely, but oh man, that voice.

Graveled and rough, the unpaved sound travels from my ears to my toes, and doesn't miss a thing in between. I take a breath and attempt to get a rise out of him.

"Hi, Jasper."

His eyes go an impossible shade darker, obscuring his pupils, and hardening to ebony marble. I smile. It's only recently that I learned J.D. stood for Jasper Dane when he was in the news, hailed a hero. Until then it had been a one-sided game of me trying to decipher the initials of the man that only went by Stiles. I never would have come up with Jasper but it oddly suits him.

"Nice to see you off duty," I say.

He doesn't answer, which causes me to fill the empty space. "I haven't seen you at Royal's before. Do you come here often?"

Jeez, Jordyn. I mentally slap my forehead. It sounded like such a cringy pickup line, I have to laugh out loud.

Stiles doesn't laugh back or even crack a smile. I've never actually seen him smile. I imagine it's all the more spectacular for being rare—like a lunar eclipse.

"You're a tough nut, Jasper."

"No one calls me that."

"A tough nut or Jasper?"

"Either."

"I'm your first. I like that."

He ignores the comment, looking anything but amused.

"I come here quite often," I say, answering my own question. "Not on the weekends, though. I'm not a karaoke fan." I make a face. "The burgers never disappoint. Have you tried them?"

"No."

"You don't know what you're missing. I always get a double stack with two patties and a slice of Canadian bacon, that's the clincher right there. And the spicy sauce." I blow a chef's kiss with my free hand. "I usually head here after a game or practice. I play field hockey... soccer too, but tonight was field hockey."

"That explains the uniform," he says, indulgently, lifting one size-twelve, make that thirteen, shoe onto the low metal rung of his stool.

"We lost. I was in a pissy mood because of it. But then I saw you and I instantly felt better."

He doesn't seem to know how to respond to that, so he doesn't.

"How's the shoulder?" I ask, sliding onto the seat next to him without an invitation. If I waited for one, I wouldn't be sitting anytime soon, or ever. "All healed?"

"Yes."

The last time I saw him, nearly two months ago, his arm was in a cast. "Thank you again for what you did."

"It's my job," he says without effect, as if saving lives is no biggie.

"Well, we're all still grateful."

His gaze shifts away. Embarrassed by my praise, I assume. I let it go to keep things light. "What are you drinking?"

"An Irish stout."

I grimace because dark beer is too strong for my tastes. "I'm a pale ale girl all the way. This one's a silky oat. Wanna try?"

His unreadable expression returns to me. "No thank you."

Okaay. This was going nowhere fast. But quitting is for wusses. I set my glass down on the bar next to his arm. There's a chunky platinum watch strapped around his left wrist and a tattoo of some sort of reptile. The tail coils around his sinewy forearm and thick bicep, before disappearing under the short sleeve of his shirt. "Is that a snake?"

"A drakaina."

"What's that?"

"A female dragon."

Interesting choice. The scaly ridges, outlined in black, are detailed and life-like. Intrigued, I reach out and touch his bare arm. *Ho-ly shit!* I damn near start breathing fire myself. I'd half expected for the scales to be cool. Instead, his skin is hotter than a ghost pepper and this close to him, he smells of citrus, spice, and sin. I want to bury my nose in his neck. I want to rip off his clothes and eat him up.

As if he can read my thoughts or is having them too, I lift my gaze to see another reaction from Stiles. Yass! Something sharp and simmering in the dark depths of his eyes. "Does your she-dragon have a story?" I ask.

"No."

I lift an eyebrow because I don't believe him. He averts his eyes again, and looking back up at the boxing match on the TV screen, raises the beer to his mouth. Even in motion there's a stillness about him. Not calm exactly, but measured.

I watch him take a long pull. Watch his bottom lip kiss the neck of the bottle and the bob of his Adam's apple work on a swallow.

"Do you have any other tattoos?"

No response. Hardly a breath. Just silence. I'm a talker, the quiet isn't my friend. Waiting him out is excruciating. Eventually, he lowers the bottle and returns his gaze to mine. That flash of something in his eyes is gone.

What was up with this man, and his hot and cold vibes? Although he's never returned any of my advances, I sense he isn't immune to me. There's a restraint that fuels those sonic waves. It pulsates in the tension arcing between us that I just know would blow the freaking top off if he were to let it loose.

"Well?" I break the silence and trace the scales of the tail, challenging him to loosen his guard. "Are there others?"

"Why?"

"I'm curious. Interested." His expression remains level but the muscles in his forearm beneath my fingertips rumble like quaking rocks.

"Haven't you heard about curiosity killing the cat?"

"Sure, I've heard it. But that doesn't scare me."

"I don't imagine much does," he says in what sounds like neither a compliment nor an insult. Then he surprises me with an answer. "I have several others—on my torso, my back, and my thigh."

"Oh." I gulp, and my eyes drop past his hard chest and abs to his thighs, and the bulge of denim. Maybe you could judge a man by the size of his feet after all. Before I get caught drooling, I look back up.

He pins me with a nuclear stare that sears my flesh.

"I'd love to see your tattoos."

"Are you always this bold?"

"Pretty much. Is that a problem for you?"

"No."

Another positive indication "So?" I ask, encouraged, and take a slow sip of my beer, chasing the cold liquid on my lower lip with my tongue.

His gaze blatantly follows the motion. "So, what?"

Time to go for it. No more games or beating around the bush. This sexual attraction is fierce and formidable. It has grabbed hold and won't be denied or abated until I thoroughly work him out of my system.

"Would you like to come back to my place? No strings attached."

It flashes again, that hot and dangerous burn in his eyes. Then just as quickly, flickers out. "No thank you."

His response delivered in the same monotone as declining a taste of beer snaps me back like whiplash.

"Sorry," he adds, not seeming sorry at all. "Women like you aren't my type."

A blow no gentler than Theodore's. And yet somehow his manages to hurt even more. Had I totally misread him or had he been playing me? Some twisted game to slap me down cold. *You aren't my type.* Can't get any clearer than that. But he didn't have to be so heartless. My instinct is to curse him out and kick his ass into next week. Only too stunned and mortified to speak, I just sit there as he places a twenty-dollar bill on the bar, and walks away.

The achy rasp of Amy Winehouse's "You Know I'm No Good" drifts through the sound system, deepening the unwelcome ache in my chest. I look across the stretch of the bar, past Cam's raised eyebrows, to where Stiles is exiting. The door closes behind him with a click I can feel rather than hear, leaving me in the chill of his rejection that had hit entirely too close to home.

ABOUT ME

I write sexy stories that are intense, provocative, and deeply sensual. The characters are complex and perfectly imperfect—that's what makes them interesting to write, and hopefully to read.

In *Fat Girl* and *A Naked Beauty*, I presented a female lead struggling with body image and self-acceptance. I think that's something most women, regardless of their size or weight, can identify with. Sadly, too many of us have a "fat girl voice" in our heads, that tells us we're not good enough or perfect enough. As a recovering yo-yo dieter, over the years, I've learned to quiet that negative voice that had distorted my self-perception. I don't view the word *fat* as derogatory anymore. That gives it too much power. As an author, inspired by the theme of loving yourself and discovering your own intrinsic worth, I want to bring my readers stories that are real, relatable, and entertaining—where strong characters with tough battles and troubled pasts tug at your heartstrings, turn you on, and have you cheering for a beautiful, forever love.

Originally from Cleveland, Ohio, I'm now a proud adopted Canuck, living in Calgary, Alberta, with my husband and daughter. The winters are frigid, but the sun shines 335 days of the year. Tanning in a parka—it happens! I studied in Toronto, and began my career in human resources before spreading my entrepreneurial wings to start up a change management consulting practice. I have loved the work and the reward of helping clients realize their visions. But my true passion has always been writing. Most nights, you will find me sitting at my computer, tapping out the countless story lines in my head.

I liken writing a great romance to a box of Godiva. Decadent and delicious! You can't stop at just one.

I love interacting with my readers. Please follow me on:

- @leighcarronauthor
- @leighcarronebooks
- www.leighcarron.com

AUTHOR'S NOTE

Fat Girl and *A Naked Beauty* are both works of fiction. However, the characters faced real issues. If you or anyone you know is struggling with body image, an eating disorder, or abuse, please know that there are resources that can help.

Consider:

- Your local hospital; they can provide you with the services you can access in your area.
- Hotlines for when you need to talk to someone outside of a friend or family member.
- Books on guidance and healing in your library, bookstore, and online.
- Support groups, such as Overeater's Anonymous, available in most communities and some offer online options.

No one should struggle through difficulties alone; it's okay to ask for help. Please don't keep silent. Reach out and talk.

With love,

Leigh

Made in United States
Troutdale, OR
03/16/2025